To Emma & Phil

Happy Reading!!

Love & Best wishes

# *Jacob's Nanny*

by
Susan Johnston

Susan Johnston

Strategic Book Group

Strategic Book Group
P.O. Box 333
Durham CT 06422
www.StrategicBookClub.com

Design: Dedicated Book Services, Inc. (www.netdbs.com)

ISBN: 978-1-61204-519-1

# *Dedication*

*This book is dedicated to Brian Goldsmith*
*(17th April 1930-7th December 2009).*
*We miss you dad.*

# Contents

# Chapter . . .

# 1

Cedar Vale High Street was alive, bustling with workers from the nearby Cedar Vale Business Park, all in search of lunch and a few rays of sun. The warming Autumnal sunshine had brought them out in force. A welcoming break from the incessant rain they had been experiencing over the past few weeks.

Kate Forrester had finally reached the front of the queue at Ritchie's Delicatessen. She flicked a stray lock of blonde hair behind her ear as the middle aged woman behind the counter starkly announced, "Next!"

"Two ham salads on granary, please," Kate responded.

"Salad cream or mayo?" the assistant tersely replied without a glance in Kate's direction.

"Salad cream, please."

"Do you want any onion?"

"Uhm...no thanks." Kate thought of the two potential clients she was meeting that afternoon and decided to spare them. She didn't particularly like working on a Saturday afternoon but then business was sporadic at the moment and in the current financial climate, couldn't be turned down just because it was the weekend.

The two sandwiches were deftly put together and handed over. She took the bags, paid the money and stepped out of the shop into the mid-day sun. Tucking one of the sandwiches into the top of her handbag, she removed the other from its wrapping and ravenously took a bite. Her eyes wandered up the high street in the direction of the bank. No signs yet, just time to take a quick look in the bridal shop window. Her best friend, Tina, was getting married in the next few weeks;

surely it would be her turn soon. How long was she supposed to wait before she too became a bride?

The beautiful, ivory coloured, silk gown virtually filled the entire window display with its full skirt and elegant train. A few tiaras were scattered around the floor on some rucked silk littered with silver sequins. Her eyes floated up and down the dress, her mind picturing herself floating down the aisle as she took another bite of her sandwich. How she would love to wear something like that. When was Alex going to pop the question? Maybe once he'd sorted out the business finances. She glanced towards the bank again. At last he was on his way back.

Kate took one last look at the dress before joining her boyfriend on his way back to the car. His face was stern and his eyebrows met at the deep furrow in his brow. She handed him the other sandwich.

"How did it go?" she asked as he walked around the car to open the driver's door.

"It didn't," he replied avoiding her eyes.

"What do you mean, it didn't? What did he say?"

Alex looked up and stared at Kate across the roof of the car. "In a nutshell, we've given you enough money now go and make some of your own."

They opened the car doors simultaneously and seated themselves inside. Alex fumbled for the keys, his eyes still blazing. He started the engine then hit first gear.

"Well, what are we going to do?" she asked anxiously.

Alex paused. He put the car back into neutral and sank back into his chair.

"Kate," he started and looked towards her. "We need to talk."

***

Richard Anderson was beside himself. His life was in turmoil and about to take a turn for the worse. He could see the situation slipping from his grasp and there was no way to retrieve it; no way to make his wife see sense; in fact it was quite the opposite. She had made her decision but he was the one who would have to live with it. He had to make all the sacrifices and juggle what was already an impossible situation.

Melissa Anderson, a well polished, good looking woman was busy throwing clothes into a suitcase opened up on the king size bed. Despite her frenzy, her dark, silky hair still sat perfectly in a knot at the back of her head. She slid open the lavish, mirrored, wardrobe door to reveal yet another row of blouses and skirts, and sweeping them all off the rail, laid them swiftly in the case.

"For God's sake, Melissa, can't we just talk about this?" pleaded Richard in a last hopeless bid.

"I've done enough talking to last a lifetime," Melissa replied. "I can't carry on like this. My nerves won't take any more."

"What are you talking about, *your nerves?* How long is it going to take to get your *nerves* back to normal?"

"Dr Rosenberg said it could take months, even years. A case like mine only comes along . . ."

"Oh, do me a favour, a case like yours. Dr Rosenberg has given you every excuse under the sun to behave like you do. What about Jacob? You're a mother, Melissa, and it's about time you started acting like one."

Melissa stopped what she was doing for a moment and stared at her husband in disbelief.

"You have no idea how I feel, do you?"

"Sure I do," Richard answered waving his hands in the air. "You're feeling trapped because you've got a child, so you want to discharge yourself of all your responsibilities, give it a medical name and jet off to the sun for some so-called rehabilitation."

Melissa turned away in disgust and continued with the task of packing her suitcase.

"Ugh, I don't know what I ever saw in you. Call yourself a doctor. You haven't got an ounce of compassion in your entire body."

She slammed down the lid of the case and heaved it onto the floor. From there she proceeded to drag it to the top of the stairs. Richard ran his fingers through his hair in desperation.

"What am I supposed to do about Jacob?" he asked despairingly after her.

"You're a clever man, Richard," she replied sarcastically. "I'm sure you'll work it out."

***

Kate stared vacantly at the floor. Alex had waited until she had been seated comfortably in their compact, detached home in the middle of suburbia; the sun still high in the sky and life still moving on outside as if nothing was untoward, before he'd dropped his bombshell.

"I'm sorry, Kate," he had said staring out of the diamond leaded window at the neatly mown lawn.

"Who is she?" she'd asked choking back the tears.

"I met her at the gym. We just got talking about the business and she said she wanted to help..."

"Oh, I'm sure she did."

". . . it just went from there."

"So she offered you money, just like that? Surely you could see that she'd want something in return."

"We got on well. One thing led to another."

Kate couldn't bear the sound of it. It was as if her whole life had been a complete farce. A joke played out at her expense. How could she possibly have missed all the signs? Or had she simply not wanted to see them in some misguided delusion that everything was rosy in their lives and running to plan.

"How long have you been seeing her?"

Alex had turned around to face Kate. He heard the pain in her voice but he knew he had to continue with what he'd set out to do. It would have been too easy to brush it aside and allow things to carry on as they were.

"A couple of months; what difference does *that* make?"

"I just wondered how long you'd been making a complete fool of me. I bet all your friends know, don't they; and what about their girlfriends, my so-called friends? Have they all been laughing behind my back?"

"I only told Chris and he promised not to say anything to anyone."

"Oh, that's big of him; all boys together."

"Look Kate, I didn't mean it to happen like this. I just wanted to save the business and it looks like she's the only option now."

Kate had looked up at him. She couldn't believe what she was hearing.

"Right, so I'm out on the street so you can save your bloody business?"

"We'll both be out on the street if I don't save it," he'd shouted. He'd had enough of defending his actions. So it was underhand and deceitful; he'd never claimed to be perfect. "You won't be out on the street, you'll find somewhere."

"I have somewhere if you hadn't noticed," Kate had replied sternly.

"Look, Kate, sometimes shit happens. Couples split up. You can't stay together just to keep a roof over your head."

"No, but couples usually split up because they don't love each other any more, not because the business is going bust," she'd answered desperately.

She'd looked into his eyes to try and search out his true feelings. He'd averted them and gone to look out of the window again.

"Oh, I see, you don't love me any more either, is that it?"

"Kate . . ." he'd pleaded.

"Is that it?" she'd shouted, baiting him for a reply.

Alex hadn't replied, he couldn't, he didn't know how to without crushing her feelings even more. He'd hurt her enough.

"I'll take that as a *yes* then, should I?" she'd finally asked him.

"I'm gonna go to Mike's for a while. I'll be back some time on Monday. It'll give you time to pack. I'm sorry, Kate, I really am. I didn't want to end it like this."

"Then don't," she'd retorted. "We can work this out."

"I'm sorry."

Alex had walked out of the room. There wasn't going to be a negotiation. He'd made up his mind and that was final. It was over. He'd made his way upstairs to pack a bag leaving Kate empty and desolate. She'd given him the best part of her life. Nine and a half years she'd spent working as his secretary for peanuts to help the business survive, and now she'd got nothing to show for it. The tears had streamed down her face. Thirty two years of age and having to start her life again. The thought filled her with dread.

***

Richard stood at the top of the stairs and watched helplessly as his wife walked out of his life. The door banged shut behind her and she was gone. The fine lines on his face were etched with worry. What was he to do now? She hadn't given a second thought to his career when she'd marched out of their home. But then, it was probably his career that had driven her away in the first place. It was hard dividing your time between a particularly demanding job and a home life. His work was like a mistress, always coming between them, taking most of his precious time. Then just over four years ago, Jacob had come along and absorbed what little time he had left. No, it was little wonder she had left him. But now he had the daunting task of setting up his practice as a new consultant while bringing up his son as a single parent. The nanny wouldn't arrive until eight o'clock on Monday morning; just as he should be starting his ward round. She would be biting at the bit to leave at five o'clock as his operating list was finishing. There was the washing, ironing, shopping, and cleaning to do in between, as well as making all the meals. How was he going to cope?

He walked into the lounge. His young son was sprawled on the floor, his crayons scattered around him and a fun size colouring book opened on the page of a happy family playing ball on the beach. Richard shrugged and shook his head at the irony.

"What are you colouring, Jacob?" he asked, crouching down on the floor beside his son.

"A picture," came the reply. Jacob was concentrating far too hard to engage in any kind of conversation.

"Jacob, mummy's had to go away for a while. She still loves you very much but she's got to get some pills to make her feel better."

"Can't she take them here?" the little boy asked quizzically.

"No, the doctor has to make sure she takes the right ones at the right time."

"But you're a doctor, can't you do it?"

"I'm a different kind of doctor. I do operations; this one helps people take medicine."

"Is she coming back then?" he replied, still focussing on his picture.

"I'm not sure, sweetheart."

He knew all too well their relationship was over, but couldn't face telling him the truth. He didn't want to give him any false hopes of her imminent return.

"Daddy."

"Yes, what is it, son?" Richard asked pensively preparing himself for the onslaught of questions that would no doubt follow.

"Erm, can you pass me the blue?"

Richard smiled. So his son hadn't been too traumatised by the news, he thought as he handed him the blue crayon he required. He ruffled his hair and got to his feet. He would now try to get his head around the ordeal that faced him.

# Chapter . . .

# 2

Richard lifted the receiver. It was Sunday afternoon and Jacob was playing with a digger in the back garden, scooping the soil up, driving it across the lawn then tipping its contents out onto the opposite flower bed. He tapped the familiar numbers into the phone then waited for the reply.

*"Hello."*

"Hi, dad, it's me."

*"Oh, hello, son, how are you?"* Donald Anderson replied in a half whisper.

"What's the matter, are you losing your voice? I can barely hear you," Richard said showing concern.

*"No, your mother's got one of her migraines. I don't want to disturb her."*

"Oh, sorry, I suppose the phone ringing didn't help."

*"No worries, son, you weren't to know. Anyway, what can I do for you?"*

Richard was hoping to invite his parents down from Scotland for the week to take care of Jacob whilst he sorted out his affairs. His mother's migraine had put that idea to rest.

"Just ringing to see how you both are, really."

*"Oh, apart from that we're fine. How's Jacob, is he still enjoying nursery?"*

"Yes, he loves it."

*"How's Melissa, is she feeling any better? Last time your mother spoke to her, her nerves were bad."* There was a pause. Should he tell his parents now that Melissa had left him or should he carry on the façade that had been his marriage? *"Richard, are you still there? Is everything alright?"*

"Yes, everything's fine, dad, everything's fine. Tell mum I was asking about her."

*"Yes, of course I will, love to Jacob, bye son."*

Donald replaced the receiver and made his way to the bedroom with the glass of water he had promised his wife before the ringing phone had diverted his attention.

"Who was that on the phone, dear?" Iris Anderson asked her husband as he stepped into the room.

"It was Richard, just calling to see how we are. I told him you weren't feeling too well," Donald replied, his eyes slowly adjusting to the darkness of the room. He placed the glass on the bedside table next to his wife and eased her up into the sitting position. He wrapped her pink, bed jacket around her shoulders and after removing the flannel from her forehead, passed her the glass.

"Did he mention Melissa?" Iris asked taking a sip of water.

"No, dear, and I gave him every opportunity."

"I wonder why he feels he can't tell us?"

"He'll tell us in his own good time. You never know, that may have been the reason he was calling us and he didn't want to worry you whilst you had a migraine."

"That's why I've got this confounded headache in the first place, because *she* couldn't wait to tell us. Oh, I do hope he's alright, I mean fancy leaving him to look after Jacob on his own when he's got his career to think about as well."

***

Richard stared at the phone. What would he do now? His parents had been his only hope. He had no other choice. He would have to take some leave and work the problem out with Rachel, the nanny. He knew she would be less than obliging. Why Melissa had hired her in the first place he would never know? She always had somewhere else to be whenever they asked her to do anything out of the normal routine. Still, this was an emergency. Maybe she would help on a temporary basis just while he sorted things out. He lifted the phone again; time to arrange cover for the week ahead.

***

Carl Walker had been making the most of his weekend off. Sprawled across the beige, leather sofa in his bachelor pad, first floor apartment, he had basked in the luxury of watching a football match while having a beer and a bowl of macadamia nuts in the sound knowledge that he couldn't be disturbed by any of the patients under his care. He was not on call this weekend and he was going to enjoy it.

Suddenly his mobile phone rang.

"What the hell ..?"

His eyes flicked to his phone on the coffee table in front of him and the name Richard Anderson illuminated at the top of the screen. Carl immediately sat up straight and pressed the green button. He knew he couldn't be seen but it just didn't feel respectful talking to his boss whilst lying on the couch.

"Hi, Mr Anderson."

*"Carl, hi, sorry to interrupt you in the middle of Sunday afternoon. I know it's your weekend off but I have a family crisis on my hands and I'm going to have to take some time out to sort it."*

"Sure, I understand," replied Carl, with one eye on the football.

*"Would you do the ward round tomorrow morning and then my clinic? I'll try and pop in some time in the morning to rearrange my operating list and put something on that you can do on your own. I'll come and find you when I get in and make some arrangements; is that okay with you?"*

Carl's attention was totally focussed on his conversation now. He was to be given a lot of responsibility and he wanted to make sure he had all the facts correct. Leading the clinic and the operating list; that was important stuff.

"Yes, that's fine, Mr Anderson. I'll speak to you tomorrow."

*"Thanks, Carl, I appreciate that."*

The phone went dead. Carl switched the television off. He picked up the can of lager from the coffee table and threw the remainder of its contents down the sink. He needed a clear head for this. This could be the make or break of his future in plastic surgery.

Richard replaced the phone. One hurdle down, nine hundred and ninety nine to go. Next on the agenda was to inform his good friend and colleague, Todd Hamer. Todd wouldn't be a problem. He'd supported him throughout as he'd discussed the ups and downs of the Anderson marriage over lunch nearly every day in the hospital canteen. That just left the Professor to inform of his plans. That would be fun. What would he say when he found out his newly appointed consultant was on the verge of a nervous breakdown following the break up of his marriage and that he'd been left with their four year old son to take care of in the process?

***

Professor Royston pulled up outside Marcelle's French bistro in the delightful village of Shadmoor. He expertly reversed his silver, Mercedes Benz into the parking space then ran round to the passenger door to let his wife out.

"Oh, thank you, Gerald, how chivalrous of you," she tittered.

"Well it's not everyday you get to draw your old age pension," he said smiling back at her.

"Now, don't spoil the moment, you tease," she replied. "I've always wanted to come to Marcelle's. Sonia Patterson, the lady captain, says it's wonderful and I can't have her eating at places that I haven't, can I?"

"Well we can only afford these prices on special occasions so make the most of it," he said winking at her. "Happy birthday, Dorothy."

"Thank you, Gerald," she replied and linked his outstretched arm.

They sauntered to the door of the restaurant taking in the beautiful view of the Shadmoor countryside. They entered the premises and were immediately met by the French waiter.

"Good afternoon, monsieur et madam," he greeted them. "Do you have a reservation?"

"Yes, Professor Royston."

"Ah, Professieur, welcome. I have your table ready."

The waiter led the way to the table whereupon the couple were met with seven pairs of smiling eyes.

"Happy birthday, mum, happy birthday, grandma!" came the chorus from the table.

Dorothy's mouth opened wide then spread into a huge smile.

"Oh, my goodness, what a wonderful surprise. Oh, I can't believe you're all here."

"We've got the day off school tomorrow, gran," shouted the youngest granddaughter, Mia. "We're staying over tonight in a hotel."

"Oh, how lovely, my look at you all. Aren't you growing up?"

Dorothy's eyes filled with tears as she took in the sight before her. Her Daughter, Nina, and her husband, Giles, with their two children, Sophie and Mia. Then there was her son, Peter, and his wife, Paula, and their son, Aaron. It was all too much. She hadn't seen them in months. She fished around her handbag for a tissue as the presents and cards were thrust in front of her.

Gerald stood back proudly nodding to his daughter and son for taking a moment out of their hectic lives to celebrate their mother's sixtieth birthday. Suddenly his mobile phone vibrated in his jacket pocket. *No, not the hospital,* he thought, *surely not.* He'd left specific instructions with his registrar to only call in a dire emergency. He discreetly checked the name on the screen. *Richard Anderson, what the hell did he want?*

"Let me take your jacket, Dorothy. I'll go and hang it up over there."

Dorothy was far too busy chatting to her family to notice that there was anything untoward happening and passed it to her husband. Gerald made his way towards the cloakroom and answered his phone.

"Richard, is this important only I'm in the middle of my wife's birthday lunch?"

*"No, Prof, just to let you know I need to take some leave next week, family business, and Carl Walker is going to be running my clinic and operating list."*

Professor Royston had an amazing ability to make you feel that whatever you had just said was so insignificant, that it wasn't worth the air time just donated to it. This was one of those moments.

"Fine," he replied. "Speak to me tomorrow, goodbye, Richard."

*"Goodbye, Prof."*

Gerald quickly replaced his phone to the inside pocket of his jacket and returned to his seat shaking his head.

"Anything wrong, dear? Giles saw you on your mobile. There isn't a problem at the hospital is there?" Dorothy asked inquisitively.

"No, no, everything's fine, now have you all decided what you're going to eat?"

***

Richard felt even worse. He had now totally put the Professor's back up, interrupting his wife's birthday lunch with his piece of *trivia*. How was he supposed to know? He was only keeping him informed. Nonetheless, he was probably going to have to pay for that intrusion some time in the near future.

# Chapter . . .

# 3

Kate awoke with puffy eyes and a blinding headache. For the second night running she'd cried herself to sleep. She stared at the suitcases lined up in readiness for her departure and another melancholy wave tore through her heart. It ached intensely. Like a nagging toothache, it constantly reminded her that she was now alone and homeless.

Her temporary accommodation, as it had been emphasised, had been arranged the previous day with a desperate phone call to her friend, Tina. She had been very quick to point out that despite the fact she was alone in the house at the moment, her fiancé would in fact be returning from his conference in Aberdeen by the end of the week and wouldn't find it appropriate her being there, since she had now split up from his best friend, Alex. Kate had duly but politely asked her what she meant by that.

"Well, it might look like we're taking sides," she had answered.

Kate didn't know what was hurting most; the fact that her boyfriend of nine and a half years had dumped her for some other woman with an open cheque book, or that her best friend felt that she owed any kind of loyalty to the two timing bastard. There was also a nagging feeling in the back of her mind that Tina was fully aware of the situation and had prepared her conditions in advance. There had been no surprise in her tone nor upset for the turmoil her friend had found herself facing. It had all been rather matter of fact and to the point. She had five days to find somewhere to live and then she was out. Despite her feelings, Kate had no other choice than to take the few nights offered to her then quickly find herself some other accommodation. The future was daunting.

It had been Saturday night when she'd found the cheque. She had spent all day sitting in the chair, watching the light fade as the evening rolled in. She hadn't moved an inch; a catatonic figure to anyone who happened to be passing by and had glanced in the window. She had finally succumbed to the darkness, and taken herself up to bed. The envelope had been sitting on the bedside cabinet.

Kate had slowly opened it. Was it a letter to explain his actions; to say how sorry he was for the hurt he had caused? No, it was a cheque for the paltry sum of two thousand, five hundred pounds. That was the price he had put on their relationship. She had worked hard over the past nine years helping to build his empire. It was his stupid mistakes and high ambitions that had ruined everything yet he was about to start his life again with a new woman in the house she had called home all these years, and she was to be ousted out with barely two months rent in her pocket.

It was the cheque that had initiated the tears with the stark realisation that she now had nothing. It had confirmed that she was out of the picture and that a reconciliation was out of the question.

She dragged herself out of bed and into the shower. Normally she would be in work now, typing her first letter, answering the phone and making sure Alex was on his way to his first appointment. But today, she would attempt a small piece of toast and a cup of tea, dry her hair, call a taxi, and deliver her bags to Tina's. From there she would find herself the nearest newsagents, buy the local newspaper, and look for somewhere to live.

***

Richard was giving Jacob his Weetabix when Rachel, the nanny, arrived. It was ten past eight. Richard stared at the clock as the keys rattled in the door. He would normally be at work by now in the middle of his ward round. How was he going to manage after this week? She was always late. It was time for the pep talk.

"Hi, Mrs Anderson, sorry I'm a bit late, there was an accident at the end of the road . . ."

*And you stopped to have a look,* he thought. ". . . and I couldn't get past for the ambulance. They'd blocked the road," she continued, hanging her coat up in the hallway. She made her way into the dining room.

"Oh, *Mr* Anderson, I didn't realise it was you. Shouldn't you be at work? Where's Mrs Anderson?"

"She's left." Richard decided he wasn't going to beat about the bush. He would just be straight with her; she would have to know sooner or later and Jacob was bound to say something.

"Left, what do you mean, left?"

"She's gone, moved out leaving me to take care of Jacob."

"But what about your job? How are you going to do that and look after Jacob as well?"

"Well, that's where you come in."

"Me? I'm only the nanny, Mr Anderson. I can't be here all the time."

Richard could see that this was going to be difficult. She wasn't the most obliging of people, in fact far from it. She had an agenda and she stuck to it. Here at eight and home at five and that was how her life functioned. She couldn't cope with variations to the norm. Change wasn't part of her make-up.

"I'm not asking you to be here all the time, Rachel. Could you maybe tweak the hours you do work slightly, just while I get myself sorted out?" he said hopefully.

"Tweak, in what way?"

"Well, I wondered if you could perhaps start a little earlier . . .?"

Richard could hear the sharp intake of breath. The furrowed line on her forehead soon followed and he still hadn't finished what he was going to ask.

"How much sooner?"

He wanted to say half an hour but, after her initial response, couldn't bring himself to as the look on her face had now turned to abject horror.

"Fifteen to twenty minutes would probably work."

"Oh, I don't know."

"I'll pay you extra."

"It's not the money although that would be nice. It's just you get yourself into a routine with the buses and everything."

"Okay, well could you maybe do it for a short period, whilst I find alternative arrangements?"

"What do you mean, alternative arrangements? You're not planning on getting rid of me are you, only I need this job?"

"No, no, Rachel, calm down. I just mean that I may need someone to sit with Jacob first thing until you arrive and at the end of the day when you leave. Mine isn't a nine to five job as you may well appreciate. Sometimes emergencies breakout or my list runs over and I have to stay late. I also have to be on call which means I could get asked to go into the hospital in the middle of the night."

"I couldn't come over in the middle of the night. My mum wouldn't let me do that."

"No, obviously not."

Richard got the distinct impression that she hadn't a clue what he was talking about and that he was wasting his time. Whatever happened though, he had a week, at the outside two, to come up with a better solution. But first things first, now he had to hand over his son to the bemused Rachel and hope that she could get past the accident at the end of the road and get him to nursery on time, whilst he went into work to organise his workload and face the wroth of Professor Royston.

***

Carl Walker was just finishing the ward round as Richard arrived.

"Morning, Mr Anderson," the sister of the ward greeted him. "Sorry to hear about your family problems."

Carl's face went a shade of crimson. What a great start to the week, his consultant now knew that he tittle tattled to the staff. He had only answered sister's enquiry as to where his boss was.

"I'll walk down to the clinic with you," Richard suggested. "Any problems on the round?"

"No, Mr Jackson's going home today and Mr North's drain can come out later, there was barely anything in it. I'm sorry about what Sister Jackson said."

"Oh, don't worry about that. They'll all know sooner or later."

There was an awkward silence as Richard thought about his predicament and Carl recollected Sister Jackson's comments. Richard spoke first.

"There are about three new patients at the clinic. I can see them while I'm here. You can join me, and then the rest are yours. Any problems just give me a ring. I can give you advice over the phone. If it's something that needs looking at, would you let Mr Hamer know. He's in theatre this morning but he hasn't got anything heavy so he can pop out any time. I've got to go and see Prof Royston before I leave."

"Thanks, Mr Anderson, I'll try not bother him."

The three patients were waiting in the clinic when they arrived. Richard grabbed the notes and made his way to the consulting room. Carl followed in hot pursuit. How he wished he could possess the cool, calm demeanour of his boss. He always looked so composed and in control.

The three patients were all straight forward cases. A diagnosis was made, investigations were booked, and follow up appointment dates discussed for the first two. The third patient was placed on the waiting list for surgery. Richard scribbled in the notes and handed over to Carl. Suddenly there was a knock on the door.

"Yes," Richard said.

A head popped around the door.

"Professor Royston would like a word, Mr Anderson," said the young nurse.

"I'll be right out," he replied.

Professor Royston was standing in the corridor with his hands behind his back. Richard emerged from the consulting room. The Professor peered at him through the spectacles at the end of his nose causing Richard to swallow a little too loudly. He didn't want to appear ruffled, but the Professor had the knack of bringing that particular emotion out in him.

"Ah, Richard. A word if you might in my office."

"Certainly, Prof."

Richard followed like a naughty schoolboy being led to the headmaster's room. Professor Royston entered first and waited for Richard to follow him before he closed the door. He offered the chair in front of the old, mahogany desk and duly took his place behind it.

"I thought you had some kind of family crisis which was urgent enough to interrupt my wife's birthday celebrations," he remarked with a hint of a smile.

"I do, Prof."

"Then what are you doing here; shouldn't you be at home sorting things out?"

"I just came in to speak to Carl. I wanted to make sure he knew what was going on before I take some leave. I've got to organise a suitable operating list for him then I'm going home."

Richard wondered whether this was the point at which he was about to receive the backlash from yesterday.

"That's very commendable of you, but I'm sure one of your colleagues could have done that. How much leave do you need?"

"A week, maybe two. Melissa's left me . . ."

"Oh dear, I am sorry."

". . . and Jacob. I have a nanny, but I'm not sure she's going to be much help under the circumstances. I just need to make a few arrangements."

Richard's head dropped. He could feel the Professor's disapproval of his marriage breakdown seeping into his blood.

"Yes, of course, Richard. You must get yourself some help. It's not easy bringing up children, but in a demanding job like ours, it's virtually impossible alone. Take the two weeks if you need them and let me know periodically how things are going. We can extend it if necessary."

Richard looked up in surprise. Maybe he had read him wrong. Maybe there was a heart beneath that red bow tie and cynical exterior.

"Thanks, Prof. That's very understanding of you. I promise I'll sort this out as quickly as possible." The two men stood up and shook hands. "Thanks very much," Richard said appreciatively, relieved at the outcome.

"Good luck, Richard," Professor Royston replied. "You're going to need it."

***

It was Tuesday morning and Kate was rudely awakened by a cup of strong tea and some warm advice.

"Morning, Kate," Tina announced in a loud whisper. "Here, I've brought you a brew. Help yourself to some breakfast then get yourself under the shower and go and find a job and somewhere to live. It's the only way you're going to get over him by moving on."

Kate opened her sleepy eyes and sat herself up in the bed.

"Oh, what time is it?" she groaned.

"It's five past eight. Now listen don't worry about both today. Concentrate on one thing at a time. Don't forget though, Chris is back Friday night. You don't really want to spend the weekend with Alex's best mate, do you?"

Was that an order or a question, Kate wasn't sure? She had however, got the message loud and clear, that by Friday, Tina's hospitality would be wearing thin and she would be required to be elsewhere.

"See you later, honey. Text me if you have any luck."

Tina disappeared out of the door to her job at the travel agents. Kate peered across at the cup of tea she'd been left, or was it coffee? She couldn't normally tell when Tina had brewed up; it was always the colour of treacle. She had this annoying habit of leaving the tea bag in the water then going off to carry out some other function. She eventually came back to find the tea stewed and, totally unphased by this, would proceed to serve it as it was. She had even been known to leave the teabag in there on occasions. This particular cup looked like she had done just that. Kate couldn't face it and decided to go downstairs and make herself another.

She rummaged in the refrigerator for something to eat. She didn't really feel like anything but with the overwhelming task ahead of her, decided that a couple of pieces of toast were probably required. Maybe if she put a touch of jam on them it might make them a little more appetising and easier to get down.

On her way to the cupboard, Kate paused to look at the notice board next to the refrigerator which was covered with photographs. She couldn't help but notice the picture of Chris and Alex leering out at the camera pulling some ridiculous face. She remembered that holiday in Crete, when they'd all gone together. Her heart sank. They'd had some good times as a couple and now she was going to have to face the world as a single person. She wondered how many of their friends would stand by her and still want to go on holiday, or even just see her now that she and Alex were no longer together.

***

Kate pulled the door to behind her and locked up. She felt a little more refreshed after her shower, but still the churning in her stomach threatened the journey. She had felt like this for the past few days and would have gladly returned to her bed given half a chance.

She placed the folded newspaper in her handbag and headed off in the direction of the high street and the nearest letting agency. She'd studied the properties to-let in great depth the previous day and couldn't quite believe the extortionate monthly rents for just a one bed roomed flat. She thought of her measly cheque which she'd banked the day before and wondered how long it would actually last her if she failed to get a job.

Kate was soon outside the letting agency. She opened the door and stepped inside. A pleasant young woman in a tight, navy blue, two piece suit and extremely uncomfortable looking stiletto shoes approached her.

"Hello, can I help you?" the woman asked politely.

"Yes, I hope so," Kate replied. "I'm looking for a one bed roomed flat to rent."

"Certainly, madam. Would you like to take a seat, and I'll take some details? Which area are you looking at?"

"Somewhere local, not very expensive."

"I see," the saleswoman said with an empathetic smile. "How much were you thinking of?"

"Around four hundred a month?"

"You won't get much for four hundred around here, in fact I doubt there's anything for that."

Kate removed the newspaper from her bag and opened it on the desk in front of her.

"There are a few I've seen in the local paper. Can you see if they're still available?"

The young woman flicked her eyes across the page and tapped a few words into her computer.

"No that one's gone . . . so has that one . . . and that."

Kate's heart sank. She knew it wasn't going to be easy. It was like booking a late holiday where all the best deals had gone and she was about to be offered the one no one else wanted; the shabby little Bed and Breakfast in the middle of nowhere with the candlewick bedspread and shared bathroom.

"Oh, just a minute, there's one here; a one bed roomed, fully furnished flat on Cedar Vale High Street over the dry cleaners. So it's just down there," she said pointing to the right.

"How much?" Kate asked expectantly.

"Three hundred and sixty five pounds per month, that's very reasonable for a one bed roomed. Would you like to view it? I'll just see if that's possible. Yes, it's unoccupied at the moment."

It sounded too reasonable. Kate's excitement began to wane. What was wrong with it and why was no one living there at the moment?

"Yes, that would be great."

"Are you free now?" she asked.

"Yes," Kate answered, unfortunately she was.

"I'll get the keys then and we'll take a look. I must admit I haven't seen the property myself yet."

Kate waited whilst the assistant retrieved the keys and slipped her raincoat over her jacket. They left the shop and went in the direction the woman had indicated, past Ritchie's delicatessen. They continued their walk past the shops. Kate couldn't bring herself to look in the bridal shop window. It held too many bad memories and countless disappointments.

They were soon at the dry cleaners. A white, wooden door with the number twelve and the letter A in gold coloured metal stood between the dry cleaners and the next shop, the newsagents. The young woman let them both in. Behind the door was a steep staircase covered in a threadbare carpet. The walls, which Kate presumed were once white, now appeared stained and yellow. The woman flicked the light switch and a bare bulb illuminated above the top step, barely lighting the way. The two women cautiously mounted the stairs.

At the top was another wooden door, the centre of which contained a panel of opaque glass; the entrance to the flat. Kate wasn't sure what she expected to find behind it; squatters maybe, a drug den, an infestation of rats and insects; none would have surprised her. Her first impressions were not positive, in fact quite the opposite.

The saleswoman let them into the flat. A musty smell instantly met them, a reminder that the place had not entertained a human being for quite some time.

"It *has* been empty for a while," said the saleswoman practically reading Kate's thoughts. "It will need a little airing."

They walked to the left, through a narrow, dark corridor into the lounge via another doorway. A tatty, leather sofa and chair filled most of the small room. A dusty Venetian blind hung in the window behind the sofa and the walls were covered in the same pot of white paint they'd used in the staircase; that too was now yellow. A folded, white, melamine table sat against the wall to the right of the window with a white, painted, wooden chair either side. This was obviously the dining table although, once it was stretched out to its full capacity, Kate wondered how you would actually move in the room. It would also involve a considerable amount of furniture moving, but then on the other hand, the unlucky person who got to finally inhabit this dump would hardly want to do any entertaining. They wouldn't possibly want to bring anyone here.

A kitchenette led off to the right through an open archway. Both woman stared blankly as their eyes met the filth and grease that had accumulated on the work surfaces and the oven hob. They daren't look inside the oven itself. The refrigerator door was laid open for all to admire the handy work of someone somewhere who had at least seen fit to give it a clean.

The rest of the flat was equally grim. They made their way back along the dark corridor in the opposite direction. Off to the left was the bathroom. In distinct need of repair and some kind of ventilation, the cracked tiles held a multitude of mould spores. Kate could see them leaking out of the grouting. A sad looking shower head hung limply over the white, metal bath and black hairs clung to the plughole. She shuddered; God forbid if this is the only place she could afford. Would a lick of paint and a bottle of bleach render it inhabitable? She doubted that very much, but still the best was yet to come . . . the bedroom.

Kate nearly gasped in horror as she entered the last room. Her eyes were immediately drawn to the single bed in the middle of the bedroom. The striped mattress looked as if the invisible man was still lying on it; it had so many indentations where the springs no longer functioned. She shuddered at the wildlife it would probably contain. A tiny, wooden effect wardrobe stood in the corner with barely enough room for a couple of jackets. Similarly the chest of drawers looked as though they would fall over if you as much as put a t-shirt in there. The curtains didn't quite touch the bottom of the window and once pulled across would probably take on the appearance of a sheet but it was the walls that filled Kate with alarm. The floral patterned wallpaper was hanging by a thread at each corner of the room forced away by the underlying damp patch and that familiar black mould.

The whole place was a million miles from the three bed roomed, detached home she had shared with Alex. Small it may have been, but it was comfortable and clean and didn't require pest control to make it habitable.

"Well, it needs a bit of attention, but it's cosy and could be made nice," the saleswoman stated rather non-convincingly.

"A bit of attention? It needs more than that I'm afraid before I would even consider it. Who's the owner, I can't believe he would offer this place for rent looking like this? It's a health hazard; he should be reported to the Department of Health," Kate replied, incensed at the woman's last comment.

"Would you consider it if the owner had it thoroughly cleaned," the woman asked hopefully, sensing that the customer must be a little desperate to entertain the place in the first place.

"I'd have another look at it maybe, but in its current condition there's no way I would move in."

Kate didn't sound too convincing. She knew in her heart of hearts that her options were few and that if she didn't get herself a job as well, she'd be lucky to have this place.

"I'll leave my number and you can let me know if the owner is prepared to do anything," she finally agreed.

Kate scribbled her mobile number on a piece of paper she found in her handbag and left it with the woman. They both quickly left, pulling the door firmly behind them, dearly hoping they would never have to enter the place again.

Kate made her way outside and quickly drank in the fresh air; deep bucket-falls of it in a bid to rid herself of the musty smell clinging to her throat. She watched the saleswoman tip toe back to her office in her uncomfortable shoes and envied her position. She was only trying to get rid of the place and would probably never have to go in there again. No, Kate had the dreaded feeling that she would be back here sooner rather than later carrying a couple of cases of her personal possessions.

She stared up at the grimy windows with the Venetian blind and shuddered at the thought of her staring out at the main road and the passers by doing their shopping. She envisaged sitting in the dimly lit lounge at night time when all the shoppers had gone home and the noise of the traffic had died down; when the loneliness set in and the walls began to close around her. A desperate wave enfolded her, tightening around her chest, threatening to stop her breathing. She took a deep breath and breathed out slowly. It would only be temporary, surely. She'd find something better soon.

Her eyes were drawn to a piece of paper hanging in the window of the dry cleaners underneath the flat; PART TIME STAFF REQUIRED, APPLY WITHIN. Could this be her passport to a better home, she wondered? She decided to give it a go. Her mood lifted slightly as she opened the door and stepped inside.

A middle aged woman with short, dark brown, curly hair and glasses looked up as she entered then carried on labelling the clothes in front of her.

"Yes," she asked after a few moments.

It seemed all the shop assistants had the same kind of attitude around here, Kate thought casting her mind back to the delicatessen.

"I've come about the job advertised in the window," Kate said politely.

"Oh, just a minute," the woman replied then walked to a door at the rear of the counter. "Sheila," she shouted above the noise of the machines in the back. "Someone's here about the job."

"Send her round, Edna," Sheila shouted back.

"Go through," the first woman ordered as she returned to her task.

Kate did as she was told. The smell of cleaning solutions was a pleasant change to her nostrils after the past twenty minutes upstairs. Through the back was a host of machinery, hanging rails and item after item of clothing. Everywhere Kate looked there was a suit or a dress gleaming and covered in polythene.

Sheila took Kate into a tiny office right at the back of the building and sat her down.

"Now, tell me all about yourself . . ."

Forty five minutes later, Kate walked out onto Cedar Vale High Street as a part-time employee of Patterson's Dry Cleaners, working opposite shifts to Edna who had reached the age of sixty and still wanted to work a few hours in preference to sitting at home every day with her husband, Harvey. Kate would work Monday, Tuesday and Friday, and Edna would cover Wednesday, Thursday and Saturday morning on the counter. She should have been elated; celebrating with a bottle of wine and some friends; the first interview she'd had and she had been given the job. But she wasn't, on the contrary. The part-time position meant that she would almost certainly have to take the flat upstairs, since that was all she could now afford.

Kate made her sullen way back to Tina's home. She decided to walk; every penny was precious now and once there, she would await the phone call to tell her whether the landlord of 12A Cedar Vale High Street could be bothered to look after his new tenant.

# CHAPTER . . .

# 4

The days were ticking by, the weekend was looming, and the inevitable was rearing its ugly head. Kate was going to have to accept the flat on Cedar Vale High Street despite the lack of communication from the letting agency. She would give them a piece of her mind when she went in there.

Tina had been overjoyed by her news of both a job and accommodation on the same day. She had spared no time at all convincing Kate that she was making the right decision.

"You have to start somewhere," she had emphasised. "You can't expect to walk into a well paid job with no experience, and as for the flat, I'll help to clean it when we move your belongings in on Friday."

Kate seemed to have no choice but to take it, wildlife and all.

***

Richard had made no headway with Rachel at all. She had agreed in principal to the extra fifteen minutes at either end of the day but had yet to arrive before five past eight. He would never be able to depend on her and as for his on call work; he couldn't even consider it bearing in mind Rachel's complete lack of co-operation.

His mind was racing as he pushed his trolley around the supermarket. He realised he'd never actually done this whilst Melissa had been around. Either she'd done the shopping or one of those lorries had brought it to the house. It was quite an education. After over an hour of mulling over brands and products, weighing up prices and special offers, he finally paid and left. How on earth was he going to fit that into his heavy schedule? He had to put it all away now.

He pulled up outside the house and flipped the boot. Mrs Miller, his neighbour, had seen him arrive home through her lace curtain and quickly took the opportunity to get the full story first hand. There had been far too many rumours flying around and she felt a certain responsibility as the next door neighbour, to put everyone straight on the matter.

"Richard, how are you?" she asked, eyeing the bags of shopping in the boot.

Richard looked round.

"Oh, hi, Mrs Miller. I'm fine, thank you."

"I haven't seen Melissa around for a couple of days, is everything alright? She hasn't had one of her turns has she?"

"She's had more than that, Mrs Miller, she's left us. I'm now Jacob's sole guardian, and what's more we haven't heard from her in . . ." Richard looked to the heavens and screwed his eyes up to calculate, ". . . five days."

"Oh, I am sorry, Richard. I know you're a very busy man." Mrs Miller was genuinely concerned. She liked having a doctor for a neighbour and the thought of him not being able to do his job, or God forbid, having to move was not something she cared to relish. "Listen, if you need any help, and I mean any time of the day or night, just give me a knock and I can sit with Jacob whilst you do what you have to do."

Richard was quite taken aback. He had thought that she was only doing the nosy neighbour routine, but she actually seemed quite concerned about him. He didn't like to admit it, but he would probably have to take her up on her offer if he failed in his quest for another solution.

"Thanks, Mrs Miller," he replied a little brighter. "You might regret that, I may have to call on your help. Jacob's nanny isn't very flexible I'm afraid. She's only a bit of a kid and doesn't really understand the gravity of the situation."

"I mean it, Richard, and I'll be upset if you don't, do you hear?"

Richard smiled appreciatively and nodded.

"Thank you very much, that's a great help."

Mrs Miller returned to her home and Richard set about putting the shopping away, with just a little less weight on his over-burdened shoulders.

***

Kate opened the door to 12A Cedar Vale High Street on a drizzling and miserable October morning carrying a bucket full of cleaning solutions, cloths, rubber gloves and bleach; the weather precisely reflecting her mood. Tina followed her in with her vacuum cleaner, brush and dustpan. The rest of the luggage was outside in Tina's car.

The assistant at the letting agency had conveniently just started a two week holiday and hadn't passed any message on about the flat being cleaned and so it was left to the two young women to take on that task.

Kate opened the door at the top of the stairs and the familiar smell of mould came rushing towards her. Tina tried hard not to show her distaste as the smell filled her nostrils. Kate glanced down at her.

"We'll soon have this place smelling like roses," Tina joked, trying to lighten the situation.

"I didn't know they did rose smelling bleach," Kate replied. "Because that's what this place is getting, totally bleached. I'll probably die of the fumes in the night."

"Don't be daft, we'll open all the windows and we can get some nice air fresheners and dot them round the place."

They started in the bedroom in order to give it enough time for the smell of the bleach to diminish before Kate had the misfortune of having to sleep in there. Kate had treated herself to a sleeping bag and two new pillows; there was no way her skin was going to make any contact with that mattress. The curtains were taken down and placed in a bag for washing. She would sleep without them tonight.

Tina went into the bathroom and stared in disbelief at the chipped tiles and black mould. What kind of friend was she to let Kate move into a place like this? It was like some kind of doss house. But then Chris would never forgive her if he came home and found they had a lodger. She took the bleach out and started scrubbing; the bathtub, the sink, the toilet, the floor, and every square inch of tile on the wall. Her arms felt like lead by the time she'd finished but it was the least she could do.

They both met up in the lounge and prepared for another onslaught. The carpet received a dousing of carpet cleaner and left to soak for more than the desired length of time, and everything wooden was damp dusted . . . with bleach. Luckily there weren't many rooms and by late morning they had left themselves with only the kitchen to finish. They scrubbed every cupboard, the oven, and the hob until their original colour could be recognised, and threw away anything that had been left behind. Nothing in the kitchen was considered clean enough to eat from. The very thought of putting one of the abandoned forks or spoons in her mouth turned Kate's stomach. At three thirty they had finally done. All the windows were wide open and the strong smell of bleach was subsiding.

Tina dotted the air fresheners around each room, then she lit an aromatic candle and placed it on the folded table in the lounge. "It looks tons better," she said less than convincingly.

"Well, at least we've got rid of that awful smell," Kate replied, still not sure that she could actually spend a night here.

The two women brought up the rest of Kate's belongings and Kate proceeded to put everything away whilst Tina went back downstairs onto the high street to the Chinese takeaway to get them something to eat.

"There you go, it looks really homely now you've put everything out," Tina lied again as she appeared around the door clutching a white plastic bag. She placed the bag of food on the worktop in the kitchen and Kate went to dish out.

"I haven't got any plates," she announced looking around the kitchen.

"It doesn't matter, we'll eat out of the cartons."

"But what with, I've only got that one knife, fork, and spoon that you lent me?"

"You have the fork and I'll have the spoon," Tina replied handing the utensil over.

They took their food over to the folded table and after clearing a space by dragging the armchair across the room, pulled out one of the leaves. They seated themselves on the white, wooden chairs and tucked in. After a while they both looked at each other. Tina couldn't gauge Kate's thoughts. She smiled sympathetically. She could understand how she could feel so upset, but then suddenly Kate began to laugh.

"What's so funny?" Tina asked bemused.

"Us, sitting here with a fork and a spoon; I can't believe that I have nothing to show for nine years with Alex. I don't even have a plate."

Tina started to laugh with her. Before they knew it both of them were laughing hysterically and tears rolled down their cheeks.

Tina felt better as she left Kate that night. They'd had something to eat and drink and Kate's sense of humour was still intact. That was the main thing. She hadn't got herself depressed about the whole situation. Little did she know that as soon as her car had pulled away into the evening rain, Kate had seated herself on the sofa and cried. It started at first with the solemn realisation that she was completely alone. Her friend was making her way back to her fiancée. They would soon be embracing each other after they'd spent a few nights apart. Alex would be with his woman, whoever she was, in their lovely warm home, getting into her bed under the sheets that she had chosen. Her thoughts then returned to her predicament and the tears started to roll; huge drops fell onto her cheeks, faster and faster they poured. She began to sob until finally the tears ran out and her body ached from the effort. Eventually with a huge degree of reluctance she made her way to the bedroom and slithered between the layers of her new sleeping bag.

Kate didn't know if she ever fell asleep that night. She couldn't decipher whether she was having a bad dream or if in fact it was actually her real life unfolding in front of her, such was its clarity.

***

Richard sat opposite his young son as they ate breakfast together. Jacob's hair stood up at right angles and his eyes looked sleepy as he shovelled his cereal down.

"Daddy," he began. "When did you say grandma and granddad are coming to stay?"

"Another week yet; next Sunday and they're going to take care of you for a few days. Will you like that?"

"Mm."

Richard had finally told his mother the whole story. Well, she had dragged it out of him. She'd rung later in the week, when her migraine had subsided and asked Richard outright.

*"Richard, how are you darling?"* she'd started the conversation, and there ended the familiarities. She was standing no more nonsense.

"Oh, I'm fine, mum."

*"No, Richard, I mean how are you; how are you coping now that Melissa has walked out? What on earth was she thinking? How are you supposed to manage on your own with a full time job and a child to look after? Well, not just a full time job, a demanding one that doesn't finish at five like other jobs. I should know, I was a doctor's wife for thirty five years until your father retired."*

Richard had been slightly shell shocked. First of all he didn't know his parents were aware of his predicament and secondly, he didn't quite know which question to answer first.

"I've had a few days off, mum, just to try and sort things out."

*"And?"*

"And what?"

*"What have you sorted out?"*

"Oh, I see; so far the nanny has said she will do an extra quarter of an hour at either end of the day," though Richard had yet to see her arrive at her original time promptly. He decided not to mention that to his mother. "And Mrs Miller, next door, has very kindly said she would pop in any time I need her."

There had been a pause at the other end of the phone.

"Mum," said Richard, checking if she was still there.

*"Is that it? Is that all you've arranged so far? Will the nanny not live in for a while, just until you find alternative arrangements?"*

"To be honest, mum, I don't think that's a possibility. Besides, I'm not sure I'd like her around twenty four seven."

*"But Richard, if it's an option, you might have to take it."*

"That's just what I'm saying, mum, I don't think it is an option."

*"Well have you asked her?"* Iris Anderson was not a woman to give in without a fight. Richard would have to come clean or this conversation would go on all night.

"Not in so many words, but she was very reluctant to do the extra hours."

*"Oh, I see. When do you go back to work?"*

"A week on Monday."

*"We'll come down and give you a hand. I'll have a word with your father. We'll probably fly down on the Sunday."*

"Really, oh thanks, mum. You don't know how relieved that makes me, and Jacob will love to see you."

*"Then it's a date. I'll ring later in the week. Is Jacob okay by the way? How's he doing without his mother?"*

"He's quiet, but I think he's alright. Kids are quite resilient aren't they?"

*"Not as much as you think, keep an eye on him. He may be bottling things up. We'll make a big fuss of him when we come down. What does he like doing at the moment?"* Iris was already mentally planning their activities.

"He loves crayoning, playing with action toys, anything like that."

*"I'll have a little shop before we come down."*

"Now don't go spoiling him."

*"I'll spoil him as much as I like, he's my only grandson, and especially since his mother has just walked out on him, poor little sweetheart. He must wonder what the hell he's done. You keep reassuring him that this is not his fault won't you?"*

"I will, don't worry."

*"Okay, son, see you in a week and keep your chin up, for the sake of Jacob if nothing else."*

"Thanks, mum, and thanks again for coming down, bye."

*"Bye."*

Richard had been so happy at the prospect of his parents coming down, but his euphoria was waning again as the seconds ticked by on this Monday morning. The realisation had set in that Rachel was once again late. He could feel the anger building up from the pit of his stomach. Two minutes past eight and still no signs. He would have to have another word with her. He wasn't fond of confrontation. It was the only part of his job that he disliked, but still, if he was to get any kind of respect from this girl, he was going to have to do it. At ten past eight, the key rattled in the door and Rachel let herself in.

"Sorry I'm late, only . . ."

Rachel didn't have time to finish. Richard, flushed and angry, concluded the sentence for her. "Your alarm clock didn't go off; there was a huge traffic jam; the bus driver was abducted by aliens. You haven't arrived on time since I've been off Rachel, let alone the fifteen minutes earlier I asked you to start. Now do you want this job or shall I get someone who can start when I ask them to because this isn't good enough for me . . . at all?"

Rachel stood motionless and stared at her boss. Jacob dropped his spoon in his bowl of cereal as his jaw lowered in surprise. Suddenly, the young girl's bottom lip began to quiver and tears started to drip onto her cheeks. She swallowed hard.

"I'm sorry," she mouthed. She couldn't speak properly for fear of bursting into tears.

"Rachel, I have a very demanding job which I'm going to have to go back to next week and I need some kind of commitment from you. I need to know that you will be here at quarter to eight in the morning so that I can get to the hospital to start my ward round. Can you do that?"

His voice was much gentler now. He didn't want the girl emotionally disturbed but he now knew that she had got the message loud and clear and that anything less than what he was asking, was not enough.

Rachel nodded this time, still not sure that she would be able to enter into conversation without crying.

"Fine, thank you. Now would you get Jacob ready whilst I tidy up in the kitchen?"

Rachel nodded again and quickly manoeuvred the little, bemused boy up the stairs. Richard carried the pots into the kitchen and placed them on the worktop. He leaned back against the sink and closed his eyes. This was so hard. He rubbed his forehead. The only light at the end of the tunnel was his parent's visit, but that's all that it was, a visit. He couldn't ask them to uproot and come and live with him. He also had to tell Rachel that she wouldn't be needed during his parent's stay. How was she going to take that? Under the present circumstances she will probably think that she was being fired. Typical, she was in the wrong turning up late every day yet here he was feeling guilty for telling her and giving her a holiday.

***

Kate's first day had been fairly successful. Sheila and Edna had shown her the ropes, then Edna had allowed her to serve several people in the afternoon alone. It wasn't rocket science but nonetheless it was an important part of the procedure since it was her duty to ensure that the correct clothes went back to the right people.

Kate was exhausted by the end of the day. She hadn't stood for so long in ages. Her previous job consisted of sitting at a computer for most of the day. She met the odd client but that was about as much walking as she did. She was almost glad to get back to her flat at the end of her first day. Tomorrow she would be alone at the front desk. Edna was beginning her new hours and had only reluctantly volunteered to work today to pass on her valuable experience.

"I'll be in the back if you get stuck with anything," Shelia had reassured her. "You'll be alright," And that was it. She was now an indispensable member of the team.

Edna had passed on her luck. That would probably be the last time she saw her for a while since they would now work opposite shifts to each other. Kate wasn't unduly upset. Edna wasn't exactly a barrel of laughs, in fact she found her quite surly and if she was a customer, would perhaps mention so. She would be much nicer.

That evening Kate took herself to bed earlier than usual. She would read her book for a while and hopefully tonight, she may be able to get a few hours sleep. It didn't come easy at the moment. She spent hour upon hour staring at the grim surroundings, thinking of every conceivable way of getting out of these four walls and into somewhere a damn site healthier. But tonight she wasn't going to have that problem for a soon as her eyes met the words her lids started to close. Before she knew it, her book was resting on top of her and she was fast asleep.

***

Richard had barely got Jacob dressed that morning when he heard the front door open. It was Rachel bright and early. He glanced at his watch, twenty two minutes to eight. He could hardly believe it. So she was capable of arriving on time. He took Jacob into the kitchen where Rachel was awaiting approval; she smiled in anticipation, eyebrows raised.

"Morning, Rachel, well done. You're actually early this morning."

"I know, I got the earlier bus."

"Well thanks for that. It makes me feel a lot more confident about getting in on time for work. I really appreciate it." Richard thought he would overdo the praise after his threat yesterday. Rachel glowed with self satisfaction. She had certainly surpassed herself today. She seated herself at the breakfast table and took out her magazine, whilst she waited for Richard to prepare breakfast for his son. Richard took a deep breath and carried on. He would bring the magazine thing up at a later date; best not to spoil the moment at this point in the day.

"I'm going to sort the washing out today," he announced. "I've got some dry cleaning to take as well. Have you got any plans when Jacob's in nursery?"

"No, not really. I usually just read my magazine or a book," Rachel replied.

Richard shook his head in despair.

"I wondered if you'd sort Jacob's bedroom out for him? There are a lot of toys and books that he's grown out of up there. He needs some room to put all his birthday presents. They've been sat around for weeks now," he suggested.

"Course, I'll do that when he gets home then he can help me. I don't want to throw away any of his favourite toys. He'd never forgive me, would you Jacob?" Rachel answered.

"I don't want to throw *any* of my toys away," Jacob complained. "I want to keep all of them."

"See what I mean. I would be in trouble if I started throwing your toys out without asking first wouldn't I?"

Rachel seemed quite pleased with Jacob's response and went back to her magazine. It was worth a try, thought Richard trying to think of something else she could do instead of sitting on her backside all morning reading. He was sure other nannies did more than this but he didn't quite know what was within her boundaries. He didn't particularly want the agency ringing him up and complaining that he wasn't sticking to the job description; unfortunately in Rachel's case, that didn't amount to very much.

***

Richard had set the washing machine in motion and was on the way to the dry cleaners with two suits and a pair of trousers to be cleaned. He wasn't sure how he was going to fit this into his schedule once he had returned to work either.

The dry cleaners wasn't far. He parked his car up on the high street and rushed in. Kate was busying herself behind the counter pinning tickets to the prepared garments when the tall, handsome, stranger walked in.

"Hi, can I help you?" she said smiling sweetly.

She'd kept her pact to be more pleasant than Edna to the customers. It seemed to be working. They soon smiled back and engaged in conversation with her.

"Could you have these dry cleaned for me?" Richard asked smiling back at the pleasant, young woman.

"Two suits and one pair of trousers, is that right, sir?"

"Yes, that's right."

"You haven't left anything in the pockets, have you?"

"Oh, I didn't think to check."

"You never know, sir; there might be a twenty pound note in there."

Richard rummaged through all the pockets and smiled again.

"No, typical of my luck at the moment, nothing."

"Yes, you and me both. They'll be ready by Friday morning, is that alright for you?"

"Yes, that'll be great."

"What name is it, please?"

"Anderson, Richard Anderson."

Kate scribbled the details on the ticket and handed it over to him.

"Just bring your ticket with you on Friday, Mr Anderson."

"Do I need to pay you now?"

"No, when you collect will be fine, thanks a lot."

"Thank you."

"Goodbye."

"Bye."

Richard was very impressed with the service. That was simple enough, it was just time consuming having to drive here and park up. Melissa had always done the dry cleaning run and made such a fuss about it.

Kate was still looking out of the window at her last customer. They didn't usually come in looking so smart and handsome. Even dressed casually he looked expensive. She wondered what he did for a living. She started to day dream as she looked at the ticket stub. Richard Anderson, he sounded important like he could be a bank manager or an accountant. She looked forward to Friday now, when he would return to collect his clothing. She hoped he didn't send his wife in his place.

***

The rest of the day went by fairly quickly. Kate was kept busy and seemed to be serving someone in her pleasant manner every time Sheila popped her head round the door.

"Everything going alright?" Sheila asked around lunchtime.

"Yes it seems to be."

"Why don't you go and get some lunch and I'll take over the counter."

Sheila glanced over the ticket stubs and admired the tidy desk.

"Well done, Kate, you're doing really well."

Kate stopped at the door and smiled.

"Thanks, Sheila. See you in half an hour."

Kate had no desire to return to her flat for lunch so she removed the bag of sandwiches from her handbag and took a seat across the road in the gardens. The air was cool but the sun was shining. She took the flask out and poured herself a cup of tea.

Sheila watched her from the window. She was a nice girl but what was she doing sitting over there when she lived in the flat upstairs. It was difficult to get to know her even though they worked in the same building. They didn't come into contact much, but she had noticed a sadness in her eyes behind that lovely smile; one that often accompanied loneliness. She wondered why she'd taken the flat upstairs on her own. The way those students had left it, it was a wonder anyone could live in there. Maybe she was running away from something, or even someone, Sheila thought drawing up her own conclusions. A customer entered the shop and her thoughts were gone.

***

Kate was tired again after another busy day but this evening it was difficult to switch off. Her mind was racing. She had more responsibilities now. Shelia seemed happy with her though which was good. Richard Anderson kept making his way into her thoughts. *Don't do anything stupid when he comes in on Friday,* she warned herself.

That night her mind refused to rest. She stared at the illuminated alarm clock by her bed and watched the hours tick by. Then she fixated on the damp patch in the corner of the room. Despite the darkness, she could still make out the black mould and the paper peeling off. She hated this room, more than any other. Probably because in this room she had nothing else to think about but the dank surroundings she found herself in. She could feel a wave of despair taking over her. How she yearned for Friday when she could get out of here and talk to people again.

# CHAPTER . . .

# 5

It was Friday morning and Richard had just put down the phone. Rachel wouldn't be coming in this morning, she had a bad cold, her mother had just informed him. *Well she was bloody fine yesterday,* he'd wanted to tell her but for some reason had decided against it. What was he going to do? She was so unreliable. He had detected a stern note in her mother's voice and wondered if Rachel had told her about his threats. It was probably her mother's idea for her to take the day off. She was making him sweat. His heart sank again. Just as he thought he was making some headway, she'd let him down again. Ah, well, his parents would be here in a couple of days to lighten the load.

He made his way downstairs to prepare Jacob's breakfast. He wanted to leave him asleep as long as possible. He'd had a difficult night last night, a disturbed sleep, maybe a bad dream. Richard didn't know for certain what had woken him but it had taken a while for him to settle again. He wandered through the dining room into the kitchen.

The pile of ironing sitting on the dining chair seemed to be getting bigger and he couldn't find the impetus to do anything about it. He'd only ever ironed a shirt, and that was badly. He'd perhaps get round to that job once Jacob had gone to bed tonight. The longer he left it, the more his mother would feel obliged to get it done and then the guilt trip would begin as if he'd left it there on purpose. No, it would have to be tackled tonight.

Jacob wandered bleary eyed into the dining room.

"Daddy, what day is it?" he asked rubbing his eyes.

"Hello, sweetheart," his father said putting down the cereal packet and picking his young son up. "How are you this morning? I thought I was going to have to come and wake you up. It's Friday today; last day at nursery and then the weekend off, how good is that?"

"When are grandma and granddad coming?"

Jacob had asked the same question every day since Richard had told him of their visit. He was beginning to wonder if his mother was right and that Jacob was suffering from Melissa's departure. Perhaps that was the reason he'd had a disturbed night last night.

"Two more sleeps and they'll be on their way."

The little boy seemed satisfied with the answer and sat down at the table waiting for his breakfast. Richard observed him from the kitchen. Why had Melissa not been in touch with him yet? Of course he was missing his mother; he was stupid not to have noticed it. It had been almost two weeks since she'd walked out without a single word. Grandma will know what to do. She will drown him in so much love and affection in the next few days, he won't have time to think of his selfish mother.

***

The journey to nursery was quiet, almost silent. Jacob gave the odd, single word answer to Richard's questions but that was all he could muster. Richard walked in with him when the doors were opened.

"Morning, Jacob," Mrs Bentley announced as he walked into the room. "Oh, good morning," she said looking at Richard.

"Morning, I'm Jacob's dad. I'll be picking him up today."

"No Rachel, is she okay?"

"Yes, apparently she's got a cold. Jacob, why don't you go and hang your coat up." Jacob walked off to the cloakroom. "He's a bit quiet this morning. I don't know if you heard that his mother has left but it may have something to do with that."

"We'll keep an eye on him; Rachel did mention something, but thanks for telling us. See you later."

Richard said goodbye to Jacob and reluctantly left him aimlessly wandering around on his own. His heart went out to him. He was just thankful that his parents would be here on Sunday to shoulder his burden and cheer their grandson up.

Next job was to retrieve his dry cleaning. Richard went straight to the Cedar Vale High Street and parked in the same place he had done previously. He could see the same girl behind the counter and decided he would pick her brains and seek out some help.

Kate saw Richard Anderson approaching the shop. She new exactly where his dry cleaning was on the rack behind her and would look ultra efficient when he produced his ticket and she went straight to the correct garments, not like someone who had only started three days ago. He was certainly bright and early; the first customer of the day. She'd added just a hint of makeup this morning although she needn't have bothered since her cheeks flushed as he entered the shop.

"Morning," she said brightly. She'd decided earlier not to use his name; that would sound far too familiar.

"Morning," he replied. "I've come to collect my dry cleaning."

She knew exactly why he'd come having thought of little else over the last couple of days. He handed over his ticket and she reached up to retrieve the polythene covered clothes hung up behind her.

"There you go, that's twenty three pounds forty five please."

Richard handed over his credit card. Kate completed the transaction and handed his card back.

"Do they have an ironing service here?" he asked hopefully.

"No, I'm sorry," Kate replied, then suddenly she had an idea. She quickly glanced behind her. "The shop doesn't have one but I could do some ironing for you if you wanted."

"Really?" Richard asked. A smile spread across his face. "That would be fantastic. Are you sure?"

"Yes, of course, I only work here three days. I've got plenty of spare time."

Kate felt giddy inside. She could hardly believe her luck, not only did she have the opportunity to raise some extra cash in order to get out of that ghastly flat, but she would also get to see Richard Anderson again.

Richard was so happy. He could visualise that perpetual pile of ironing disappearing overnight, and not only that, it would never be there again longer than it needed to be.

"I don't suppose I could be really cheeky and ask you to do the ironing at my home could I, it's just I have a very demanding job and a four year old son and I'm finding it really difficult to fit everything in at the moment?"

*Even better,* thought Kate.

"Of course, how far away are you? I don't have any transport you see."

"Oh, don't worry about that, I'll send a taxi for you."

"Really, you'd go to those lengths just to get your ironing done?"

"I certainly would. You won't believe what a relief this is."

Kate was making all kinds of assumptions in her head. He obviously wasn't married, or maybe he was married and she's left him to look after their child. She still hadn't worked out his occupation but that wouldn't take long, not now she was actually working for him.

"When do you want me to start?" she asked, carefully trying to hide her excitement at the thought of doing some ironing.

"As soon as possible, before we actually sink under a mountain of laundry."

Kate managed a laugh. She thought that was appropriate and not too forward under the circumstances.

"What about tomorrow, or would you prefer to leave the weekends free?" she said.

"Tomorrow is perfect; I was hoping you were going to say that. My parents are coming over on Sunday and I would love to show them that I was actually coping." Richard laughed this time. At last his luck was changing. She seemed such a nice girl, talkative and obliging. "Would two o'clock be alright for you?"

"That's fine, I've got no other plans for the weekend."

"Where shall I send the taxi?"

"Here, I'll wait outside." Kate had no intention of letting him see where she lived.

"Are you sure? I can send it to your home."

"I don't live far away."

"Great then, I'll see you tomorrow. Oh, by the way, I don't know your name."

"Kate, Kate Forrester."

"Richard Anderson, but please, call me Richard."

Richard scooped his dry cleaning off the counter and with one last goodbye, left the building. Kate wanted to laugh and cry at the same time. She couldn't believe that she could be so happy at the prospect of doing some ironing. It was a chore she'd hated when she lived with Alex, but how she looked forward to it now. She would do it so well, the job would be hers for life.

***

At two o'clock the following day, Kate was waiting patiently outside Patterson's Dry Cleaners. A private taxi pulled up at the kerbside and she quickly ran across to ensure it was hers. She didn't want to be late on her first day.

"Taxi for Kate Forrester?" she asked hopefully.

"Yes, booked by a Mr Anderson, is that right?"

"Yes, that's right."

She climbed in the back. For some reason her heart was racing. Why was she so nervous? She felt like she was going for an interview for some high flying job, not ironing a few shirts. The taxi pulled away and she watched the flat disappear. Then it dawned on her why she was so nervous; if this didn't go well, she would be staying there indefinitely, and that was not an option she cared to think about.

A few minutes later the taxi drew to a halt outside a large, detached, Victorian residence the side of which faced a vast open park.

"How much do I owe you?" she asked the driver.

"It's already paid for, love," the driver replied.

Kate inwardly smiled and thanked the man. She made her way through the ornate, cast iron gate and up the garden path. She stopped for a while to catch her breath, then knocked on the door. Moments late the door swung open and Richard was there to greet her.

"Kate, come in. It's good to see you."

"Thank you."

It was good to see him, she thought. He was her saviour, dragging her away from that awful place. She followed him into the hall and immediately the contrast between the flat and Richard's home were apparent. It was warm and clean, with expensive décor. Richard took her coat and hung it on the hat stand in the hallway just next to the staircase.

"Follow me," he beckoned.

He led her through a doorway, past a room to the left which was obviously his office with its mahogany wooden desk and laptop, into the dining area. There she spied the pile of ironing, teetering way above the rim of the basket ready to fall at any moment.

"Would you like a drink before you start; tea or coffee?" Richard asked.

"I'll have a coffee please, but if you don't mind I'll get cracking. There's quite a bit here and I'm sure you don't want me here all night as well."

"Oh, I know, it's so embarrassing, but I'm absolutely useless at it."

"Don't apologise, if you could do it, I'd be out of a job."

"No, you don't have to worry about that. I wouldn't have the time to do it anyway."

Kate set about her work and soon was chipping away at the pile. Suddenly a little face appeared around the door.

"Ah, this is Jacob. Jacob meet Kate, she's going to be helping us. I wondered how long it would take before you came to have a look at what was going on."

"Hello, Jacob. Nice to meet you," Kate said to the little boy. "And how old are you?"

"I'm four," he replied shyly. "My grandma and granddad are coming tomorrow to stay for a few days."

"I think your daddy told me, that's great isn't it? What are you going to do with them?"

"I'm going to colour and play with my toys."

"Really, I used to love colouring when I was young."

"Are you good at it?"

"Not too bad."

"Jacob, why don't you go and do a lovely picture and you can show it to Kate when she has a break?" Richard interrupted.

"Okay, and you can take it home with you if you like," Jacob said excitedly.

"Oh, I'd love to, that would really brighten up my flat. Will you put lots of colour in it for me?" Kate replied.

"Yes." Jacob ran off in order to complete his mission.

"That's the most he's said all week," Richard commented. He looked thoughtful. "His mother walked out on us and I think he's becoming a little withdrawn. He's really excited about his grandparents coming. I just hope it doesn't upset him too much when they have to leave."

"You'll just have to make a huge fuss of him and take his mind off it," Kate suggested.

"I know what you're saying but my job is so time consuming it's quite difficult to do that."

"Just make the most of the time you do have." Kate smiled. "Here am I sounding like an expert. I don't even have kids of my own and I'm trying to tell you what to do."

"No, it all helps, Kate. Sometimes you can't see what's happening when it's right under your nose. It quite often takes someone else to point these things out."

Kate couldn't believe how easy he was to talk to. She had been ironing for a good half an hour and they hadn't stopped talking apart from the odd occasion when Richard would grab a handful of clothes and take them upstairs to put away.

The break was a welcome one. She could feel the twinge in her back after standing for so long in one position. At that point Jacob walked into the dining room proudly displaying his picture.

"Wow, Jacob, have you done that yourself?" she asked.

"Yes," Jacob replied.

"Are you sure, only I saw your daddy leave the room once or twice?"

"No, daddy you didn't help me, did you?"

"No, definitely not."

"Well I've never seen such a beautiful picture by a four year old."

Jacob's smile spread the full width of his face lighting up his eyes. Richard stood back and smiled with him. It was infectious watching his son looking so happy at last.

"And am I really allowed to keep it?" Kate asked staring at the picture.

Jacob nodded. He was too happy to speak.

"Okay, Jacob, Kate's going to finish off now, would you go and do me one of those lovely pictures?" asked Richard.

Jacob disappeared again and Kate reluctantly finished her chore. She would have loved to stay and chat for longer. It was so lonely in that flat hour after endless hour with not a soul to speak to. At least she had this job now to break the endless tedium.

As she finished the last items, Richard swooped in again to take them upstairs. He quickly returned.

"So Kate, do you want to take the job on? I'd certainly like you to."

"Well if you're happy, I am. When do you want me here?"

"What days did you say you worked?"

"Monday, Tuesday, and Friday. I can be free any other time."

"What about Wednesdays at three o'clock for say a couple of hours?"

"Perfect."

"I'll send the taxi to the same place, is that okay with you?"

"I'll be waiting."

"I'll get your coat. Jacob," he shouted. "Kate's leaving now, are you going to say goodbye?"

Jacob ran out of the lounge and threw his arms around Kate.

"Ahh, that was lovely. I've got my picture, Jacob," she said waving it at him. "I'm going to put it straight on my wall when I get back."

"Bye, Kate."

"Bye, sweetheart."

Richard looked on in shock. He had never seen his son show anyone that kind of affection before, not even his mother. He'd purposely asked her to come in the afternoon so that his son could see her again. He had a certain feeling that she might be good for him.

"Daddy, is Kate coming again?" he asked his father as they waved her off in the taxi.

"Yes, son, for a long time I hope."

***

Kate's faith in human nature had just been well and truly restored. *What a lovely family,* she thought as she made her way back to her flat clutching her picture. She glanced down at it again. He must have used every colour in the box, just like she'd asked him. Poor little thing not having his mother around. How could she walk out on such a beautiful little boy? She was going to make a fuss of him when she saw him next Wednesday, she was sure of that.

# Chapter . . .

# 6

"Grandma, granddad, Kate came yesterday and I drew her a picture and she's going to put it on her wall," shouted Jacob barely pausing for breath.

He was jumping around the hallway excitedly as his grandparents struggled through the doorway with their luggage. Richard leaned forward and took the smaller case from his mother.

"Who's Kate?" Iris asked as she threw her arms around her young grandson.

"She came yesterday to do the ironing; another of my recruits. She works at the dry cleaners on the high street and very kindly volunteered to come and help me out."

"Mm, sounds like she made quite an impression on someone," Iris laughed.

"She was great with Jacob, and she was only here a couple of hours. They got on really well."

"Never mind all this talk about Kate," Donald Anderson moaned. "Get that kettle on. You hardly get a thimble full on these flights."

Richard laughed.

"One strong cup of tea coming up, dad."

***

"So, my little sweetheart, what have you been up to since I last saw you?"

Iris and Donald had settled themselves into their room and were now seated on the sofa in the lounge enjoying a nice cup of tea with biscuits. Jacob stood in front of his grandma with a car in each hand ready to show her.

"Mummy left and we haven't seen her for a long time. She's gone to get some medicine," he replied with his eyes still fixed on the cars. He was demonstrating the opening doors on the little, red, sports car.

The three adults looked at each other concerned.

"Well, guess what granny has brought for you," Iris exclaimed, quickly changing the subject. "Go and get that bag over there and have a look inside."

"Crayons!"

"And."

"A colouring book!"

"Of."

"Lightning McQueen, daddy, it's a Cars colouring book!"

"Wow, how good is that?" Richard exclaimed.

"Granny, I'm going to do Kate another picture because she wants to make her flat look nice."

"Well I do hope we get to meet Kate whilst we're here. I'm very intrigued."

***

Kate stared at the picture on her bedroom wall. She smiled inwardly. It was like her link to the outside world; an imaginary umbilical cord connecting her to the Anderson household. It had certainly pumped life back into her; seeing his little face light up when she told him how good it was. How wonderful fate was. Just as she thought her world had crumbled, a chance meeting with Richard Anderson had turned it upside down. She was now actually looking forward to something. She would count the hours down before she could go back next Wednesday.

***

Richard arrived back at work bright and early on Monday morning. He had left a multitude of instructions with his parents who had ushered him out of the door stating firmly that they had managed to bring him up and would cope perfectly well. Richard didn't doubt that, he only hoped that Jacob would with yet more change.

"Morning, Carl, morning, Sister Jackson," he announced as he breezed on to the ward.

Sister Jackson looked in awe at the man approaching then scurried after him whilst Carl Walker brought up the rear pushing the metal trolley of notes with him.

"How's everything been whilst I've been away? Any problems?"

Sister Jackson had taken her position next to Richard as they spoke to each patient in turn. She always insisted on doing the ward round with him. No one else was allowed that privilege, which all worked rather well until she was off duty, then no one new how the ward round proceeded, thus making the Sister look even better when she returned as everything would then revert to running smoothly again. No other consultants were treated in this way, not even the Professor. He practically had to insist that she accompany him.

Richard was well aware of Sister's fondness for him. He could see the glint in her eye and the faint blushing of her cheeks every time he spoke to her. He made every move to keep her at arms length though; she wouldn't require much encouragement, that's why he always insisted on calling her Sister Jackson, not Cynthia as she had asked him to do on many occasions.

They finally arrived at Ronald Burton's bedside who was patiently waiting in the side room.

"This is Mr Ronald Burton," Carl explained. "Sixty two years of age, non smoker. Mr Burton has considerable skin loss over the tibia with exposed bone. He's for a gastrocnemius flap or possibly a free flap on your trauma list this afternoon."

"Good morning, Mr Burton," Richard said introducing himself. "I'm Mr Anderson, the consultant. Do you mind if I have a look at your leg?"

"Not at all, doctor," Mr Burton replied.

Sister Jackson swooped in and removed the dry dressing from his leg. A raw wound about the size of a tablespoon was exposed. Richard could see the bone showing through.

"How did this happen, Mr Burton?" he asked inspecting the wound.

"A concrete paving slab fell over and unfortunately my leg was underneath it."

"We need to cover the wound up; we can't have bone showing like that because there's a risk that it might get infected. We've got two options here. We are going to see whether we can swing some tissue round from the back of your leg. If we do that then we'll have to cover the area left by that flap with a skin graft. We'll take that from the same thigh; keep the work on the one leg. If that particular flap isn't suitable then we may have to take tissue from the muscle in your back and plumb it into your leg. We'll need to cover that with a skin graft as well. Any questions Mr Burton?"

"Only one, doctor. Will it be sore afterwards?"

"The anaesthetist will give you a machine to ease any pain. He'll explain that to you when he comes to see you." Richard tapped him on the shoulder. "See you this afternoon."

Outside the room Richard dished out his orders.

"Carl will you sort out the consent form and make sure it mentions the skin graft. I don't want the same problem we had the other week with Mr Vickers. Sister can you make sure that dressing is done immediately, we don't want any infection in that bone. Thanks a lot."

Richard started to walk away before Sister Jackson had time to ask any more awkward questions about his private life. At that point Todd Hamer walked onto the ward.

"Richard, good to see you back, how's things?" he asked shaking his hand.

Richard spied Sister Jackson hovering in the background waiting for his reply.

"Todd, good to see you as well," he replied manoeuvring him out into the corridor.

"Things have definitely been better. I'm glad I caught you though, who's on call this weekend; can you remember from the rota?"

"Yes, it's me, why?"

"I couldn't swap with you could I? My parents are over for a few days and they could look after Jacob for me this weekend. I haven't exactly made much progress sorting cover out yet."

"Hey, these things take time. If Jayne and I can do anything to help, just give us a call."

"It's a bloody miracle I need at the moment, but thanks for the offer. Oh, I have actually found someone to do my ironing so things are looking up slightly."

"There you go; it's not so bad after all."

"No, I just wonder how long old Royston will see it like that."

***

Wednesday was finally here and Kate waited patiently for her taxi. How she had looked forward to today. Her picture still hung on the wall in pride of place reminding her that life wasn't that bad after all.

Iris Anderson opened the door to her.

"Ah, you must be Kate. I've heard so much about you from my little grandson here."

Jacob's head appeared beneath his grandmother's arm. Kate was overjoyed. So Jacob had talked about her when she'd gone, she thought.

"Yes, that's me," she replied. "Hello Jacob, how are you today?"

"I'm fine," he said shyly.

"Are you going to do me another picture? I need one for my living room now. Your other one has brightened my bedroom up so much."

"Do you want a lot of colour on it again?" asked Jacob almost giddy at the idea.

"Yes, please, as many as you've got."

Jacob ran off in pursuit of his crayons whilst Kate went in and took her coat off.

"Come in, Kate, and I'll put the kettle on. Thank you for taking the trouble over Jacob. He's a bit lost at the moment," the older woman said.

"It's no trouble, Mrs Anderson, he's adorable."

"I know he is, mind you I'm a bit biased him being my one and only grandson. I do miss him terribly though. We moved up to Scotland before he was born. We both love that part of the world and couldn't wait to retire up there, but now I think we may have to look into moving back down here."

"The only thing about living long distances away is that you probably spend longer at any one time with your family. My mum lives in Spain and I get to spend a week with her at a time but then I don't see her for months."

"Precisely, it's all or nothing."

The two women chatted easily over a cup of tea then Iris left her to carry on with her job whilst she went to check on Jacob. After a while she popped back into the room.

"The pictures coming on very nicely; he's taking so much care over it."

"Bless him." Kate was touched.

She put the finishing touches to the last shirt and was finished. Jacob arrived with the picture.

"Here you are, Kate; this is Lightning McQueen and Mater in Radiator Springs."

"Oh, Jacob, you are going to be a wonderful artist. That's so neat. Where did you get this lovely picture from?"

"Grandma and granddad gave it to me but you can keep this one."

"Is that okay with grandma and granddad?"

Jacob turned round to seek their approval.

"Of course, after all that hard work, Kate deserves a picture doesn't she?" Iris said happily. She could see a bond building between her grandson and this young woman and had no intention of breaking it.

***

Richard's taste of freedom was coming to an end. Rachel would be back on Monday. He'd spent the last two weeks making as good an impression on Professor Royston as he knew how, bowing and scraping to his every whim, even going as far as chairing the Theatre User's meeting in his absence. But alas it was time for his parents to leave and it was difficult to decide who was most upset.

"Now you put your foot down with that young girl if she starts, what's she called, Rachel? Remember, you're the boss."

"I know mum, but what if she walks because she doesn't like what I have to say? I tell you these days the employees hold all the cards."

"Nonetheless, you've got your career to think about and she's supposed to be the nanny, helping you not the other way round. Now, if you need us again just give us a call." Richard was tempted to ask them outright but he knew they were tired. His father was already in the taxi waiting to go back to the airport. Jacob was fine in small doses for his grandparents, but all day every day had taken its toll. "In fact if the worst comes to the worst," his mother added, "I'm sure Kate would help you out. She's such a nice girl and you're right, Jacob thinks the world of her."

Richard heard what his mother had just said. It wasn't such a bad idea after all. She seemed to like her short visits. It also seemed that Kate had won the hearts of his parents as well.

# Chapter . . .

# 7

Richard arrived at one fifteen on the dot for his afternoon list. He was met by Janey Vickers the theatre manager.

"Hello, Mr Anderson, I'm afraid Mr Donovan's orthopaedic list is running a little late. Your list is going to be delayed slightly," she said apologetically.

"Oh, no, how long will he be?"

"He reckons he'll be finished by two."

"Two o'clock? Is there not another theatre I could use?"

"No, I'm afraid not. We'll get the first patient down and be ready to go as soon as possible."

Richard felt cold. This was the last thing he needed. With his current arrangements he required everything to run like clockwork. He sighed deeply. "Have you got a copy of the list Carl?" he asked his registrar.

Carl fished the copy out of his briefcase and handed it over.

"I could do with swapping the order. If we do Mrs Arnold second then if necessary you could finish that one. I need to be around when we do Harry Lee. Could you arrange that while I speak to my secretary?"

Carl disappeared to a phone whilst Richard left the department. He arrived back ten minutes later to a perplexed looking young man.

"I'm afraid the anaesthetist has given Mr Lee something to drink and we can't do him until three o'clock."

"Oh, God," Richard remarked running his fingers through his hair. Frustration was starting to crush his spirit. What did he do now? His thoughts went back to his mother's suggestion about Kate. She would be at the house at three o'clock.

Maybe he could ask her to step in; he knew for certain that Rachel would be less than obliging.

***

Kate had not met Rachel yet. She was hoping to form another friendship through the family, having managed to bond with everyone else so far. She'd even had a very pleasant conversation with Richard's father despite his absence throughout most of her visits.

"Hi, I'm Kate," she announced brightly to the young girl opening the door.

"Hi, I'm Rachel. Mr Anderson told me to expect you, come in."

Jacob must be in the lounge, Kate presumed, as she heard the sound of the television in the background. Rachel seated herself at the dining table and continued flipping through her magazine.

"Where's Jacob?" Kate asked somewhat puzzled. She was hoping to trigger Rachel into acknowledging that she'd left her young ward alone.

"Oh, he's watching his favourite programme on television, he's fine in there."

The ironing board and iron were out waiting for her. Richard must have done that in the morning before he left for work. She took the small, plastic jug to the kitchen to fill it with water. The sink was still stacked high with dishes from breakfast. Kate could see the milk left in the bottom of the bowls.

"Rachel, why haven't you washed these pots yet; they're from breakfast?" she asked in disgust.

"It's not my job to wash pots; I'm here to look after Jacob."

*Well you're not doing that either,* Kate thought.

"He's at nursery all morning; you could have done them then."

"It's not up to me to wash someone else's dishes," she replied irritably. "You do them if they upset you so much."

"I will do after I've finished this ironing."

Kate was incensed. What on earth had she been getting away with, and what exactly was she being paid for? She felt a moral obligation to look after Richard's interest take hold of her. If this is how she acts when someone else is here, what does she do when she's alone with Jacob, take an afternoon nap?

The two women didn't speak again despite being in the same room. Kate became more and more incensed with every flick of a page and every pop of chewing gum. She banged the iron down hard which seemed in turn to irritate Rachel all the more.

Once Kate had finished, she laid the clean, pressed clothes in a pile on the edge of the table and tidied up. She still had three quarters of an hour to go before her taxi arrived so she decided to clean the kitchen up. She couldn't leave it like that for Richard to come home to. Rachel still hadn't moved.

"Does Jacob want a drink?" she finally asked as she wiped down the kitchen worktops.

"He'll come and get one if he needs one."

Kate was on the verge of some heinous deed when the phone rang. Rachel managed to peel herself away from her magazine to answer it.

"*Rachel.*" It was Richard on the other end. "*I'm going to be late, my list has been delayed, I wonder, can you stay back tonight to take care of Jacob?*"

He heard that familiar gasp and instinctively knew the answer.

"No, sorry, I've already made arrangements to go out."

*"I thought as much . . . ,"* he paused for thought. Kate was his only hope. "*Could you put Kate on, please?*"

"Kate!" she bellowed from the hall. "Mr Anderson wants to speak to you."

"Me?" Kate asked and took the receiver.

"*Hi, Kate, it's Richard. I'm sorry to drop this on you, but would you be able to take care of Jacob for a while? My list is over running and I have to do the last patient. Normally I'd leave my registrar to do it but it's a difficult case."*

"Of course, I'd love to," smiled Kate. Her obvious delight reflected in her voice.

Richard was overjoyed to hear the words. At last someone who was willing to help him out.

*"Kate, you're a star. I can't tell you how relieved I am. Would you mind giving him something to eat as well and I'll try not to be too late. The number's by the phone to cancel the taxi. Thank you so much."*

"No problem, there's no rush."

She would much rather be here looking after Jacob than back at that awful flat alone.

*"Thanks, Kate."*

The phone went dead.

"You shouldn't have done that; you're only making a rod for your own back," Rachel remarked. She'd been hovering by the phone listening in to the conversation.

"Why?"

"Because he'll ask you again. He's already asked me to work longer hours. Quarter of an hour at the beginning and end of every day. Mrs Anderson would never have done that."

"No, that's why he's asked you, because Mrs Anderson isn't here anymore and he needs all the help he can get. Anyway, it's my business if I want to help out. I'm going to see if Jacob's alright—haven't you got a magazine to finish?"

Rachel didn't detect the sarcasm in Kate's tone and merely saw it as an opportunity to do just as she'd been asked. Jacob was still transfixed to the television.

"Hi, Jacob," Kate said as she peered around the door to the lounge.

She'd not been in this room before. It was tastily furnished with a brown, leather, corner sofa and two arm chairs. An antique, oak, apothecary, coffee table sat in the centre of the room and a hole in the wall fire glistened with glass coals. Jacob was curled up in the corner of the sofa; his knees tucked under his chin.

"Kate!" he said gleefully jumping up. He ran across the room to hug her around the waist.

"How are you? Guess what, I'm going to look after you while daddy finishes work. He's going to be a bit late home, is that alright?"

"Yes, can we do some colouring or play a game?"

"Of course we can. Will you show me all your games when we've had something to eat, then we can decide what to play?"

"Yes." Jacob was excited again. Kate had the best ideas.

"First of all though, you have to tell me what you want to eat."

"I like Shepherd's pie."

"Well, let's see if we have enough food to make shepherd's pie shall we? We could save some for daddy for when he gets home."

***

Richard arrived home two hours later. As he opened the door, the delicious aroma of home cooking filled his senses. He immediately felt hungry. Suddenly the sound of hysterical laughter filled the air.

"Oh, no," he heard Kate proclaim.

He popped his head around the door of the lounge and Jacob was rolling around the floor in tucks of laughter. Kate was staring in disbelief at the Snakes and Ladders board.

"Daddy," he shouted, and went running towards him.

"What were you just laughing at?" Richard asked.

"Kate got a three and she landed on a snake and it was number ninety nine. She had to go all the way back to number six. That means I might win."

"Oh, poor Kate."

Kate was laughing as well now. She was enjoying every minute of her time with Jacob.

"By the way, there's a good smell. What have you had to eat?"

"We had shepherd's pie and we made some for you," said Jacob.

"Really, thanks Kate."

"Well, we made plenty to go around. I hope you don't mind me going through the cupboards. Jacob said it was his favourite."

"Not at all, especially if you've made me some as well; I'm starving. We love shepherd's pie don't we Jacob. It's one of the few things we all eat."

"Daddy, can we have another game of Snakes and Ladders before I go to bed?" Jacob pleaded.

"Well, I suppose so," Richard conceded. "But only on one condition. That I can play as well. You finish this game off while I go and warm my meal up and then we'll have one last game."

"Hurray," shouted Jacob.

Richard didn't have the heart to refuse. Jacob was having so much fun with his new friend, his worries momentarily put to the back of his mind.

Richard soon walked in with a steaming plate of food just in time to see Jacob's victory dance.

"I won, daddy. Kate was only on number eighteen."

"He's too good for me at this game," smiled Kate.

Richard shovelled his food down ravenously in between the shake of the dice as they started their next game. Before long both the food and the game were finished and Jacob was being ushered up the stairs to bed.

"Say thank you to Kate for looking after you," said Richard half way up the stairs.

"Daddy, can Kate read me a story?"

"Kate might want to go home, son," Richard replied. "She's already exceeded the call of duty by several miles."

Richard turned round and smiled at Kate.

"I don't mind at all; if it's alright with you."

"Please, daddy, please."

"Okay, if Kate doesn't mind."

At that point Richard's mobile phone rang in his office.

"Oh no, who's that at this time? I won't be a minute, Kate, would you just help him to clean his teeth for me?"

"Sure."

She could hear that he wasn't happy.

"Are you sure that *I'm* on call? I thought it was Mr Hamer tonight," he said, panic starting to rise in his voice.

What was he going to do? Surely he couldn't ask Kate for any more favours. She'd already done enough. It was his only choice, apart from Mrs Miller next door and he knew without even asking who his son would prefer to take care of him.

"Kate, I couldn't ask you for yet another favour could I?" he said interrupting the start of the story.

Kate looked up from the book.

"Apparently I'm on call tonight. I didn't think I was; I thought I'd changed them all."

"You go; I'll take care of Jacob."

"Are you sure?"

"Positive."

Kate could see the weariness in his eyes. She so wanted to help him. This was the only way she knew how to; by letting him do his job in the safe knowledge that his son was being well cared for in his absence. She was growing quite fond of her new 'family'.

It was well after midnight when Richard returned home. The house was silent. He could just make out the faint light of the lamp in the lounge through a crack in the door.

Kate was asleep in the chair; her head bent to one side. Richard felt a pang of guilt slice through him. What was he asking of this poor, young woman? He'd been out for far too long but then what could he do? He was torn between his work and home and neither were getting his full attention.

He made his way into the kitchen and flicked the kettle on. The place was immaculate; not a thing out of place, unlike the way he'd left it this morning as he'd rushed out of the door.

Kate stirred from her sleep. The noise of the boiling kettle had disturbed her and she knew Richard was finally home.

"Kate, I'm so sorry about the time," he apologised.

"It doesn't matter, Richard, honestly. I'm more than happy to help."

"I've just boiled the kettle, do you want a drink?"

"Yes, please, I'll have a cup of tea then I'll get going."

"No, I wouldn't dream of sending you home in a taxi on your own at this time of the night. There's a spare bed upstairs, you must stay here."

"Okay," said Kate pleasantly surprised. She hadn't expected to be sleeping over when she'd set off this afternoon.

Richard poured her a cup of tea.

"Was Jacob alright?" he asked.

"Yes, he went straight to sleep. He's so good."

"He's very fond of you, Kate."

"He hardly knows me."

"He knows; kids have good intuition."

"His pictures really cheer me up you know." Kate looked down. She didn't want him to see the tears welling up in her eyes but Richard had already seen a sadness emerging from them. *What's wrong Kate,* he longed to ask? *What's happened to make you so sad?*

She finished her drink quickly before he could ask any questions.

"I think I'll go to bed now. Remember, anytime you need help just let me know. It's absolutely no trouble."

"I'll show you to your room," Richard offered then paused for thought. "You wouldn't want to help me out here on a more permanent basis would you? I'm really struggling to keep my head above water, what with work and looking after the house. I feel like I've been neglecting Jacob. The place already looks tidier after you've been here for just one evening."

"Yes, of course I would, but how?"

"What I was thinking was, if you worked here on Wednesdays and Thursdays, your days off, you could stay overnight and I could maybe do my on call then."

"Sounds perfect," she laughed. "When do you want me to start?"

"The sooner the better as far as I'm concerned. How about tomorrow? We'll talk about it over breakfast. Kate, you don't know what a relief this is." Richard was more than pleased with their arrangements. "I'd better show you to your room hadn't I or we'll both be fit for nothing tomorrow."

Kate slid between the luxurious sheets and rested her head on the soft pillows dressed in Melissa Anderson's old nightie, and fell into a deep contented sleep. One night a week away from the flat was going to be bliss; one wonderful night when she wouldn't have to stare at the mouldy walls and smell the damp creeping into her bones. She was so happy. She blessed the day she'd bumped into Richard Anderson.

Richard couldn't believe the difference Kate Forrester had made to his life. He'd only met her a few weeks ago and already doors were opening. He could now do on call every Wednesday night; without Kate that would have been virtually impossible. She would be doing his cleaning as well as his ironing. She'd probably do the shopping if he asked her knowing Kate.

Richard fell asleep a much more contented man that night. Maybe things were looking up after all. He certainly wouldn't have to rely on Rachel as much which was a blessing in itself.

***

Kate could hear the distant beeping of an alarm clock. She slowly opened her eyes and smiled. It hadn't been a dream after all. She was lying in the spare room of Richard Anderson. It was still dark outside and raining but that didn't take away the exhilarated feeling she was experiencing just by being in this beautiful, sumptuous bedroom. This would be her room every Wednesday, she thought dreamily. She would be so excited when it was time to pack her bag next week.

She met Richard at the breakfast table in the spare clothes he had found for her. He was starting to prepare Jacob's breakfast.

"Morning," Kate said brightly.

"Ah, morning, did you sleep well?" he asked.

"Like a log. That bed is so comfortable. Listen, have you got anything else you need to do? I can make Jacob's breakfast."

Richard couldn't believe it; she and Rachel were like chalk and cheese.

"Thanks, Kate, I could eat my own. I don't usually get the chance. By the way, I meant to give you this last night before I was rudely dragged back to work."

Richard held a key up and handed it to Kate. She slipped it into the pocket of her jeans and carried on with breakfast.

"Thanks, I'll clip it on my key ring."

Kate was so proud. She now had her own key to Richard Anderson's home. She could barely hide her joy. She was now truly a member of the household.

***

It was the following Tuesday and Professor Royston was seated behind his mahogany desk, contemplating his next phone call. Surely his wife was being a little optimistic hoping that their family would all join them again this time to celebrate their fortieth anniversary. He had emphasised this to his wife during their planning discussions, but she had seen fit to allocate him the job of persuading them all. She would see to the organisation of the party so it was the least he could do.

*Why was it so important to have their children and grandchildren there,* he had thought? There were plenty of other people they could invite. He had hoped to try and change her mind but she was adamant and fairly confident of their attendance. He wished he had her faith and enthusiasm.

"We all had such a lovely time at my birthday," she had reminded him.

He was not quite as confident. He dialled the number and waited. It was Nina, his daughter, who answered.

"Hello, Nina," Gerald began.

"Hello, dad, what do you want?"

"Another favour."

"What now, dad?"

"As you know it's our fortieth wedding anniversary in three weeks and your mother was planning a celebration . . ."

"Oh, dad, I know what you're going to say but we've all just been over there for mum's birthday. You can't expect us all to drop everything and come over again, surely."

"Well, you mother doesn't think it would be much of a celebration without you all."

"Can't you just take mum away for the weekend or maybe go somewhere nice for a meal. That place was good where we went, what was it called, Marcelle's?"

"I think your mother was hoping for a bit of a party."

"It's not fair, dad, we've got things to do at the weekend. The kids have activities and it's the only time Giles has off. He doesn't want to spend half his leisure time running up and down the motorway."

"No, I quite understand, dear, but this is a one off. We might not be around for the next big one," he laughed half heartedly.

"I'm sure you will and I'm sure you'll manage perfectly well without us. Mum will understand. Now listen, dad, someone's at the front door so I'll have to go. You and mum take care, speak to you soon, bye."

Gerald looked at the receiver then replaced it. Where did she get that attitude from? Couldn't they all put themselves out on the odd occasion for their mother? Hadn't she given them years of her own life when they'd been growing up tending to their every need; running them here, there, and everywhere as teenagers; and what thanks did she get? He despaired of his children. Was it their fault that they'd grown up spoilt and thoughtless? It wasn't that long ago that he and his wife were used as babysitters on a regular basis, before they'd all decided to up and move miles away.

He could feel the anger rise in him. What was he going to tell Dorothy? She'd been planning this party in her head for months now, she will be so disappointed. He decided that he would leave that conversation until he got home and would vent his frustrations elsewhere. He made his way down to the clinic, each step expressing his displeasure. Someone would pay for his daughter's thoughtlessness.

"Ah, Richard, just the man. Consultants meeting, tomorrow morning at seven. Don't be late will you? I've got an eight thirty start tomorrow in theatre and I've got a few points on the agenda to bring up."

"Seven o'clock?" repeated Richard. Immediately his mind went into panic mode going through all the options he had available. Rachel didn't start until quarter to eight, theoretically; Kate would get there about eight o'clock. His only option was to call on Mrs Miller next door. "Right, Prof, I'll be there."

Richard went round to see Mrs Miller that evening. He took Jacob to introduce him just in case he should wake up and find her in his home in the morning.

"Hi, Mrs Miller," Richard said as she peered round the door. "It's Richard from next door. Sorry to disturb you."

"Oh, Richard, do come in. And this is Jacob, my, aren't you growing up to be a handsome boy?"

"Mrs Miller, remember when you very kindly offered to help us out."

"Of course I do, Richard, and it still stands."

"That's really kind of you. I wonder if you could help me tomorrow morning. I have an early meeting which I really can't miss and it's before the nanny starts."

"Yes, of course I can, what time would you need me?"

"About six thirty?"

"Six thirty's fine. I'm usually up around that time anyway."

"Thanks, Mrs Miller, you've saved the day. See you in the morning."

"Bye, Richard, I'll be there."

Sure enough, at six thirty the following morning there was a little tap on the front door. Richard was already dressed in his suit.

"Come in, Mrs Miller, I've made you a cup of tea."

"Oh, thank you, Richard. My, don't you look smart? You look quite the part."

Richard smiled. He led Mrs Miller into the lounge and handed her one of Rachel's magazines which she'd left behind. They did come in useful sometimes. "Rachel will be here about seven forty five. I'm hoping to pop back before I start my list, just to see that Jacob's up, so it shouldn't be for too long."

"Don't worry, I can manage."

"Thanks, Mrs Miller, I appreciate this. Bye for now."

***

At eight o'clock, Kate stepped out of the taxi, walked up the path, and knocked on the front door. She paused as she thought she had heard the sound of crying coming from inside the house. She knocked again. Yes, it was crying and was becoming increasingly hysterical. It was obviously Jacob, but why was he in such a state, where was Rachel? She opened the door with her key to find Jacob at the top of the stairs, red faced with tears streaming down his cheeks, splashing onto his pyjamas.

"Jacob, what's the matter?" she asked running up the stairs towards him.

"I want daddy," he sobbed barely catching his breath.

"Well daddy must be somewhere, or Rachel, have you called them?"

"I keep shouting him and he won't answer. Has he gone like mummy?"

"No, sweetheart, of course he hasn't gone. Your daddy wouldn't leave you for the world. Come here."

Kate sat on the top step and reached out for the little boy. He climbed onto her knee and cuddled into her as she rocked him to and fro. Eventually his sobs subsided and turned into sniffles. Moments later Kate heard the key in the door and Richard walked in. She stared in disbelief.

"Where've you been?" she asked anxiously. "Jacob was crying his eyes out when I arrived."

"I've been to a meeting," Richard replied unaware of the situation.

"A meeting? Well who was looking after him?" she asked incredulously.

"Mrs Miller from next do..." They both stared at the closed door of the lounge. "Oh, no," Richard began and walked through the dining room towards the door.

Kate picked Jacob up and followed him. She stopped as Richard opened it slowly. Mrs Miller's lifeless body lay in the chair, her right arm hanging down beside her and her head resting to one side. Richard looked in shock at Kate.

"She isn't?"

"I think she is," he replied walking into the room.

He stepped up to her cold body and placed a finger on her neck. There was no pulse. He felt her wrist—nothing. He slowly closed her eyes and turned around.

"I don't believe it," he muttered. "It looks like she's had a stroke; her mouths drooping at the corner. He came out of the room rubbing his forehead and sat on one of the dining chairs. Kate placed her arm around his shoulder.

"Are you okay?"

Richard put his elbows on the table and placed his head in the palms of his hands.

"Oh, Kate," he finally said. "She was only doing me a favour, poor lady. She was a lovely old dear. I'm glad you're here; I don't think I could cope with this and take care of Jacob. Where the hell is Rachel?"

"Shall I get Jacob ready and you can phone the ambulance?"

"If you don't mind, Kate; that would be great. It would be better if he wasn't here when they come for her."

Kate walked Jacob back towards the stairs. She glanced at the notepad on the table by the phone in the hallway.

"Richard," she called out. "Look at this."

Richard came to the foot of the stairs and read the note on the pad written in capital letters out loud. "RACHEL NOT COMING TODAY, HAS A COLD." Mrs Miller had taken the message.

"Another cold, she seems to be cursed with them. The second one this month. That's it, I've had enough of her; she's going. As soon as I find another nanny, she's out of here." He paused, "Kate, you don't want to be Jacob's nanny do you?"

"Me? But I don't have any qualifications to be a nanny," Kate answered.

"Yes, Kate, please, Kate," said Jacob jumping up and down.

Richard smiled affectionately at his son. "He thinks the world of you, what else do you need. Rachel has NVQ's coming out of her ears and she sits and reads a bloody magazine all day."

"Well, if you think I could do it, of course I will."

They both smiled as they helped each other out yet again.

"I think you'd be great at it."

***

By the time Kate returned from the nursery, the ambulance had arrived and the ambulance men were removing Mrs Miller from the lounge on a stretcher. A white sheet was draped over her body. Kate gave a sympathetic nod to the two men and they solemnly nodded back. She steadied the door for them as they encountered the two steps down to the garden path and noticed the odd flicker of curtains from the neighbours. Today was the first time she had actually seen the kind, old lady. Richard was helping a policeman with his enquiries. He had promised to go round personally to Mrs Miller's son and break the sad news. Richard was grateful for that. He seemed like a nice, sensitive young man.

"Thank you, Mr Anderson, that's all we need for the moment," the young policeman said.

"No, thank you for being so prompt."

Richard saw him to the door then returned to the dining room where Kate had taken it upon herself to make a strong cup of tea.

"Thanks for looking after Jacob this morning. I'm just glad he didn't wander into the lounge before you arrived," said Richard.

He took hold of the mug of tea being handed to him and sat down at the table. Kate sat opposite him. They both sipped their drinks silently pondering over the morning's events wondering what the next move was to be. Richard could almost hear his mind ticking over. He'd already asked Kate to be Jacob's nanny, could he possibly go one step further?

"Kate, I know I've probably asked far too much of you already, but I've been thinking." Kate looked up from her tea. "I know you've said in the past that you don't like your flat; what would you say to moving in here and being like a live in nanny-cum-housekeeper? I couldn't risk that situation happening again like this morning."

Richard watched Kate's face intently as his proposition registered. To his surprise Kate's eyes filled with tears. Soon the tears were sliding down her face.

"Kate, are you alright?"

She nodded helplessly. She couldn't speak she was so happy. Richard ran into the kitchen and soon returned brandishing a box of tissues.

"Is that a yes then?" Kate nodded again. "Come here," he whispered.

Kate stood up and Richard threw his arms around her. He held her tightly against him whilst she silently wept. All her pent up emotions and sadness slid away in the tears she shed and soaked into his shirt.

"Kate Forrester, you are the best thing that has ever walked into my life."

# Chapter . . .

# 8

How Kate would enjoy handing back the keys of the flat to the letting agency. She didn't care if she lost the rest of the months rent; to be rid of its musty smell and yellow, damp walls would be compensation enough.

Richard had insisted on driving her there after taking the morning off. No one had minded after he'd explained the trauma of poor Mrs Miller. Kate had reluctantly accepted the lift. She had no desire for Richard to see the place she had called home for the past few weeks. What would he think of her living in such a dwelling?

"I'll have to phone Rachel up at some point today. I can't say I'm looking forward to that conversation," he said apprehensively.

"Why don't you do that whilst I pack my stuff away?" Kate offered, seeing the chance to keep Richard from entering the place and seeing it in its full glory. It wouldn't take her long to load her few possessions into a couple of suitcases.

"Okay, I'll give you a lift to carry things down."

"Don't worry, there won't be that much."

His conversation was brief and to the point. Rachel's mother had taken over from her daughter and quoted her rights several times, but neither of them could argue at the fact that Rachel hadn't fulfilled her role and had refused to co-operate, a requirement that had become very apparent. He'd explained the morning's events and the phone had gone very quiet at the other end. A promise of two weeks pay had sealed the deal and Rachel was history leaving the path free for Kate to move in and begin her duties. Richard was pleased with himself. It hadn't cost him as much as he'd thought. He jumped out of the car and followed Kate's footsteps up the gloomy staircase. He opened the door at the top and entered the flat. The damp smell hit him as he took in the surroundings. He could hear Kate to his right so he made his way into the bedroom.

"Oh, Kate," he said sympathetically as his eyes were drawn to the décor. He looked at the damp patch in the corner near the ceiling where the paper hung off. "I didn't realise it was like this. No wonder you can't wait to get out of here."

Kate looked around her. "You should see the rest of it. At least I'm going in the right direction, out of here. Imagine how I felt when I first moved in." She tried to be light hearted about the whole thing. She had hoped that Richard wouldn't actually see the place.

"What happened, how did you end up in here?"

"I'd been living with someone for the best part of nine and a half years and working for him. The business wasn't doing well and the banks didn't want to know so he turned to this woman at the gym who offered to help him; only she didn't just want to help him with the business, so I got the push and this was all I could afford."

"Didn't he help you out?"

"He gave me a cheque for two and a half grand; he said that was all he could afford."

"But surely you were entitled to more than that after nine years."

"It was either that or the business would go bump. Hey, I don't want his money now. I don't want anything to do with him anymore; he's history. I've made a new start and if you don't mind me saying, I think it's rather a good one."

Richard smiled. "Come on, let's get you out of here and throw the keys back at the crooks who let this place. They want locking up."

Kate put the lids firmly down on the cases. Jacob's two pictures were nestled on the top. Richard grabbed one in each hand and carefully picked his way down the steep flight of stairs. He loaded them into his car which was parked by the kerb opposite the doorway and then caught Kate up just outside the letting agency. He held the door for her and followed her inside. She scanned the room for the woman with the uncomfortable stilettos who was seated at a large desk by the window.

"Can I help you?" the woman remarked feeling two sets of eyes upon her.

"Yes," Kate began. "I've brought the keys back for 12A Cedar Vale High Street, the flat over the dry cleaners. I've got somewhere else to live now."

"Yes, somewhere that's clean and hygienic," Richard added.

The woman flushed slightly as she recalled the condition of the flat and the conversation she'd had with the owner; "*If she wants it cleaning it will be another fifty per month*". She had chosen at the time not to mention the offer, merely to forget about the whole thing and hope the woman renting had done the same.

"I'm afraid you'll have to give a months notice on that property," she replied with a complacent smile on her face as she scanned the computer screen in front of her.

"I'm not staying there another minute, let alone a month. Would you if you had the choice?"

"That's beside the point madam," the woman started. "The vendor . . ."

"We don't give a damn about the vendor," Richard interrupted. "He's obviously some unscrupulous thief who doesn't care one iota for his tenants. If he wants to complain about it I can put him in touch with the Department of Health and my solicitor. Now I think you'll find that Miss Forrester here is owed two weeks rent so if you want to organise that with the vendor I would appreciate it. Oh, and before you say she's not entitled to that, I may just be letting my solicitor know about *this* place as well; renting that health hazard out to a vulnerable young woman. I bet the papers would be interested too."

The sales woman was completely flustered as all eyes in the room now focussed on her to see what her next move would be.

"I'll see what I can do," she mumbled.

"Thank you," Richard said politely and taking Kate's arm, led her, slightly stupefied out of the premises.

Once outside, the fresh air brought Kate back to her senses.

"Thanks for that, I think I was about to be ripped off, wasn't I?"

"I'm afraid so, Kate. Still, you may not see your two weeks rent again from that crooked bastard, but it's a small price to pay to be out of there."

Kate wanted to hug him, throw her arms around him like he had done to her earlier that day, but instead she had one more obstacle to face; resigning from her job at Patterson's Dry Cleaners.

"Do you want me to come in with you in case you have any problems?" asked Richard.

"No, I'll try and handle this one myself," she laughed.

Inwardly Kate was a bag of nerves. They had every right to make her work her notice and then where would that leave Richard? He'd already fired Rachel. She took a deep breath and walked into the shop. Edna was at the counter. She looked surprised to see Kate.

"Hello, what are you doing here? Surely you're not missing the place," she joked.

"No, I've come to see Sheila, is she in?"

"Yes, she's round the back, go through." Edna looked intrigued.

Sheila noticed Kate as she appeared from behind the machines.

"Hi, Sheila, could I have a word with you?"

Sheila guided Kate into the office away from the noise of the working area. She signalled a chair for Kate to sit on.

"Anything wrong?" Sheila asked concerned.

"I need to hand my notice in. I'm really sorry, Sheila, but I've got another job where I'm going to live in and they need me as soon as possible."

Kate clutched her hands in her lap and waited anxiously for the reply. Sheila thought of the flat upstairs where she'd been living. She couldn't blame her for wanting to get out of that place as quickly as possible, but it did leave them in a dilemma.

"You know, you're supposed to work two weeks notice to give us chance to get someone else in to fill the gap," Sheila pointed out.

"I know, Sheila, and if necessary I'll fulfil my contract, but if you have any other solution I would be so grateful, you see . . ."

Kate explained all about Richard and his estranged wife; how Jacob hadn't seen his mother in weeks; how she'd taken on the job of ironing and from there it had snowballed; she told her about Rachel and her magazines and how unreliable she was and finally she told her about poor Mrs Miller and her stroke that morning.

Sheila listened patiently. She was fond of Kate; she was a nice girl. Suddenly she had an idea.

"Just a minute," Sheila said and walked out of the office. "Pam, can you just let Edna off the front counter, I need a word with her."

Moments later Edna entered the office.

"Did you want me, Sheila?" she asked looking worried. She'd still not worked out why Kate was there.

"Edna, is your Gail still looking for a job?" Sheila asked.

"Yes," replied Edna. "She was made redundant two weeks ago," Edna explained to Kate.

"Could she start here tomorrow?"

"I'll give her a ring now," Edna said excitedly. "I'm sure she will."

Kate started to breathe rapidly. She hadn't expected this at all. She'd been going over every option in her mind ever since Richard had made his proposition. Edna nipped out of the room to make the call. She soon returned elated.

"She's over the moon. She'll start as soon as possible."

Kate's smile stretched across her face. She stood up and hugged the bewildered Edna. She still hadn't heard Kate's news yet.

"That's settled then," Sheila announced. "Kate's leaving, Edna. Would you be able to show Gail the ropes tomorrow like you did for Kate?"

"Course I will, I don't want my own daughter making a mess of the job, do I?" she laughed.

"Thank you, Sheila, for being so understanding. I really appreciate it, and my new boss will as well."

She shook hands with Sheila and tapped Edna on the arm as she left on a good note.

"I'll probably see you more now, when I bring the dry cleaning in."

"Bye, love," shouted Edna as she closed the door behind her.

Kate returned to the car, a broad beaming smile on her face.

"Did it go alright?" Richard asked impatiently.

"Yes, I can't believe it. I was sure they'd ask me to work two weeks notice but they had someone in mind for the job, Edna's daughter, and she was ecstatic about it so I'm free to start now."

"Thank God for that. I was just wandering what we'd do if you'd had to stay on, I mean I could hardly ring Rachel and say 'I know I've just fired you but would you mind working a couple of extra weeks whilst Kate works her notice'?"

They both laughed.

"Oh, I'm so pleased that's all over. It'll be time to get Jacob soon," said Kate.

"Yes, it will," Richard replied glancing at the clock on the dashboard. "I'll come with you to nursery and introduce you to the staff; they need to know who's picking the children up; then I'll get back into work. Goodness me, what a morning. I'll be glad to get in there for a rest."

***

The Caribbean island of Antigua was covered with a beautiful, azure sky and bathed in a layer of warm sunshine. A gentle breeze rustled the leaves of the palm trees standing alongside the lush, green grass.

Melissa Anderson stretched out on her padded sun lounger by the poolside and felt the heat penetrate her skin. She adjusted her yellow bikini to reveal as much spray tanned body as was decently possible, and closing her eyes, brushed the loose, brown hair from her forehead with her fingertips. This was heaven, she thought indulgently.

Her mother arrived by her side and placed a tall glass of iced gin and tonic on the small table beside her.

"There you are, darling," said the older woman. "A little aperitif to keep you going before dinner."

Melissa opened her eyes and sat up. She lifted her sunglasses and squinted slightly as she looked for the glass.

"Thanks, mum. You know coming here makes me feel so much better. This should be the cure for all ailments."

Her mother smiled. She knew her daughter all too well and that she needed little in the way of encouragement to fly out here and bask under the sun's rays all day.

"If you're feeling better, darling, why don't you give Richard a call and arrange a time to see Jacob when you get back? You don't want to leave it too long."

"Oh, another week won't make any difference. I'll phone him when I get home. I don't want to upset myself while I'm here. Dr Rosenberg says I should just take some time completely away from anything that could possibly set me on edge—you know, recharge the battery."

Melissa took a sip of her drink, slipped her sunglasses back on then repositioned herself on the sun lounger in preparation for another hours sunbathing.

"I'm sure Dr Rosenberg didn't mean for you to completely neglect your son for several weeks when he was coming up with his bright ideas." Or had Melissa put her own interpretation on his words. "Your husband's got a job to do. He shouldn't be coping on his own," her mother argued.

"He's got Rachel, he's not alone. Anyway, Jacob's at nursery half the time."

Valerie Charles despaired of her daughter. When was she going to get real and take her responsibilities seriously? She was in grave danger of losing her child completely although in her present state of mind, she doubted whether she actually gave a hoot. All that mattered to Melissa at the moment was her confounded 'illness' and pampering to its every whim. Valerie even doubted that there was an illness at all; she had possibly experienced post natal depression after Jacob was born, but that was over four years ago now. Apart from that, all she could think of was that she was suffering from Richard neglecting her in favour of his work.

"Maybe you could phone him before you leave, just so that your father and I know what's going on. Jacob's our grandson, you know. We have a right to know if we're ever going to see him again." Valerie's cool exterior was beginning to waver.

"Of course you'll see him again, mother. Richard will be begging me to take him off his hands when I get back; especially when the long summer holidays come along. We'll be able to come and see you and dad. I could bring my new man over for you to meet."

"Out of the frying pan and into the fire. I thought it was man trouble that got you into this mess in the first place."

"They're totally different, mum. All Richard cares about is his job."

"Well don't go making the same mistakes twice over, for Jacob's sake."

Valerie left her daughter to continue relaxing and made her way back into their luxurious bungalow she and her husband had retired to. Her daughter didn't seem to possess any maternal feelings whatsoever. Maybe she did have some kind of illness. She knew when Melissa was four years of age she wouldn't want to have been separated from her for so long. Right at this moment though, she would quite happily relish the thought of waving her off, back on a plane to England.

Her husband was at the island in the centre of the kitchen tossing a green salad. He looked up in anticipation as she entered the room.

"Well," he asked. "Any luck?"

Valerie shook her head. "She's just not facing the facts. She's got this wild idea that Richard is waiting anxiously by the phone for her to contact him and that when she does she'll be having Jacob when and if she wants him. If truth be told she's going to get a very rude awakening when she loses that child completely."

"Do you want me to have a word with her?"

"I honestly don't think it will make any difference. I know she's our daughter, Jack, but I can't help feeling sorry for Richard. She's left him high and dry. How's he supposed to do his job and care for Jacob at the same time? He doesn't work nine 'til five. He's a doctor and sometimes that means round the clock care. And as for that poor little boy; he hasn't seen or heard from his mother in weeks." Valerie sighed and shook her head again. "Do you think *we* should ring him just to show we care?"

"I don't know, Val, we might be treading on someone's toes. Melissa would never forgive us if she thought we were taking sides."

***

Professor Royston had decided to leave it a couple of days before he broke the news to his wife. He could visualise the look of disappointment on her face and it pained him to think that he could do nothing about it. It was Dorothy who broached the subject over breakfast on the Friday morning.

"Oh, by the way, Gerald, did you manage to speak to Nina about the party? I completely forgot to ask you."

"Yes, I did," Gerald replied uneasily. He hadn't concocted a decent excuse yet and was rather put on the spot. "I'm afraid they can't make it."

"What do you mean they can't make it? We haven't set a date yet. Ring her back later and say we'll set the date around them whenever they *can* make it. It doesn't have to be on that particular weekend."

"I think she said they would be busy all around those dates, Dorothy. We might just have to go ahead without them this time."

"But it wouldn't be the same without them all. We had such a lovely time at my birthday. I'm sure they'll reconsider if you just arrange it a little better."

Gerald was beginning to get agitated. Why couldn't his wife see a refusal when it was so blatant? He didn't want to be blunt but if that's what it took he was going to have to take that approach.

"Dorothy, I'm afraid they're not coming. Nina made it quite clear that they have other commitments at the weekend and that Giles will have spent all week travelling and would prefer not to do so at the weekend as well, so let's just find an alternative to them being here; either a party without them or we could go away for a few days somewhere nice, maybe Paris or Amsterdam. I'd much rather do that than to have to bow and scrape to our selfish daughter and son-in-law. It would appear that they were quite willing to accept our help when their children were young but aren't quite so keen to pay us back now they don't need us any more."

Dorothy stared in disbelief at her husband. Was he really saying that their children didn't want to come to their Ruby wedding anniversary party? But why wouldn't they? Surely every child would want to celebrate the fact that their parents had been together for forty years. It didn't happen too often these days. Should she give it one more shot or would she actually push Gerald over the edge? She decided to try.

"Do you think if I gave them a ring it would help; just to explain a few details you might have overlooked?" she chanced.

"No, Dorothy, I don't, and what's more, I wouldn't give them the satisfaction of thinking we are desperate for their company."

Dorothy could feel the tears welling up. She sat silently for a while, contemplating the news, then got up to go and fetch a tissue. Gerald could hear her sniffling in the kitchen and felt a huge wave of sadness. He resented his children at that point for breaking their mother's heart but more so for not being here to pick up the pieces.

Dorothy couldn't believe what she was hearing. She would wait until Gerald left for work and then ring Nina herself. She knew what Gerald was like. He had probably lost his temper as usual and got the wrong end of the stick, and Nina, being as pig headed as her father, had dug her heels in and refused to come. No, she would smooth the situation over then continue with her arrangements. She needed to book the golf club soon or it would be taken. She felt a little better now, and went back to see her husband off.

Gerald had his suit jacket on ready to go to work. He was waiting for her in the hallway. She wouldn't tell him of her intentions; he'd only try to dissuade her. She should have done this herself in the first place. Arrangements weren't his strong point although he had done a good job of her surprise sixtieth birthday gathering; she had to give him that.

"Are you alright, Dorothy?" he asked pensively, noticing the tissue in her hand.

"I'm fine," she replied straightening his bow tie. "Now, off you go and don't you be worrying. You've enough to do at work."

*That should do it,* she thought ushering him towards the front door. Gerald felt a little happier. She was a good soul, his wife; never one to let things bother her, he thought. But, if truth be told, she had just learned to cope over the years. Being upset was a sign of weakness in the Royston household and was not to be tolerated for longer than a couple of hours at the most.

As soon as the door closed and the car engine started, Dorothy went straight to the phone and dialled her daughter's number. It was Nina who answered.

"Hello, Nina, it's mum here."

*"Hi, mum, you're early. I'm just getting the children ready for school."*

"I won't keep you long, dear. I know your father rang you the other day about our anniversary but I want to make sure he has given you the facts correctly. The date hasn't been set yet so if there's a better one for you . . .?"

*"Mum, I told dad to make arrangements without us. It's too far to keep dragging the kids at weekend and Giles has done enough driving throughout the week."*

So Gerald was right, they had no intention of coming.

"Oh I see; so let me get this right, you wouldn't be coming over whatever day it was on. Is that what you're saying?"

*"Yes, mum, it wasn't that long ago we were over for your birthday."*

"Okay, while you're on, have you had any thoughts about Christmas? It'll be upon us before we know it."

*"Yes, we're having Christmas here. You and dad are quite welcome to come but you'll have to find somewhere to stay. Giles's parents will be having the spare room."*

Dorothy paused. So the arrangements had already been made with Giles's parents. She wondered how long it would have been before they were privy to them, if at all.

*"Mum, are you still there?"* Nina asked irritably.

"Yes, I'll let you go and see to the children now. We'll speak again about Christmas."

*"Bye, mum."*

Nina put the phone down and without a second thought went to tend to her children.

Dorothy was devastated. Two snubs in one fell swoop. Where had Nina learned to be so insensitive? She had just succeeded in making her feel like an annoying little child at a sweet shop who had been humoured with a few chews instead of the box of chocolates she'd been asking for. She dabbed the tears rolling down her cheeks and walked into Gerald's office. The pile of menus, guest lists, and seating plans sat patiently on the corner of the desk awaiting her attention. Without a moment's hesitation, she swept them up and dropped them into the waste paper bin. There would be no party this year nor any Christmas celebrations with the family. This year Professor and Mrs Royston will indulge themselves and to hell with everybody else.

***

Gerald Royston could not get the picture of his wife's face out of his head when he told her that their children would not be making the effort to come and celebrate their anniversary with them. It haunted him all morning. His secretary could sense the tension as she greeted him.

"Morning, Prof. How are you today?" Marjorie Goldman said cheerfully.

"I've been better," he grunted as he swept past her and entered his office. "Marjorie, where are Richard and Todd this morning? I need to speak to them." He had subconsciously decided that someone was going to suffer for his children's thoughtlessness.

"They're both in clinic. Do you want me to get them on the phone for you?"

"No it's alright, Marjorie; I'll go and see them myself."

***

Todd Hamer met Richard walking down the main corridor on his way to clinic clutching a paper cup of steaming coffee in one hand and his brief case in the other.

"Morning, Richard. How are you today?" Todd asked in a sympathetic manner.

"Ah, morning, Todd. I'm fine thanks for asking. In fact, the best I've been for ages."

"Really, what's happened to you then? The last I heard some old lady had died in your living room and you had to take the morning off to sort things out."

"Oh, yes, *that* was bad. Poor Mrs Miller; she was looking after Jacob whilst I came to that early morning meeting and then suffered a massive stroke and died."

"So what have you got to feel so pleased about?"

"Jacob has got a new nanny, and I've got myself the best housekeeper ever."

"My God, have you won the lottery? How can you afford all those staff?"

"Not those, Todd, one person, Kate Forrester. Remember the girl at the dry cleaners who came to do my ironing, her. I got rid of Rachel; she was just about useless and Kate started yesterday. Jacob absolutely dotes on her and she makes the best shepherd's pie this side of the English Channel."

"Shepherd's pie, eh?"

"Yes, well that's all she's made so far, but it was delicious."

"And what's for dinner tonight might I ask?" Todd asked intrigued.

"As long as it's not a tin of soup or a ready meal, it will be better than what I've been used to over the past few weeks." The two men laughed as they arrived at clinic. "Doing anything nice over the weekend?" Richard asked, turning the conversation towards his friend.

"I'm taking Jayne out tonight to that Japanese restaurant on Atherton Road. Her sister's babysitting. We haven't been out in ages on our own so I've got a table booked for seven o'clock."

"I believe you've got to book well in advance to get in there."

"Yeh, you bet, three weeks ago."

"We never got to go there; Melissa didn't like Japanese food and I always wanted to try it."

"Ah, gentleman, just the people I wanted to see." Professor Royston spotted them at the end of the corridor. "I want us all to get together at around five o'clock to discuss the Hand Surgery Seminar we're hosting after Christmas. The sooner we get started on it the better."

Todd went white. "I've got plans for this evening, Prof, do you need all of us?" he asked hopefully.

"Won't take long old chap. You alright for that time, Richard?" he asked knowing full well that Richard's home arrangements had been decidedly difficult to orchestrate recently.

"Yes, Prof, no problems. I could let Todd know of any decisions made."

Professor Royston looked a little perplexed. He thought it was Richard who was having the difficulties. Nonetheless, he would endeavour to make someone else's life as difficult as his own was at the present time, so he took full advantage of the opportunity.

"No, I think we should all be there. I'll go and let Raj and Elizabeth know. See you later."

He turned and walked off in the direction of theatres to inform the other two consultants of their evening entertainment.

"The bastard," Todd exclaimed once the Professor was out of earshot. "Why doesn't he get a bloody life? Just because he's got nothing better to do all weekend."

"You've still got a bit of leeway there. You're not eating until seven. I mean how long can he take to discuss the seminar? We haven't even got a venue for it yet."

***

At six forty five Todd sneaked out his mobile phone and under the cover of the huge conference table texted his wife: NOT GOING 2 MAKE IT, PLS CANCEL REST, WE'LL EAT AT DOG & DUCK 2NITE. His heart sank and his anger rose.

Richard watched as his friend glanced at his wristwatch for the umpteenth time. He could sense his indignation seeping across from the next chair.

"Look Prof . . ." Todd suddenly started.

Richard put his hand across his forearm in a bid to stop him from verbally attacking his superior.

"Yes, Todd?" Professor Royston asked calmly, taking quiet solace in the fact that he'd finally managed to obtain some kind of reaction from one of his colleagues.

"Why don't we do a video link from the operating theatre to the lecture theatre so that we don't have a crowd of people around the table, half of whom can't see a thing?"

"Good point, Todd. What do the rest of you think of that?"

All were in agreement.

"Okay, Monday we'll make a start on putting that together. Would you liaise with Medical Illustration, Todd, and I'll get my secretary to book the lecture theatre? Well, I think we've made good progress this evening. That was well worth getting together. Thanks all, I'll let you get back to your loved ones now."

***

Richard pulled up outside the house and smiled at the warm light greeting him outside the front door. He couldn't remember ever having used that light before. It conveyed a whole host of things to him, but most of all it said welcome home and it doesn't matter that you're late. It was the first time he had arrived home at this time and not felt guilty about being away too long.

He rushed up to the door to avoid the heavy drizzle and let himself in. The house was quiet except for the sound of Kate's voice in the distance. He slowly pushed the lounge door open and stepped inside. Jacob was cuddled up under Kate's arm on the sofa, listening intently to the saga of the Whale and the Snail. What a lovely scene it made; such a difference from Rachel and her magazines. Neither of them noticed Richard, such was their concentration on the book.

"Evening, you two," he said with a broad smile on his face.

"Daddy!" Jacob shouted and ran to give him a hug.

"Hi, Richard, how was your meeting?" asked Kate, making her way towards the kitchen.

"Unnecessary, I have to say, but when Professor Royston shouts we all jump. It was great to see his face though when he asked me to go and I told him it would be no problem.

That was worth hanging around another two hours for. The only trouble is, Todd, one of the other consultants was supposed to be going out to dinner and had to cancel, so he wasn't too pleased."

"Well unfortunately for you, you're going to have to have warmed up lasagne."

"Sounds great to me."

"But, on a positive note, Jacob has decided he likes lasagne as well."

"Really," Richard asked looking at Kate first then Jacob. "Really, Jacob, have you tried Kate's lasagne?"

"Yes, and I had carrot and cucumber sticks as well and I like them too."

Richard laughed. As he sat down to his piping hot meal with a small bowl of salad and a glass of red wine moments later, with his young son seated opposite him chatting away happily, he thanked his lucky stars for Kate Forrester.

***

Gerald Royston had got stuck in traffic on the way home. It had been a miserable, wet journey and a small accident on the Webleigh roundabout had blocked the route. It was almost eight o'clock when he finally pulled onto the driveway. His own fault, he thought; he certainly wouldn't be telling any of his colleagues about this on Monday morning.

The house was in darkness and a nagging feeling tapped at his subconscious. Where was Dorothy? Why didn't she have any lights on? She was usually watching television at this time of the evening or reading something.

He quickly put the key in the lock. His hand was trembling slightly as he turned it. He went straight into the kitchen and flicked the light on. A solitary plate covered in aluminium foil, stood on the granite worktop. He made his way into the lounge. Dorothy was sitting on the sofa fast asleep, with several brochures draped across her lap.

"Dorothy," he said in a loud whisper.

Dorothy slowly opened her disorientated eyes. "Oh, Gerald, where on earth have you been? I was expecting you ages ago."

"There was an accident on the way home. What are you doing in the dark, I was worried about you?"

"I must have drifted off."

"What are all those brochures?" he asked turning the table lamp on.

"Holiday brochures."

"Yes, I gathered that, but where for?"

"Anywhere we want to go, preferably over Christmas."

"Christmas, but what about the family; we always spend it with the children?"

"To hell with the family, Gerald, this is our life and if we want to go to the Caribbean for Christmas, then that is exactly what we will do."

"And what about the party?"

"*This* will be our party, Gerald," she said waving the brochures at him. "We'll have a far better time, just the two of us."

Gerald smiled and kissed his wife on the forehead.

"Good for you. I'll take a look at them once I've had something to eat."

Gerald was relieved to find his wife in reasonable spirit but wondered how much of her new found tenacity was fuelled by abject disappointment.

# Chapter . . .

# 9

Kate loved her new job. She enjoyed running the house, making sure it was clean, doing the shopping, putting it all away neatly, the wonderful smell of freshly laundered linen, playing with Jacob, taking him to nursery and even better, the little look of joy on his face when she picked him up, but most of all, she loved the sound of Richard's key in the lock in the wonderful knowledge that he was home. The thrill she experienced every time his head appeared around the door and greeted them both was second to none. She even loved the look of pleasure when she placed his evening meal in front of him. If she was truthful with herself, which at the moment she was trying desperately to avoid, she was beginning to have feelings for him and would do absolutely anything he asked. Pleasing him and his son was her new aspiration in life.

Kate was careful not to overdo it though. She didn't want to appear too obvious; no, just the right proportion was required and it seemed to work. Jacob was a new child. He was no longer introverted and quiet like he was when his mother had just left, but had blossomed again into the funny little character he was before her disappearance. He never mentioned her now. Richard had always been happy enough to talk about her but the questions had recently dried up and that was good enough for him. Richard seemed much calmer these days, even contented. There was no panic in the mornings getting Jacob ready and looking at the clock desperately awaiting Rachel, and certainly none in the evenings on the occasions he was late. All in all it was a very happy household.

Kate looked forward to the weekends most of all, especially if Richard wasn't on call and could spend some time with them. It was so much fun playing board games, colouring, and building Lego together. She even gave herself the luxury of pretending they were a family although no one would ever know that: that was her secret.

And so it was, with grave dissatisfaction, on one Saturday afternoon in the middle of November, that Kate succumbed to having to attend Tina and Chris's wedding. She was half hoping that Richard would be on call and she wouldn't be able to go, but he had made sure he was available when Kate had told him the date. She never took any time off for herself and she deserved it. Little did he know that she was actually dreading it. It would be the first time she would come face to face with Alex since they'd split up and the very thought of it filled her with apprehension.

She hadn't thought very much about him over the past few weeks. Not since she'd met Richard. His face had faded somewhat from her mind and the happy times they had shared were now overshadowed by their last few days together. He had become an unpleasant memory and one that Kate would rather shake from her mind completely. Today was going to unhinge all that. Today he would be in the same room, eating the same food, drinking from the same bar, and talking to the same people. It wasn't as if they were just passing either. They had both been invited for the whole day, so at two o'clock she would get her first glimpse of him, and he would still be there at midnight, totally inebriated by that time and making a complete nuisance of himself, just like he used to do when they were together. She was madly in love with him then and it used to annoy her, so this was going to be ten times as irritating.

Just after midday Kate reluctantly went to get ready. She had insisted on giving Jacob his lunch whilst Richard finished off some correspondence but after that, she had run out of excuses to delay the inevitable.

"Now don't start cleaning anything when you get up there," Richard warned. "Just get ready."

He was beginning to have an awful feeling that she was going to back out of this wedding at the last minute and he didn't want that on his conscience. Kate ran the shower in the bathroom then stepped under in an attempt to inject some enthusiasm. Her thoughts kept returning to Alex which spurred her on. She wasn't going to look a mess in front of him. She was going to show him what he was missing.

Soon her shoulder length, blonde hair was styled, her makeup applied to perfection and her new closed donned. The flattering, fitted, grey trouser suit with powder blue blouse was finished off with matching shoes and bag. She looked at her reflection closely in the mirror and was pleased. She could make her entry to the wedding safe in the knowledge that Alex *would* give her a second glance.

Kate made her way downstairs and into the lounge.

"Okay, I'm ready," she announced.

"Wow, Jacob, look at Kate. Doesn't she look pretty?" Richard enthused.

Kate laughed and her cheeks flushed with pleasure at the thought of Richard admiring her.

"Oh, wait a minute, Kate," he said rushing into the kitchen. "You haven't put your flower on." He picked up the yellow carnation and pinned it to her lapel.

"Thanks," said Kate. "I would have forgotten that." She could smell the faint aroma of aftershave as he leaned towards her.

"There you go," he smiled. "You look great."

She wished he was coming with her as her ally. Why did she feel like she was about to enter the lion's den?

"Come on, Jacob, get your coat on. We're going to drop Kate off."

"You don't have to, you know. I can get a taxi."

"We want to, Kate. Unfortunately I can't pick you up. This one will be in bed by that time, hopefully."

They all piled into the car and Kate's fantasies of being a family came flooding back to her; mum and dad in the front and their little boy in the back, on their way to a family wedding. But alas, the journey was over all too soon, they were outside the church, and Kate would have to make that solitary journey across the road without them. Her stomach lurched as she watched the procession of people making their way to the ceremony.

"Now listen, Kate, go and enjoy yourself and don't worry about what time you get back. You won't disturb us, we both sleep like logs."

Kate was missing Richard's reassuring tone already.

"Thanks for the lift. See you tomorrow, Jacob," she said turning round to the back seat.

"Bye, Kate," came the little voice. "See you tomorrow."

Was that a sulk Richard noticed on his face? Surely he wasn't upset because Kate was going out and he had to spend the day with his dad.

"Bye, Richard," she said and closed the car door behind her.

The wind bit at her face as she crossed the road. She briefly turned to wave to her make-believe family as they disappeared in the car, then looked around for a familiar face. There was none to be seen outside so she ventured into the church. It was cold but peaceful inside. The organist played quietly in the background. A few people were nodding their heads in conversation but Kate didn't feel the need to join in. She was quite happy to inconspicuously slide onto the back pew. The less people that saw her the better at this stage. Sympathetic nods were the last thing she needed.

Alex was already seated three rows in front and to her relief he had seen fit not to bring his new partner. Mike Fenwick was to his right. He and Alex had been friends since childhood, and was the man Alex had stayed with the night they had split up. He'd always been on his own throughout their relationship so Kate had never really got to know him that well. Mike had only visited when Kate was out or occasionally dropped by to meet up on the way to the pub.

Not surprisingly, to Alex's left was Chloe Jones, Wade Garrity's girlfriend. Chloe had always had her eye on Alex. It hadn't mattered whether Kate was there or not; she would unashamedly flirt as soon as Wade's head was turned. She had wondered whether Chloe was the mystery woman in Alex's life but then had comforted herself with the knowledge that she didn't have that much money to bail him out of trouble. Wade's presence next to her now confirmed any nagging doubts. Kate had never really considered Chloe as one of her friends like some of the other girlfriends, merely an annoying distraction who wouldn't hesitate to stab you in the back given half the chance.

Chris was seated on the front pew in his best bib and tucker, talking with his best man John Patrick. Kate smiled as she saw him adjust his tie every few seconds and smooth down his hair. He was a complete bag of nerves. Such a contrast from the usual arrogant, young man who paraded himself like a peacock every time he went out. Kate always felt that he had been responsible for the cooling off of her relationship with Tina. He had questioned every move she had made once he had decided that he wanted to settle down, who she was going out with, what time she would be back? He was a control freak and seeing him now in this vulnerable state amused her.

Suddenly the organ struck up loudly and blasted out the first few chords of The Wedding March. The congregation stood as Tina appeared at the back of the church clinging to her father. She looked stunning in her strapless, white, lacy wedding dress with a beaded tulle shawl wrapped around her shoulders; a little too frilly for Kate, but nonetheless beautiful. Her tiara glittered as the sunlight filtered through the stained glass windows and her long, auburn hair, curled into ringlets, danced around her shoulders.

Tina and her father set off down the aisle followed by two sweet little flower girls dressed in pink. They each carried a posy of pink flowers selected from the bouquet Tina was carrying, and had a circlet of the same flowers perched on their heads.

Chris stood in front of the vicar now with John by his side fidgeting with his hands this time; he adjusted his tie one last time as Tina arrived by his side.

Kate stared at the back of Alex as the wedding service began. Was this what she'd really wanted with him; a wedding with all the trimmings, or was it just because Tina and Chris were tying the knot that she'd felt that it was probably her turn next? She had spent the best part of nine and a half years with him yet throughout that time he had barely changed. He'd still gone out with his mates every Friday night and most Saturdays come to think of it, unless she'd complained sufficiently. Thursday night was their time out as a couple which inevitably involved meeting up with other couples. Kate would then spend the evening talking to the females whilst Alex parked himself at the bar talking to the males. They would always go home early because it was work in the morning. She couldn't believe that she had been prepared to spend the rest of her life in that perpetual rut. She even remembered with embarrassment half begging him to keep her in that monotonous lifestyle on that fateful day. Even though she wasn't in a relationship, life with Richard was far more interesting.

Once the service was over and the happy couple had filed out of church the congregation stood to leave. It was at this point that Alex got his first glimpse of Kate. He had surreptitiously been looking for her throughout the service and deduced that the only place she could be was behind him. Kate pretended she hadn't seen him and kept her eyes fixed on the floor, but she could feel his burning into the side of her head. She now had the upper hand and would plan her moment carefully when she actually decided to acknowledge his presence. She made her way to the end of the pew and managed to file into the passing throng before he had time to get level with her. She was soon outside in the cold wind, fighting her way past the crowd that had gathered around Tina and Chris, searching out a quiet spot to hide away in.

Suddenly a voice caught her completely off guard.

"Hi, Kate, how are you?" It was Alex. He had watched her disappear to the edge of the churchyard and decided to get the formalities out of the way. Kate jumped; she hadn't expected anyone to speak to her let alone Alex.

"Oh, I'm fine thanks, and you?"

"Yeh, not bad. You look well."

"Thanks."

Kate was finding it difficult to talk to him. Nine and a half years together, yet after just a few weeks apart, they had nothing in common anymore. They paused to watch as the photographer assembled the bride and groom with various combinations of guests, then quickly snapped away before the cold took hold.

"I can't believe they've finally done it, can you?" Alex asked nodding in the direction of the newly weds.

Kate shook her head. She stole a quick glance at him. He looked a little older than she remembered; a little more worn and his brown, wavy hair was cut shorter than usual, but he was still good looking and would turn her head if she didn't know him better.

"How's the business doing?" she asked intrigued.

"It's back on its feet, thank God," he replied. He knew better than to thank the person who was really responsible for its salvation.

"I see you haven't brought her with you, I'm glad about that. That would have been really uncomfortable."

Alex looked a little embarrassed.

"No, I didn't think that would be very tactful, besides, she wasn't invited. How about you, did you find yourself a job?"

"Yes, I've had two would you believe. The first one was just an interim thing but I'm fine now."

"Good, I'm glad. Listen, I don't know if you've made plans but would you like a lift to the reception? I've only got Mike in the car."

"No, it's alright," said Kate. She didn't have the faintest idea how she was going to get there, but she certainly didn't want to rely on Alex.

"Seriously, it's not a problem," he insisted.

Kate could feel Chloe Jones's eyes upon her. She looked across at her and quickly interpreted the look of envy in them.

"Okay, thanks," Kate finally submitted and followed him to the car throwing a knowing glance across at Chloe. There, that was one less person she would have to speak to at the reception.

Mike sat in the passenger seat and Kate slid into the back.

"Hi, Kate," Mike said turning to speak to her. "How are you?"

"I'm fine thanks, Mike," she answered a little surprised. That was the most he had said to her in nine and a half years.

"It's nice to see you again."

"Thanks."

She wished she could say the same for him but she didn't feel like she really knew him. In fact, she had never given him a second thought since she and Alex had split up. She had no reason to. The rest of the journey was spent making polite conversation and talking about the weather until Kate's mind drifted to Richard and Jacob. She wondered what they were doing now. Richard had said he might take Jacob to the park but it was so cold. She hoped that he would remember to put his thick winter coat on; that wind was freezing.

"Did you manage to find somewhere to live, Kate?" Mike asked, interrupting her thoughts.

"Yes thanks."

"Good."

Alex cast a stern look at his friend. What business of his was it where Kate lived? He'd never took the slightest interest in her before. Mike was oblivious to the glare and carried on with his inquisition.

"How's your mum, does she still live in Spain?"

"Yes, she's fine thanks. It's quite good for her out there; she suffers a bit from arthritis."

"Is that why she moved there?"

"No, she met someone who lived out there. They run a restaurant."

"I wish you'd told us that before we went on Chris's stag weekend to Benidorm. We ate at some real dives.'

At last they were at the hotel and Kate could relieve herself of her interrogator.

"Thanks for the lift," she said and quickly went inside to warm up. A champagne reception greeted them and Kate helped herself to a glass. Mike watched her as she disappeared whilst Alex found someone else in the car park that he knew to chat to.

Kate spotted a seating plan by the doorway to the reception hall and decided to spend some time studying it. It would save her having to talk to anyone else. Her conversation with Mike had been somewhat laboured due to the fact that she'd never spoken to him before at length and hadn't a clue as to what they had in common. She removed the journey from her mind and diverted her attention to the names on the board.

"Mr Arthur Herbertson, Mr David Phelps," she read out loud, who the hell were they whom she had been placed in between? Her eyes swept over the rest of the table. She didn't recognise any of the names. Just out of interest she looked for Alex's seat and found it in the midst of seven other familiar names including Chloe Jones. Kate was livid. How dare she be cast aside like she was no longer deemed fit to share the table of the 'friends'. Who had made that decision?

Kate could no longer think rationally, only that a conspiracy was in the making. From that moment on, it was all she could think about. She resented being treated like an outcast. She could hear the roar of laughter coming from the bar and knew that it was probably Alex who was entertaining them; the betrayal stung even more.

Kate spotted Tina's mother and before she could disappear into the ladies' toilets, Deidre Irvin was by her side. "Kate,

I thought it was you, love, at the back of the church. How are you? Tina told me all about you and Alex; I'm so sorry. I thought you two were together for life, didn't you? Tina did as well; it's funny how things turn out isn't it?"

So many questions, Kate thought.

"I know," she replied and then waited for the next burst of conversation.

"Have you looked at the seating plan? I believe it took ages to sort out. Let's have a look, where are you? Oh, there you are between Uncle Arthur and cousin David. You'll be alright there, well away from Alex," she said in a loud whisper, nudging Kate as she scanned the room for her ex.

Kate started seething again about the wretched seating plan. So it wasn't Deidre who was responsible. Wait until she found out who was.

Suddenly there was a small commotion over by reception and the newly wed couple entered through the sliding doors into the hotel lobby. Tina adjusted her train and they made their way to the doorway of the dining hall. This was the part where everyone had to traipse past them one by one and congratulate them. Kate wished they would just get on with it. She'd had enough already and barely two hours had gone by. She stood in line with the rest of the guests and waited her turn. It was all so false, she thought. She would no sooner line up and volunteer to kiss Chris than she would to clean his shoes, yet here she was, dressed in her finery, queuing up with the rest of them, awaiting that very 'pleasure'.

It was ages before she reached her turn. She was famished by the time she got to the front. Maybe she should have taken Richard's advice and had a quick sandwich before she set off.

"Congratulations, Tina," she gushed and hugged her friend.

"Thanks, hone, I'll speak to you later," Tina promised.

"Alright, Kate?" Chris asked as she arrived in front of him.

She quickly pecked him on the cheek and walked into the dining room. The rest of her table were already seated. They all stared at her as she read her name card and sat down. She took a deep breath and smiled.

"Hi, I'm Kate."

"Hello, Kate," said Uncle Arthur. "We were just wondering who you were. Are you on the bride or groom's side?"

"I'm a friend of Tina's," she replied.

"I see," Uncle Arthur continued. "We're all Chris's family. I'm his uncle, his mum's brother and this is his cousin on his mum's side, David."

Kate nodded at David who politely nodded back then continued his conversation with what she presumed was his wife on his left hand side. Oh great, thought Kate, not only did she not know anyone, they were all Chris's relatives so nothing in common there either. She felt like standing up and going home.

A bowl of carrot and coriander soup, chicken fricassee with seasonal vegetables and duchess potatoes, followed by a dish of sherry trifle were all eaten in silence as communication dried up with Uncle Arthur, and the rest of the table seemed less interested in Kate than the family members seated in their immediate vicinity. She gratefully accepted a cup of coffee as she listened indignantly to the laughter coming from two tables away, Alex's table. She swore they were doing it on purpose, particularly Miss Jones, throwing her head back every two minutes and looking in Kate's general direction. Surely she'd heard all Alex's jokes before, everyone else had.

At last it was time for the speeches. At least everyone would have to be quiet now. Kate noticed that Chris was starting to adjust his tie again as his big moment approached. Funny, she thought he would have loved this part, all eyes focussed on him; the centre of attention. She smiled to herself again. She was going to enjoy watching him squirm.

John Patrick stood up and banged a spare fork against his champagne glass. Everyone went quiet except for Alex's table.

"Hurray, come on, Johnny," they heckled.

Chris's mother stared over in abhorrence at the disruption; Chloe threw her head back again and laughed; John looked petrified. He had been Chris's friend since they were children and although Alex probably spent more time with him now, Chris thought he owed John the role for longevity of friendship. In hindsight though, Alex would have been the better choice. He was much more confident in front of an audience.

John coughed and began his speech. He started from where he and Chris had first met, in the front garden of David Swindel's house chasing a stray cat, and slowly, very, very slowly built up the story until the vast majority of the gathering had virtually fallen asleep. Kate couldn't believe that no one had thought to sensor the speech such was its length, and total lack of humour. Wasn't the best man supposed to make everyone laugh? Finally he toasted the bride and groom and everyone clapped heartily with relief. The only positive side Kate could see about the speech was that the time it had taken John to deliver it, had given Chris more time to sweat over his.

The family and friends all stood to raise their glasses to the bride and groom, and then it was Chris's turn. His neck had started to turn a blotchy red as he loosened his tie in preparation. No one heckled this time; they could see his unease. He looked down at his pieces of paper on the table before him and felt for his cuff links.

"Thanks, John . . . for the toast . . . and the speech . . . yeh . . . it was great to hear all those memories . . . erm . . . it's great to see everyone here, er, today . . . erm."

Tina looked up at her new husband and then at the pieces of paper littered across the table. He'd obviously written them on his stag do, inebriated. They were totally illegible.

"What are you doing?" she whispered to her new husband. "Thank the parents or say something."

"Yeh . . . we'd just like to thank our parents, erm . . ." he looked down at Tina again. "And for all the presents."

"The flowers," Tina mouthed.

"Oh, yeh, we've got some flowers for our mothers." He paused whilst the bouquets of flowers were brought in and given to the two smiling mothers. He looked at Tina again.

"Toast the bridesmaids." She was starting to look awkward.

"And can you raise your glasses and be upstanding for the bridesmaids."

She closed her eyes as his embarrassing speech drew to a close.

"Oh, I think we've got something for the bridesmaids as well . . . have we?"

The bridesmaids were given their gifts and Chris sat down to a trickle of applause since no one was quite sure whether he'd finished or not.

"That was shit wasn't it," he said to Tina. "I was so nervous, I couldn't read my notes."

Tina felt a pang of sympathy for her husband and just hoped that her father's speech would make up for the last two. She kissed him lightly on the cheek and reassured him that every groom was the same.

"Do you think?" he asked.

"I know they are."

He felt a little better and took his tie completely off. He could relax and enjoy himself now that his major role was over.

Kate took no satisfaction from watching stage fright completely ruin Chris's performance; far from it. She thought she preferred his arrogant self than the one she'd just unfortunately had to witness.

Tina's father ultimately came to the rescue and delivered a speech second to none. The audience laughed loudly at his jokes, probably because there was finally something humorous to laugh about. He briefly reminisced about his daughter as a young girl and about the time he had met Chris when he had walked into his home for the first time and been lost for words; being careful to make no reference to his recent speech. He welcomed Chris into the family on behalf of himself and Deidre and hoped they would be very happy together. The applause resounded round the room and the guests began to mingle.

Kate's table soon cleared to go and talk to the rest of the family seated on the next table. She suddenly felt very exposed and alone. The seating plan now showed its true colours. Tina was first to notice and made her way across the room. She sat beside Kate who was gazing thoughtfully into her wine glass.

"Thank God that's all over and we can get down to some serious drinking," Tina began before taking a large gulp of champagne.

"Oh, hi, Mrs Holloway, how are you?" Kate replied.

She felt more comfortable now that someone had come to talk to her although she realised that she could not expect the company of the bride for any length of time. She would be expected to make her way evenly throughout the guests.

"How's it going?" Tina asked referring to Alex's presence in the room.

Kate had no desire to ruin the day and explain that it wasn't Alex's presence that was making things difficult, merely the perfunctory seating plan which had placed her with an ensemble of relatives who she neither knew nor cared to get acquainted with, and Alex two tables away with all their friends. It had probably been Chris's idea to take the easy option and remove Kate from the potential cauldron before any harm was done, but there was no need. She was an adult after all unlike some she could mention.

"It's fine, honestly. He actually gave me a lift here so we can't be all that bad," she explained.

"How did you manage that?"

"He just came out and asked me. I could hardly refuse since I hadn't even thought myself how I was going to get here. By the way, I love your dress."

"You'll get to wear one, one day; I know you will."

"Yeh, one day maybe, when they find out the moon *is* made out of cheese."

"Seriously, you will and there's one thing I *can* be certain of."

"What's that?" asked Kate.

"Your husband's speech will be a damn site better than mine."

The two girls laughed.

"I've never seen Chris so nervous," Kate smiled.

"I know," Tina answered. "It'll certainly put him off ever leaving me. He'd never want to go through that again. Listen babe, I've got to circulate; I'll speak to you later. Will you be okay?"

"Yes, sure I will. See you later."

Tina disappeared and Kate was alone again, but not for long this time. She hadn't noticed Mike Fenwick approaching from across the room.

"You look like you're on another planet," he remarked. "Mind if I sit down?"

Kate could hardly believe it. Mike had barely spoken to her in the past nine and a half years yet today here he was again, making some kind of special effort. She was grateful to him in some ways; there was still an hour to go before the evening guests arrived, which was a long time to sit on your own.

"Sure, take a seat," said Kate offering him the chair next to her.

"I'm sorry about you and Alex . . ."

"Oh, thanks."

"He's actually more stupid than I gave him credit for."

Kate looked up in surprise.

"What do you mean?" she asked.

"Giving you up, he must be mad. I'd never give you up if I was going out with you."

Suddenly Kate felt very uncomfortable. She hoped that that wasn't some kind of chat up line and quickly tried to gloss over his last comment. She was beginning to regret how she had encouraged him to sit down now.

"It was probably the best thing in the long run; I bet we're both happier now than we ever were when we were together. Sometimes these things just run their course and there's nothing else to do than to split up."

"I haven't met his new woman yet you know. He won't introduce me to her."

"Why, do you want to meet her?"

"He's one of my best friends. Wouldn't you introduce your new partner to your friends?"

"Maybe, it depends."

"On what?"

"On whether I thought my friends would like them or not. Maybe he doesn't think you'd get on, or maybe he's just not ready for you all to meet yet."

Kate couldn't believe she was talking about Alex's new girlfriend and defending his actions to his best friend. Was this some kind of reverse therapy she was experiencing?

"I always got on well with you didn't I?" Mike asked still a little bemused.

"Well sure you did," Kate replied.

She was beginning to wonder if Mike was on some parallel universe. She couldn't believe she was talking to the same person. Was he actually deluded and had made up this imaginary relationship they had shared or did he actually think that the odd grunt or wave of the hand constituted a friendship? He was obviously capable of much more as he had proved today.

"What would you do in my situation?" he asked.

"I wouldn't worry about it. He'll introduce you when he's good and ready."

Mike pulled his chair up a little closer to the table and Kate sank back in hers. He looked like he was here for the duration now and she had nowhere else to go. She looked across the room and saw Wade nudge Alex and nod his head in their direction like a silly teenager. The whole table turned to look. Kate chose to ignore them and carried on her counselling session, although she wasn't quite sure now who was counselling who.

"I've always liked you, Kate," Mike continued. He reached across and lightly touched her hand. Kate felt like he had just jabbed a needle into her. "It's like you just get to know someone and then they walk out of your life." There was an embarrassing silence as Kate thought of the best, most sensitive way of getting rid of him. "I don't suppose you'd like to go out one night would you, now that we're both on our own?" He finally plucked up the courage and asked.

"I don't think that would be a very good idea, Mike. It would be a bit awkward with you being one of Alex's best friends don't you think?"

"Alex doesn't need to know."

His face was very serious now. Kate stared at him; she'd never really taken that much notice of his features before. She'd never really thought he was that interested in women, but now she was seeing him in a different light. He was quite pleasing to the eye with his short cropped, dark brown hair, dark eyes, straight nose and full lips. If she hadn't met Richard and was still in that horrendous flat, she might have been slightly tempted now, but her life had taken a different course and Alex and his friends were not part of it anymore.

"Mike," she began.

"Shh, you don't have to say anything yet. Just think about it."

"Mike, I . . ."

"I'll speak to you later, I'd better get back to that lot or they'll think I'm ignoring them," he interrupted.

Mike scraped his chair back and made his way back to Alex's table, obviously not wanting to hear Kate's refusal. She now had time to think of a feasible excuse to let him down lightly, but she was also alone again and looking vulnerable sitting by herself. She half wished he hadn't mentioned anything about going out together and that she still had his company at the table. Kate decided to take a walk, even if it meant going outside in the freezing cold. Mike's eyes followed her as she made her way to the door.

It was dark outside now as well as cold. Kate pulled her jacket tightly around her and headed through the door in the foyer. A couple of taxis had pulled up dropping off some of the evening guests. She felt a slight relief as she realised that she was over halfway there. Only the evening reception to endure then she could return to the haven of Richard's home.

"You're not going already are you?" came a voice in the darkness.

Kate quickly turned to see Wade smoking behind a wall of the hotel.

"No, just getting some fresh air."

"You and Mike seem to be getting on well."

"We're just talking that's all," Kate replied tersely. She couldn't believe them; they were like a bunch of schoolchildren pairing people off. "It's nice of him to bother."

"Wade, what are you doing?" Chloe had spotted Kate going outside and had come to make sure her and Wade weren't getting up to anything.

"I'm having a cig," he answered irritably.

"Oh, Kate, there you are. You seem to be going through all the men today. Just thought I'd better check. You've got to keep your eye on these single ones."

"It's not the single ones you have to worry about in my experience, Chloe," Kate replied referring to her ever flirtatious eye on her ex-boyfriend.

"What do you mean by that?" asked Chloe, now incensed at Kate's impudence at answering her back.

"If the cap fits."

Kate was purposely talking in riddles to completely flummox Chloe. She knew she didn't have the intelligence to know what she was talking about; she also knew that she could quite easily be drawn into a slanging match which would be completely inappropriate at her friend's wedding, and was definitely not Kate's scene so she decided to end it and walk away. She carried on her walk up the driveway until Chloe and Wade disappeared back into the hotel.

"I never liked that bitch when she was going out with Alex. I like her even less now."

"Why, because she thinks you've got your eye on Alex or because she just played you at your own game?"

"Oh that's nice, stick up for her why don't you. That's why I don't like her because she just turned you against me."

"You just said you didn't like her when she was going out with Alex, that's got nothing to do with what just happened then."

Kate could still hear them arguing despite the wind whistling in her ears. She couldn't wait for the evening to end.

A steady stream of taxis had started to file into the hotel grounds and Kate glanced in each one to see if there were any friendly faces in them. She walked back inside as the cold started to eat through her jacket, profoundly aware that she was still on her own.

The wedding party had moved into another room filled with tables and chairs and a small, wooden dance floor at the far end. The bar area to the right, just inside the door was already surrounded. With the lights dimmed and vibrant, flashing, coloured lights arising from the dance area, the party was about to begin. The DJ blew into his microphone. "One two, one two," he said deafeningly.

Kate knew that signalled the end of any audible conversation. She decided to have one last, long drink and then make her apologies and go.

"Kate, what do you want?"

Mike was at the front of the queue and about to be served. She couldn't face lining up with everyone else so she accepted his offer of a drink.

"White wine spritzer, please," she said.

Alex was standing behind him and fed the drinks back to the table they had commandeered. Mike paid and brought her's over personally.

"Thanks for that," she said smiling. "I'd have been there all night. I'm useless at a bar."

"Why don't you come and join us?" he asked hopefully.

"No thanks, Mike. I don't think I'd be too welcome. I've just had words with Chloe outside."

"What about?"

"Something and nothing. You know Chloe; she doesn't necessarily need a reason."

"Have you thought anymore about what I said?" he asked staring at her.

Kate felt a little uncomfortable again. He moved in closer to her until she could feel his breath on her face.

"I'm not really ready for any kind of relationship at the moment, Mike. I've only just got myself sorted out after Alex and I split up and I just need a bit of time to myself."

"Well that's not a *no*, is it? What if I give you my number and you get in touch with me when you feel ready?"

"Yeh, that's probably the best idea," said Kate relieved that she had appeased him now and he wouldn't ask her again.

"Come out here, I don't want that lot staring."

He led her out into the reception area and found a piece of paper and a hotel pen. He scribbled his number down and passed it to her. She quickly placed it in her handbag before anyone else could see.

"Now why don't you go and sit with everyone else and stop worrying about me?" Kate ordered with a grin.

"I'll see you later," he replied winking at her.

He seemed happy enough with their arrangement, Kate thought. She went back into the room to find Alex grilling Mike. He didn't look too pleased. Kate decided to go and sit with Deidre, Tina's mother. She might talk a lot but she was the safest option at the moment. Deidre was pleased to see her again and despite the topics of conversation, Kate was happy to discuss the state of youths today, varicose veins, and Dancing on Ice for the rest of the night. She settled herself into a chair and didn't move again until she had finished her drink.

It was approaching nine o'clock and Kate doubted whether she could face Mike at the bar again. She had caught his eye several times and looked away quickly before he had time to make any kind of contact. Surely he wouldn't ask her to dance. That would be far too obvious in front of Alex. She had managed to drag her white wine spritzer out for the duration and the urge to go home was now at its strongest.

Tina had drifted over to speak to her mum and Aunty Vera. She made her way around the table towards Kate.

"How are you doing, babe?" Tina asked putting her arm around her friend's shoulder.

"If you don't mind, Tina, I'm going to go soon. I don't know about you, but I'm exhausted."

"It's been a long day. I know it's been hard for you; when you end up talking to my mum all night I know things are bad."

"Hey, you, you cheeky beggar. We've had a nice chat haven't we, Kate?" Deidre remarked rather taken aback.

"We certainly have. We've put the world to right tonight haven't we, Deidre?" laughed Kate. "Anyway, thanks for inviting me, I wouldn't have missed today for anything."

"Aw, thanks, hone, it wouldn't have been the same without you. I just wish it could have been easier for you. I really miss you on Thursday nights, you know. It's not half as much fun any more."

"Oh, come on. You've got Chloe to talk to. What more could you want?"

"Exactly."

The two women laughed and Kate got up to leave. She hugged Tina tightly. Despite all, she was still her closest friend and Kate intended to try and keep it that way.

"Say goodbye to Chris for me, I don't really want to go over there."

Chris was sat with Alex and the rest of the friends, pouring down the beer and getting louder and louder. Tina looked back at Kate.

"He'll be fit for nothing on his wedding night," she moaned.

"You'd better get over there and tell the barman to water his beer down. Bye, Deidre, bye, everyone," Kate shouted to Tina's mum and the rest of the aunties.

At last she could excuse herself and go. She felt elated as she disappeared out of the door towards the telephone booth to book her taxi home. She decided to wait outside in the cold, night air. Her head was banging after shouting all evening and straining to hear what the others were saying.

It was quiet outside and a light drizzle filled the air. The faint thudding of music could still be heard in the background. Suddenly the automatic doors to the hotel slid open and Mike appeared before her.

"Are you going already?" he asked walking towards her.

"Yeh, I've had enough now. My ears are ringing."

He stood in front of her and his eyes stared deep into hers.

"You will ring me won't you?" he said slipping his hands around her waist.

He moved forward and pressed what seemed like his entire body against her. Then his lips were on hers. Kate tried to move away but she was blocked by the wall. He was kissing her harder now. His hands moved up and held her face steady. Kate finally managed to push him away.

"Mike, what are you doing?" she asked angrily.

"It's just a goodnight kiss."

"Well don't," she snapped at him.

"You alright, Kate?" came a voice from the doorway.

It was Alex. Mike jumped back as if he'd just received an electric shock.

"I'm fine thanks," she replied, relieved to see someone; it didn't matter who.

"You coming back in, Mike?"

"Yeh, I was just getting a bit of air."

"And the rest," Alex answered indignantly.

His eyes followed Mike as he walked past him into the hotel, his shoulders slumped and his head lowered like a little boy about to get a ticking off from his mother. Alex stepped outside.

"Thanks for that," Kate said gratefully.

"What was that all about?"

"It was probably partly my fault. I haven't exactly discouraged him all day, but . . . he was the only one who took the trouble to talk to me."

"Is that why you're leaving so early?"

"Yes, a wedding can be a very lonely place on your own, despite all those people," Kate replied. A lump came to her throat.

"I'm sorry. I just didn't think you'd want to speak to me."

"There were others in there as well as you who could have said something. Seems like I'm the black sheep now you've dumped me."

"Hey, it's not like that."

Kate's taxi pulled up. She took one last look at Alex.

"See you around." She attempted a smile.

"Yeh, take care of yourself." His voice was softer than usual, almost caring.

Alex watched the taxi pull away and felt like he'd let her down yet again. He was beginning to make a habit of it. He wondered if he would still have been with her had the business not failed; in the back of his mind he knew the answer.

***

Kate didn't look back. She was on her way home and it took the length of the journey to compose herself after Mike's advances. She eventually smiled with relief as the taxi pulled up outside the house and she could see a light on in the lounge.

She flicked her shoes off in the hall. Richard was reading a medical paper in the lounge slouched on the sofa in a pair of grey jogging pants and a white t-shirt. Some gentle, classical, piano music played in the background. He lifted his reading glasses up as she appeared around the door.

"Kate," he said quickly looking at his watch. "It's only twenty past nine; what are you doing back so early?"

"I'm sorry, have I disturbed you?"

"Yes and I'm glad you did. This is the most boring paper I've ever read. How did your day go?"

"It was really hard work," sighed Kate. "I can't say I actually enjoyed it."

"Oh, you poor thing. Sit down, I'll get you a drink and you can tell me all about it."

Richard arrived back moments later with a large glass of chilled, white wine and Kate settled back in a contented haze as she recollected the day. He was so easy to talk to. She could feel her headache ease as the tension slipped away and the wine brought about a relaxed feeling of euphoria. Richard listened intently. He found Kate so entertaining when she opened up and started recounting her stories. He'd never seen her tipsy before and it made him smile.

". . . so I went outside for a breath of fresh air and to get away from Mike, bumped into Wade who was having a quick cigarette and then Chloe appears from nowhere and thinks I'm trying to have a sneaky tête à tête with her boyfriend..."

Richard laughed heartily. He was enjoying this conversation.

". . . so we had words and then she had words with Wade; honestly it was a right fiasco."

"Sounds like you could do with another drink; fancy a nightcap?"

"Yes please, I think I could manage one more."

Kate had no intention of ending her evening with Richard prematurely. What had started as a disaster, was now turning into an extremely pleasant night. It was rare to catch him in such a relaxed mood; he was usually rushing somewhere or doing masses of paperwork when he was at home.

She took a sip out of the second glass of wine.

"I think I can safely say now that that's the last time I will go out for years; I'm completely drained."

Richard laughed again.

"While we're on the subject of arrangements, have you made any for Christmas day?"

"No, not yet."

"So you'll probably be spending it here," he suggested hopefully.

"If that's okay with you?"

"Thank God for that. I thought it was going to be just me and Jacob on our own. I'm sure he'll be much happier now he knows you'll be there too."

Kate had been dreading the festive season this year; the first time she'd been alone. It had suddenly become much more appealing.

"Oh, and I'll be cooking," Richard added. "It's your day off so if you want to make other arrangements, now's your chance."

Kate laughed this time. She certainly had no desire to go anywhere else now, even if it meant having beans on toast.

It was past midnight when the two finally parted company and went to bed. Kate lay awake for ages dreamily reliving the past few hours, trying to remember every piece of the conversation which had made Richard laugh. Tina and Chris's wedding was in the distant past now and could remain there as far as she was concerned.

Richard was in no hurry to fall asleep either. He'd thoroughly enjoyed his evening once Kate had arrived home. He couldn't remember a time when Melissa had made him laugh like that or even when they'd had such a long conversation. He was beginning to grow very fond of Kate Forrester.

# Chapter . . .

# 10

Valerie Charles placed her bags of shopping on the kitchen worktop and went outside to find her husband. She glanced at the phone as she walked past it—no messages. Jack was beside the pool in a pair of shorts, the rest of his body exposed to the warm sunshine. His book was beside him on the sun lounger and his eyes were closed.

"Jack, have you heard anything yet?" his wife asked anxiously.

Jack opened his eyes and sat up.

"No, not yet."

Valerie shook her head.

"She said she'd ring as soon as she'd spoken to Richard. She was supposed to contact him yesterday."

"You know what she's like, Val. Time waits for her not the other way round."

"I bet Richard and poor little Jacob are beside themselves by now. She thinks of no one but herself that girl. I'm going to ring her; I can't stand this any longer."

***

Richard and Jacob were play fighting in the lounge. Kate could hear the giggling from the kitchen. The smell of roast beef, Yorkshire pudding and roast potatoes permeated the air.

"Take that, and that," Richard shouted as he tickled Jacob under each arm.

Jacob screamed with laughter as he tried helplessly to fend his father off. Suddenly the phone rang in Richard's office. That usually meant that he was required at work and Kate looked at her cooking in despair. Not another microwaved meal, she thought. She didn't like it when he was dragged away unexpectedly.

"Richard," she called reluctantly. "The phone in your office."

"Oh no, I hope that isn't work, that dinner smells delicious."

He ran to the office before the call transferred to the answer machine.

*"Hello, Richard, it's Melissa."* Richard was speechless. *"Richard, are you there?"*

"I'm sorry; who did you say it was again?" he asked seating himself at his desk.

*"It's Melissa,"* she repeated.

"Oh, Melissa, I'm sorry I didn't recognise your voice, it's that long since I've heard it."

*"Very funny, Richard, I wondered if I could speak to Jacob?"*

"Absolutely not. Surely even you couldn't expect to disappear out of his life for nearly three months and then just breeze back in as if nothing's happened."

*"I haven't been well but I feel much better now."*

"No doubt after a substantial holiday in Antigua."

*"I have been to visit my parents, yes, but only to recuperate. I wasn't partying every night if that's what you're insinuating."*

"I wasn't thinking that at all, I merely pictured you on a sun bed every day with a large glass of Martini by your side, being pampered over by your long suffering mother."

*"Honestly, Richard, I didn't ring up to be insulted, I just wanted to see my son."*

"Then you shouldn't have rung up and expected everything to be handed to you on a plate like you normally get. Jacob has been through enough since you walked out—three months ago. You can do this by the book or not at all."

Kate could hear Richard's raised voice from the kitchen and decided it probably wasn't the hospital beckoning him. She'd never heard him use that tone before.

*"Very well, maybe I could come over one afternoon after nursery when Rachel is there to see him then."*

"Rachel doesn't work here any more."

*"Really?"* Melissa asked surprised. *"Well how are you managing, and I didn't mean for that to sound condescending?"*

"Very well, no thanks to you or Rachel. She was useless, lazy and totally uncooperative."

*"Not while I was there she wasn't."*

"No, you see, Melissa, while you were here she didn't have to do anything untoward. Unfortunately my job doesn't finish at five to five and there the problems began. Jacob's got another nanny now and we're all doing fine."

*"Oh, I see. Could I maybe see him at the weekend then?"*

"No, we're busy this weekend Christmas shopping."

*"Midweek?"*

"No, I want to be there when you see him. I want to make sure he's not upset, and he goes to bed early when it's nursery the day after."

*"What about the next weekend then?"*

"I'm on call."

*"Then that takes us up to Christmas day."*

Richard was adamant she wasn't going to call the shots. He was going to do that in his own good time, without being forced into a corner.

"No way, there's no way you are making a grand entrance on the biggest day of the year. I'll have to think about it and let you know. Leave me your number and I'll get back to you."

*"You have my mobile number, don't you? I'm sorry you feel so bitter but I just wanted to be right before I saw him. I don't want to let him down again."*

"I'll call you."

And with that, Richard put the phone down. His heart was racing. How dare she think she can just waltz back into his life?

Kate heard the slamming of the receiver and went to see if everything was alright. Richard had his head in his hands. She dared to put a hand on his shoulder.

"Are you okay, Richard?" she asked tentatively.

"That was Melissa wanting to see Jacob." He paused momentarily whilst he tried to collect his thoughts. "I don't know what the best thing to do is. Should I let her see him and risk her disappearing again or do I tell her where to go and then have Jacob ask me in a few years time why I stopped him seeing his mother?"

"It's difficult since you don't know what frame of mind she's in. Maybe you should just let her see him when you are around. Like you say you don't want Jacob to hold it against you in years to come," Kate replied trying to find the words to reassure him.

"She wanted to see him on Christmas day would you believe? The bloody nerve of that woman."

"When I was younger and my parents had split up, I used to see my dad on Boxing Day. It was like another Christmas Day in a way because I got some more presents but it wasn't quite as exciting. It's just a suggestion but it might keep everyone happy."

"You might be right, Kate. She could come round on Boxing Day for an hour or so. It's usually a nothing day anyway. I'll call her back and tell her after I've given her time to sweat a bit longer. Don't say anything to Jacob yet will you though, there's still time for her to let him down again."

"Of course not; I'll go and finish dinner."

He smiled up at her. "Thanks, Kate." It was good to have someone to share his thoughts and troubles with. Under normal circumstances he would still be mulling over that conversation with Melissa. Now he'd come to a decision and was looking forward to his roast dinner.

***

Melissa stared blankly at the phone, not quite understanding what had just happened. Was Richard managing without her? Had she left it too long before contacting them? What was she going to tell her parents? She had been so self assured that everything would fall back into place and that both of them would be relieved that she was back in their lives. She looked down at her trembling hands only this time it wasn't her 'condition' that was worrying her, it was Richard's decision.

***

Dorothy Royston was preparing for her Caribbean Cruise. She was half-heartedly searching for the correct sun cream factor and a new bathing costume; not an easy task the week before Christmas. Her enthusiasm for the holiday had waned somewhat following the telephone conversation with her daughter and son. She'd started the day off rather more upbeat when she broke the news to her husband at work.

"Guess where we're going for Christmas." She'd said to him over the phone.

He'd half expected her to say Nina's house. He didn't think she would actually go through with the alternative plan.

'*Let me guess,"* he's replied. "*Dorset."*

"No, I told you we weren't going to Nina's."

*"Go on then, tell me."*

"Just a minute, let me put my glasses on, are you ready . . ." Gerald was intrigued. Why on earth did she need her glasses to name their holiday destination? ". . . Antigua, St Kitts, Martinique, St Lucia, Barbados, and Grenada, doesn't that sound wonderful?"

*"I'll say it does, when do we go there?"*

"On Friday, for two whole weeks."

*"That's marvellous, Dorothy. Leave it with me and I'll sort the rota out."*

***

Gerald had put the phone down but was a little concerned. Had his wife thought this through properly? It was all very well in embryo but when it finally came down to it, would she still feel as elated once she'd told the children. The answer to that question was soon answered with her next phone call to Nina.

***

Dorothy couldn't wait to tell her daughter after their last conversation. She'd show her what it felt like to have your family put you second best. Unfortunately, Nina didn't share her mother's fervour.

*"What do you mean, you're going away for Christmas? We always spend Christmas together as a family."*

"I know we do, dear, but this Christmas your father and I thought we'd treat ourselves since it is our Ruby anniversary year and we didn't have a party in the end."

*"But I thought you and dad were going away for your anniversary not for Christmas. It won't be the same without you, and the kids will be so disappointed."*

Peter was no better when she spoke to him.

*"Christmas?"* he'd said disgruntled. *"You can go away any time of the year, why do you have to go at Christmas? We were all going to meet up at Nina's."*

"Well I'm sure you won't have a shortage of people. Giles's parents will be there."

*"Exactly, you remember Giles's parents, don't you? They can't speak properly, their mouths are so full of plums."*

"Peter, that's a little unkind."

*"Sorry, mum, but it won't be the same this year. This will be the first time we haven't seen you and dad at Christmas time."*

Dorothy had felt totally deflated. She'd wanted to show her children that it didn't matter whether they wanted them or not, they were still capable of having a good time on their own. She hadn't realised how important their presence was and instead she was left feeling as if they were neglecting them all to go off on holiday and enjoy themselves in the sun, leaving them to fend for themselves on Christmas Day.

How her children loved to play the sympathy card and make them feel guilty when the need arose. One minute they didn't want to be inconvenienced by being dragged away from their comfort zones to celebrate an important occasion, and the next they desperately needed them to fulfil the requirements of the Festive Season; that being all the family together, present and correct.

She had spent the whole of the Christmas period shopping for presents that she could fit into a reasonably sized box to post over to Nina's house. In hindsight perhaps she should have run it by them first. But it was done now and they would just have to manage without them. Maybe next year when they start inviting people over to stay, they might think of their own parents first instead of Giles's.

***

Richard pulled the loft ladder down and made his way up the steps.

"They're up here somewhere. I'm just not sure which boxes they're in. Just a minute, if I can find the light switch. There we are, that's better, I can see what I'm doing now. Right I've found the tree and the tree decorations, but I'm sure there are more."

"Send the tree down, we can make a start with that, can't we, Jacob?" said Kate.

"Yes, daddy, can we have the tree?" Jacob shouted, jumping up and down and clapping his hands together.

Kate caught the boxes as they were lowered from the loft and carried them downstairs.

"Found them!" she heard Richard shout from inside the roof.

"What's that?" she shouted back.

"I've found the rest of the decorations. You carry on and I'll bring them down."

Kate unpacked the artificial tree and slowly put it together on the floor in the lounge.

"Right, Jacob, let's test the lights before we start putting them on." She plugged the lights in and they all glowed satisfactorily in their different colours; red, green, blue, and yellow. Jacob's face lit up in delight. He ran to the foot of the stairs. Richard was nearly at the bottom with his first box of decorations.

"Daddy, the lights work, come and see."

"Great, you carry on, Jacob, I'll follow you with this box," Richard said peering over the top of it.

"I'll drape the lights around the tree, Jacob," Kate said, "and then you can help put the baubles on."

Jacob went straight to the box of baubles to line up the ones he was going to put on first. "Look at this one, Kate, it's like glass, you can see through it."

"It's beautiful isn't it?" she replied trying to concentrate on evenly spacing the lights.

"Look at this one, it's got glitter on."

"Oh, that's lovely."

"Look at this one, Kate, it's like a bell."

Kate speeded up. She was going to be here all night at this rate individually inspecting every tree decoration. Suddenly Richard's mobile phone rang and Kate instinctively knew that he would soon be on his way to the hospital.

"Kate, that's my call, there's someone with a glass cut to the wrist."

"Okay, we'll carry on if that's okay with you?"

"Of course it is, it was never my forte, hanging up the Christmas decorations," he smiled. "It's a woman thing."

Kate looked at him suspiciously.

"Did you ask someone to ring you round about this time? I bet that wasn't the hospital at all, was it?"

Richard laughed out loud.

"Now do you honestly think I could be that devious? I'll see you at closing time, erm I mean when I've finished." Kate laughed this time and shook her head. "Bye, Jacob, daddy's got to go to work. You be a good boy for Kate and go to bed when she tells you."

"Bye, daddy, see you," he replied not even looking in his father's direction. He was far too busy lining up his next bauble.

"He's obviously missing me already, see you later, Kate."

"Bye, drive carefully." Kate watched him as he walked away. "Right, Jacob, let's make the house look really special for when daddy gets home."

They worked so hard that Jacob looked tired by the time they'd finished.

"Let's turn the main light off and see what the tree looks like in the dark." Kate flicked the light off and Jacob stared in awe as the beautiful lights twinkled on the tree catching the tinsel and making it sparkle. The candle arch stood proudly in the window, lit for all passers-by to see. Garlands of holly and pine cones hung from the wall lights and wreaths adorned the ornate candles. They placed one on the dining room table in place of the bowl of fruit and one on the table near the telephone. Kate had never seen such exquisite decorations. She remembered as a child making paper chains to hang from the ceiling and wrapping tinsel around all the pictures on the wall. There was nothing like that in the Anderson household. Each bauble alone must have cost a fortune. Melissa Anderson obviously had expensive taste.

Kate and Jacob sat on the sofa staring at their hard work as Jacob ate his supper.

"Doesn't it look beautiful in here, Kate?" he uttered.

"It certainly does, Jacob. I think you are fantastic at putting Christmas decorations up."

Jacob looked very pleased with himself. He didn't think he'd done that much but if Kate said he had, that was good enough for him and that is what he would tell his dad when he saw him tomorrow.

Jacob's eyes were drooping as he laid in his bed listening to Kate read his bedtime story and for the first time she was able to put the book down before the end as his eyes closed and his nostrils began to purr. She pulled the duvet under his chin and kissed him gently on the forehead. His mother would soon enter his life again and she wondered if they would still share this special bond that had been created out of nothing or whether she would walk in and take back what was hers.

***

The house was quiet when Richard finally made it home. He flicked the kettle on, leaned against the worktop, and rubbed his aching neck. It was hard looking down a microscope for so long; one artery, two veins and a median nerve repair, not to mention the multitude of tendons to piece together, were a lot to do when you only had a junior registrar to assist. He swore the scrub nurse would have been more help.

He walked towards the lounge with his cup of steaming tea in an attempt to unwind before he made his way up to bed. Kate had left the lights on by the look of things he noticed. He opened the door and stopped, gazing like a small child at the site before him. His eyes filled as he saw the fairy lights on the tree then the candle arch in the window magically lighting the room. The glass coals glowed in the fire and the room looked almost mystical. He sat down and drank in the aura. Kate always went that one step further to make things special.

Finally, he reluctantly switched off all the lights and wearily climbed the stairs up to bed. He stopped outside Kate's door. Should he knock and thank her for all her efforts. He waited a while and listened to see if he could tell whether she was still awake, . . . then decided not to disturb her and carried on to bed.

Kate could hear him outside the door. Her breathing quickened. How she would love him to open it and come into her room. Then she felt embarrassed just thinking about it. He was totally out of her league, far too good for her. He would never see her as anything other than the nanny, or would he?

***

The next morning Richard was up early preparing breakfast. Kate heard him in the kitchen and quickly got herself ready to find out what he was doing.

"Richard, I'll get breakfast ready," she said as she met him in the kitchen.

"I've got a long list waiting for me today. I just wanted to make sure I had a decent breakfast inside me. I thought I might as well prepare yours and Jacob's at the same time."

"Thanks for that. I'm going shopping today, anything you want to add to the list?"

"Do you think we've got enough for Jacob? Maybe you could get a few stocking fillers for him if you see anything suitable." Richard was facing her now. She knew he had something on his mind.

"No trouble, anything else?"

"You wouldn't mind wrapping his presents while he's at nursery would you? I'm absolutely hopeless at it," he asked tentatively.

"Of course I will," she smiled. "Where are they all?"

"In the top of my wardrobe and his bike is in the garage. I don't know what you can do with that to make it look like a present. It's too big to wrap."

"I'll get a big bow for it and tie it to the handle bars."

"Good idea, see, I knew I'd hired you for some reason."

"Oh thanks, glad I could be of some use."

"By the way, thanks for doing the decorations with Jacob. They looked lovely last night when I came in; took me back to my childhood."

***

Kate spent an hour wrapping presents then dashed round the supermarket before she had to fetch Jacob from nursery. She'd resume the task when Jacob was in bed tonight. It pleased her to think that she was making Richard's life easier. He had been working so hard lately. She couldn't wait for Christmas Day when they could all be together.

# Chapter . . .

# 11

Kate rose on Christmas morning to the smell of roasting turkey. The aroma filled the air and immediately she felt a delicious hunger pang. A broad smile spread across her face. It was the day she had been waiting for. The day the three of them were going to spend together and no one else was invited.

She hadn't heard Jacob's footsteps yet, she thought, as she glanced at her alarm clock. Eight fifteen. He had been so excited the previous evening as she and Richard had prepared a little tray containing a glass of sherry, a mince pie and a carrot for Rudolph with him. She'd laughed as he'd lain in his bed and squeezed his eyes together trying his hardest to go to sleep so that the morning would come quicker. Yet here it was and no sign of him.

She pulled on her dressing gown and wandered downstairs.

"Merry Christmas," Richard announced as he saw her approaching the kitchen.

"Merry Christmas," Kate replied with a smile.

Richard walked up to her and kissed her on the cheek.

"Something smells good," she said, savouring the moment.

"I only hope it tastes good. It's been cooking an hour already."

"Is Jacob not up yet? I can't believe he's slept in; he was so excited last night."

"I know, he was probably exhausted. I'll give him a bit longer."

"Need any help with anything?"

"Absolutely not. I told you, this is your day off."

Suddenly a bleary eyed little boy appeared at the foot of the stairs, a soft Winnie the Pooh dangling by his side.

"Daddy, can I have a drink?"

Kate and Richard swung round to see him.

"Jacob," Richard shouted. "Have you forgotten what day it is?"

Jacob's eyes opened a little wider. They could see the cog start to move in his brain as it began to dawn on him that it was Christmas Day. All of a sudden the penny dropped and his eyes lit up.

"Has Father Christmas been ?" he squealed with delight.

"I don't know," Richard joked with him. "Shall we have a look?"

He brought him into the kitchen and there on the tray was an empty glass, a plate containing a few crumbs and half a carrot.

"He's been, Kate, he's been," he whooped with glee.

"Come on then," Richard said as excited as he was. "Let's see if he's left you anything. Have you been a good boy?"

Jacob nodded enthusiastically.

"Has he, Kate?"

"The best," Kate answered following them into the lounge.

Richard opened the door and there in front of the Christmas tree were Jacob's presents all beautifully wrapped and waiting to be opened.

"Daddy, a bike, he's brought me a bike!" Jacob walked over to his bicycle complete with stabilisers and Lightning McQueen splayed down the side. "It's a Cars bike, Kate, look."

Kate could barely contain the tears in her eyes as he intricately inspected his present. She lifted him onto it and stood beside him as he pedalled across the room.

"We'll be able to go to the park and have a ride later if the weather stays dry," promised Richard. "Would you like that?"

"Yes, daddy, can I open some more presents now?"

"Of course you can, come on."

Richard scooped him off the bike and Jacob ploughed into the rest of the presents announcing every one as he threw the paper into the middle of the room.

"Thanks for being here, Kate," Richard finally said as the last few presents were unfolded. "It wouldn't have been the same with just the two of us. And thanks for helping me with all this."

"It's my pleasure, Richard, honestly. If it hadn't been for you two, I'd be on my own in that flat today."

"It's funny how things turn out isn't it. Just less than three months ago I was in a real state trying to juggle my life around, and you were in that grotty flat. We were total strangers, yet here we are sharing the same house and helping to make each other's Christmas a happy one."

He stared thoughtfully at her then smiled. Kate didn't know what to say. At that moment she would have gladly welcomed the world to stand still. She wanted him so much with his blue eyes and handsome face, yet had to console herself with the fact that although he needed her just as much as she needed him, unfortunately it wasn't in the same way.

"Daddy, can we open this," Jacob asked interrupting the moment and waving a Doc Hudson car at him.

"Course we can, in fact Kate will open it with you whilst I check on the turkey."

Moments later Richard returned to the lounge.

"Jacob," he said. "Why don't we give Kate her presents?"

"You've got me a present?" Kate asked delightedly.

"Yes," replied Jacob diving under the tree. "We put them under here at the back so you couldn't see them."

Jacob handed Kate a small parcel and an envelope.

"Thank you," she said taking hold of the gifts. "There might be a couple more under there."

Jacob dived back under the tree again and emerged with two more presents; one small, the other much larger.

"Which one do you want?"

"This one." Jacob pointed to the bigger present and gave the other to his father.

Richard opened his first.

"Oh, thank you, Kate. That's amazing, I was running out of this," he said holding up his favourite aftershave.

"I know, I saw it was nearly empty in your bathroom when I was cleaning."

She was so thoughtful.

"It's very expensive, Kate, you shouldn't have spent so much."

"Of course I should. This is my family now."

Kate was a little embarrassed exchanging gifts. She hadn't had a clue as to what to get Richard. He seemed to have everything, then a moment of inspiration had come and sorted the problem. Jacob was a little different. She had seen so many things that he would like but she wanted it to be special. Jacob was tearing the paper off, then his jaw dropped.

"Daddy, look, a Cars racing track. You can race Lightning McQueen and Doc Hudson."

"Wow, that's fantastic, we'll have a go this afternoon shall we?"

"Can we open it now, daddy?"

"Later Jacob, we'll go for a walk before we have Christmas dinner then it doesn't start getting dark, you can take your bike."

Kate loved that idea. Her family dream sprang into her head once again.

"Kate, you haven't opened your presents yet," Jacob pointed out.

Kate looked at the present and then slid her finger along the sealed end of the envelope. Inside was a voucher. She read it out loud:

A Pampering Day : Take the whole day to relax with our special treatments. In the morning a Pedicure and Hot Stone Back Massage followed by Three Course Lunch. In the afternoon complete your special day with a Manicure and then finally the ultimate Deep Cleansing Facial.

Kate cried out with joy. "Oh, how lovely. I've always wanted to go to one of these places. I can't wait."

"That's from me, Kate," Jacob grinned.

"Really, what a fantastic present."

"You deserve it, Kate, you work so hard," Richard added.

"You've got another one there, Kate. Do you want me to open it for you?" Jacob asked barely able to contain himself.

"Jacob, haven't you opened enough presents for today?" Richard stepped in.

"Why don't you help me?" Kate compromised. She didn't want to overrule his father, but she didn't want to see him disappointed either.

They both opened the parcel to reveal a small box. The word Garners was written across the lid in gold letters, the name of the jewellers shop in town. Kate's heart began to race. Richard had bought her jewellery. She looked up at him and he gently smiled back at her. She slowly opened the box and inside was the most exquisite necklace she had ever seen. A fine gold chain with a diamond droplet encased in a gold clasp. She gasped, she'd never possessed anything so beautiful before. She could feel a huge lump rise to her throat and tears prick at her eyes.

Richard looked concerned. "Do you like it Kate?" he asked espying the look on her face.

Kate shook her head. "It's absolutely gorgeous," she replied, a tear escaping down her cheek. She wiped it clear with the sleeve of her dressing gown. "I can't believe you've bought me this."

"Do you want to try it on?" Richard asked taking the box from her. "Here, let me fasten it for you."

She turned her back to him and lifted her hair. She could feel his hands upon her neck and closing her eyes, absorbed their touch.

"There, go and take a look."

Kate stood in front of the mirror above the fire. She lifted it up and admired its beauty.

"It's beautiful, thank you so much, and thank you Jacob for my wonderful day out. This is just the nicest Christmas I've ever had."

After a hearty breakfast of bacon butties, the three of them set off to the park. Richard wheeled the new bike across the road and then Jacob led the way pedalling as fast as he could.

"Slow down, Jacob, you're going to fall off," Richard shouted chasing after him.

Kate laughed as she watched Richard tear off at full speed. She'd never seen him running before and it made a comical sight, him charging along waving his hands. Jacob wasn't aware of the dangers. He had his helmet, knee and elbow pads on and was prepared for any eventuality. Finally, Richard caught up with his son and duly chastised him.

"Jacob, it's your first time on this bike, now just slow down and wait for me."

Kate wandered happily along behind them. This had been the most perfect Christmas Day so far; Jacob's face as he'd opened the lounge door, the presents, bacon butties for breakfast and then a walk with her 'family'. They would have dinner about three o'clock and then relax and play games or watch a film on television. How she wished that this was how it would be forever, just the three of them.

Richard waited for Kate to catch up.

"Right, it's your turn to keep up with him. I'm exhausted."

Kate laughed. "You need to spend more time at the gym," she answered him, running to catch Jacob.

"Oh yes, and when would I have time to do that, in the middle of the night?"

***

They had had such a lovely morning by the time they got back to the house. Their cheeks were glowing and each of them felt a hunger pang that would do justice to their Christmas dinner. Kate helped Jacob in with his bike and Richard headed straight for the kitchen to resume his duties as chef for the day. The roast potatoes were slid into the oven and the final preparations were made to the vegetables.

Kate spent the next half hour fixing Jacob's race track together and wondered why she had bought such a complicated present. Jacob patiently played with the cars as she spread the instructions and the pieces around the floor trying to look like she knew what she was doing. Richard finally came to the rescue and between them they completed the track. The batteries were inserted and the race began.

Jacob was mesmerised as he tried to follow the cars speeding round. After a while he stopped the racing and positioned all the rest of his cars around the track trying to create a scene from the film. Kate began to ponder over where they were going to keep the track now it had been assembled, as it took up a considerable amount of the lounge floor and she didn't relish the thought of having to put it together again every time he wanted to play with it.

Finally the call came for dinner and after the promise of being allowed to open several more games in the afternoon, Jacob was reluctantly prised away from his Christmas presents.

They sat around the oak table in the dining room, Richard at the head and Kate and Jacob either side. Richard carved the turkey and Kate spooned out the vegetables for her and her little companion. Once their plates were fit to burst they started to eat. There wasn't a sound to be heard.

"Well, there's a sign of good food," said Kate after a while. "When everyone goes quiet."

"It doesn't taste too bad does it?" Richard said sounding quite surprised.

"Too bad? It's delicious."

They finished eating and Richard stood up to clear the plates away. "Oh, no," he shouted from the kitchen.

Kate looked up. "What's wrong?"

"I forgot the crackers," he sighed holding one up at the kitchen door. Kate laughed. "Let's pull them now before we have our dessert," he suggested.

"Yeh," Jacob agreed clapping his hands.

***

The afternoon brought about a master class in Kerplunk, courtesy of Richard.

"Well, you're a dark horse," Kate pointed out. "You never told me you'd had a misspent youth playing Kerplunk."

"Yes, there's still quite a bit you don't know about me, Miss Forrester," he teased.

"Really and what would that be?" she replied playfully.

"Just wait and see, I may surprise you every so often."

Kate laughed out loud. Jacob sulked because his father wouldn't let him win. Richard set the game up again.

"I don't want to play again, daddy," Jacob said walking back to his cars.

"Oh, so it's just Kate and me is it? Well do you know what happened when I was a boy and used to play this game every night before I went to bed?"

"What?"

"I didn't win every time. Every third or fourth game, I used to lose."

Jacob mentally calculated how many games they'd played then a smile crept across his face.

"Can I play?" he said enthusiastically this time.

They all sat down for a fourth game and Richard carefully studied the sticks, this time to see which one would bring all the marbles crashing down. After a while he found it and slowly started to pull.

"Oh, no, I don't think I like this one," he teased.

"He's got to carry on, hasn't he, Jacob?"

Jacob was totally focussed on the stick his father was pulling.

Plop!

One marble fell.

Plop, plop!

Two more fell.

Jacob's face lit up as it dawned on him, his father had *that* stick.

One slight more pull and the whole lot came thundering down. They poured into the tray and then spilled over the edge onto the carpet. Jacob couldn't contain his delight. He clapped his hands with joy and danced around the room.

"How many did you get, Kate?" he said excitedly.

"I got four."

"I only got two." His eyes were wide with the knowledge that he had finally won. "I won, daddy, I won, Kate."

The two adults laughed at his antics.

"Can we play again? Please, can we play again?"

It was too much for Richard, he wasn't used to losing at this game and as he resumed his winning streak, Jacob gradually lost interest and the game finished.

They played with Jacob's new toys for the rest of the day and by bedtime, he had managed to open and play with every single one. He was shattered by this time and his eyes were closing as a big yawn took over him. Despite his efforts to stay awake, he was asleep by the time his head hit the pillow.

Richard and Kate returned to the lounge.

"What do you fancy to drink, Kate?" he asked heading towards the kitchen.

"I'll have another glass of that wine we had for dinner if there's any left," replied Kate. "It was really nice."

"Yes, it was nice wasn't it? It was one Todd recommended," he agreed.

He brought two glasses in and placed them on the coffee table.

"I don't want to spoil today, but *she's* coming tomorrow and I think we should talk about what we're going to do."

"In what way?"

"Well I was thinking that you and Jacob could be upstairs when she arrives, it would give me chance to have a quick word with her and find out exactly what she's got planned. Then I'll come up for Jacob and maybe you could make a pot of tea and bring it in."

"Of course I will."

"How long do you think I should let her stay the first time?" asked Richard. He'd been pondering over the details since she'd rang on that fateful day.

"I don't know, maybe a couple of hours."

"Yes, I think that's enough for her first visit." He took a deep breath and reached for his glass of wine. "But for her, today's been pretty good hasn't it?"

"I can't tell you how much I've enjoyed it. I was dreading Christmas. I was sure that you and Jacob would be away or that you'd be inviting someone over and I'd have to find somewhere else to go. I've never seen a child on Christmas morning before. It's absolutely magical—Jacob's face when he saw everything by the tree. We should have captured it on camera."

"I know, I haven't taken one picture today, it completely slipped my mind."

They talked some more, but after a while, like Jacob, the tiredness took over and they both headed off upstairs. It wasn't long before Kate was between the sheets of her comfy bed. She couldn't stop thinking about the day despite her desire to go to sleep. What would have happened if she hadn't bumped into Richard at the dry cleaners? Would she really have had to spend Christmas in that mouldy old flat staring at the black patches on the wall? She thanked her lucky stars for the wonderful day she had just spent. The only damp patch on the horizon now was tomorrow's ordeal with Melissa.

***

Richard wasn't his usual, cheerful self the following day and Kate knew why. It had started the previous evening and escalated. Now the day had arrived he felt decidedly uneasy. The past three months hadn't been simple, far from it, but between him and Kate, they had made things a lot less fraught. His son was a happy little boy again and life was looking good.

Now Melissa was back on the scene and about to turn their perfect world upside down. He knew she would. Even though he'd told her that he was calling the shots, she wouldn't be able to stay in the background for long. Melissa had to be centre of attention and where Jacob was concerned that meant announcing to all that she was his mother. She would force her way back into his affection whether he liked it or not and gently push Kate aside.

As far as Kate was concerned, she would probably be treated as a second class citizen. Melissa had been used to 'staff' all her life and had been brought up to understand that they were there to work for you not to engage in chat and befriend. The mere thought of it turned Richard cold. He couldn't bare the idea of Kate being spoken down to. She was very precious to him and despite Melissa's unquestionable disapproval, he would do everything in his power to ensure that didn't happen.

It was almost three o'clock and Richard was keeping one eye outside to make sure there were no surprises. He wanted to give Kate the nod as to when to take Jacob upstairs and didn't want to frighten the poor boy. He had been pre-warned about his mother's visit that morning. Richard had left it as late as possible in case she called off at the last minute. It hadn't upset him or on the other hand, excited him either. He had merely took it in his stride and continued playing. He had that many distractions at the moment, very little seemed to bother him.

At three on the dot, a car pulled round the corner and drew up outside the house.

"Kate, I think she's here," he shouted from his office.

Kate swiftly took Jacob upstairs. He'd willingly followed her with the promise of a game of hide and seek. From upstairs she could hear the doorbell ring then the exchange of words. There were more voices than she'd anticipated. Had she brought someone with her? She decided to concentrate on their game rather than try to listen to the conversation. The voices soon diminished as Richard led them into the lounge.

It was Jacob's turn to hide. Kate closed her eyes and counted.

". . . nineteen, twenty, coming ready or not."

As she turned around, Jacob was in front of her seated on the bed with his knees tucked under his chin.

"That was mummy at the door wasn't it?" he said solemnly. "Will she be cross at me for not speaking to her for a long time?"

"Jacob, what on earth makes you think that? Mummy was the one who had to go away because she wasn't well. She wasn't allowed to speak to anyone, but she's much better now. That's why she's come to see you."

Jacob smiled but it wasn't a happy one, it was more of relief that he wasn't in trouble any more. Kate's heart went out to him. He deserved better than this. He was a good little boy who needed stability in his life, not a mother who drifted in and out as the whim took her. She hoped for Jacob's sake that it didn't happen again.

Richard tapped on the bedroom door. "Jacob, are you ready to come and see mummy?" He noticed Kate sat on the bed next to him. "Everything alright, Kate?"

Kate nodded. "He just thinks mummy might be cross that he hasn't spoken to her for a while, but I've told him she won't be. She's just been poorly and she's better now."

Richard shook his head. Typical of Melissa to make others feel uncomfortable for her failings.

"Come on, sweetheart. Mummy's not cross with you at all. She can't wait to see you and she's brought some presents for you which Father Christmas left at her house. By the way, Kate, she's brought her boyfriend with her, no doubt as moral support, would you believe. Could you make one more cup? Tea will be fine."

Jacob slid off the bed and held his father's hand as they went downstairs.

Kate went into the kitchen and prepared the tea. She poured the water into the teapot and left it to brew as she carried the tray of cups and a bowl of sugar through to the lounge. She slowly pushed the lounge door with her foot. Luckily Richard hadn't closed it properly behind him. Then her mouth dropped open, the tray tipped forward, the cups and the sugar crashed to the ground, smashing into pieces as her eyes fell on Alex seated in the chair nearest the door.

"I'm so sorry, Richard," she cried out in alarm.

"It's fine, Kate, don't worry," Richard reassured her.

Alex sprung to his feet and offered his help. "I'll give her a hand," he insisted to Richard. "You carry on here."

Alex was in the kitchen before Kate had time to recover. She was shaking by this time and her mind had completely emptied as to what to do next. She followed Alex to the kitchen.

"What the hell are you doing here? Don't tell me Melissa is the blank chequebook?" she hissed.

"Ssh, honestly, Kate, I had no idea you worked here, I promise."

"Look what you've made me do. I look totally incompetent now in front of your girlfriend."

"Kate, please don't say anything. I'll help you clean it up. You just prepare another tray and I'll tell them I saw you catch the handle of the door, I'll make something up but please don't say anything."

Kate stared at him in disbelief. Was he trying to tell her that Melissa wouldn't look too favourably at her boyfriend being the hired hand's ex? Her hand was still shaking as she set the tray again. Alex disappeared into the lounge to clean away the debris.

"Alex, what are doing?" Melissa asked incredulously.

"It's okay, Melissa, I'm just helping. I could see exactly what happened. She just caught the door handle as she came in."

Richard looked puzzled at Alex's intervention. He passed him and went into the kitchen to find Kate.

"Kate, are you alright?"

She was visibly trembling. "I'm so sorry, Richard. I look like a complete amateur."

"Hey, it doesn't matter. Alex said he saw you catch the door handle as you walked in."

"But all the cups are smashed."

"So what, they're only cups. No one's hurt." *Except for my feelings,* thought Kate. "Come here, I'll take the tray this time."

"Do you mind if I go and get some fresh air. I feel dreadful."

"Not at all, just take your time. Melissa usually has this effect on people," he smiled.

Kate rushed to the hallway, grabbed her coat, slipped on her shoes, and went out into the cold, afternoon wind. The icy breeze on her face was welcome. She took a deep breath, crossed the road to the park and started walking. The further away she was the better. Once the house was out of view, she sat down on one of the wooden benches and placed her head in her hands. The tears rolled down her face. She was unable to stop them, as if the pent up emotion was escaping from her body. She couldn't decide whether it was the humiliation of dropping the tray in front of Melissa, or the shock of seeing Alex. Maybe a combination of both was to blame, or maybe it was the untold disappointment she felt for letting Richard down.

***

"So that's the new nanny or housekeeper, whatever you call her, is it?" Melissa asked, still looking a little shocked after all the commotion.

"We call her Kate," Richard snapped back in her defence.

"That's the trouble with you, Richard, you're far too familiar with the hired help. You treat them all like family. She shouldn't be calling you Richard, it should be Mr Anderson."

"What, like Rachel, you mean?" said Richard incensed. "It doesn't matter whether they're useless or not, just so long as they're respectful. Well, I happen to have a lot of respect for Kate, she's more than the 'hired help' as you call her, she's a good friend and she dragged me out of the shit that you left me in."

The room fell silent and three stunned faces turned towards him, the stark animosity almost visible. It was Jacob who broke the cold silence.

"Daddy, where's Kate gone?"

Richard put his hand to his mouth and closed his eyes as it dawned on all of them the reason they were there.

"She's gone for a walk, Jacob, to get a little air."

"Can I go with her?"

His parents hung their heads in shame. Their behaviour around him had been abysmal. Melissa finally came to her senses. She was gaining nothing by insulting Richard's choice of nanny, in fact quite the opposite. She was in danger of not being invited back and needed to back track very quickly.

"Richard, I'm sorry for that. I had no right to criticise. I'm in no position to do that now and Jacob is obviously extremely fond of Kate. She seems to be doing a marvellous job. I suppose I'm just trying to stir things because you've managed so well without me and I don't feel . . . part of Jacob's life anymore."

Richard couldn't believe it. Was Melissa actually eating some humble pie and apologising for being a complete bitch. This was a first. Alex sat by quietly pleased at his girlfriend's attempt at grovelling. He knew exactly why she'd done it; to manipulate the situation towards her own ends. It was nothing to do with Kate's performance as a nanny, but he would deal with that when they were alone, not in front of Richard. Neither of them must know that there was any connection between him and Kate.

Melissa and Alex stayed another hour. Richard kept one eye on the clock. Where was Kate, he thought? It was getting dark outside and the temperature was plummeting. He disappeared periodically to look out of his study window. The park was visible from there, but there was still no sign of her. He was beginning to worry.

Alex sensed Richard's uneasiness. Was Kate waiting for him to go before she returned to the house? Perhaps he could do the decent thing and wind things up.

Melissa was sitting on the floor playing cars with Jacob. She couldn't ever remember sitting like this when she lived here; in fact, she couldn't really remember ever playing with her son, that was the nanny's job. She always had something else to do; something more important, or was it? Was there anything more important than spending time with your child? She was enjoying herself now and was quietly annoyed for causing a scene before. Why did she always have to pass comment on other people? Kate was probably a very nice person, and what did it matter whether she called Richard by his first name or his last as long as Jacob liked her and she was good with him.

"Melissa, do you think we should make a move?" Alex suggested whilst Richard was out of the room. "You don't want to overstay your welcome first time. Maybe Richard will let you come again if we go before he kicks us out?"

"Yes, you're probably right. I'll have a word with him and see if I can come again. Would you like to see mummy and Alex again, Jacob?"

Jacob nodded nonchalantly and Melissa could see that she had a huge mountain to climb trying to convince her son that his mother was back to stay and not about to run away again. She could also see that he had developed a special bond with his nanny, a bond she'd never seen before in him. The whole household was different. There was an air of calm about it, which she had disturbed somewhat today. Richard wasn't going to take too kindly to that. She would have to make some changes; he seemed a far more contented man than he had ever been before, as if her absence hadn't been that much of an ordeal.

"Well, I'll go and talk to daddy and try and arrange another time to come and see you."

She watched her son hoping for some kind of response, but his apathy continued. She quickly left the room leaving Alex alone with him.

"So what do you and Kate get up to then, Jacob?" Alex asked.

"We play Snakes and Ladders and Kerplunk, but daddy always wins that. We colour and draw and stick things. And she reads me bedtime stories."

Alex's eyes clouded over. She would have been a great mother to their children, he thought. If only the business hadn't failed, he would have still been with her. He'd been a complete fool, and now he'd asked her to keep this huge secret. How many times was he going to let her down? The only consolation he could take with him was, that despite everything, she'd picked herself up and had got a good job with beautiful living accommodation thrown in.

Melissa found Richard on his way back from his study, a look of concern etched on his brow.

"Everything alright, Richard?" she asked equally concerned.

"Yes, fine."

"Alex and I are going to go now. I wonder . . . do you think I could see Jacob again, soon?"

Richard was sure that he had heard an ounce of compassion in her voice. Gone was that self assured, arrogant woman that had entered his home and in her place was one desperate to see her son again, but not quite sure whether it was going to be a forgone conclusion or not.

"Yes, you can, as long as you're quite clear as to the rules. I'll be present for the first few visits and they'll take place in this house, then we'll take it from there."

She was genuinely relieved and pleased. She had assured her mother that he would be eagerly awaiting her to take Jacob off his hands but that was as far from the truth as she could have imagined. He was coping admirably with his new nanny and Melissa was left feeling slightly surplus to requirements and out in the cold.

"Of course, Richard, whatever you say."

***

It was dark by the time Kate watched Melissa and Alex get back into their car and pull away. She still wasn't sure if she was ready to return to the house such was her disappointment at letting Richard down, but finally the cold was too much to bear and she emerged from her shelter behind the huge oak tree and walked back across the road. She opened the door and Richard appeared from his viewing point in the study.

"Kate, where have you been? I was worried about you." He could see her red eyes and knew she had been crying. "Come here."

He wrapped his arms around her.

"I'm so sorry," she whispered again, her body shivering from the cold. "I ruined everything didn't I?"

"Well actually, no you didn't," Richard began still holding her tight. "She left here very impressed with you, and pleading to see Jacob again."

"Really?" Kate answered him pulling away.

"Really, so that means that you and I make a very good team."

She smiled at him this time. She did feel slightly better. "How's Jacob?"

"Missing his nanny, but apart from that, unscathed."

"So it went alright then?"

"It was fine and I've made it quite clear that if she wants to see Jacob again, she does it on our terms, not hers."

"Wow. How do you feel?"

"Better now that first visit's over, oh, and by the way, that was thanks to you as well. You were the one who suggested she visit today, so thanks for that. Now let me get you a warm drink, you must be freezing."

Kate didn't think she deserved any thanks, but nonetheless, she was happy things had gone well. She wished she could tell Richard the real reason that she had made such a fool of herself, but for Alex's sake, kept quiet.

The phone rang as they sat themselves down with a warm cup of coffee. Richard picked it up.

*"Richard."*

"Hi, mum, how are you?"

*"Hello, son. Just called to see how the visit went?"*

"It went okay. We had the odd word here and there but for most of the time she was fairly civil, which must have been quite an ordeal for her."

*"Now, now, Richard. How was Jacob?"*

"He was fine, no problems at all."

*"And what about when she left?"*

"He didn't bat an eyelid. I'll tell you, mum, she's got her worked cut out there. It's not going to be plain sailing getting that relationship back. I think Kate's replaced her in his affections."

*"I'm sure you're right, Richard. Kate has a far more stable influence over him than she ever did. Talking about Kate, your father and I were wondering if she would like to join us for New Year?"*

"Well, she's right here, I'll ask her." Richard put his hand over the phone. "Kate, my mother wants to know if you want to come up to Scotland with us at New Year? It's just for a couple of nights but it'll be a nice break."

"I'd love to if that's alright with you?" she replied suddenly very excited at the prospect of seeing his parents again.

"Sure it is. Yes, mother, she'd love to."

*"Oh, splendid, that's a date then. Better go, your father is waiting for his dinner, bye, Richard."*

"Bye, mum."

***

Iris Anderson replaced the receiver and with a contented smile, felt very pleased with herself.

"Well, that's sorted that little problem out," she announced to her husband.

Donald Anderson was sitting in the conservatory, diligently doing a Times crossword from a book he was given for Christmas. They were such a challenge, particularly the cryptic ones.

"I'm sure that's a bit underhanded, Iris. I don't think Richard will take too kindly to your little plan."

"He won't know any different. It's only a dinner party when all's said and done. We're not sending him off on a blind date. Anyway, I'm sure Kate won't mind babysitting; it is her job after all."

"We'll see. Don't blame me though if Richard decides not to come."

"He'll have to come when I accept the invitation. You don't let the Harper's down when they've been kind enough to invite you. It's not the done thing."

"I'm sure Richard doesn't think as highly of the Harpers as you do, dear. He is a consultant now and has made bigger decisions than that."

"Mm, he's getting a little too attached to that nanny. I may have to get her on board first then she can help me persuade Richard."

"Just as long as he's aware that I had nothing to do with it."

Iris giggled.

"Of course, but wouldn't it be marvellous if he ended up going on a date with Ingrid. She's a lovely looking girl and such breeding. She doesn't live too far away from Richard either."

# CHAPTER . . .

# 12

Richard reluctantly went back to work the following day. He would have loved to have spent more time with Jacob and all his new toys. Time seemed to be moving so fast these days. He was growing up and spending precious time with him over Christmas had made him realise what he was missing.

He had enjoyed Kate's company as well. They shared a very close bond now and she was such a comfort to have around. He felt that he could discuss anything and everything with her. He was actually looking forward to visiting his parents now that he had her to chat to along the way. She would certainly keep Jacob entertained whilst they were there.

The ward was virtually empty over the Christmas period. He had committed himself to a couple of day case, operating lists which were mainly trauma and skin cancers, but only minor operations so that the patients didn't have to stay in. After all, who wanted to be in hospital whilst everyone else was out celebrating?

He entered the ward and the first person he saw in the office was Todd.

"Morning, Richard," said Todd brightly, happy to see his friend. "Had a good holiday?"

"Yes, it was great, thanks. Just the three of us on Christmas day, and it was perfect."

"Three of you, is Melissa back?"

"No, I mean Kate."

"Oh, I see, very cosy.'

"It's not like that; she's just a good friend."

"You don't spend Christmas day with just a good friend."

"You do if she lives in your house."

Sister Jackson was hovering in the background pretending to concentrate on some district nurse referrals. She hadn't heard this Kate mentioned before. Who was she, spending Christmas day with Richard and living in his house?'

"Fair enough, what are you doing for New Year?" Todd continued.

Richard looked a little sheepish. "We're all going to my parent's house in Scotland for a few days."

Todd looked across at him and a wry smile appeared on his face. "Say no more."

"Seriously, Todd, there's nothing going on. She's not interested in me like that."

"Well, why would she be spending all her spare time with you then? Surely a nanny has days off, but she chooses to spend her's with you."

Carl Walker came into the office and Richard set off on his ward round quickly pursued by Sister Jackson. His mind was elsewhere though, back at home, wondering if Kate's reasons for spending the holidays with them were as Todd had insinuated or simply because she was lonely and had no other option.

***

Dorothy Royston was gazing trance-like at the clear blue sea over the port side of the ship. The sun warmed her bones and should have calmed her troubled mind, but it was failing somewhat. She couldn't seem to get her children's disappointed voices out of her head. They were on their way to Martinique; they'd already seen the beautiful islands of Antigua and St Kitts, so why was she feeling so down. She just couldn't seem to help herself.

"A penny for them," came a voice behind her. Gerald had brought over two glasses of iced Martini and lemonades.

"Oh, nothing, dear, just thinking about the children."

"Like you've done every second of this holiday. For goodness sake, Dorothy, you've got to let them go if you're going to enjoy this trip. We're visiting some of the most beautiful places on earth and all *they* are doing is making you miserable."

"I know, they have this remarkable talent for it. When I spoke to them on Christmas day they made me feel like a leper."

"That's because we brought up two spoilt brats who are so used to getting their own way, they can't understand why we didn't drop everything to run across to Dorset when they demanded it. Well, we're here now, so let's just try and enjoy it."

"You're right, Gerald, of course you're right."

Dorothy took a sip of her drink and resumed her vacant expression as she stared out to sea. Gerald stood back helplessly watching. He would love to give those two a piece of his mind only at this moment in time, his feelings were running so high he would probably succeed in alienating them forever.

***

Richard loaded the car with the suitcases and strapped Jacob into his booster seat along with his fleecy blanket and pillow. It was late evening by the time they were setting off. He usually did this journey through the night so that Jacob could sleep all the way. Richard was used to being awake all night, his years of on call had taught him the art of endurance.

"Have you got everything, Kate?" he asked as he locked the front door.

"Yes, hopefully. If I haven't it's too late now."

They both settled down in the car and Richard tapped his flask of black coffee. "Yes, that's all I need for the journey," he smiled, and they were off.

Once they'd hit the motorway, Kate could feel her eyelids become heavy. She'd been looking forward to the journey, having Richard all to herself for several hours, but now the drowsiness was taking over. She yawned.

"Why don't you tip the chair back and have a sleep? It's a long journey. That's why my parents either fly or go by train. I just find it easier to drive, especially with all Jacob's belongings."

"Do you not mind? Some company I am, as soon as we hit a straight road, I fall asleep."

"How's Jacob doing in the back?"

Kate looked round to see Jacob's head resting comfortably on his pillow and his eyes shut tightly.

"He's out for the count."

"That'll be it for the whole journey now. It's much easier taking him at this time than trying to entertain him for the entire trip during the day. No child can sit still for that length of time. Would you mind pouring me a coffee just in case you do decide to nod off then I won't have to disturb you?"

It wasn't much further down the motorway that Kate finally gave in to the motion of the car and fell asleep leaving Richard to enjoy his own company. He briefly glanced across at her and smiled to himself. They were so comfortable in each other's presence now. He wondered what he ever did without her. The stress had been stripped away from his life leaving him to be able to concentrate on his job and enjoy the precious time he had with his son.

He enjoyed his evenings with Kate, just the two of them. She was a pleasure to have around. There was never the risk of being chastised because dinner had been ruined, or that he'd left dirty dishes in the sink. The pressure was off and he was a far better person for it. They were just two adults who had a mutual appreciation of each other.

His mind started drifting to places where it had no right to go. What if they weren't just good friends, what if she didn't work for him, would he encounter a different kind of attraction? She was a good looking woman with an unbelievable personality. His heart started to quicken at the thought of them together. What if Todd was right and she was thinking the same? Surely they couldn't let such an opportunity just pass them by.

A few drops of rain fell on the windscreen; the automatic wipers immediately swept them away. Soon the drops were falling faster and the rain started. Richard groaned, surely not mile upon mile of darkness in the rain. What with that and no one to talk to, the journey would seem endless. He glanced in the mirror at Jacob, he was still sound asleep with his head tipped to one side. As he looked up, a car appeared from nowhere in front of him. Richard swerved quickly to avoid it. Kate was shaken from her sleep.

"Sorry about that," Richard said as a surge of adrenaline ran through his body. "That guy mustn't be doing above forty in the middle lane. Honestly, there's nothing on the roads. What is he doing driving at that speed in this lane?"

"In this weather as well, what's wrong with the inside lane?" Kate replied. "When did it start raining?"

"About five minutes ago."

Kate noticed that the cup of coffee was empty and went to pour him another. Maybe he was feeling drowsy like she had been with the hypnotic street lights flashing by overhead. The darkness and the wet conditions weren't helping with visibility either making it a fairly miserable drive. She would make every attempt to stay awake now for the rest of the journey.

***

They finally pulled into his parent's drive early the next morning with two very tired people in the front seats and a very lively customer in the back.

"Granny, granddad, we're here," Jacob shouted at the front door.

"Ssh, Jacob," Richard whispered. "People are still asleep."

Kate couldn't believe the size of the house for just the two of them. It was like a Scottish manor house nestling in the middle of the countryside. She couldn't wait to explore the place once they'd had a decent rest.

Richard tapped gently on the front door and waited. There was no answer at first; luckily the rain had ceased. Finally a weary looking Iris Anderson opened the door in her dressing gown.

"Granny, we're here," Jacob shouted again, forgetting the locals still fast asleep.

"Sweetheart, how lovely to see you. Come on in all of you. Have you driven straight up?"

"Well, we had a couple of stops but not for long. We didn't want Jacob to wake up. He's had a great sleep," said Richard.

"How are you, Kate, I bet you're shattered aren't you?"

"Oh, I'm not too bad thanks. I had a quick forty winks on the way."

"Well listen, you two, if you want to have a nap, your father and I will look after Jacob."

"Thanks, mum, maybe a couple of hours will be nice after a cup of tea."

"I don't know, like father like son," Iris laughed and went into the kitchen to put the kettle on.

"Richard, you're in your usual room and Kate's next to Jacob's. I'll show you where to go," Iris said after they'd finished their drinks.

Iris led the way up the staircase to a large landing. Kate admired the pictures of the Scottish landscape as she walked past each one. They eventually came to their rooms.

"Now the bathroom's down there and there are towels in your room, Kate. Have a nice sleep."

"Thank you, Mrs Anderson, that's very kind of you."

Iris went back downstairs to see to her grandson. Kate quickly caught Richard before he disappeared into this room.

"Give me a knock before you go downstairs won't you? I don't want to stay asleep all day."

"Course I will," he smiled. "See you later."

Kate was so tired she failed to take in the beautiful surroundings she had found herself in and even more so, the breathtaking view from the window. Her head hit the pillow and everything else was a distant memory.

***

She woke to a tapping noise on the door and the wind whistling through the trees outside. She'd had a strange dream which had disturbed her. One she couldn't quite remember the details of however hard she tried. It was just sitting there in the back of her mind. Disorientated at first, it finally dawned on her what the tapping noise was.

"Kate, are you awake?" It was Richard, his voice still sounding weary.

"Yes, I'll be down in a minute."

"Okay, see you downstairs."

Kate went into the bathroom. A large, ornate mirror hung over the sink unit. She opened her toiletry bag and inspected her face in the mirror. She would quickly freshen up, removed the black mascara smudges under her eyelids, and then join the family downstairs.

"Are you going to let Jacob see in the New Year tonight?" Iris asked her son.

Donald was in the conservatory playing cars with Jacob.

"I'll see how he goes. If he's tired, I'll just take him to bed."

"Ah, Kate, how are you feeling after your sleep?" Iris asked as the young woman walked into the lounge.

"A bit more refreshed, thank you, but I'll tell you again at midnight."

They all laughed although Kate knew that if she remained in Richard's company, she would quite happily stay awake all night again.

"Why don't I make us some lunch?" Iris suggested and disappeared into the kitchen.

"Do you want some help?" Kate asked; she wasn't used to sitting around and being waited upon.

"No, Kate, you have a rest. Maybe you could help me tomorrow."

Donald could hear the conversation from where he was sitting in the next room. He knew what that was all about. Tomorrow she would be preparing Kate for her part in persuading Richard to 'get his life back'—whether he wanted to or not.

Richard wandered into the conservatory. His father had been very quiet since their arrival. He seemed to be keeping out of the way for some reason as if engaging in conversation might force him to divulge something he wasn't permitted to.

"Everything alright, dad?"

"Yes, I'm fine, son. Just playing cars here. Tell me again, which one am I supposed to be."

"That's Sheriff, dad."

"Granddad, you can be Mater as well and I'll be Lightning McQueen and Sally."

"Right you are, Jacob, I'm going to get some petrol . . ."

Richard left them to play. His father obviously wasn't in the mood for chatting with the adults which wasn't unlike him, that was his mother's department, but still he hadn't seen him for a while, he could make a bit more of an effort. He joined Kate back in the lounge. She was staring out of the window at the view over the glen. She turned as Richard entered the room.

"What a fantastic view, isn't it?" she said to him.

"Yes, a bit bleak in winter, but the summers are lovely around here."

"Whose is that house you can see in the distance? It's like a mansion."

"Oh, that belongs to the Harpers. They're the ones with all the money around here. I think they own most of the land you can see."

"How do you get that kind of money, to be able to own half of Scotland?"

Richard laughed. "It's not quite half, but I know what you mean. I think a lot of it was inherited but you still have to be a fairly good manager to keep it all. They've invested well in stocks and shares and I think they rear prize winning cattle." Richard looked up beyond the house as his memories came flooding back. "See that road up there with the kind of hair-pin bend?"

"Yes, the one just behind the house."

"That's right, that's where I trashed the car on the way home from the pub one night."

"Agh," Kate gasped. "Were you drunk?"

"No, more's the pity, I hadn't had a drop. Melissa didn't speak to me for weeks after."

"Why not? Surely it couldn't be your fault if you hadn't had a drink."

"No, but it was her car I was driving. We had to hire another one to get home then have hers delivered. It cost us a fortune."

"Oh, I see."

"Lunch is ready," came the shrill cry of his mother.

They followed her into the kitchen where a large oak table was set out with hot vegetable soup, warm bread rolls, and ham and cheese sandwiches.

"Oh, Mrs Anderson, this is lovely. Just what you need on a cold day."

"Do call me Iris, dear. Now, sit yourself down and tuck in." They didn't need to be asked twice. Jacob helped himself to a plate of ham sandwiches and hungrily munched his way through them. "Oh, Kate, I hope you like haggis because that's what we traditionally eat up here for New Year."

"I must admit, I've never had it but I'll certainly give it a try. Mm, this soup is delicious."

"It's home made," Iris answered, basking in the compliment.

"Grandma, do I have to have haggis?"

"No, darling, I've got fish fingers for you."

Jacob was satisfied with the answer and continued with his sandwiches. Richard noticed his father was still very quiet. He'd made little in the way of conversation since they'd arrived.

"How's the weather been up here, dad? Has there been any snow yet?"

"It's been bloody awful," Donald replied grumpily.

"Donald, watch your language in front of Jacob." Donald nodded and continued with his soup. "Yes, it's been raining for over a fortnight now and it's so cold. You can't go out without dressing for an arctic expedition."

The afternoon went by and still nothing from his father. Richard was beginning to worry. This was going to be a long evening, struggling to find a topic of conversation his father was prepared to discuss. Maybe his parents would give up on the New Year and leave him and Kate alone to celebrate together. He quite liked the idea of that. It would give him an opportunity to find out what she really felt for him.

Contrarily, his mother seemed to be in a completely opposite kind of mood as if she had some amazing, exciting secret that only she was privy to. He wished she'd let her husband in on it and try and cheer him up.

***

Jacob gave in at about ten o'clock. He had every intention of running out of the back door and in through the front to bring in the New Year but his eyelids had other ideas and Richard carried him, already clad in his pyjamas, fast asleep to bed.

Just his mother and father to go and then he would have Kate all to himself, Richard thought deviously. Kate seemed to be enjoying herself despite his father's melancholy mood. She was like that though; she would never make anyone feel uncomfortable by airing her true feelings in public, not like his father.

Finally the moment arrived that Kate had been waiting for, the big countdown to New Year 's Day when she could kiss Richard for the first time. How she wished his parents weren't in the same room watching his every move. All four of them sat glued to the television.

"Ten . . . nine . . . eight . . . seven . . . six . . . five . . . four . . . three . . . two . . . one, Happy New Year," the presenter shouted.

"Happy New Year everyone," Iris announced, and went straight to her son. "Happy New Year, Richard."

Richard kissed his mother on the cheek. Donald made his way to Kate.

"Happy New Year, Kate," he said giving her a big hug and a kiss on both cheeks.

Richard shook hands with his father and Iris and Kate embraced each other. Iris sat down next to her husband and tapped him on the hand. Richard approached Kate under the watchful eye of his mother.

"Happy New Year, Kate, thanks for everything."

"Happy New Year, Richard," Kate smiled back.

He put his hands on her shoulders, drew her towards him and kissed her tenderly on the lips. Not a quick peck, as one would have expected, but a lingering kiss which definitely lasted a few seconds, Kate thought.

Kate nearly swooned, Donald smiled sentimentally, Iris was horrified. What on earth was he doing kissing his nanny in such a fashion? It was time for them all to retire to bed before any more feelings spilled over and led to something else. She would have to put her scheming into action sooner rather than later tomorrow morning.

***

Kate found sleep hard to come by that night. How could she even contemplate closing her eyes and obliterating the past few moments without reliving them a hundred times or more. Richard had kissed her. Not the type of kiss an employer gave to his employee, but one that had hidden meaning and just a hint of passion.

Eventually the encounter started to blur and she reluctantly fell asleep. Her hopes of a wonderful dream about the two of them together were shattered when the strange nightmare from earlier haunted her for the rest of the night.

***

Kate lay on her bed the following morning waiting for signs of life downstairs. She heard the sound of pots rattling in the kitchen and decided to get up. Iris was in the kitchen preparing breakfast.

"Morning, Iris," Kate said as she peeped around the door.

"Morning, Kate," Iris replied brightly. "Did you sleep well?"

"Yes, thanks," she lied.

"I'm glad you're down first, I wanted to ask you a favour." Iris had been preparing her speech over several days now and was prepared for every eventuality. "I wondered if you would kindly baby sit for Jacob tonight."

"Of course I will."

"That's wonderful, you see we've been invited to the Harper's for dinner and they aren't aware that Jacob is here as well. They've always wanted to meet Richard and it's not often that he's up this way."

The name Harper rang a bell for Kate. The house in the distance—that's where she'd heard it before, it belonged to them.

"No, that's not a problem at all. We like our evenings together, we'll play hide and seek if that's alright with you. We're running out of different hiding places at home."

"That's settled then. I just need your help in persuading Richard to go."

"Why's that?"

"Well, he won't want to leave you two behind, I'm sure of that."

"Of course I'll help you convince him. We'll be fine; Jacob will have a much better time here," Kate smiled.

Iris clapped her hands together. Kate could see that this was a very important and prestigious invitation, one Iris couldn't afford to miss out on.

"I told Donald that it was about time Richard got out there again and started meeting people. Melissa didn't waste any time finding herself a new man, why should Richard hang about waiting." The smile slowly started to fade from Kate's face. What was all this talk about meeting people? Iris only mentioned a dinner party with the Harpers. What exactly had she just committed herself to? "Now you will help me convince him won't you? Ingrid Harper is such a lovely, young woman. They'd be perfect for each other and I believe she doesn't live too far away from Richard."

Kate felt like Iris Anderson had just put her hand inside her chest and was slowly squeezing the life out of her heart. She had just inadvertently promised her host that she would help her push the man she had fallen for into the arms of another woman and there was nothing she could do about it. How could she tell her that she was in love with her son and she didn't want to help her any more, now that another woman was involved? Iris had set her heart on this dinner date and, as it would appear, on her son settling down with virtual aristocracy, certainly not a nanny. That would never do for Iris Anderson.

The room suddenly filled with the rest of the family but Kate hardly noticed them. She had mentally joined Donald in his melancholy place. Iris was exuberant enough for both of them. Donald could tell that they'd had their little chat the moment he walked into the kitchen, and that Kate had agreed to go along with it—whether she liked it or not.

"Richard," Iris began, placing a plate of warm toast on the table. "We've been invited to the Harper's for dinner this evening . . ."

"Oh, we are going up in the world," Richard retorted sarcastically; Iris chose to disregard his comment.

". . . Their daughter, Ingrid is up for the holidays and Kate has very kindly offered to baby sit for Jacob whilst we go."

Both men looked at Kate. Donald doubted the word 'offer' was ever used in the conversation but Richard couldn't believe what he was hearing. Kate ignored both their stares and busied herself spreading some strawberry jam on Jacob's toast.

"Kate?" Richard was waiting for her comment.

"Yes, Jacob and I are going to have a game of hide and seek whilst you're all out."

Jacob looked up from his breakfast, his eyes searching the room and his mind already in motion as to where he was going to hide first. This was going to be the best holiday ever. He'd never had the luxury of an adult and a whole host of new hiding places to himself before.

"But I haven't said I'm going yet," Richard objected.

"You should do, you'll enjoy yourself." Kate's mouth was opening and the words were spilling out but she had no control over them, just some inane desire to please his mother.

"Very well, I'll go," he agreed, his eyes blazing as he continued to stare at Kate. Why was she encouraging him if she knew there was going to be another woman there? Had he got it totally wrong; did she not have any feelings for him after all?

"Wonderful," his mother blurted out, unable to contain her excitement. "I'll ring and confirm just as soon as we've had breakfast."

She'd already done that of course, such was her faith in Kate's powers of persuasion, but she didn't want to appear presumptuous. A fake telephone call wouldn't do anyone any harm.

Kate wanted to cry in despair. Richard seemed so angry with her. Should she just have kept out of their family matters; was that why he was cross? After breakfast, she followed Jacob into the conservatory. He was her only ally now and she would spend the rest of the day with him. She could bury herself in his fantasy world. It was a far better place to be than her own right now.

Richard was alone with his mother in the kitchen still seething. A nagging feeling was clawing at the back of his mind.

"Is that why you invited Kate up here, mum, to baby sit whilst you set me up on a blind date?"

"Not at all, we invited her because she's practically one of the family."

He didn't believe her for one minute.

"Was she aware that this Ingrid would be there when she offered to look after Jacob?"

"Yes, of course she was. Richard, what are you trying to say exactly?"

"I'd just like to know how the conversation went. I don't like the idea of bringing Kate up here for a break and then asking her to work."

"I didn't ask her to work, she offered. Richard, I don't like what you're insinuating. Now Kate is more than happy to stay here with Jacob so shall we just drop the subject?"

***

Kate and Richard barely spoke for the rest of the day. Kate could hardly bring herself to look at him. He should have stood up to his mother and refused point blank to go. He'd already betrayed her in her eyes, even before he'd set off, and she despised Ingrid Harper with a passion, whoever she was?

She felt sick to the stomach when he appeared before her later that day looking smart and extremely handsome in his grey trousers and white, open neck shirt. She could smell the delicious aroma of his aftershave, the very one she had bought him for Christmas, and knew that she was going to struggle to play the part of the woman who didn't give a damn, if she could play it at all.

"Bye, Jacob," he said, taking a quick sideways glance at Kate. It was her last chance to tell him she didn't want him to go. "Now you be a good boy for Kate, won't you?"

Jacob couldn't wait to begin his game of hide and seek. He'd been told he had to wait until they'd all gone before they could start so he was anxious for them to leave.

"Right, let's get this over with," Donald muttered to his son whilst adjusting his tie.

Richard wondered whether this evening was the cause of his father's dolefulness over the last couple of days.

Iris made a dramatic entrance in her best dress and a neat row of pearls around her neck. Kate could sense the excitement grip the air as she walked into the room.

"You two have a lovely evening. I've shown Jacob a few good hiding places so you've got your work cut out for you, Kate."

Kate half heartedly smiled in response. She wished she could share her enthusiasm but she had never felt less like doing so. She took one last glimpse at Richard before he turned to leave. No woman in her right mind could ignore how handsome and distinguished he looked. Suddenly an overwhelming fear of loss came over her.

As soon as the door shut behind them, Jacob was raring to go

"Kate, you count first and I'll hide."

"Okay, Jacob, off you go. I'll count to twenty."

Kate turned around and started to count whilst watching the car pull away through the bay window; Richard driving, his father in the passenger seat and his mother waving her arms in the back. She was responsible for that. If she hadn't gone along with Iris's plan, she was sure Richard would still be here now, joining in their game.

". . . nineteen, twenty, coming ready or not." Kate made her way upstairs. She knew Jacob was up there, she could hear him giggling.

***

The Andersons arrived outside the Harper's mansion. Richard stepped out of the car and immediately began to admire the outside of the stone building.

"My, this is some place," he uttered. "I've never seen it up close before."

They walked along the gravel path and knocked on the huge wooden door. Bea Harper was busily overseeing the setting of the dining table in the main dining hall.

"Now make sure you place Ingrid next to Richard," she whispered to her housekeeper. "Mrs Anderson and I have been discussing them and we think they'd get on rather well together." She heard the knock at the door and went to answer it.

"Iris, lovely to see you. Come on in, all of you," she beckoned.

"Bea, meet my husband, Donald and this is Richard, my son."

"Lovely to meet you both. Do come into the lounge, let me take your coats." They were handed over to the housekeeper. Bea was pleasantly surprised. Iris had been right about her son.

"My husband won't be long, but Ingrid is in here."

Ingrid was looking through a book on antiques beside a huge, roaring, log fire as they entered the lounge. Richard glanced around at the ostentatious surroundings before his eyes rested on the young woman. She put her book down and went over to greet them. Her dark brown eyes flashed up at him as she shook his hand.

"Pleased to meet you, Richard," she smiled, seductively pushing her brown hair behind her ear.

Seconds later Bea's husband came into the room.

"Ah, darling, at last. This is my husband James. James, this is Iris, Donald her husband and her son, Richard."

"Evening, good of you to join us," James remarked. "Anyone for a drink? How about a whisky to warm you up, Donald?"

Richard found the only vacant chair which just happened to be next to Ingrid. He wondered how much more of the rest of the evening was going to be stage managed.

"So, I believe you're a doctor, Richard, is that right?" Ingrid asked already engaging in her own private conversation.

"Yes, I'm a surgeon."

"Oh, how exciting, what kind of operations do you do?"

"I'm a plastic surgeon."

"Really, how fascinating. So do you do face lifts and liposuction?"

"Amongst other things, but not in the NHS. I mainly do hand surgery and lower limb trauma. I do the odd face lift in my private practice."

"You must be awfully clever."

Richard smiled slightly embarrassed.

"What do you do?" he asked doubting whether she'd ever done a days work in her life.

"I help to run an antiques business and I do quite a lot of work for various local charities, mainly Shadmoor Hospice."

"Shadmoor, is that where you live?" Richard was intrigued.

"Yes, when I'm not here. I must admit, I do like the tranquillity of this place, but Shadmoor is a lovely village. Do you know it?"

"Yes, I don't live far from there, Cedar Vale."

"Really, I know Cedar Vale very well. There's a Japanese restaurant there which is absolutely divine."

"On Atherton Road, I know exactly the one you mean."

"Have you been?"

"No, but I hear the food is out of this world."

"Oh, we must go sometime. They do the most delicious sushi."

"I believe it's quite hard to get a table."

"Oh, don't worry about that, Richard. I can pull a few strings."

Iris and Bea looked at each other approvingly. They seemed to be getting on nicely and had already established they were practically neighbours.

"I'll just go and see if dinner's ready," Bea mouthed to Iris.

It was only a moment before she returned to take them through to the dining room. Richard, not too surprisingly, found himself next to Ingrid at the table. He didn't mind, he was quite enjoying her company. They chatted easily throughout dinner, not really taking much notice of the carefully prepared dishes they were eating.

***

It was Jacob's bedtime and Kate took him up to his room and read him his bedtime story. The characters seemed to merge into one bleary fog as her mind drifted from Richard's kiss to the strange look on his face as he'd left this evening.

"Kate, you missed a bit," Jacob complained as he flicked the page back.

"Sorry, Jacob, I'm not concentrating am I?"

"What does that mean, Kate?"

"It means I'm thinking about something else and not what I'm doing."

"What are you thinking about?"

Your father, she wanted to say. He should be here with us and not with some other woman who will never think as much about him as I do. But she didn't say it, Jacob would never have understood. She would just have to let her heart continue to ache, like it had done for the past few hours.

"Nothing in particular," she uttered and carried on reading.

Once she'd finished the story, she sat with Jacob for a while on the edge of the bed. She smiled affectionately as she watched him feign sleep with his angelic face screwed up tightly. He was such a beautiful little boy; definitely his father's son. Now every time she looked at him she could feel the tears well up in her eyes. What if Richard likes this other woman; what if Jacob does too? She couldn't bear the thought of losing them both.

***

"What a delightful evening, wasn't it, Donald?" Iris enthused, stepping back into the house.

Kate was straining to hear from her bedroom. She'd left her door slightly ajar for that very reason.

"Yes, very nice," Donald replied with slightly more ardour than before.

"You two seemed to be getting on very nicely, setting up a date."

"It's just a meal, mum; nothing serious. She knows the owner of a Japanese restaurant in Cedar Vale and can get us a table. It's really difficult to get in."

Kate's stomach lurched. So they got on well enough to see each other again. She hated the woman, despised her. She'd ruined her life. Richard should be hers. Why had she listened to his mother?

***

It was a lonely journey home the following day. Richard seemed like a stranger to her. He was acting as though he'd taken on another persona; that of a man who was no longer single but in a meaningful relationship. He had an air of confidence about him ignited by the admiring glance of another woman. Even the way he spoke to her was different like she was someone who he was merely acquainted with and hadn't yet got to know; like they were starting all over again, meeting for the first time.

***

Donald and Iris had waved them off from the front doorway.

"Well, that was rather successful though I say it myself," she'd remarked smugly. "I think they all had a good time, especially Jacob despite us going out and leaving him. Kate's a marvel with him isn't she?"

"I thought Kate was a little quiet today," said Donald.

"Maybe she was still tired after missing that night's sleep. Remember, she's not used to it like Richard."

# CHAPTER . . .

# 13

Gerald and Dorothy Royston opened the front door and dragged their suitcases into the hallway. They were exhausted after their journey home. Dorothy collapsed onto the sofa and waited for her husband to bring her a cup of tea.

"Mm, it's never the same abroad is it?" she smiled. "That first cup of tea when you get home is always the best."

"Yes, you're right. I think it's the milk."

"Shall I ring the children and tell them we're home?"

"It's up to you, Dorothy, but if I was you, I'd leave them to sweat a bit longer. They practically ruined the holiday with their dramatics, no, leave them. I don't know about you but I'm going to have a lie down for a while. That journey certainly took it out of me."

Dorothy smiled at him. She wished she could have an ounce of his attitude. He wasn't bothered what Nina and Peter thought of them, in fact, quite the opposite. He was quite prepared to tell his children exactly what he thought of *them*.

It wasn't long before she heard the faint purring sound of her husband snoring. If she was going to ring them, then now was the time. She knew she wouldn't rest until she'd made that call and found out exactly where she stood with them. It had been difficult on Christmas Day phoning from a pay phone in the middle of a busy harbour. She tapped in the numbers and waited for someone to answer. It was Giles who picked up the phone.

"Hello, Giles, it's Dorothy."

*"Hello, Dorothy, did you have a good time?"*

Dorothy thought she heard a hint of bitterness in his voice although she could have been mistaken.

"Lovely, thank you. Is Nina there?"

*"Just a minute."* He put his hand over the phone and mouthed to Nina. "It's your mother; do you want to speak to her?" Nina shook her head. She was up to her eyes with the children and didn't need any more distractions. *"She's a bit busy at the moment, Dorothy. Can she ring you back some time?"*

"Yes of course, no problem. Could you just let her know we've arrived back safely?"

*"Will do, bye, Dorothy."*

"Goodbye, Giles."

Dorothy replaced the receiver. A bad feeling started to grow in the pit of her stomach. Why hadn't Nina spoken to her? It wouldn't have taken a minute. She would try her son and see if she got the same response from him.

*"I'm sorry; your call can't be taken at the moment. Please leave your message after the tone."*

"Hello, Peter, it's mum here. Just to let you know we've arrived back home. Call me when you get a moment. Love to Paula and Aaron."

Neither of the children returned their mother's call that day, nor the next. Dorothy was devastated. She didn't tell her husband that she'd called them. He would have been annoyed, rung them back and played hell. No, she would have to let this eat away at her alone.

***

Alex pulled up outside the house. He could see Melissa chatting away on the phone through the window and wondered how the telephone company would survive if she ever left the country. He stuck his head around the door and waved. She waved back and, looking exceedingly happy, replaced the receiver.

"Good news?" he asked hanging his jacket up on a hook in the hallway. He smiled at her as she came into the hall to greet him.

"Yes, my parents are coming over in a few weeks. I can't wait for you to meet them. They were going to stay in a hotel but I told them they might as well stay here. We've got the room haven't we?"

Alex's smile slowly faded. He didn't do the parent thing very well. He was always glad that Kate's mother had lived in Spain and very rarely came over to visit. But here were Melissa's parents actually staying with them.

"How long for?" he asked trying to sound upbeat.

"Only a week or so. They can't wait to see Jacob."

"How's that going to work? I thought Richard had set some ground rules."

"I'll have a word with him. I'm going over tomorrow, I'm sure he'll understand. Besides, he used to get on really well with mum and dad. Maybe he would bring Jacob over here."

Oh, my goodness, thought Alex; parents, son and an ex-husband all in one weekend. He started to think of excuses to be elsewhere, places he might go, people he could visit. The whole idea was too daunting. At least he had a few days to hatch a plan.

"I'm going to go and start making that spare room habitable. I might nip out later and get some new bedding and curtains," Melissa continued—and she was gone.

Alex went into the kitchen to prepare himself a sandwich. Had he jumped in a little too quickly asking Melissa to move in with him? Maybe he should have given himself a bit more time to play the bachelor and all that that entailed; football on television with a few mates round and plenty of lager, clothes left where they were taken off, going down to The Dog and Duck whenever the need arose, having an Indian takeaway and leaving the empty containers on the worktop until the following day. He'd barely had a week alone before she was in rearranging the furniture and making the place smell nice with her scented candles and pot pourri.

Then again, perhaps he was being a little harsh on her, after all, she had just bailed him out of debt to the tune of twenty five thousand pounds, and there was still more if he needed it. He would do his best to brave the week in question and welcome her parents, after all, it wasn't many men who were lucky enough to have their potential mother-in-law live in a luxury villa thousands of miles away, with the possibility of seeing them only once or at the most, twice a year.

***

Kate first encountered Ingrid Cecilia Harper about five days after they'd returned from Scotland. Richard was on call and she wasn't expecting him back until late. Jacob was in his bed fast asleep and Kate had just flicked the television on to see if there was anything interesting to watch. Suddenly a knock at the door disturbed her viewing.

She opened the door and there stood Ingrid under an umbrella, dressed in her finest cashmere coat. Kate knew it was her, her face was perfectly made up and she could smell her expensive perfume.

"Oh, you must be the nanny," were her first words. "Is Richard in?"

"No, he's been called out. I'm not sure when he's back," Kate replied, equally terse as she guarded the front door. There was no way this woman was getting past her without a fight. "Did you want something?"

The two women's dislike of each other was now mutual. How dare this woman speak to her like this?

"Would you tell him I've booked a meal for us at the Japanese restaurant like I said I would? No, on second thoughts, I'll ring him." Ingrid smiled smugly, turned on her heels and left without a word of goodbye.

*How rude,* Kate thought as she slammed the door behind her. She leaned against the closed door. Her heart was beating rapidly. Suddenly everything was so real. This imaginary woman, who Richard had mentioned in passing, now had a face and a voice, albeit a pompous one. She was attractive and well bred and perfect for him, and now Kate was nothing more to him than the hired help again. *She'd* made that quite clear. She hadn't even called her by her name. *Oh you must be the nanny*—the words filled her head and stung her self esteem. What a bitch.

***

Ingrid was more than troubled following her brief visit to Richard's house. He hadn't mentioned that the nanny was a young, good looking woman. When Richard had spoken of her, her immediate image of Kate had been that of a much older woman with grey wispy hair tied back in a bun; someone who was fond of baking bread and cakes then eating her produce, which consequently reflected in her rotund appearance. That was the type of nanny Ingrid had grown up with as a child. Not like this one, she was quite the opposite. She had to speak to Richard as soon as possible. She couldn't have that woman getting in there first and spoiling her surprise. If she wasn't mistaken, she could have sworn there was a bit of jealousy floating around. Her call was soon answered.

*"Hello, Richard Anderson speaking."*

"Richard, it's Ingrid."

*"Oh hi, how are you?"* Richard stood up as soon as he heard her voice and walked out of the coffee room. This conversation was not for the ears of the rest of the theatre team.

"I'm fine, thank you. Your housekeeper tells me you're at work."

*"Yes, I'm on call. We're about to do a case when theatre becomes available. When did you speak to Kate?"*

"Just now, she wasn't very forthcoming as to how to get hold of you so I thought I'd use your mobile phone number. I hope I'm not interrupting anything."

*"No that's fine."*

"I just wanted to say that I'd managed to get us a table at the Japanese restaurant on Saturday evening at eight. Can you make it?"

*"Umm, yes I think so. I can't think of any other plans, no, that would be great. That was quick. I thought you had to book weeks in advance."*

"You do. Let's just say I know the management."

*"Very handy, I'll look forward to it."*

"Shall I meet you at your place now that I know where you live? We could get a taxi then we could both have something to drink?"

So, she'd been round to the house and met Kate face to face.

*"Great, what time?"*

"Around seven forty five."

*"I'll order a taxi for that time."*

"See you then."

*"Yes, bye."*

Richard pressed the red button on his phone and smiled to himself. She wasn't lying when she said she could pull strings. Wait until he told Todd. He still hadn't managed to get there after cancelling his reservation following Professor Royston's impromptu meeting. He'd booked again but it wasn't for ages yet. He made his way back into the coffee room.

"Any news, Carl?" he asked his registrar.

"About twenty minutes; they're just sewing up."

Richard looked at the clock. Perhaps he'd give Todd a call now whilst he was waiting.

***

"Have you spoken to the children since we got back?" Gerald asked.

He was flipping through the photographs Dorothy had got printed earlier that day.

"No, not yet."

"Haven't you rung them yet? That's a good one of the sunset in Martinique. You did well there, Dorothy."

Dorothy was either going to have to lie to her husband or admit that they still hadn't rung her back. It was over three days now and she had been experiencing a sickening feeling in her stomach for the entire duration.

"No," she replied solemnly.

"Honestly, Dorothy, you fretted about them all holiday and let them ruin the whole damned thing. I thought you'd have rung them by now."

Dorothy decided to tell him the truth or he would pester her for the rest of the evening. "Well actually I did. I rang them the day we got back, when you went for a lie down and they still haven't returned my call. There you have it; that's what they think of their mother and father for not being around on Christmas day."

Dorothy could feel a large lump rise in her throat and the threat of tears stung her eyes.

"What, you phoned them three days ago and they still haven't rung you back?" Gerald was looking at her in disbelief.

"Yes, precisely."

Gerald placed the photographs on the coffee table, marched to his study and closed the door behind him. Nina answered his call.

"It's your father here."

*"Oh, hello, dad. How was the big cruise?"*

"Don't sound so bloody sarcastic."

*"Dad!"* Nina was shocked.

"Never mind, dad, your mother rang you three days ago to tell you we were back."

*"I know, Giles answered the phone."*

Gerald was a little rocked. He hadn't realised that she'd actually spoken to someone.

"And why didn't you speak to her?"

*"I was seeing to the children. I was going to ring her back and then something else cropped up..."*

Her father now had the upper hand back. He was far more comfortable in this position.

"That was three days ago, Nina. You and your bloody thoughtless brother managed to ruin our holiday over your pettiness. So we didn't come over for Christmas day, so what? You're grown ups now, you can manage without us. Your mother and I have put you two first all your lives and where did that get us? The first time you didn't get your own way you sulk and spoil everything. You both owe your mother an apology and if it isn't forthcoming, I swear to God I'll take the pair of you out of the will and you'll end up with nothing for your troubles. Is that understood?"

*"Yes,"* Nina replied. *"You've made your feelings perfectly clear."* And with that, she put the phone down.

"Well done, Gerald," Dorothy said angrily, standing at the door of the study. "I think you've just succeeded in losing our children for ever."

"I'm sorry, Dorothy, but I had to say something. I couldn't stand back and watch them hurt you like they were doing."

"That's the trouble in this house; everyone has to say something. No one could keep their inflated opinions to themselves, apart from me of course, and where did that ever get me? Trodden on by all of you. Good old mum, she's got no opinions of her own, she's got no feelings. Well I have Gerald. I want my family back, not alienating. Couldn't you have kept money out of it? If they do ever speak to us again, we'll think they're doing it just to get back in the will."

Gerald could hear the slamming of the bedroom door as Dorothy left him floundering in the doorway and retired early. There was something else for her to worry about now; not when they would ring, but whether they would ever ring again? Nina was as stubborn as her father and Peter usually did as he was told. He'd been fickle all his life.

Gerald remained downstairs rubbing his bemused forehead. What had he done wrong besides tell his children exactly what he thought of them? Suddenly he felt a sharp pain pierce his heart. Clutching his chest, his face contorted for what seemed like an age as the spasm took hold of him. He closed his eyes as it peaked then breathed with relief as it started to subside. It wasn't the first time he had experienced chest pain over the last year but that was the worst episode by far. Blasted children, he needed to take things easy not get himself worked up like that.

***

Kate had been experiencing a dull ache in her heart ever since Richard had announced that he wouldn't be in for dinner on Saturday because he and Ingrid were going out to eat. It had been Friday evening when he had eventually got round to telling her. It was funny really; he felt as if he had to gain her blessing or he wouldn't be able to enjoy himself. Kate had feigned a pleased expression for him and Richard had taken that as his nod to proceed with the relationship.

The doorbell rang at precisely seven forty five and Richard flew down the stairs to answer it.

"Hi, come in," he said with a huge smile on his face.

Kate could hear her from the kitchen. Her pretentious voice was already grating on her nerves. She hated her, not just because she was dating Richard, but because she had taken the Richard she knew so well away from her. They didn't have their cosy little chats any longer, or sit up into the early hours drinking wine and reminiscing of days gone by. He had suddenly become spoken for and had better things to do than to talk to a silly nanny.

Ingrid followed Richard into the dining area.

"Right, Kate, we're off now. Don't wait up." Jacob came running into the room from the lounge. He stopped when he saw Ingrid and went to hide behind Kate.

"Hello, young man," smiled Ingrid, but Jacob had nothing to say to her.

"Say hello, Jacob," Richard instructed.

"Hello," he said shyly then disappeared back into the safety of the lounge.

*Good for you Jacob,* thought Kate. *Young man? Who does she think she is?*

The horn of a taxi could be heard outside.

"We'd better get going, Richard," said Ingrid throwing a smug smile at Kate. "We don't want to lose our table."

Kate could feel the bile rise in her throat. Could he not see through her? Had the lure of a table at the Japanese restaurant completely fooled him?

The door closed behind them and through the kitchen window, Kate could see her touch his arm. Despair sank into her heart. She would be no fun for Jacob tonight. She couldn't bring herself to raise a smile let alone join in any games as she resolved to being back where she was when she and Alex first split up only this time it was worse. She hadn't even got off the starting block with Richard and now she would have to witness, first hand, every step of his confounded courtship.

***

The restaurant was buzzing with the chat of diners. Japanese waiters lithely mingled between the tables delivering delicious looking dishes and removing empty plates. Richard was enthralled. He'd never experienced such an atmosphere in a restaurant.

He gazed around at the wooden panelled walls and partitions, at the authentic lanterns over each table and the Japanese fans, spread out on the walls whilst they waited to be seated. The waiter soon arrived and greeted Ingrid like a long lost friend.

"Ah, Miss Harper, very pleased to see you. Your table is ready."

The waiter bowed and waved his arm in the direction they were to follow. He led them to a table for two in a quieter corner of the restaurant and held the chair for her to sit down. They both took their seats and began to look at the menus which were handed over.

"You've obviously been here before. He knew who you were straight away," said Richard peering over his menu.

"You could say that. If truth be told, I'm not that keen on cooking so I do come in here rather a lot. They do wonderful takeaways as well and after a long day at the auctions, it's nice to chill out over a lovely shrimp noodle."

Richard cast his eye down the menu.

"So, what do you recommend?" he asked, not having the faintest idea of what to order.

"Well, I suggest we start off with a bottle of warm sake and then I'm going to have the Miso soup starter followed by . . . the shrimp tempura."

It all sounded a little too vegetarian for Richard's liking and didn't help him in the slightest.

"Mm," he replied as he scoured the meat dishes. "I think I'll start with the pan fried pork dumplings and then I'll have the teriyaki beef as my main course. I'll leave it to you to order if that's alright. I don't fancy making an idiot of myself the first time I come in here."

She smiled across at him. What a stroke of luck it had been, both being in Scotland at the same time. Her mother had mentioned the Andersons and their son before but she hadn't for a second thought he would be so handsome *and* a plastic surgeon. How she will love bragging to her friends and the ladies at the Marclough Charities Society about him.

The waiter came across and she placed their order. Ingrid handed back the menus and, resting her elbows on the table, looked into Richard's eyes and said seductively, "So tell me all about plastic surgery."

Richard couldn't believe his luck. A beautiful, young woman who was interested in him and his work, and could get them into this restaurant at the drop of a hat. He wanted to ring Todd immediately and tell him. He hadn't been too pleased when Richard had gloated to him about getting the table tonight.

The waiter arrived with the sake and poured them each a cup. It soon warmed Richard's throat and filled his head with an overwhelming feeling of euphoria as he drank it a little too quickly. Ingrid poured him another cup from the porcelain bottle and looked on admiringly as he carried on with his animated, descriptions of certain surgical procedures he'd performed. His graphic attention to detail was second to none. She was glad she wasn't too squeamish, but even more pleased when the starters arrived and they could discuss the food instead.

"Here, try some of this," Ingrid offered as she leaned across the table with a spoonful of Miso soup.

"I don't know if I'm quite ready for bean curd," Richard replied bracing his taste buds for an onslaught of flavour.

"Go on, try it," she urged him.

Richard opened his mouth and was duly fed.

"Mm," he said not quite sure. "Not bad, but nowhere near as nice as the dumplings. At least I can say I've tried some now, that's a first."

Ingrid giggled. She felt so comfortable with him on their first date. She hoped it wouldn't end after the meal. She could stay with him all night. "Do you want to try mine, or am I right in thinking you're a vegetarian?"

"Not strictly speaking, but I'm leaning towards that way. I will try a bit of yours though, it looks delicious."

Richard reciprocated with his offering. If his mother could see him now she'd have him married off. They were soon faced with their main course and Richard tucked in heartily. It was one of the nicest meals he'd ever eaten. He went into raptures after every mouthful until Ingrid couldn't resist it and stabbed her fork into a piece of beef.

"Oh no, I'm going to have that the next time we come here. So much for the vegetarianism."

Richard registered the sentiment—the next time *we* come. He must be doing something right on his first date in years. He rounded the meal of with a tempura banana and they both shared a pot of green tea served in an exquisite little teapot with a bamboo handle and a crane painted on the side.

"Thank you, Ingrid," Richard finally said as they made their way to the door. "I thoroughly enjoyed that. I've been meaning to come here for years."

"I know it was wonderful, wasn't it? The only thing is, all the rest of the meals we have now will be downhill after that."

They both laughed as they made their way to the high street in search of their taxis home. Ingrid linked her arm through Richard's as she braced herself against the cold. He smiled as he looked down at her. He didn't want the evening to end so soon either.

"Fancy a drink at The Dog and Duck?" he asked hopefully.

"I'd love one."

Ingrid didn't care where they were just as long as they weren't going their separate ways. He held the door open as she walked in and both were glad to see a roaring fire in the snug.

"You grab a seat and I'll get some drinks. What would you like?"

"I'll have a glass of white wine, please."

She sat as near to the fire as she could and rubbed her hands together. Her finger tips tingled as the warmth seeped in, and her cheeks glowed in the firelight. She looked across at Richard, so tall and distinguished leaning against the bar.

Richard glanced over at the tap room on the opposite side of the bar. A couple of men were playing pool at the far end of the room and three more sat around a table chatting. He recognised one of their faces. No sooner had it registered who the man was, when he stood up to get his own drinks. He looked across in Richard's direction.

"Alex, how are you? I thought I recognised you then," said Richard.

"Richard, what are you doing in this neck of the woods? I wouldn't have had this place down as your local."

"We've just been to the Japanese Garden for a meal."

"I believe it's really nice there. Melissa won't go though, she doesn't like Japanese food."

"No, I know."

"Yes, of course you do, sorry."

"No, don't apologise." Richard handed over his money as the barman placed the drinks in front of him. "Take care—nice to see you again," he nodded.

"Yes, you too."

Alex tried to peer round the bar to see who he was buying the second drink for.

"A friend of yours?" asked Ingrid as Richard returned to the table.

"Not really, he's my ex-wife's boyfriend."

"Ah, that's reassuring to know."

"What is?"

"That your ex-wife has a boyfriend. It means she's not likely to reappear on the scene again claiming you back."

"Make that, *not ever* likely to reappear on the scene again. That little chapter in my life is well and truly closed, especially after the way she treated my son recently."

"Really, how do you mean?"

"It's a long story."

"We have a long time."

Alex returned to his table with two pints of lager and a pint of orange juice. Chris grabbed a glass off him as he sat down.

"Where's Mike?" Alex asked looking round.

"He's gone to the little boy's room. Cheers mate; we'll make this our last one shall we? I told Tina I wouldn't be too late home after being away all week." Mike was heading back to the table. "Who was that bloke you were talking to at the bar? He looked a bit too educated for you to know."

"Cheeky get, you'll never believe who that is. That's Kate's boss, Richard Anderson and Melissa's ex," he replied in a loud whisper.

Mike just about overheard the conversation. He'd seen Alex talking to Richard. So that's who he was. He'd heard rumblings that Kate had become a nanny for some doctor.

"What are you two whispering about?" he teased.

"Alex was just saying . . ." Alex kicked Chris sharply in the shin underneath the table, ". . . that we were going to make this our last drink."

"Fine by me," Mike answered him. So they didn't want him to know who the tall stranger was at the bar. Alex didn't trust him with the truth did he not? He downed his pint of orange as quickly as he could then made his excuses. "Right, that's me. I'm going to make a move. You two might be able to walk home from here, but I've got a long journey ahead."

"Yeh, right, Mike. It's about ten minutes, mate, to your place," Chris pointed out.

*Not the way I'm going,* Mike thought. He picked his helmet from beneath the table, said his goodbyes and made his way to the car park.

"Tell me again why you've just nearly crippled me," said Chris rubbing his leg.

"After your wedding, the less Mike knows about Kate the better."

Richard and Ingrid had managed to get prime position now in front of the fire and were nicely thawed out. It took Richard back to his medical student days, sat in the local pub with a pint of best bitter. All that was missing was his university scarf and ill-matching clothes.

Eventually time ran out for them and the barman rang for last orders.

"One more drink?" Richard asked pointing to his empty glass.

"No, I'm fine," she replied. "But you have one."

"No, I suppose we'd better go and sort some taxis out before all the pubs empty and everyone starts fighting for one."

Despite their reluctance to part, they both made a move towards the door. The taxi rank was just around the corner. They took the short cut through the pub car park, then Richard suddenly stopped.

"I've had a lovely evening. I thought it would be strange to go out with someone again after so long, but it's not."

"Does that mean you want to see me again?" asked Ingrid.

She gazed up at him, and like a love struck teenager, felt slightly infatuated. She hadn't imagined, in her wildest dreams, ever feeling this way about a man. Previous encounters had all been so dull and boorish. Here she had found someone with a sense of humour, who was interesting but most of all, showed sensitivity. That was one of the hardest things to find in a man.

"Yes, of course I do. It's my birthday on Friday, why don't we do something then?"

"Really, oh yes, let's. I'll book something and let you know. I'm sure you're far busier than I am."

"Okay, I'll leave that to you."

They looked at each other tenderly. Should he kiss her on the cheek or had they established that they were a couple now and that would appear far too formal? He needn't have worried about his dilemma. Ingrid led the way. She reached up, placed her arms around his neck and softly kissed his lips.

Richard closed his eyes. He hadn't been kissed like that for years. For a brief second he thought about Melissa. Had she ever kissed Alex like that—was she capable of such affection?

"I'll see you on Friday, Richard," she said.

She knew she'd had an effect on him.

"Yes, I'll speak to you before then, goodnight."

Ingrid ran on ahead to claim the first taxi and Richard stood back and watched her with her brown hair bouncing around her shoulders. She waved to him quickly as she disappeared into the cab and she was gone.

Mike was watching from the back of the car park; a sinister looking figure in black leathers and helmet. He kick started his motorbike, pulled down his visor and emerged from the darkness. He edged his way towards the exit and waited for Richard to climb into the next available taxi.

"Thirty two Richmond Avenue, please," Richard instructed the driver. "Just opposite the park."

The taxi pulled away, unaware of the motorbike following. Mike kept a safe distance so as not to raise any suspicion. He focussed his eyes on the back of Richard's head, concentrating. He didn't want to lose them. This was his only chance to find Kate again. He couldn't understand why she hadn't phoned him; she'd said she would at the wedding. He had to find her. The taxi drove on.

Eventually it pulled up opposite a park. Mike stopped the bike a few houses down and cut his lights. He switched off the engine and waited.

"Keep the change," he heard as Richard emerged and walked the few steps to his home.

Mike lifted his visor and peered at the number on the wall by the door. *Thirty two,* he memorised, *thirty two Richmond Avenue.* He waited whilst Richard entered the house for maybe a quick glimpse of Kate, but none was to be had. The door closed behind him and within minutes, the hall light was switched off and downstairs was left in darkness.

Mike was disappointed but elated at the same time. He'd made a massive discovery tonight and now he had a new purpose back in his life. He fired up his engine again and spun his bike around setting off in the direction of his flat.

***

Kate was in bed when Richard had arrived home. He was a little despondent; he'd wanted to tell someone about the restaurant although maybe Kate wasn't the right person for that. He still hadn't decided whether she was pleased for him, having found himself a girlfriend, or not. She certainly hadn't been too amicable towards Ingrid earlier that evening. Maybe it was just a matter of time. They'd get used to each other. He went to bed satisfied with his reasoning. He'd tell her in the morning.

***

Mike looked around his flat. He disgusted himself. How could he ever bring Kate here with the place looking like a pig sty? The sink was brimming over with dirty dishes and the worktops hadn't been cleaned for days. He looked for some washing up liquid under the sink. One by one, he removed the dishes from the sink and stacked them to one side, then filled it with soapy water and began to scrub each piece of crockery clean. Once he'd put everything away, he bleached the surfaces. Tomorrow he would start on the lounge, polishing and vacuuming before he set off back to Richmond Avenue.

# CHAPTER . . .

# 14

The doorbell rang. She was certainly prompt, thought Kate, putting away the lunch dishes. Richard would get that. He was so keen last time to orchestrate events and besides, she was hoping to make herself scarce after her last meeting with Melissa.

Suddenly Richard was just outside the kitchen, his mobile phone clasped to his ear, signalling towards the door. Kate took a deep breath and reluctantly went to answer it.

"Hi, Kate," Melissa said. "Am I early?"

"No, I think you're just on time. Richard is on the phone, he won't be long. Come in."

Kate felt very strange inviting the woman into what was recently her own home. But Melissa didn't seem to mind, in fact, she was quite amiable.

"Thanks, Kate."

"Can I take your coat, Mrs . . . ?"

Melissa put her hand up.

"Please, call me Melissa, it's much less formal."

"Okay, I will."

Melissa handed over her coat. Jacob appeared from the lounge wondering who Kate was talking to.

"Mummy," he shouted and ran towards her.

"Darling."

Melissa knelt down and held her arms open to him. He gave her a hug and then went straight back into the lounge to continue playing. Kate felt a wave of compassion for the woman as she rose to her feet looking decidedly rejected. She half smiled at Kate.

"I suppose it was more than I got last time," she said.

"You should spend some time playing with him. That's what he likes best, playing games. Are you any good at Kerplunk?" asked Kate.

"No, absolutely awful."

"Then we need to go and have a game with him. He hates playing with his dad because he always wins."

Melissa giggled. "Really, don't you mind?"

"Not at all."

The two women walked past the study where Kate could hear Richard talking to Ingrid. Where was he now whilst Melissa was with his son? He barely left her alone with Jacob the last time she was here and now look at him, like a love-struck teenager talking to his girlfriend on the phone, completely distracted.

"Melissa, I didn't mean to sound condescending then. I mean Jacob's your son and here am I telling you what you should be doing. That must have sounded awful."

"Please, Kate, don't apologise. Any advice is welcome. I just want to get him back on my side and you know him better than anyone at the moment."

Melissa sounded genuinely sincere. Kate was actually beginning to like her despite all her bad press. They both went into the lounge and Jacob could be heard from the study, shouting with delight at the prospect of beating his mother at a game.

Richard heard the commotion. His curiosity was getting the better of him and he was keen to finish his conversation in order to see what was going on.

"I'd better go, Ingrid, my ex-wife has just arrived and I want to make sure Jacob's alright. He was a bit upset the last time he saw her," he said in a low voice.

*"Oh, just before you go, Richard, do you have any preference as to where you want to eat on your birthday?"*

"No, just surprise me," he replied trying to hurry the conversation on.

*"I can't wait you know. I had such a lovely night yesterday. It seems such a long time until Friday."*

"I'd see you before then but I've got quite a lot on at the moment. We've got a hand meeting coming up which the hospital is hosting so we've got one or two planning meetings this week."

*"It doesn't matter; I know you're a busy man. I'll give you a ring sometime during the week and let you know how I'm getting on with the reservation."*

Screams of laughter resounded from the lounge and Richard could wait no longer.

"Yes, you do that," he answered. "Bye for now, Ingrid."

"*Yes, goodbye, Richard.*"

Richard sighed as he put the phone down. He couldn't afford too many of those conversations. He was hard pushed for time as it was. He could picture her sitting alone in her home with nothing better to do than to chat all day. He rushed to the lounge to find out what all the frivolity was about. His mouth dropped as he discovered Melissa, Kate and Jacob all sitting on the floor playing his favourite game, laughing and joking as if they'd been friends for life.

"Erm, can anyone join in this game?" he asked a little peeved at being left out.

"No, daddy. Mummy's playing instead of you and guess what, I'm beating her."

"Well, that doesn't surprise me; your mother never could play this game."

Kate threw Richard a stern glance. Melissa chose to ignore his comment; she had a favour to ask of him later and didn't want to upset him unnecessarily. All three went back to the game and Richard suddenly felt like a spare part. He decided, after the look he had just received from Kate, that maybe he should have been a bit kinder. He might then get a look in. He asked if he could join in the next game and to his surprise, Jacob agreed as long as he didn't cheat and look at the straws before he pulled them out. Richard reluctantly conceded and he found himself having a very pleasant afternoon in the company of his ex-wife, nanny and son.

Melissa had had a wonderful afternoon by the time she had to leave. She'd come on leaps and bounds with Jacob and had forged herself an unexpected friendship with Kate. Even Richard had spoken to her civilly. But now it was time to ask of her favour.

"Richard," she began as she put her coat back on. "My parents are coming over in a couple of weeks to stay and I wondered if you'd let Jacob come over to our house to see them?"

Kate was half listening to the conversation from the kitchen as she washed the remaining cups left over from this afternoon's tea. She had managed to carry the tray in without dropping it this time and had been thoroughly relieved.

Richard thought for a second. "I think I'm on call that weekend, Melissa. I can't really commit myself to bringing him over in case I get called out."

"Oh, I see," said Melissa looking disappointed. "I don't suppose you'd let Kate come with him would you?"

Kate looked up from the sink horrified. Take Jacob round to her old house, but what if Alex was there? She tried to think of an excuse why she couldn't possibly do that, and apart from telling the truth, she couldn't think of single reason against it. It was a perfectly good idea under the circumstances.

"Uhm, I'm not sure . . . oh, I don't see why not. Jacob would love to see his grandparents again. I'll ask her . . . Kate, do you have a second. You wouldn't mind taking Jacob over to Melissa's next week would you? I'm on call and his grandparents are over from Antigua."

"It's in two weeks," Melissa pointed out. "If that's alright with you Kate?"

"Yes, of course, I meant two weeks," said Richard shaking his head. "Is that okay?"

"Yes."

Kate felt like a wild animal that had just been cornered. What else could she say?

"That's wonderful. Mum and dad will be so pleased. I'll speak to you before then, Kate. Alex will come and pick you both up."

Kate went cold. She could feel the hairs standing up on the back of her neck. How could she have let herself get into such a situation, but on the other hand, - had she actually have any choice in the matter? Alex would probably be furious when he found out what they had in store for him.

Melissa left the house very pleased with herself. She waved enthusiastically at her estranged husband and her new ally as she went past the window back to her car.

"She's a different woman," Richard said in disbelief. "I don't think I've ever seen her laugh like that before. Kate, you're a marvel."

Kate's mind was fixed firmly in the future, two weeks to be exact. She didn't relish the thought of spending all afternoon trying to keep the secret that she knew the house they were in like the back of her hand and its occupant for that matter.

"Do you want me to stay with Jacob all afternoon when we go to Melissa's or can I leave them to have a bit of time to themselves?" Kate asked hopefully.

"I don't see why you can't leave him. I don't think her parents would let her do anything stupid. Val and Jack were always quite decent people. Just make sure he's settled will you. If he starts to panic when you leave, maybe you should reconsider."

"Yes, of course. I wouldn't leave him if he was upset."

***

It was Friday morning and Kate woke Jacob up a few minutes earlier than usual.

"Jacob, wake up, it's daddy's birthday."

Jacob's eyes slowly flickered.

"Where's my present, Kate?" he asked sleepily.

"I've got it here, come on, I can hear daddy downstairs."

Jacob slid out from under his duvet, put on his Cars slippers and Scooby Doo Dressing gown which grandma and granddad had bought him for Christmas, and followed Kate downstairs. As they reached the bottom step, they began a chorus of Happy Birthday.

". . . happy birthday, dear daddy, happy birthday to you."

"Thanks, you two," Richard laughed. "What a lovely surprise."

"Daddy, we've got you a present."

"Kate, you shouldn't have," he said happily taking the parcel.

"Of course I should. We chose it together didn't we Jacob?"

"Really."

Richard suddenly realised that Kate had taken over Melissa's job. His wife probably hadn't even remembered it was his birthday, let alone bought a present for her son to give to him. Yet here was Kate making sure everything was just right as usual. It didn't matter what it was, the sentiment itself was overwhelming.

"Can I open it now?" Richard asked, taking care not to allow his emotions to show.

"Shall I help you, daddy?" asked Jacob. Before he could answer Jacob had torn through the paper and uncovered a grey, woollen sweater.

"Thank you, it's lovely," he said holding it in the air to examine it. "Thanks Kate, you've obviously got great taste."

Kate smiled. There were two cards to open. One hand written by his son and the other from Kate.

"Have you written that by yourself, son?" Jacob stood by proudly nodding. "I can't believe you can write already. You haven't even started school."

He read the words in Kate's card and paused for a second, then walked towards her and kissed her lightly on the cheek. Kate then watched as he embraced his son. He had been touched by her efforts, she could tell. Maybe there was an inkling of hope for her after all.

"What time will you be home?" she asked.

She placed a finger over her lips as Jacob nearly exploded with her question. He hadn't quite got the idea of surprises yet.

"The usual hopefully. You know I'm going out later, don't you? I won't want anything to eat."

"No, I know, that's fine."

***

After nursery that day, Kate took Jacob, as promised, straight to the supermarket. They'd scanned the birthday cakes the week before and had a rough idea of the one they were going to choose. Jacob headed straight for it.

"It's here, Kate, can we get this one?"

"A Scooby Doo cake, are you sure you want that one?"

Jacob nodded and screwed his face up in delight.

***

Richard's list wasn't going according to plan. The first patient had drunk a cup of tea when the new health care assistant had handed them out on the ward mid morning so he had to go last. The next patient consequently hadn't been admitted as the nursing staff on the ward thought she was going second on the list, and to cap it all, the anaesthetist had been called away to assist with a difficult intubation. At five o'clock, the last patient was just going on the table.

"It's typical," he said to Carl. "When you need to get off on time, and everything to run smoothly, you can guarantee it doesn't."

"Are you going out tonight?" asked Carl.

"I'm supposed to be. Birthday celebrations."

"Oh, happy birthday."

"Thanks, some way to spend it, cooped up in theatre still operating."

***

Kate picked up the phone; it must be Richard, she thought.

*"Is Richard there?"* Ingrid snapped without any kind of introduction.

"No, he's not back from work yet. He must have been held up."

*"Well obviously. We have a table booked for eight o'clock. He'll have to come straight here from the hospital at this rate. Get him to ring me if he calls."*

"We've got a cake for him. He said he'd be coming home first."

*"It's hardly the same thing is it? We're not going to miss a reservation at Marcelle's for a piece of birthday cake."*

"It's just, Jacob wanted . . ." the phone went dead.

Kate felt a surge of hatred rise through her body. That woman is so rude, she thought. She doesn't possess any manners. If that's what money does for you, then you can keep it.

Kate turned around to see Jacob stood behind her.

"Was that daddy?"

"No, sweetheart, it wasn't."

"Is he coming home yet?"

"Not just yet, he must have been delayed at work."

***

Richard had just finished the Dupytren's contracture. It had been a difficult one. The diseased tissue had twisted itself around the nerve in the palm of the hand and despite the late hour, he was pleased he hadn't left Carl to do it.

"Can I leave you to sew up, Carl; I just need to make a couple of phone calls?"

"No problem, Mr Anderson," Carl replied. "Enjoy what's left of your birthday."

"Thanks a lot. Thanks, everyone, have a good weekend."

Richard returned to the coffee room and switched on his mobile phone. Three messages, all from Ingrid. He tapped her number in and waited.

*"Richard, at last, I was getting worried."*

"Sorry, Ingrid, my list was a disaster today. What time is it? Seven fifteen."

*"Yes, our tables booked for eight. I've spoken to Kate and told her you'll be coming straight here. She was fine about that."*

"Oh, really, I was hoping to nip home and get changed."

*"You haven't time, Richard. I'll meet you at the restaurant. We'll probably just have time for an aperitif."*

"Okay, I'll be there in about half an hour."

***

Kate looked at the clock. It was fast approaching Jacob's bedtime and still no signs of Richard. They must have gone straight to the restaurant. Jacob would be so disappointed.

"Jacob, I think daddy must be very busy tonight. Do you want a piece of cake now and we'll light the candles tomorrow when he's home?"

"Okay," he said despondently. "Can I have a piece with his eye on?"

Kate carefully cut round Scooby Doo's eye and placed it on a plate for Jacob, then covered the rest of the cake in a layer of aluminium foil and placed it on the worktop in the kitchen. The little boy sat in his pyjamas and dressing gown eating his cake, still hoping in vain that his father would return home soon and they could light the candles.

"Jacob, it's time for bed now."

Jacob looked forlornly in Kate's direction. Her heart went out to him. He'd been so excited about the cake. Why couldn't both his parents get their act together at the same time and put him first? He'd been through so much recently. That damned interfering woman had crawled her way into their lives and was now continually trying to turn Richard's head. It wasn't fair.

He solemnly made his way upstairs, giving the cake one last glance.

"We'll do it tomorrow. Daddy will be here in the morning and he can blow his candles out then."

***

Richard arrived home about midnight. He'd left his car at Ingrid's and taken a taxi home. Ingrid had ordered champagne and he didn't have the heart to refuse it. They'd gone back to her house following a delicious meal and completely lost track of time.

"Why don't you stay?" Ingrid had offered.

Richard wasn't quite ready to progress to that level of the relationship yet and had declined but still managed to share a few intimate moments on the sofa as well as a few glasses of wine.

Tiredness had finally overcome him and he had made his excuses to leave, but not before he'd had his arm twisted to agree to accompany her to an auction the following day. The taxi horn had sounded outside and Richard stood to leave.

"I'll see you tomorrow around eleven-ish." She now had his car on her driveway, he had to come back.

"I'll be here," he'd smiled, gave her one last kiss and left.

In the back of the taxi, he'd stared down at the gold watch she'd given him as a birthday gift. It must have cost her a small fortune. He'd only known her a couple of weeks.

The house was in darkness apart from the hall lamp and the light above the hob in the kitchen. Everywhere was neat and tidy as usual. Richard went into the kitchen to get a glass of water to take up to bed. He hated waking up with a hangover. A few glasses of wine soon had that effect on him these days. The plate covered with aluminium foil intrigued him. He lifted the foil at one corner and looked underneath. His Scooby Doo birthday cake, with one small slice missing, met his eyes.

"Oh, my God," he said out loud.

He felt so ashamed, so thoughtless. He'd been out celebrating, and hadn't even given a thought to his son, that he might have wanted to celebrate as well. So that's why Kate had asked him if he was coming home after work.

Richard continued to stare at the cake. Why was his life getting complicated again after he had just sorted it all out? Why was he being asked to split himself in two? He suddenly realised that he hadn't even told Kate that he wasn't coming home after work—Ingrid had. What had she said? He didn't dare think about it. He'd make it up to them tomorrow.

***

"Was he upset?" Richard asked Kate as they met in the kitchen the following morning. He pointed to the cake.

"A bit disappointed. I'm afraid he couldn't wait any longer for a piece."

Richard smiled. "I'm sorry Kate, I should have called you. Ingrid said she'd sorted it."

"Did she?" Kate mused.

Richard looked up worried. "She did tell you, didn't she?"

"Oh, yes, she told me alright." Kate didn't want to tell tales outside class. Enough said, she went to wake Jacob up. He was already heading down the stairs.

"Is daddy here, Kate?"

"Yes, he's in the kitchen."

"Can we light the candles now?"

Bless him, she thought, he must have been thinking about them all night.

"Maybe we could light them at lunch time, then we could have a piece of cake at the same time. We don't really want cake for breakfast do we?"

"What's that, you two, what are you whispering about?"

"The cake," mouthed Kate. "We'll light the candles at lunch time."

Suddenly Richard remembered his prior engagement. It had sounded reasonable at the time he'd arranged it in a slightly inebriated state late last night, but now it felt like he was abandoning Jacob again.

"Kate, I'm sorry, I've agreed to meet Ingrid at eleven. That means I'll have to get a taxi about ten thirty. My car's at her place."

Kate looked at the clock. They had an hour before he had to leave.

"We'd better do it now, Jacob," she said smiling at him and rubbing the top of his head.

Luckily, Jacob was so excited, the part about his father leaving in the next hour had completely slipped by him.

"You're going to Melissa's with Jacob anyway, aren't you? I'm not going to miss him for that long."

"That's next week."

"Oh, no."

They lit the candles on the cake amidst a mixture of emotions. Jacob was elated, Kate felt the whole thing had fallen completely flat and Richard had a sickening feeling in his stomach. Why had he agreed to see Ingrid again when his son needed him? He wasn't going to see him much next weekend either.

Richard and Kate solemnly ate sponge cake with jam and cream and a sickly topping of sugary icing for breakfast.

"I must admit, I've never had birthday cake for breakfast before," said Richard trying to lighten the atmosphere. "It's delicious, I think I'll try it again."

Kate forced a smile but Richard could see that haunted look reappearing in her face again. The look he'd seen when they'd first met. Gone was the sparkle in her eyes that greeted him when he walked in from work. Now only the lonely, sad stare was present poorly camouflaged by her inane smile. Had he got it wrong in Scotland? Had he missed something deeply significant? She had practically urged him to meet Ingrid, yet now she seemed so flat, deflated almost, as if the light had gone out inside her again.

He was painfully aware of the time and how it was flying by.

"I'll just grab a quick shower, you don't mind do you?"

What a stupid question, he thought. Of course she minds, you're leaving her alone to take care of your son again. Despite his dilemma, he carried on. He'd committed himself now and there was nothing he could do—apart from make it better the next time perhaps.

***

Kate's only consolation that weekend was that Richard had gone out with Ingrid in the new jumper she had bought him. Quite a compliment really, that it was good enough for her.

She and Jacob had spent a pleasant afternoon at the park. Jacob had taken his bike and Kate had once again raced around after him. She'd suggested trying without his stabilisers, but that suggestion had been put on the back burner as he'd come round a corner a little too fast with the stabilisers on, and the whole thing had fallen over. Jacob wasn't hurt, he had so much protective clothing on, but it had shaken him up enough to want to keep his extra set of wheels firmly in place.

By rights, Sunday should have been a far better day. Richard was around, he wasn't on call, and with the amount of time he had spent with Ingrid this weekend, he should have devoted the whole day to Jacob—if he could only get off the phone. Ingrid seemed to have the knack of spending the entire phone call thinking about something to call him back about later. Kate could sense Richard's irritation by the end of the third call.

"Fancy a trip to the park, Jacob?" he asked. It was obviously a form of escape.

"Can I take my bike, daddy?"

"Yes, of course you can. Come on, let's give Kate a bit of peace."

Kate was crestfallen. Normally it would just be taken for granted that she would go along with them. Did they look too much like a family for Richard's liking now? Suddenly she was being excluded; something else to thank Ingrid for no doubt.

Over the following week, Richard spent most of his time at home on the phone. There wasn't an evening where Ingrid didn't telephone and Kate felt the distance between her and Richard growing ever larger. Her moment of hope when he'd opened his birthday present was fading into a distant memory. She even wondered whether it had happened at all. His actions and words were becoming vague and soon she feared she would forget them altogether.

Before she knew it, the day she had been dreading was upon her. Melissa rang in the morning to make sure Kate was still happy to accompany her son.

*"Alex will pick you and Jacob up about eleven thirty if that's alright with you, Kate?"* Melissa said.

Kate could hear the excitement in her voice. Melissa had wallowed in her parent's approval when she'd picked them up at the airport the day before and told them of the arrangements. They had been so relieved. Finally their daughter seemed to have put her 'condition' to rest and had started concentrating on her son for the first time in her life. It hadn't been as straight forward as she'd thought, winning his affection back. She still wasn't quite there apparently, but with the help of her new friend, Kate, the nanny, she was well on her way.

"We'll get a taxi. Please don't trouble Alex."

"*It's no trouble, Kate, it's the least we can do after all your help. Now don't worry yourself. We'll see you shortly."*

The day was getting worse by the minute. Richard had disappeared to work for the day and now Alex was on his way to collect them. Kate looked at the clock; only half an hour to go.

"Come on, Jacob, we'd better get ready. We're going to see grandma and granddad soon."

Jacob didn't need telling twice. He'd been looking forward to his visit all week. He was very fond of both sets of grandparents.

Alex was soon at the door. "I'm sorry, Kate, this wasn't my idea."

"I know, I tried to tell her we'd get a taxi but she wasn't having any of it. Come on, Jacob, let's go."

They sat in the car silently, Kate fixating on the passing houses and shops, not quite knowing what to talk about.

"Everything alright with you?" Alex asked.

He was genuinely interested but unfortunately it came across as prying.

"Yes, fine, why?"

"Just asking."

"If you're wondering whether I've got over throwing the tea tray all over the floor and not being able to explain myself, yes, I have. Even Melissa's quite friendly towards me now," Kate replied in a lowered voice. She didn't want Jacob telling any tales.

"I know, she thinks you're wonderful for what you did on her last visit."

"What did I do?"

"You got Jacob to accept her again and that was huge."

"All I did was play a game with them."

"Doesn't matter what you did, Kate, apparently it worked wonders. She even said she got on fairly well with Richard and that was thanks to you as well."

Kate looked mystified. She shrugged her shoulders and continued looking out of the window until the journey ended. Soon she would be able to leave them all and disappear for an hour or so. She could feel the nerves begin to flutter in her chest as they pulled up outside her old house.

Kate stared vacantly at the front of the house. It hadn't changed from the outside. She wondered what Melissa had done to the inside or did they had similar tastes. She doubted it very much. Melissa would probably have spent a small fortune titivating the place.

"Come on, Jacob," said Alex opening the rear door of the car.

Kate stirred herself and stepped out on to the pavement. Pensively, she walked up the pathway to the door. Alex stood to one side as she made her way inside. The first thing she noticed was that the mirror in the hall had moved and made way for a much more ornate one. Kate wasn't sure whether she liked it or not—maybe a bit over the top for this style of house. Apart from that, the décor was virtually the same.

Melissa had seen the car arrive and appeared at the lounge door.

"Jacob, darling, come here while I give you a big hug." Melissa knelt down in front of her son and threw her arms around him. She took off his coat as Jacob looked cautiously around him. "Hi, Kate, thanks for bringing him," she smiled. "Come on in and we'll put the kettle on. Come on, Jacob, grandma and granddad are in here."

Jacob looked around to make sure Kate was still there with him. Kate was worried, he looked nervous. She wouldn't be able to leave him as he was at the moment. Slowly, he peered around the door. She needn't have worried. Inside the lounge, Jacob took one look at his grandparents and ran towards them.

"Oh, Jacob," his grandma squealed, delighted at his reaction. "How wonderful to see you. My, aren't you a big boy now?"

"Hi, Jacob," his grandfather said next. "How are you, little fella?"

"Granddad," said Jacob. "I've brought my colouring book to show you."

"Fantastic," his grandfather replied. "I love colouring, can I help you?"

"Mum, dad," Melissa interrupted. "This is Kate, Jacob's new nanny. Kate these are my parents."

"Lovely to meet you, Kate," her mother responded first. "We've heard a lot about you, and it's all good before you ask."

Kate smiled. "Nice to meet you both."

"Now, Kate, you take a seat and I'll fetch a drink, tea or coffee?"

"Tea would be lovely."

Kate scanned the room. How familiar it looked, yet strange. The foundations were the same, the wallpaper, carpet and most of the furniture to Kate's surprise. It was the finer details that had Melissa's signature on them. Scented candles of all shapes and smells covered the window sill and the fire surround, interspersed with oil burners and incense sticks. Funny, Kate never had Melissa down as that type of person. She began to visualise her sat on the floor in the lotus position with her eyes closed humming in meditation. She wondered what Alex made of it all.

An original watercolour of a tropical sunset hung above the fireplace; Antigua presumably. Where had the print of Monet's garden been demoted to? She loved that picture, despite the fact that it had started to fade from the sunlight that filtered through the window. Maybe she should have taken it with her. She didn't have much to show for all those years with Alex.

Alex seemed to have made himself scarce. She hadn't set eyes on him since she'd arrived. Maybe it was a bit too much for him as well. Melissa brought in the drinks and placed them on the coffee table.

"Help yourself to biscuits," she offered.

"Melissa, if you want some time with Jacob on your own that's not a problem. I'm sure you don't want me to sit here all afternoon," said Kate. She felt like she was sitting in judgement of them all, ready to report back to Richard.

"Don't worry, Kate, it's fine. I don't want to upset Richard," she said quietly.

"I've already okayed it with Richard. He said there's no problem. I'll go and look round the shops on the high street, or go and get a bite to eat for lunch."

"Really, Kate, you asked Richard if you could leave him with us? That's so kind of you. I don't know what to say."

Kate smiled kindly. "I'll come back for him in a couple of hours. Is that enough time for you?"

"Of course it is. Listen Kate, you've been kind enough to do that for us, why don't you let Alex take you for something to eat? He could take you for a pub lunch, that's the least we could do for you. The weather isn't all that nice for mooching around the high street. The Dog and Duck has a lovely warm fire I believe."

"No, it's fine honestly."

"Kate, it's no trouble. Alex, you'll take Kate for a spot of lunch won't you? I'm sure you can find something to talk about," she laughed.

Alex had reappeared at the doorway. "Course I will, come on, Kate. The Dog and Duck do a really good beef and ale pie."

Kate caught Alex's eye and wondered what he was playing at. He always used to have that when they went in there. Surely he wasn't serious about taking her. Not with the risk of one of his friends being around. Kate finished her drink then stood up to follow him. And was that a touch of resentment she'd detected in his tone?

"I'll see you later, Jacob."

Jacob was happily colouring with his grandma and didn't pay much attention to Kate leaving much to his mother's relief.

"Bye, Kate," he replied.

"He'll be fine, Kate; he's got his grandparent's to play with."

"And his mother," Kate reminded her. "Of course he'll be alright."

Melissa's eyes glassed over. Kate was such a nice person. She winced at the way she'd mocked her the first time they'd met.

Kate left Jacob to continue playing and went outside to the waiting car with Alex positioned behind the wheel.

"I'm sorry about this," she apologised. "This was never meant to happen. I offered to leave Jacob so I could get out of my old house, not to go out to lunch with my ex."

"It's not your fault," he insisted. "It's mine. If I'd come clean in the first place then we'd never be in this situation.

The only trouble now is that it's too late to say anything. The moment's gone. She'd go mad if she found out now, especially as I'm about to take you out to lunch."

Kate thought about their predicament. He was right; it *was* too late to say anything. Nonetheless, he was the one who would have to live with it. No wonder his friends hadn't met Melissa yet. He was scared to death of what they might say.

"Where *are* we going for lunch, by the way, and please don't say The Dog and Duck? I couldn't bare any comments from the likes of Chloe or Chris."

"Do you honestly think I'd take you in there to suffer an interrogation from that lot? I thought we'd go to Barnaby's over at Waterley Bridge."

Suddenly Kate laughed out loud. Alex briefly glanced over at her.

"It's ironic really isn't it? I've probably spent more time with you since we split up than when we were together. All that time you used to spend in the pub or round at Chris's. I hardly saw you some weekends. Even at work we were like ships that passed in the night. I mean, when was the last time we went out for a meal on our own? I can't remember, can you?"

"What do you mean; we used to eat out every weekend?"

"Not on our own. Tina and Chris were always there."

Alex thought for a while.

"No, you're right; we didn't go out on our own very much. That's probably where we went wrong. We should have spent more time together . . ."

". . . and less at the gym."

Kate's little dig didn't go unnoticed. They were quiet for a while before they pulled into the car park at Barnaby's. Kate noticed the selection of pizzas and burgers on the menu outside and wondered if he would ever actually grow up.

Inside, Kate studied the menu for a meal that would suit an adult female and not a prepubescent young boy. She plumped for a chicken sandwich which came with a side order of salad.

"Do you bring Melissa here?" she asked him knowing full well what the answer would be.

"No way, Melissa wouldn't come here. We eat at Marcelle's or the Italian on the high street."

"You should both bring Jacob here one day, when Richard allows it of course. He'd love it."

"I'll tell Melissa, thanks for that. You're really trying to help her aren't you?"

"A child needs his mother," she replied diplomatically.

She didn't know herself why she was helping Melissa. Maybe she had inadvertently changed sides since Richard had deserted her or maybe she was actually beginning to like her. She wasn't entirely sure. One thing she did know was that she preferred Jacob to be in the company of his mother and Alex rather than the dreaded Ingrid. There was something about that woman that she didn't like and it wasn't just the fact that she had stolen Richard's affection.

Kate and Alex passed an hour chatting easily over their meal and a cup of coffee. It had been less of an ordeal than she'd anticipated. She felt quite sad when they got up to leave and had to return to continue their façade back at the house.

"I suppose I'll be expected to take you and Jacob home."

"Oh, don't put yourself out," she joked.

They both laughed as they got back into the car.

***

There were three messages on the answer phone when Kate and Jacob got back home. Kate instinctively knew who they were from and chose to ignore them. She would relish watching Richard's face after a hard days work, coming home to that. Some would say she was hounding him, constantly phoning and leaving instructions for him to call her back. *Never mind*, Kate thought, *he'll soon get fed up of it.*

Kate was about to compliment herself on a rather successful day, when Richard returned from work.

"Hi," he shouted from the door.

"Hi, Richard, we've only just beaten you."

"How did it go?"

"Very well, Jacob really enjoyed himself."

"Did you leave him?"

"Yes, I went out for lunch with Alex, would you believe?"

"Alex?" Richard said abruptly. "Why Alex?"

"It was Melissa's idea. I think it was a thank you for taking Jacob."

"Oh," he exclaimed sounding rather put out.

Richard seemed more perturbed about Kate's lunch date than the fact that Jacob had enjoyed his day with his mother and grandparents.

"There are three messages on the phone for you?"

"How do you know they're for me?" Richard asked trying to sound amusing.

He flicked the button and listened as Ingrid's voice bleated out. *"Hi, Richard, just ringing to see how you are—call me."* Bleep.

*"Hi, Richard, presuming you must have been called out, missing you –call me."* Bleep.

*"Richard, it's me again. You seem to have been out for ages. Maybe we could grab a drink tonight if it's not too late—call me."* Bleep.

Richard stormed into the kitchen and opened the fridge door. He grabbed a bottle of cold, white wine and slammed it onto the work top.

"I thought you couldn't drink when you're on call," Kate reminded him.

He closed his eyes, returned the bottle to the fridge and flicked the kettle on. "What I'd give for a long glass of cool, white wine right now."

"Aren't you going to call her?" asked Kate practically taunting him.

"No, and if the phone rings again, let it go to answer phone first. I'm not going anywhere tonight besides my bed."

***

Ingrid stared blankly at the phone. Surely he was home by now—I mean how long does it take to do an operation? She delicately sipped from her wine glass and ran her fingers through her thick brown hair. Staring out of the window, she thought of a dozen things he might be doing now and none of them involved plastic surgery. Her heart started to race. It was too much. She picked the phone up and pressed redial.

"*Hello*," came a little voice.

Richard and Kate both stared at each other in horror. He ran from the kitchen but before he could prompt Jacob into lying about his whereabouts, his cover had been blown.

"Daddy, it's for you."

"Thanks, Jacob," Richard said reluctantly taking the hand piece. "Hello."

*"Richard, it's me; you've been a long time."*

"Yes, it was a nasty case. I've only just got in."

*"I was wondering whether you wanted to go out for a drink?"*

"Not really, Ingrid. I can't drink when I'm on call. Besides I haven't seen Jacob all day and I think Kate's just preparing us all something to eat. I'll see you mid-week, how does that sound?"

"*Like a long time away, but I'll survive I suppose. Call me tomorrow.*"

"Okay, bye."

Ingrid stared menacingly at the phone. So he preferred to spend the evening with Kate did he? She'd show her that she was not someone to tangle with. It was time to get rid of that woman.

***

Richard put the phone down.

"Did that sound really bad?" he asked. "I'll make it up to her next week. I'm too tired to do anything tonight."

Kate felt disappointed. She was hoping that he might be getting tired of Ingrid and her persistent phone calls, but it looked like he was just too physically tired tonight to be bothered with anything much.

***

Despite his fatigue that night, Richard fought hard to get to sleep. His mind wouldn't switch off. Was it the case they'd done earlier that day or was something else bothering him and slipping into his subconscious? Kate and Alex, why had they had lunch together? Surely Melissa wouldn't have suggested that.

# CHAPTER . . .

# 15

Dorothy Royston had adopted a sombre mood since her husband's phone conversation with their daughter. She couldn't bring herself to feel anything anymore. She had become numb from the head down and there was nothing her husband could say to put things right again. The damage had been done and only a visit from their self-centred children could possibly put things back on track.

He had tried everything, even cooking to bring her round but he was worried this time that he had gone too far. Even *he* thought that maybe this was more than just a bad mood and that there might be something physically wrong with his wife.

He sought the advice of a friend of his, Dr Flynn, a clinical psychiatrist who worked at the hospital. He couldn't make a true diagnosis without actually seeing her, but his first thoughts were depression. Gerald had agreed with him and if he were to pinpoint a time when this first took hold he would have said when they were on holiday; Christmas day to be precise, when his daughter had took it upon herself to castigate her mother for failing to attend the festivities. How dare she, how dare *they* for that matter, bring this upon their own mother.

***

Dorothy was seated on the armchair, staring out of the window not really focussing on anything in particular. There were days when she could spend several hours in this catatonic state, but today, a picture had suddenly caught her eye on the window sill beside the vase of wilting lilies. She walked towards the photograph and picked it up. The faces of her family smiled back at her. All four of them; Gerald, Nina, Peter, and herself captured having fun on holiday in Italy several years ago. A nostalgic smile fleetingly crossed her face then almost as quickly disappeared as a wave of sadness threatened to engulf her once again.

Gerald entered the room and noticed the look of hurt in her eyes. His heart sank; he felt partly responsible for her pain yet helpless to do anything about it.

"How are you feeling, Dorothy?" he asked concerned.

"Oh, you know," she answered non-specifically.

"I've had a bit of an idea," he said, trying to lift her spirits. "How about we invite a few people round for something to eat; just a little gathering for our anniversary?"

"Oh, I don't know, Gerald. All that cooking and preparation, I don't know if I could cope with it at the moment."

"We could get caterers in; let them do all the hard work."

"And what about the cleaning up afterwards? I don't think so, Gerald."

Gerald scratched his head. He wasn't beaten yet, one more crack at the whip.

"What about a meal out then, somewhere like Marcelle's? You enjoyed it there didn't you?"

"Yes, I did enjoy it, but I had my family with me then remember. It wouldn't be the sa . . ."

"No it wouldn't be the same, Dorothy, but maybe that isn't such a bad thing. If it isn't the same, it might take your mind off things; give you something to look forward to. Have a think about it, dear; you never know it might just cheer you up a bit."

He thought he might invite some of his work colleagues. He was all too aware that he hadn't been very charitable towards them recently; maybe this might build a few bridges.

"Okay, I'll think about it."

Dorothy thought that was sufficient to appease him and disappeared into the kitchen before the topic of a final decision reared its ugly head.

***

"I'd love to go, Richard," Ingrid said catching a glimpse of herself in the mirror. She adjusted her hair as she continued her conversation on the phone. "Friday you say, what time do you want me ready?"

*"I'll pick you up about seven thirty. It's only five minutes away from your place."*

"Tell me again what the occasion is."

*"Professor Royston's fortieth wedding anniversary. His wife's called Dorothy."*

"Do you want me to get them a present? I'm sure I could find them something from the shop."

*"Yes, that's a good idea,"* Richard said thankfully. That would save him a job.

"I'll pop round tomorrow with something, just to make sure it's suitable. Maybe we could go out for a drink."

Richard hadn't seen that coming. He had hoped that he might have a few nights to himself so that he could devote some time to his son, but how could he refuse now that she had offered to find a present?

*"Okay then,"* he reluctantly relinquished. *"Make it about eight o'clock then I can spend some time with Jacob."*

"I know, why don't I come around a little earlier than I can meet him properly. I'll have to get to know him sometime, won't I?"

Ingrid seemed to be speeding along at a faster rate of knots than Richard would have liked. She appeared to have some unmitigated plan to try and absorb all of his free time. It hadn't been long since Kate had entered Jacob's life. It was too soon to introduce another woman. Nonetheless, he didn't want to upset her a second time so he agreed.

***

Ingrid arrived at seven fifteen precisely. Jacob was in his pyjamas waiting to go to bed when Richard led her into the lounge. Kate looked up in surprise. She hadn't been expecting her; Richard hadn't mentioned she was coming.

The smile on her face immediately disappeared as the two women made eye contact.

"Jacob, Ingrid's come to see you again, say hello," Richard instructed his son.

Jacob did as he was bid then turned towards Kate for reassurance.

"Hello, Jacob, I've brought you some sweeties," Ingrid said handing over a bag of sugared jellies.

Kate started to simmer. She eyed the bag and without further ado said, "He can't have those now, it's bed time."

Ingrid recoiled in shock. "Surely one or two won't make any difference."

"Please, Kate, please, daddy, can I have some?" Jacob pleaded.

"They're full of sugar," continued Kate.

"Kate," Richard said firmly stepping in. "He can have a couple."

"But he's cleaned his teeth."

"Well he can clean them again."

Kate was stunned. She couldn't have been more hurt if he'd walked over to her and slapped her across the face. He'd never raised his voice to her before. She stood up and retreated to the haven of the kitchen, humiliation emblazoned across her face. As she stormed past Ingrid she could sense the victorious smirk she would be wearing. She glanced quickly at Richard, his face was stony; she'd never seen him like this before. That bitch, how dare she turn Richard against her?

In the kitchen, Kate poured herself a glass of water from the tap and quickly drank it, savouring the coolness against the heat of her skin. Her hands were shaking slightly. What would she do now? She could hardly go back into the lounge, not now she'd left the room in such an atmosphere. She could hear them talking through the closed door; Ingrid saying something, then Richard replying. Suddenly the door opened and Richard was in front of her.

"You know that wasn't really necessary, Kate," he said sternly. "Ingrid was only trying to make friends with Jacob."

*More like trying to buy him,* thought Kate. "You didn't have to speak to her like that." His voice was softening as he focussed on Kate's trembling bottom lip. "Let's all try and get on, that's all I'm saying." Kate nodded. She was in danger of losing her composure and she had no intention of doing that in front of Ingrid. "Come on back in the room. We're going out for a drink now. We'll leave you to get Jacob to bed."

Kate felt like she'd just walked out of the headmaster's office after a severe reprimanding and the rest of the school were watching her. She followed him back into the lounge and took her seat on the other side of Jacob, who was making his way through the packet of jellied sweets since there was no responsible adult present to stop him. Ingrid was next to him now talking about nursery, her considerable unease with children shining through.

"Well, Jacob, it was lovely to meet you again. I'll see you very soon," she said hopefully. "Shall I bring you some more of those sweeties?"

Jacob nodded eagerly, unable to speak for the amount he had in his mouth. Kate slowly seethed. She wondered if that last comment was for her benefit. How she hated that woman. Richard sensed the tension once again and decided to remove the fuse.

"Right, Ingrid, shall we go? I think it's Jacob's bedtime now."

He smiled half-heartedly at Kate but she couldn't find anything in her to return the gesture. Instead she took his cue and bundled Jacob off to bed.

Richard had failed to notice that Ingrid hadn't mentioned the Royston's anniversary present let alone brought it along for him to inspect.

***

Later that evening, after Jacob had finally gone off to sleep following his sugar fix, Kate sat on the leather suite and muddled over the evening's events. What exactly had happened? She'd certainly lost Richard for good now; he had shown no hesitation in siding with Ingrid. But where did that leave her? How safe would her job be if that woman got her way and moved in? But then, on the other hand, would she want to stay? The very idea of Ingrid being that close to Richard made her feel nauseous, and the thought of losing her precious job filled her with dread.

***

Richard felt bad the whole evening. He'd never spoken to Kate like that before. After all she'd done for him, he should have handled it better, but Ingrid had this annoying habit of making him react in ways he didn't want to. She'd urged him to say something, so what had he done in the heat of the moment, he'd said something, and now he regretted it. Kate was right, he shouldn't have encouraged Jacob to eat sugary sweets before bedtime and then leave her to try and get him to sleep. He'd apologise when Ingrid was safely out of earshot.

Ingrid was triumphant. She'd certainly got a reaction out of Kate tonight, storming off in a huff. How gallant Richard had been sticking up for her like that. She felt like they'd moved on in their relationship leaps and bounds just by that simple action. Kate Forrester won't be queen bee for much longer, she thought happily.

***

The guests were gathering at Marcelle's; friends, relatives, colleagues and their partners, but there was a depressive tone to the proceedings. Dorothy couldn't work up any enthusiasm for the event and strive as he might, Gerald couldn't quite convince her to try, not even for the duration of the party. Ingrid was the first to notice. She had a keen eye for human nature.

"That woman's got a face like a wet weekend. I thought she was supposed to be celebrating her wedding anniversary; she looks like the cat has just died," she whispered to Richard.

Richard was a little more sympathetic.

"I know," he agreed. "She doesn't look well at all. I hope there's nothing serious going on."

Gerald coaxed his wife to the table and sat down beside her. The waiter came round with the menus. Richard surreptitiously nudged Todd at the table and moved his eyes in Dorothy's direction. Todd nodded in agreement.

"She looks terrible," he mouthed to Richard.

Jayne, Todd's wife was trying hard to think of something to talk to Ingrid about. She had always tried to get on with the partners of her husband's friends but Richard had always posed a problem. He seemed to attach himself to women who thought they were far superior to everyone else in the room. First of all Melissa, and now this Ingrid woman; why did he find it so difficult to find someone normal who she could get on with? She enjoyed Richard's company but shied away from it because of the baggage that went with it.

"How's the antique's business going at the moment, Ingrid?" she asked once she'd decided upon her meal.

"Oh, you know, like everything else at the moment. Antiques are the first thing to go when people are losing their jobs and can't afford their weekly shop," Ingrid replied, her eyes never leaving the menu. "I may have to go and see mummy and daddy for a sub soon." She smiled dryly then slowly folded the menu back. "What do you do?" Ingrid finally looked at Jayne; a long, cool stare that left her feeling slightly uneasy.

"I'm a housewife, we have two children."

"Oh, a kept woman. I couldn't bear that, being at home with the kids all day. I think I'd probably go out of my mind. We always had a nanny when we were children."

"I'd sooner look after my children on my own, especially as I have the opportunity to stay at home with them." Jayne could hear herself competing with Ingrid. She hated that kind of conversation over the dinner table. It was meant to be interesting and entertaining not competitive. She decided to end it there and then and talk to the men instead.

"What are you having, Todd?"

The evening progressed and Jayne distanced herself further and further from Ingrid. She made a mental note never to be talked into inviting them over for dinner.

Poor Dorothy had barely said a word all evening. Gerald was becoming increasingly irritated at her lack of hospitality but the truth was, she just didn't have the energy to be bothered. He'd seated her next to Sonia Patterson, the lady captain, purposely. If anyone could draw her out of this gloom it was Sonia, but even she had no effect. Sonia had taken to talking to Consultant Raj Puli to her right. He was far more receptive to her tales of Shadmoor Golf Club and the dry cleaning business.

Elizabeth Chambers, the fifth plastic surgeon around the table, was the only one who got anywhere near breaking the ice around Dorothy. She was sick to death of listening to Richard's girlfriend droning on about her pampered life and had totally switched off to her. Her heart went out to Dorothy. She obviously didn't want to be here and she knew full well how her husband would have dragged her along without a second thought to her state of mind. Gerald Royston was like that. He didn't care about sensitive things like feelings. She wondered how many of his impromptu meetings were a result of his wife's obvious depression.

Once the eating had been completed and Gerald was making his way around the table, circulating amongst his guests, Elizabeth moved up a couple of chairs so that she could seat herself next to Dorothy. The older woman looked up and smiled gratefully.

"Thank you for tonight, Dorothy. It's been a lovely meal. I haven't been to this place before. It's the opposite end of town to where I live."

"Oh, it's nice to see you all. I don't get to see Gerald's colleagues much these days. He seems to keep you all away from me. Do you think he's trying to tell me something?"

Dorothy managed a half-hearted smile again, but it all seemed such an effort. Elizabeth put her hand over Dorothy's clenched fist.

"Maybe you should get out more," suggested Elizabeth. "We should have a monthly get together, although I'm not sure Richard should bring his other half."

"Oh dear, do you not get on?" said Dorothy.

"It's the first time I've clapped eyes on her and I hope the last. She's a spoilt madam if you ask me."

Dorothy's eyes briefly lit up at the thought of a bit of gossip, then the light was gone, distinguished, never to emerge again until it was time to go home. It came as a huge relief when her husband thanked everyone for coming then finally declared the evening over.

Richard, Todd, Ingrid and Jayne all walked back to Richard's waiting car parked outside Ingrid's home. Ingrid felt slightly aggrieved at the fact that he'd offered to bring them. She was hoping he might stay the night. The dilemma of whether to invite them in for coffee was resolved when Jayne announced they'd have to get home for the baby sitter. She wasn't going to risk being summoned into Ingrid's thus drawing the evening out even further.

"Well, I can see why that poor woman is so miserable," Ingrid offered on the walk back. "Having to live with him would be enough to tip anyone over the edge."

"Ingrid, that man is a very well respected professor," Richard objected.

"Maybe so, but he wasn't exactly the life and soul of the party was he?"

*Neither were you,* thought Jayne.

"There's obviously some underlying problem there, don't you think, Todd?" Richard asked showing concern.

Todd agreed. "Oh, without a doubt. She needs to see a specialist. The poor woman couldn't leave quick enough. I hope she doesn't get any earache from old Royston once they're on their own. You know what he's like?"

***

The tears streamed down Dorothy's face as her husband hurled his objections at her.

"You were embarrassing, Dorothy. Everyone at that table could see how miserable you were. How do you think that made me look? Surely you could have made an effort for one night."

"I'm sorry, Gerald, but I never asked to go out tonight. I said I wanted my children with me but you wouldn't listen would you?"

"Oh, stop sniffling, woman. Anyone would think I'd just asked you for a divorce, not treated you to a beautiful three course meal with family and friends. Honestly, Dorothy, I take you on a Caribbean cruise, then this and you're still unhappy and still going on about those blessed children of ours."

Silence followed for the remainder of the journey. As they arrived home, Gerald stormed out of the car, opened the front door, marched upstairs, and slammed the door to the spare bedroom. Enough was enough.

***

"Shall I see you tomorrow then?" Ingrid asked Richard before he jumped into the car.

"I need to spend some time with Jacob tomorrow. I've hardly seen him at all today."

"Well as long as that doesn't mean time with Kate as well, I suppose I'll have to wait until Sunday."

"Look, Ingrid, Kate lives with us. I have to see her every day. Please don't make an issue about that."

Ingrid could feel one of her petulant sulks coming on. She had sensed a bad feeling about Kate ever since she had started to see Richard. She hated the fact that they lived in the same house and that Kate had constant access to Richard whereas she virtually had to book an appointment to see him.

"Okay, point taken; I'll see you Sunday. Maybe we could go to the cinema for a change. I'll check up on what's on and give you a ring," said Ingrid.

Richard hadn't said yes to Sunday but as Ingrid had virtually got it planned already, he agreed again. He noticed her dates never included Jacob and that was a worry to him. She couldn't exclude him forever.

Ingrid planted a kiss on Richard's lips and whispered goodbye. Richard was a little uncomfortable at her public display of affection in front of Todd and Jayne. He quickly got into the car and turned on the engine. With one hand raised in farewell they drove off. Jayne briefly waved from the back seat but Ingrid had turned to go into the house by that time. She wasn't going to lose any sleep over it, in fact she secretly hoped that was the last time she saw Ingrid Harper.

"Everything okay, Richard?" asked Todd in the passenger seat noticing the flustered look on his face.

"Yes, I think so. Ingrid and Kate don't get on too well . . ." *A woman after my own heart,* thought Jayne. ". . . and Ingrid's starting to give me a hard time about being in the same house as her. I told her we all come as a package but she can't quite grasp the situation. I think she sees Kate as a threat."

Todd looked thoughtful. "Tell me again why you're not going out with Kate?" he questioned.

"What?" Richard quickly glanced over at Todd. "What's that got to do with it?"

"Because it seems to me that the answer to all your problems is to be with her. You like her, she likes you, Jacob likes her and she likes him. What's the problem?"

"Todd," Jayne said from the back of the car. "It's not really for you to comment, is it?"

"No, that's fair enough," Richard stepped in. "But there's just one problem, Kate's not interested in me."

"That's what you think Richard but . . ."

"There's no 'buts' about it, she practically threw me at Ingrid in Scotland. Anyway, what's wrong with Ingrid?"

"She's complicating your life, old chap. You seemed much happier before you met her."

# CHAPTER . . .

# 16

Richard couldn't believe he'd just wasted the last two hours of his life watching the lousiest, most nauseating 'woman's' film he'd ever had the misfortune to see. He was tired and irritable. He could have spent that time with Jacob, but instead he'd been rail roaded into watching what he considered a load of sentimental rubbish.

"Do you want a coffee before you go?" asked Richard somewhat tactlessly.

Ingrid could sense his prickly mood and put it down to the stresses of work.

"I'd rather have a glass of wine," she replied widening her eyes and fluttering her lashes.

"That's not such a good idea when you're driving. I'll put the kettle on."

"It seems silly to drive all that way home at this time of night."

"It's only ten thirty."

She was making no progress with him tonight. She glanced around her.

"Looks like we've got the place to ourselves. *Kate* seems to have gone to bed," she said, sarcastically stressing the word Kate.

"Come on, Ingrid, you don't have to be like that. Kate is a vital part to the smooth running of this house."

His very words cut through her like a knife.

"We won't need her when we're eventually living together. I can run the house and take care of Jacob." Richard looked up in surprise. Where had she got that idea from? "Well, you shouldn't have to creep around wondering whether she's gone to bed or not. When I was young, my nanny had her own quarters, not the run of the house like her. She just takes liberties expecting to use every room as if she owns the place. It's your home, Richard, not hers."

At that point the door to the lounge opened and Kate appeared clutching her book.

"Kate," said Richard, wondering whether she'd heard Ingrid's outburst. "We didn't think you were still up."

"Obviously not," she replied, and there was his answer. She'd heard every thoughtless word. She fled past them both, her eyes filled with tears, and headed towards her room.

"Kate," Richard cried as she passed.

"Leave her," Ingrid ordered. "She'll come round."

Richard stared after her. What had they done? How were they going to make amends after this?

"Why did you have to say that?" he asked angrily.

"I didn't know she was there."

"Well precisely, if you didn't know, you shouldn't have said anything. There was always the chance she could have heard."

"Oh, for goodness sake, Richard, don't be so melodramatic. She'll have forgotten all about it in the morning. But that is precisely what I was talking about. You shouldn't have to watch what you say in your own house just in case the nanny happens to overhear."

Kate was devastated. As soon as she was in the confines of her bedroom, her heart broke and the tears flowed down her cheeks. The time she had been dreading was upon her. How she hated that woman, and Richard for that matter for entertaining her.

Richard could hear her sobs from the foot of the stairs. He was pacing the floor like a caged animal wondering what best to do.

"Come and sit down, Richard," said Ingrid coolly.

"I can't leave this until morning. I have to say something."

"That's what she wants. She wants you up there, knocking on her door, grovelling for her forgiveness. That gives her the upper hand. Richard, this is your house and she is your employee. If she can't handle that then you should let her go."

"She's not just an employee, she's . . ." Richard stopped himself before he went too far.

"What?"

"She's a friend."

He stared into space as it dawned on him. She was far more than just a friend only he had been too stupid to realise. The thought of losing her now was unthinkable.

Suddenly the sound of a horn beeping outside made them both look up. A door opened upstairs, and Kate emerged carrying both suitcases containing all her possessions. Her eyes were red and swollen when she finally lifted them up to look Richard in the face.

"Would you send my wages on to this address?" she said handing Richard a small piece of paper and her key. She took one last disdainful look at Ingrid and left, closing the door firmly behind her.

"Kate, please," called Richard after her, but his cries were futile. She was already in the taxi outside instructing the driver as to her destination.

"So she'll come round will she, forgotten all about it by morning?" Richard was beside himself. "What am I supposed to do tomorrow now? I have to leave for work at seven thirty. Who's going to get Jacob ready and take him to nursery?"

"I'll do it," Ingrid offered. She was more than pleased to be able to help out. That meant she could stay over night. She tried to hide the look of glee on her face.

"You, but you don't even know where nursery is."

"Then tell me. Richard, this is what would have ultimately happened, it's just come a bit sooner."

He chose to ignore her comment again and turned to organising the sleeping arrangements. There was no way he was sharing a bed with her tonight after the way she had behaved.

"Okay," he said calming down slightly, knowing she was his only option at this moment in time. "I'll explain what happens in the mornings and where to take Jacob, then you can take my bed and I'll sleep on the sofa."

"Surely that's not necessary. We're consenting adults you know."

"I don't want Jacob waking up in the middle of the night and finding us in bed together. I don't want to have to start explaining that to him."

"Okay, whatever you say."

***

As the taxi pulled up outside Tina's house the front door opened and her friend stood waiting for her. Kate paid the driver then dragged her heavy cases up to the front door.

"Come on in, you look awful," said Tina as she inspected Kate's swollen eyes.

"I feel it. I can't believe I've gone."

The two women hugged each other and closed the door behind them. It was going to be a long night as Kate went through the whole story from Scotland and that kiss, to half an hour ago.

". . . but the worse thing is," Kate finally said, "I don't want to leave Richard and Jacob. I think the world of them both; it's her I can't stand. And I certainly can't work there if she moves in, which it sounds like she has every intention of doing."

"Listen, babe," Tina said rubbing the back of Kate's hand. "This'll look different in the morning. Why don't we go to bed and talk about it tomorrow. I'm sure we can work something out."

***

That night a raging storm howled around the house. The wind whipped through the trees bending them so far, they looked like they would snap. Richard lay awake listening to the noise. It was as if Mother Nature was venting her anger at the two of them for what they had done. He couldn't get the vision of Kate's distraught face out of his mind. When he thought back, he hadn't actually said anything incriminating, but he certainly hadn't shut Ingrid up. He had allowed her to ramble on about dismissing Kate and that in itself was a crime of equal proportion. She would hate him by now. She'd probably never want to step foot into this house again and who could blame her, but then again, how on earth was he going to manage without her, and what would Jacob say? She had been his guardian angel, sent down to help him out in his moment of need. And look how he'd repaid her.

A crashing noise in the garden broke his thoughts. He stood up from his makeshift bed and went to look out of the window. One of the fence panels had blown off and broken the window in the shed. He would have to get that fixed tomorrow before his garden became a thoroughfare for all the local thieves, who would now, quite easily, be able to help themselves to the contents of his shed. Normally Kate would sort that kind of thing out whilst Jacob was at nursery, but Ingrid would have her work cut out tomorrow taking care of him and would probably freak out at the prospect of a list of jobs to do as well.

His life had taken a turn for the worse again and it was noticeable that it was the absence of Kate that was causing it. He was missing her already, not just because she knew how to run his house better than he did and take care of his child for that matter, but just because he was missing her; her casual talk, her laughter, her sensitivity, in fact everything about her. She wasn't like Ingrid, always trying to be smart and pretentious. She was natural, caring and funny. He didn't have to think twice as to whether Todd and Jayne would like her; he knew they would and he knew they didn't like Ingrid. She was more an acquired taste, preferable to those who moved in her circles. Did he really want to estrange his closest friends because of his choice of girlfriend? He knew that they wouldn't be getting an invitation from them for dinner as a couple any time in the near future after Ingrid's performance at the Royston's party?

He peered at his watch in the darkness, trying to make out the time from the fluorescent tips on the hands. It was either quarter past five or twenty five past three, he couldn't quite make it out. He was hoping it was the latter, he hadn't had a wink of sleep yet and he knew he had a full list tomorrow.

***

Jacob opened his sleepy eyes and yawned. It was still dark in his room but the light was on downstairs so he pulled on his dressing gown, grabbed Tigger by the arm and made his way down the stairs. He could hear the clinking of pots in the kitchen and went to surprise Kate. He crept up to the kitchen door and shouted, "Boo!"

Ingrid jumped then turned around. "Hello, Jacob, you're very lively this morning."

Jacob looked in horror as he came face to face with the woman who kept taking his father away from him.

"Where's Kate?" Jacob asked. A hint of distress had entered his voice.

"Kate's had to go out."

"Where's daddy?"

"Daddy's at work, like he is nearly every morning when you get up."

"I want Kate." Jacob started to back up until he bumped into the dining table. "I want daddy."

"It's alright, Jacob," Ingrid said crouching down to his level. "Daddy and Kate will be back soon." The name caught in her throat as she pleaded with the young boy to try and see reason. "I'm going to take you to nursery this morning so you eat your breakfast and then we can get ready. Come along, sit at the table."

Jacob clutched Tigger into his chest and took the seat farthest away from Ingrid. She placed a bowl of Rice Crispies in front of him then went in the kitchen for some milk.

"I want Kate," he started to shout again and then in temper, tipped the bowl over. Rice Crispies scattered all over the table then dropped in their multitudes onto the floor. Ingrid's head whipped round.

"Jacob, what are you doing? That is so naughty. Kate isn't here so you're just going to have to put up with me this morning. Now pick those Rice Crispies off the floor or I shall ring your daddy and tell him what you've just done."

Jacob's bottom lip began to quiver then the tears started to roll down his cheeks.

"I want daddy," he started to cry and soon he was hysterical. He flicked the rest of his cereal off the table with Tigger then stood up and started to stamp on them with his feet.

"Jacob, stop it immediately." Ingrid ran into the hallway and picked up the phone. "See Jacob, I'm going to ring daddy and tell him and he will be very cross when he gets home."

He suddenly calmed himself and sat back on his chair, his face still wet from the tears and his snotty nose running towards his mouth. Ingrid quickly wiped the tears away and then his nose.

"There," she said cringing at the damp tissue as she deposited it in the waste bin. "That's better, now are you going to eat some cereal or do you want toast instead?"

"I want chocolate," he sulked.

Ingrid thought of the evening she'd given him sweets at supper time and the control Kate had tried to exert over his eating habits. In hindsight Kate had been right and after what she'd just experienced, she too would have been annoyed if a visitor had tried to give her child sugary sweets at bedtime. Nonetheless, chocolate at this moment in time would be a success. At least he would have eaten something. She compromised with a piece of chocolate cake and a drink of orange juice and agreed to forget the Rice Crispie incident if he behaved himself from now on.

***

Richard glanced at his phone. Everything must be running smoothly at home, no messages yet. His heart sank—no message from Kate either, but then what did he expect? Todd met him as he arrived at the clinic doors.

"Morning, Richard, everything alright? You look like you've just lost a twenty pound note and found a fiver."

"Kate walked out last night," Richard blurted out. "So Ingrid's been looking after Jacob this morning."

"What happened?"

"She overheard Ingrid bad mouthing her."

*That bloody woman again,* thought Todd. "What did she say?" Todd couldn't believe Richard was still with her. She was slowly ruining his life, taking over bit by bit.

"She as good as said that when she moves in we won't need Kate any more."

"And what did you say; she's not moving in is she?"

"No, she isn't, but before I had chance to say anything, Kate appeared from nowhere, ran upstairs, packed her things and was gone."

"I don't know what to say, Richard. You are going to get her back aren't you?"

"Of course I am, I just don't know how at the moment. If I go and see her and Ingrid finds out she'll walk out on me. Then if Kate won't come back I'll be left with no one to look after Jacob."

"Looks like you've got a lot of decisions to make, Richard. I know what I'd do in your shoes if that's any consolation."

Richard looked thoughtful and made his way to his consulting room, not really taking any notice of Todd's advice. He had to make a phone call to get the fence and the shed window fixed before his clinic started.

***

Kate woke late with a blinding headache and puffy eyes. She and Tina had drowned her sorrows the night before and now she was regretting it. She'd still not heard from Richard and the longer his silence, the more the reality sank in.

She went downstairs to the kitchen in search of fluids. Any would do as long as they weren't alcoholic. Chris was seated at the table in the kitchen greedily eating a bacon and sausage sandwich whilst reading the newspaper, donned in a short blue, towelling bath robe, boxer shorts and white socks.

"Morning," he mumbled through a mouthful of breakfast. His thick mop of blonde hair obviously hadn't seen a brush as yet this morning.

"Morning, Chris." Kate was surprised to see him and not her friend sitting there. "Where's Tina?"

"She's gone into work. She said it would be better to go in sooner so she could get off earlier. Help yourself to some breakfast."

"That's alright thanks; I think I could only stomach a cup of tea. Look, Chris, I'm really sorry about invading your space. I promise it won't be for long. I just need to get myself sorted out."

Chris shrugged his shoulders. "Doesn't make any difference to me, I'm away for a few days now," he replied and returned to his paper.

Kate didn't bother herself further trying to make conversation. Normally she would make the effort in someone else's house but this morning she neither had the energy nor the inclination. She poured herself a cup of tea and took it back to her room. She'd wait until Chris made himself scarce before she went back downstairs.

***

Mike was starting to panic. *Where was Kate this morning,* he thought frantically as Ingrid left the house dragging Jacob behind her? Surely he hadn't missed her moving out. He'd never be able to find her again and then what would he do with himself every morning. His whole day would be disturbed now wondering what had happened to her.

***

Ingrid's patience was rapidly running out. Jacob had not co-operated one iota this morning playing her off against Kate and his father constantly. They had arrived at nursery twenty five minutes late and he had treated her to the biggest temper tantrum she had ever witnessed. Mrs Bentley had lifted him screaming and crying into her office and closed the door whilst another member of staff had comforted Ingrid and taken her back to her car. The other children had stared aghast at his outburst, never having seen him like this before. Five minutes later, Jacob had calmed himself sufficiently to draw a picture of himself, Kate and his father playing football at the park opposite their house.

Ingrid's eyes glazed over as she peered through the windscreen of her car. It was only nine thirty in the morning and her nerves were jangled. How on earth was she going to manage for the rest of the week? The unthinkable fleetingly entered her head. She was the only person apart from his father that Jacob wanted. He hadn't even mentioned his mother this morning, only that damned woman, Kate. She hated to admit it, but they might actually need her back.

***

Kate forced a Scotch pancake down her throat and called it lunch. She had no appetite to speak of whatsoever. She half-heartedly flicked through the pages of the daily paper she had just bought at the local paper shop, until she reached the 'flats to let' section. A part of her was still hoping that Richard would call and beg her to come back, although Ingrid would have to go and that was hardly likely to happen considering the amount of times he had sided with her recently.

She skimmed down the row of vacant flats and her eyes widened as they rested on the words 12A Cedar Vale High Street. Pleasant, one bed roomed flat overlooking the high street. Fully furnished, gas central heating, £385 pcm. So he'd put it up another twenty pounds a month, the thieving scum. The thought of moving back in there was not an option. She wondered if anyone had had the misfortune of living there since she'd been at Richards. Her heart sank as she thought about Richard again and his lack of communication. Her mind was in turmoil. Maybe she would wait until Tina returned from work, then they could sit down and discuss the whole thing. She would know the best thing to do.

***

Ingrid glanced at the clock. Only half an hour more and she would have to go and fetch Jacob from nursery. The thought was chilling. Where had the last couple of hours gone? Just time to have one more strong, black coffee and then she would face the wroth of her four year old tormentor once again.

From the safety of her BMW Z4, Ingrid could see the queue of mothers and child minders waiting to collect their little darlings from the nursery, chatting easily in their cliques. She wondered which one Kate fitted into. There was no way she was going to join them. Anticipating the reception she was about to receive, she hung back until the last of them had departed, then she walked into the building.

Jacob was seated with one of the helpers at a table doing a jigsaw puzzle with his coat on ready. Mrs Bentley greeted her. "Ah, here you are. He's all ready for you."

Ingrid smiled uneasily then cautiously approached him. "Hello, Jacob," she said warily.

"Where's Kate?" he snapped back.

"Jacob," Mrs Bentley scolded sensing another tantrum on its way. "That's not very nice."

"I want Kate," Jacob persisted and the tears started to roll down his face again.

Mrs Bentley gently took his arm and tried to coax him towards the door but he pulled against her. His face reddened and he started to scream.

"I WANT KATE, I WANT KATE."

Ingrid looked on, mortified. She had never been in a situation like this before where she didn't have control and she had no idea how to deal with it. She felt an anger begin to bubble up and cloud her better judgement.

"Jacob, stop it. You are being so naughty. Now I will tell your daddy if you don't put an end to this behaviour and get into the car with me. Kate isn't here so I am picking you up and if you don't stop it, I will tell her never to come back again."

Everyone, including Jacob stopped what they were doing. There, thought Ingrid, that's done the trick—but far from it. Jacob's lip started to shake and he was now sobbing hysterically.

Mrs Bentley picked him up and sat him on her knee.

"Now, now, Jacob," she said rubbing his hand. "It's time to go home and this lady is here to take you." Ingrid thought she heard a bitterness in her tone as she mentioned 'this lady'. "Now you don't want to upset daddy and Kate do you when they hear what you've done?" Jacob had calmed down slightly and he shook his head. "Well in that case, you go home and the sooner you get there, the sooner you can draw a lovely picture for Kate for when she gets back."

That did it. He climbed down off Mrs Bentley's knee and headed towards the door. Ingrid held out her hand to him but he pulled his away in an exaggerated move which suggested that she might have won the battle but she was not going to win the war.

The short journey back to the house was in silence which suited Ingrid fine. Once back home, Jacob went straight to the lounge, took out his crayons and colouring book and carefully began to colour a picture for Kate. It was going to be the best he'd ever done so that she would never leave him again.

Ingrid was quite pleased with herself and the tranquil atmosphere she had created. Richard would be proud of her if he walked in now. She decided to venture the question of some lunch now that she thought she had gained his trust.

"Jacob, what would you like to eat? You must be starving after all that hard work this morning."

"I'm colouring," came the brusque reply.

"But you need to eat as well."

"I don't want anything, I'm colouring."

"Why don't I get you something and you can eat and colour at the same time?"

There was no reply so Ingrid took that as a positive and went into the kitchen. She poured some crisps into a bowl and prepared a sandwich. She carefully placed them next to Jacob on the floor of the lounge and took a step back, ensuring she didn't disturb his concentration. Jacob briefly glanced at them and continued with his task. Ingrid heaved a sigh of relief. Another hurdle jumped, she thought. At least he hadn't thrown the food back at her.

***

Richard was waiting for the first patient on his afternoon list to be anaesthetised.

"Patient's just going on the table, Mr Anderson," Carl said popping his head round the corner of the coffee room.

There was no response. Richard was miles away—wondering how he was going to tell Ingrid this evening that he was going round to the address on the piece of notepaper, to get Kate back. He had every right to, she was Jacob's nanny and it was nothing to do with Ingrid who he hired or fired. They weren't at that position in their relationship for her to make such a decision.

"Mr Anderson, the patient's going into theatre," Carl repeated.

"Oh, thanks, Carl," Richard answered emerging from his trance. "I'll be right there."

***

Ingrid hovered around the kitchen wondering whether to go back into the lounge to make sure Jacob had eaten his lunch, or to just leave him while he was settled. She shook her head. Who was she trying to kid, telling Richard to get rid of the nanny because she would do the job just as well? She was only half way through the day and she was mentally and physically scarred. She secretly admired Kate in a way. She managed to do this day in and day out. The boy wanted and respected her; how had she achieved that? How had she managed to set routines and boundaries? Right at this moment, Ingrid would consider it a major success if he'd eaten the sandwich she had put in front of him, and the crazy thing was, she didn't have the courage to go and find out. Maybe she would put it to Richard later that perhaps she was a touch hasty, planning Kate's exit.

Suddenly the lounge door opened and Jacob appeared. His eyebrows were still furrowed and he carried his picture by his side.

"Have you finished, Jacob?" Ingrid tentatively asked. "May I have a look?"

"I'm putting it in my bedroom for Kate. I'm going to give it to her when she reads me my bedtime story."

"That's a nice idea. I'm sure she will be very touched."

Ingrid had resigned herself to the thought that Kate was coming back now and she was just biding her time alone in Jacob's company. She took the opportunity to look in the lounge and see what he'd eaten for his lunch. To her horror, the crisps had gone and only one bite of the sandwich. Chocolate cake for breakfast and crisps for lunch, what would Richard and Kate think of her?

Jacob was soon back downstairs. "I want to go to the park," he demanded.

Ingrid glanced out of the window. The trees were still bending in the wind. It was hardly the weather to go playing on swings and roundabouts. "Maybe another time, Jacob, it's not a very nice day today. Are you going to eat your sandwich?"

"I don't want it, it's horrid. I want to go to the park."

"Okay, but don't blame me if you get cold."

"I want to take my bike."

"Fine."

She dressed him in warm clothes and safety helmet and retrieved his bike from the garage. They carefully walked across the road before Jacob mounted and was off.

"Not too fast, Jacob," Ingrid shouted behind him. "I don't want to lose you."

But Jacob wasn't listening. He pedalled as fast as he could until he pulled further and further away from his pursuer. Ingrid looked on in trepidation. Not only had she given Jacob the worst possible diet today, but now she was about to lose him. She ran after him, her legs beginning to tremble at her lack of exercise. She was jogging as fast as she could, breathing hard, sucking in huge amounts of air.

"Jacob, stop," she yelled as loud as she could, whilst gasping for breath.

The cold air bit at her throat as she stopped and leaned over, her hands placed on her knees in exhaustion. She could just about see him in the distance. One more bend and he would be gone. She began running again, but the cold was burning her lungs now.

"JACOB, JACOB, STOP."

It was no good; he was out of sight and the light was beginning to fade. An overwhelming feeling of nausea swept though her. She wanted to be sick as a hundred thoughts ran through her mind of paedophiles hiding in the bushes, abductors waiting in cars for unsuspecting little boys... the list went on. Richard would never forgive her if he came to any harm. A surge of adrenaline reached her legs and she made it around the corner.

The first sight that greeted her was Jacob's bike, abandoned on the floor. But where was Jacob? He was nowhere to be seen. Suddenly a dog barked and Ingrid glanced across the field. There he was, kneeling down stroking the West Highland Terrier belonging to an old lady.

"What's she called?" Ingrid could hear him saying.

"She's called Mitzie."

"Can I stroke her?"

"Yes, of course you can, she won't bite."

"JACOB," Ingrid shouted.

Jacob and the old lady looked round.

"Is this your mummy?" the lady asked.

"No, I don't like her," he replied, suddenly being reminded that he was trying to escape and now she'd caught him up.

"Oh dear," the lady replied. "Well, nonetheless, it looks like she's been looking for you so perhaps you'd better go."

"Okay, bye, Mitzie," he said stroking the dogs head.

"Goodbye, dear."

"Jacob, don't you ever do that again," screamed Ingrid.

"I was only stroking a dog."

"I don't mean stroking the dog, I mean racing off like that. I couldn't see you. What if that old lady had been a nasty person who wanted to take you away?"

Jacob started sulking and went to get his bike.

"Oh, no you don't, young man. You're not riding that thing again. I'm not chasing after you like some lunatic. You can walk with me."

She grabbed his hand and dragged him along, his legs nearly lifting off the floor, back in the direction of the house. The old lady stood by watching, pondering as to whether she should intervene or not.

"Come along, Mitzie, time to go," she smiled down at her companion.

"I swear to God I'm going to tell you daddy what a naughty boy you've been today. Do you do this for Kate?" Ingrid ranted at him.

"No," he replied solemnly.

He knew he was in trouble now. He desperately wanted Kate back. He would never have ridden off like that for her. She was far too precious to him to risk her displeasure. Yet despite him being a good boy, she had left him. She'd been gone far too long now for her to have simply gone shopping or to be visiting someone. He started to get worried.

What weren't they telling him? What if Ingrid was looking after him tomorrow as well—and the next day? What if Kate never came back?

The old woman discreetly followed them back to the main road, and watched as they crossed over and entered the large house opposite.

Back inside the house, Ingrid made her displeasure known in no uncertain terms. She was shaking with a mixture of rage and fear.

"Do you have anything to say for yourself, young man?" she asked in anger. Jacob looked up to her with his big blue eyes and shook his head. "Then go into the lounge and think of something and make it good because I am so cross with you at the moment. Imagine if a policeman had seen you racing off like that, he'd have had something to say to you."

It was Jacob now who looked in fear. What if he was put in prison? What if he never saw Kate or his daddy again? He started to cry.

"Now what?" asked Ingrid. "It should be me who's crying, not you. You're not the one who's just run halfway round the park chasing after you."

"I don't want to go to prison," he yelled at the top of his voice. "I want Kate."

Ingrid could feel the muscles in her neck and shoulders tighten. The headache started slowly, then rose to a crescendo of magnanimous proportions. All she wanted to do was lie down in a darkened room, alone. She rubbed her temples in a circular motion with her finger tips and left Jacob to contemplate his actions in the lounge while she made herself a cup of herbal tea. No sooner had she poured the hot water into the cup and breathed in the soothing camomile aroma, when there was a knock at the door. Funny, she wasn't expecting anyone. She half hoped it might be Kate, grovelling for her job back. She opened the door and froze with her mouth agape. Her heart started to thump wildly in her chest.

"Good afternoon, madam; is this your property?"

"No, it's my boyfriend's, why do you ask?"

"May I come in?" The policeman stepped past her before she had time to answer and towered above her in the hallway. He removed his hat and tucked it under his arm. He took out a small notepad and flicked through the pages until he found the one he required.

"Could I ask you your name, madam?"

"It's Ingrid Harper."

"Is there a young boy living in this residence?"

"Yes, he's my boyfriend's son, Jacob," Ingrid replied closing the door.

"Is he here now?"

"Yes."

"Could I see him?"

"Of course, officer, can I ask what this is all about?"

"We've received an anonymous phone call referring to an incident earlier today, where a small boy was seen being mishandled by a woman. The caller followed the two people referred to, back to this address." Ingrid could feel her legs trembling beneath her and looked for something to steady herself on. "Are you aware of any such incident, madam?"

"Yes, I am," Ingrid tried to regain her composure. "I'd taken Jacob to the park and he'd ridden off on his bike so fast that I couldn't keep up and I lost sight of him. I eventually caught up with him round a corner, told him off and dragged him back to the house, which I suppose could have been misconstrued as 'mishandling', but I can assure you, officer that it wasn't. I was just frantic with worry that I might lose him."

"I see, madam, nonetheless, I would like to see the boy in question, please."

"Yes of course, he's in the lounge, follow me."

The policeman followed Ingrid through the house into the lounge where Jacob was still sniffling about the prospect of going to prison. His eyes widened as he watched the tall officer follow Ingrid into the room.

"Hello, young man," said the officer. "My name's PC Brooks, but you can call me Sam. You look a bit upset, are you alright?"

He sat on the sofa next to the young boy. Jacob shied away and sat cowering as far from him on the sofa as he could.

"She said I might go to prison, but I just want Kate and daddy back."

Ingrid closed her eyes in despair. Could things get any worse?

"And who is Kate?"

"She's my nanny."

"Where is she?"

"I don't know."

The officer looked round at Ingrid.

"She left last night. We all had words and I ended up looking after Jacob for the day whilst things calmed down," she said quietly.

He nodded knowingly. Ingrid could practically read his thoughts. The situation was looking grimmer by the second; disagreement with the nanny, altercations in the park, it made her sound like some kind of reprobate.

"Did you run away from this lady in the park?"

Jacob shook his head. Ingrid was mortified. Why was he denying it? It had only just happened.

"I was on my bike," he answered, deciding he quite liked the policeman and it didn't look like he was about to send him to prison. After all, why would he tell him his name if he was going to lock him up?

"Ah, I see, and you went a bit too fast for her to keep up with you?" Jacob nodded this time. "Did you hurt yourself at all?"

"No, I got off my bike to stroke a dog."

This seemed to satisfy the young man. He smiled and stood to his feet. "Everything seems to be in order," he continued. "The person who rang was only being cautious. You can't be too careful these days; you see, any physical contact can be seen as assault so it's probably best not to give the public any cause to worry."

"Thank you, officer Brooks, for your concern. I'll see you to the door."

The policeman replaced his hat and left the house. Ingrid closed the door behind him and stared vacantly in front of her. Her shoulders started to shake and before she could stop herself, she was sobbing inconsolably. Tears of shame rolled down her face and onto the floor. The humiliation was too much for her. Accused of assault on a child, she couldn't believe it. It was as if she'd just stepped outside her body and was looking down on a surreal nightmare enacted by herself. How could a child of four years old, reduce her to this? She turned around, picked the phone up and dialled Richard's mobile number. He answered it immediately from the confines of the coffee room.

"Richard, get yourself home immediately."

*"Ingrid, Ingrid is that you?"*

"Yes it is, and if you don't get home soon, I will walk out of here and leave your son to fend for himself, I swear I will."

*"Ingrid, what on earth has happened?"*

"I've been subjected to food all over the floor, a temper tantrum in front of the whole nursery, charging round the park and the final straw, a visit from the police. Now please come home and sort this mess out."

*"Right, I'll be twenty minutes. Just let me sort my list out."*

The phone went dead. Carl was seated beside him and overheard Richards part of the conversation.

"Is everything alright, Mr Anderson?" he asked concerned.

"Not really, Carl. I need to go home. Sounds like there's a bit of an emergency. Can I leave you to do the last case? It's just an extended carpal tunnel." He drew the line of incision on his wrist with his finger tip. "Usual dressing with a plaster of Paris, volar slab."

"That's no problem, Mr Anderson. I've done a few before."

"Great, I'll ring you later to make sure everything's okay. Tell the anaesthetist for me will you?"

Richard quickly went to get changed and left the building with a churning feeling in his stomach. He knew Ingrid wasn't cut out to look after children, but this sounded serious—the police—how had she managed to get the police involved?

He was true to his word. Twenty minutes later he was pulling up at the front door.

***

Tina had returned from work and she and Kate were having a cup of coffee and contemplating Kate's next move.

"Why don't you stay here until the end of the week, and if he hasn't been in contact by then, start looking for something else? Chris is away for a few days and I'm certainly not going to force you out into a cesspit like the last flat you had."

"Thanks, Tina, I really appreciate this. That cesspit, as you call it, is still up for rent. I saw it in the paper this morning only he wants more money for it."

"You're kidding me." Tina paused for a moment and smiled. "I know it's not the best circumstances, but I'll enjoy the company. I hate being alone when Chris is away."

***

Richard burst through the door, to find Ingrid still crying in the kitchen. His eyes scanned the room for Jacob.

"Ingrid, what's the matter? Where's Jacob?"

"He's upstairs in his room, I sent him there and that's the only peace I've had all day. I'm sorry Richard, I know he's your son and you love him dearly, but that boy is hateful. You'd better get Kate back because I am certainly not looking after him tomorrow."

Richard glanced up quickly. *Get Kate back, did he hear her correctly?*

"Oh, I see," he replied taking umbrage at her caustic comments towards his son. "I thought you wanted to get rid of her."

"Well I've changed my mind. She is obviously some kind of miracle worker with that boy. He has been asking for her all day and quite frankly, they're welcome to each other." Richard stood back aghast. "I'm sorry, Richard. I didn't mean to say that, that was horrible. It's just that I've had the worst day ever. He threw his breakfast all over the floor then stood on it, had a tantrum both going and coming back from nursery, left me in the park and because I was cross at him for disappearing, some hapless member of the public called the police and accused me of child abuse. I had to spend fifteen minutes explaining myself to some young officer as to why I grabbed Jacob's arm to prevent him from running away again."

More tears rolled down her face and Richard felt a pang of sympathy. He put his arms around her and kissed the top of her head.

"I'll go and have a word with him."

"No," she insisted, waving her hand in the air. "Please, go and get Kate first. I need to go home and have a lie down."

"Okay."

***

Tina had started to cook dinner, well, she'd thrown a couple of jacket potatoes into the microwave and was mashing some sweet corn into a tin of tuna.

"Shall we have a bottle of wine to go with this; it might just drown the taste?"

Kate managed a smile. Tina had never had much in the way of culinary skills. Her cooking was nearly as bad as her cups of tea. They were disturbed by the sound of the doorbell.

"You get that and I'll finish off the tuna," Kate offered.

Kate could hear voices but couldn't quite make out whether they were male or female. Tina was soon back in the kitchen, her eyes wide.

"It's for you, it's Richard . . . he's gorgeous," she mouthed.

Kate started to breathe rapidly and it was all she could do to stop herself from smiling.

"Did he say what he wanted?"

"No, just that he wanted to speak to you. He's in the hall."

Kate opened the kitchen door and sure enough, Richard was stood in front of her, still dressed in his suit with a long overcoat shielding him from the rain.

"Hi, Kate." He smiled when he saw her.

"Richard, what are you doing here?"

"I've come to apologise. I'm so sorry for what happened. I don't know if you can ever forgive me but we both, that's Jacob and I, want you back . . . desperately."

Kate could see the old Richard for a moment, the one she'd known on the way to Scotland. She would have gladly walked out of the house with him, there and then, but there was still one problem casting a huge shadow over the whole sorry mess.

"What about Ingrid? Does she know you're here?"

Kate was trying to gauge his feelings for her. Was she still in the picture or had things cooled down after yesterday?

"She looked after Jacob today, and I think she wants to go home to have a nervous breakdown. Apparently he asked for you all day . . ." Kate smiled to herself, ". . . and somehow the police were involved at one point."

"WHAT, what happened?"

"Oh, she lost it with him; he'd raced off on his bike and disappeared for a while so she dragged him back home and someone reported her."

Kate put her hand up to her mouth to stem the flow of laughter. Richard smiled at her. "She's hopeless with him." Suddenly he was serious again. "We need you, Kate, please come back."

Kate thought for a moment.

"I don't know if I can be in the same house as Ingrid. She can't stand me."

"Oh, believe me, Kate, after today, I think she has a new found admiration for you."

"Really?"

"Really."

"Okay then, but Tina's just made me something to eat."

Tina burst out of the kitchen.

"I'm sure Richard can get you a takeaway on the way. It's not exactly Gordon Ramsay is it?"

"Thanks, Tina," Richard said gratefully.

"I'll go and get my cases then."

Kate ran upstairs whilst Tina made the most of her few seconds alone with Richard. She was soon at the top of the stairs carrying her worldly goods in her old battered cases. Richard ran up the stairs to carry them down whilst Kate said goodbye to her friend.

"Thanks, Tina, for looking after me again."

"No problem. Hope everything goes okay."

The two women hugged each other.

"Thanks, Tina," said Richard as they left the house.

Tina closed the door behind them, thankful her friend was going to be alright but already missing her company.

***

Ingrid didn't move from the kitchen for fear of disturbing Jacob upstairs thus risking the chance of him coming down and repeating his histrionic behaviour all over again. She was so pleased when she heard the sound of the front door and the voices of Richard *and* Kate. She walked out to meet them, but before she managed to get there, the sound of footsteps could be heard upstairs. Jacob had heard his beloved Kate first.

"Kate," he shouted with joy running down the stairs.

Kate smiled up at her little friend. She presumed that his naughtiness was the reason she was back, but nonetheless, she'd missed him and wallowed in his welcome as her eye caught Ingrid in the hall doorway.

"Hello, Jacob," she laughed as he threw himself at her and squeezed the life out of her.

Ingrid could only stand back and admire. After the day she'd just experienced, she would loved to have had that connection with the boy. Instead, she couldn't wait to get out of the place and anaesthetise her weary head with a large brandy. She presumed he couldn't wait to see the back of her as well which saddened her. Her relationship with Richard somewhat depended on them getting on. She couldn't see a future without that possibility. But she'd work on that another time. Her head would burst if she didn't get out soon.

"Hello, Kate," Ingrid ventured in the middle of all the salutations.

"Hello, Ingrid."

"Thank you for coming back. I'm so sorry for upsetting you yesterday. I wasn't thinking properly."

Kate breathed deeply. She had nothing to say in answer to the woman, she wasn't about to forgive her although, as a gesture, she felt she should prompt Jacob into saying something.

"Jacob, do you have something to say to Ingrid?"

"Sorry," he said with his head tilted down and his eyes on the floor.

Ingrid merely nodded and walked past them both.

"I'll see you on Wednesday," she virtually whispered to Richard.

"I'll walk you to your car." It was the least he could do under the circumstances.

Kate took Jacob through to the lounge and seated herself next to him on the sofa. "So, what happened today? Ingrid seemed very upset when she left."

Jacob looked glum. "I didn't want her to look after me, I wanted you. If you'd have been here I wouldn't have been naughty," he replied, applying his childlike logic to the situation.

"But that's not the point, Jacob. Whoever is looking after you, you should be a good boy." Jacob looked thoughtful. "I suppose in a way this is my fault. I should have told you that I wouldn't be here. It must have been a bit of a shock waking up and finding someone else looking after you, but sometimes unexpected things happen, and you've got to be a big boy and cope with them."

"Well, she wasn't very nice to me."

"Why not?"

"She got the policeman to take me to prison, but he was nice and he didn't."

"Jacob, they don't take little boys like you to prison."

"Do they not?"

"No."

Richard walked into the room at that point with a stern look on his face. "Well young man, what have you to say for yourself?"

"Kate said it was her fault."

"What?" asked Richard flabbergasted.

"She said it was her fault for not telling me she wouldn't be there, but that I was still a naughty boy for what I did."

Richard looked at Kate and shook his head.

"Don't ever do that again, do you understand me?"

Jacob nodded and considered himself told. He thought he'd got off pretty lightly considering his behaviour today but he wasn't about to say anything that might lessen his chances of a reprieve.

"I think it's time we all had something to eat. Are you hungry, Jacob?" said Kate.

"Yes, I'm starving."

"What have you had to eat today?" she asked, intrigued as to what Ingrid had made for him.

"Chocolate cake and crisps?"

"What?" both adults said simultaneously.

"I had chocolate cake for breakfast and crisps for lunch. I had one bite of sandwich but I didn't like it so I left the rest."

"I'll go and make something," Kate decided before the conversation took a dive into deeper waters.

She disappeared into the kitchen and started to rummage through the cupboards to find something that would make a meal for all of them. Time was ticking by and Kate thought it best that Jacob had an early night tonight after the day he'd just had.

Richard took his chance and followed Kate into the kitchen.

"Thanks for coming back, Kate," he said quietly so as not to let Jacob hear. He didn't want him to find out the real reason for Kate not being there today.

Kate spun round. Richard was looking at her intensely.

"I'm glad you came for me."

"You know I was going to come round and ask you to come back whether Ingrid had had a bad day or not. I was going to come after work. It's just not the same when you're not here." They were staring at each other now. "I should have stood up to Ingrid. I'm so sorry."

"It's alright, Richard. I know you would never have said anything like that. The thing that worried me was that she was calling the shots. If she gets to do that, my job will never be safe."

"As far as I'm concerned, your job will always be safe."

He moved towards her, slid his arms around her waist and squeezed her tight. Kate folded her arms around his shoulders and held him too, for what seemed like an eternity. He felt so good, close to her like that. Then, without warning, he was looking into her eyes. She could feel the intensity burning into her. He focussed on her lips and suddenly he was kissing her; a loving, caring kiss that Kate wanted to go on and on forever . . . but she had to pull away.

"Richard . . . you have a girlfriend."

"Yes," he sighed, reluctantly walking away.

Kate smiled and watched him as he made his way back to Jacob. He turned around for one last look and caught her smiling at him. He winked slowly and for the first time since Ingrid had arrived on the scene, she felt an overwhelming connection. The last few seconds would stay with her forever; she would run through them over and over again in a bid to get every detail just right.

# Chapter . . .

# 17

Melissa had just returned from a full days shopping with her mother. They were both laden down with bags. Her father, Jack, was seated by the window reading the paper and is eyes rolled as he focussed on the shopping.

"What's the matter, dad?" Melissa asked him. "You should have come with us if you want to control the amount mum spends."

"You know your mother; she has this amazing talent of sneaking off and buying things when I'm not looking. She's just as bad when I'm there. I might as well enjoy the peace and quiet before I get the credit card bill."

Both women laughed and took their purchases upstairs before Alex had time to see them when he came in from work.

"Do you think we'll get the chance to see Jacob again before we go or do you think that's pushing it a bit with Richard?" Val asked her daughter as they spread their new clothes over the bed to admire them.

"I was going to give him a ring later and ask. Maybe I could speak to Kate and she could have a word with him. She seems to have a bit more influence than me."

"Would you try Melissa? It would be a shame to come all this way and only see him the once."

It was Kate who answered the phone. *"Oh, hi, Melissa. How are you?"*

"I'm fine thanks. I wonder, could I speak to Richard?"

*"He's not in at the moment. He's still at work. Can I get him to ring you when he gets home?"*

"Yes, I just wanted to ask him if my parents could see Jacob again before they fly back home?"

*"I'm sure he won't mind. When are they going back?"*

"On Saturday."

*"Leave it with me, I'll have a word with him."*

"Do you not mind?"

*"No, of course not."*

"Thanks, Kate, that's so kind of you, bye."

*"Bye, Melissa."*

***

Melissa was glad Richard wasn't in. Kate would do a much better job of convincing him than she would.

"I've had a word with Kate, mum. She's pretty sure she can arrange it."

"Oh, that will be nice. It's such a long time until the summer holidays, that's if he can come."

"Hopefully by then I'll be able to have partial custody," Melissa thought out loud.

"Don't presume anything dear and then you won't be disappointed. We'll be pleased if we get to see him before we go home."

***

It was later that evening when Richard returned the call.

"I believe you want Jacob one night." He sounded rather abrupt and Melissa knew she had to tread carefully.

*"Yes, Richard, my parent's were wondering if they could see him again before they go home, they're leaving on Saturday?"*

The mere mention of her parents seemed to pacify him. He had always got on well with them. His mood soon mellowed and his voice took on a different tone.

"That's fine. I'll bring him round on Friday when I get in from work."

*"That's great, thank you."*

Melissa was a little disappointed. He could arrive home at any time. What if he was delayed at work? It could be seven, eight o'clock and then it would be his bedtime. At that point, she heard voices at the other end of the phone.

"Just a minute, Melissa, Kate says she'll bring him round earlier then he can have a bit longer with you. What time are your parents leaving?"

*"We're taking them to the airport at ten on Saturday."*

There was a pause again whilst Richard considered something.

"Do you want Jacob to stay with you overnight so that he can come with you? He might like a trip to the airport to see his grandparents off."

*"Oh, Richard, do you not mind? That would be wonderful. Thank Kate for me as well would you for bringing him over. I can't tell you how much I appreciate that, really I can't."*

Richard was overcome with his wife's gratitude. He'd never heard her be grateful for anything before unless if was very expensive.

"She sounded pleased, Kate, really pleased. She said thanks for taking him over. Do you not mind?"

"Not at all and now you won't have one eye on the clock all the way through your list. Imagine if you got off late, we'd be picking him back up to go to bed before he'd got there."

"You're right, as usual."

She smiled at him, still remembering his kiss from the day before. In fact, she'd barely thought about anything else all day.

"Did they come and do that fence panel and the shed window?"

"Yes, they arrived just as I was about to go for Jacob, so I had to leave them to it. They seem to have done a good job."

"I'll have to paint that panel this weekend if I get chance. By the way, I forgot to tell you, I won't be in for dinner tomorrow," he said nonchalantly flicking through his mail. "I'm going to a charity do with Ingrid and she wants to leave early. She's helping to set it up. I'll probably end up putting chairs out and folding napkins."

He started to laugh but Kate wasn't listening as a pang of jealousy ripped though her. Just at the point where he'd mentioned Ingrid's name, she had lost interest and gone to find Jacob in the lounge. Her disappointment was now complete. He was still seeing Ingrid and that equated to his kiss meaning absolutely nothing.

***

"I don't believe it," Melissa announced.

"You don't believe what?" asked Alex, just walking in after a hard day at the office.

"Richard has agreed to let Jacob stay overnight on Friday. He said it would be nice if Jacob came with us to the airport so that he could wave mum and dad off."

Her parents were overjoyed. Their daughter had finally done something right where Jacob was concerned and she was being rewarded for her efforts.

"That's wonderful, dear. There's hope for the summer holidays yet," her mother said waving her crossed fingers in the air.

***

Ingrid had finally recovered from her day with Jacob. Her tension headache had subsided by the following morning—although the medicinal brandy had left its mark with a slight hangover. She was ready again to pursue Richard and keep the 'precious' Kate as far away from him as possible. She was well aware that removing Kate from the Anderson household was not an option for the time being, so her task now was to eliminate Richard from the house by going on as many dates as she could concoct.

She'd already covered Wednesday evening with the Marclough Charity Dinner. She would pick him up early and make sure she delivered him back home when everyone else was tucked up in bed, that's if she couldn't persuade him to stay the night. Funny, he seemed a little reluctant to do that at the moment. Maybe he needed to get back for Jacob.

She would have to get her thinking cap on and get the next date planned. Maybe she would drop that on him on the way to the function. She didn't want to leave it too late into the evening in case she got distracted, or worse still, he got drunk and forgot. It was never the same arranging these things over the phone. It gave him too much of an opportunity to say no.

She rummaged through her wardrobe looking for something extra special for him tomorrow night. There was a bit of fixing to do after her poor performance as child minder. Maybe she would take Jacob some more of those sugary sweets that Kate despised so much. He seemed to like them. That's the closest she had come to any kind of bond between them, when they had sat together on the sofa after Kate had fled the room. It would be a kind of 'olive branch', a little something to say 'no hard feelings', 'let's start again'. Yes, she would do that.

***

Gerald Royston poured himself a bowl of Corn Flakes. Gone were the days when his wife would have a cooked breakfast prepared before he'd finished shaving. He'd enjoyed scrambled eggs on toast or a bacon sandwich with a mug of piping hot tea every morning for as long as he could remember. Now Dorothy could barely get out of bed in time to wave him off.

He poured the cold milk on his cereal. He always wished he'd liked hot milk, especially on days like this when you could see your breath in the air outside, but he didn't like the way it made the flakes go all soggy so he persevered and quickly drank his tea afterwards in order to warm himself up.

Dorothy appeared at the door in her nightie and dressing gown.

"Oh, I'd have done that, Gerald."

"I think I can pour myself some cereal, Dorothy. Get yourself a cup of tea and take the paper back up to bed with you. You should take it easy."

"Take it easy, I don't do anything but these days. I can never seem to get myself going."

"Why don't you go shopping this afternoon? Buy yourself something nice like a dress or a top."

"I don't think so; it's no fun on your own."

"Why not ask Sonia Patterson to go with you? She loves shopping, so her husband says, and he should know." Gerald laughed at his own joke and continued with his breakfast. Dorothy ignored his last suggestion and went back to bed. She wasn't in the right frame of mind for Sonia today, she was far too frivolous. All she felt like doing was going back to sleep. She was so shattered by the sleepless nights, lying there wondering if her children were ever going to call her again. The day times seemed to be spent catching up on lost sleep. It was all a vicious circle and try as she might, she didn't know how to get out of it.

A terrifying thought had crossed her mind several times in the last few days. What if she needed help and had to be admitted onto a psychiatric unit? She knew she needed to get her act together or Gerald would start intervening with his medical colleagues. He'd always been friendly with Patrick Flynn, the clinical psychiatrist. They'd known each other since medical school. If he got wind of what was happening, who knows where she would end up. She pulled the quilt over her head to try and blank out the thought.

***

Kate dropped Jacob off at nursery.

"It's so good to see you again, Kate. I don't think Jacob was too enamoured with that lady who brought him yesterday," said Mrs Bentley tactfully.

"Don't you think so?" Kate asked hopefully. If Jacob didn't like Ingrid, could there really be a future for her and Richard. "I must admit, she's not the easiest person to get on with."

"No, to be truthful, she didn't come across as very friendly. It's no wonder he kicked off like he did."

Kate fought to keep the smile off her face and said goodbye to Jacob.

"Bye, Kate, will you be coming for me?" he asked before she left.

"Yes, don't worry, I'll be here."

"See what I mean," Mrs Bentley added. 'He's petrified she'll come back. She's put the fear of God in him, poor little thing."

The two women smiled knowingly then Kate made her excuses and left. She was on a mission. She'd had an idea for the afternoon and was about to search the garden shed for some matching fence paint. She and Jacob were going to paint the new fence panel to save Richard the trouble at the weekend. He worked hard enough during the week. He deserved some time with Jacob on his days off.

***

The shed had been disturbed since it had lost its window the previous weekend. The joiner had moved things around and the wind had blown half the leaves from the garden in there. She would clean it out and hopefully come across some paint.

After about an hour the shed was restored to its former glory and Kate stood in the garden with her pot of fence paint making sure it matched that already on the other panels. The colour was the correct match so she put it to one side with a couple of brushes for later. She just had time to clear the breakfast dishes and tidy up inside before going back for Jacob.

He was ready with his coat on eagerly awaiting her return. He shouted as she appeared at the doorway. "Kate, I'm here.

I've drawn you a picture." He was waving the picture in his hand as Kate approached. He flattened it out on one of the small tables to show her. "That's me, that's you and that's daddy."

Kate felt choked as she just about made out her and Richard holding hands behind the little figure of Jacob. Mrs Bentley strolled over to them.

"Do you think he's trying to tell you something?" she smiled and nodded at Kate.

Kate could feel herself flush. It was alright for her to have these kinds of thoughts but when it became the talk of the nursery . . . The other nursery staff started to giggle as she carried Jacob's picture for him. Had they all been discussing it? Kate couldn't wait to get out of the door.

"Do you like my picture, Kate?"

"I love it, Jacob," she replied. "I love all your pictures, they're so colourful. Do you remember that one you did for me when I lived in that flat and I put it on my bedroom wall?"

"Yes."

"Well, I've still got it and I'll always treasure it."

"I'm going to show this to daddy when he gets home."

"I think Ingrid will be with him so maybe keep it until tomorrow when he's on his own. We're going to do some painting this afternoon."

"Are we?"

"Yes, but not on a piece of paper, we're going to paint the new fence panel with some special paint which will preserve it for longer."

"What does pweserve mean?"

"It means keep it looking good for longer."

"Can I help?"

"Of course you can, I'm going to need your help or we won't get it done before daddy comes home from work. We want it to be a surprise. We'll have something to eat first because we'll need all our energy to do this job. What do you want for lunch?"

"Erm, a ham sandwich and some grapes, please."

"That's a good boy and lovely manners as well."

Jacob sighed proudly. He was so happy to have Kate back with him. He never wanted another day like Monday ever again. He seemed to have got away with his behaviour where his father and Kate were concerned, although he hadn't seen Ingrid since. The idea of her coming round later made his tummy feel a little queasy. What if she was horrible to him again? Maybe he would hide somewhere, possibly the shed if they were going to be in the garden, then he wouldn't have to see her. The longer he left it, the more chance there was that she might forget.

After a quick lunch they went into the back garden. The new fence panel jumped out at them, bare and patiently awaiting its coat of paint. Kate took the lid off the pot and looked in dismay. It was so watery. *She* was going to have trouble not sloshing it everywhere, never mind her little helper. Jacob, dressed in an old pair of fleecy tracksuit pants and his recently downgraded winter coat, took the first dip. He carefully moved across the soil to the fence and applied the paint, barely spilling a drop.

"Well done, Jacob, good boy," said Kate about to copy his technique.

They both stood on the flower bed in front of the fence chatting away together. Jacob related the whole of Monday step by step, safe in the knowledge that there would be no further repercussions—Kate had promised him that, and he believed every word she said. They had nearly finished around four thirty when the light started to fade.

"Kate, would you do that bit down there, I don't want to paint the post?"

"Of course I will."

She bent down and dabbed a bit of paint in the corner. As she went to stand up, Jacob turned back to the fence with his brush fully loaded and ready to go. He wiped it straight across Kate's face, a line of Rustic Oak from one side to the other. Jacob looked horrified as he realised what he'd done. Kate looked shocked at first then started to laugh and before long they were both in hysterics.

"Jacob, what do I look like?" she screamed.

Jacob couldn't speak for giggling. At that point, Richard and Ingrid arrived at the house. He'd managed to leave work early and was heading for the shower when he heard the laughter from the back garden.

"Is that Kate and Jacob, what on earth are they doing?" he asked turning towards Ingrid.

"It sounds like they're laughing."

Richard opened the back door and there were Kate and his son, tears streaming down their faces.

"Daddy, look at Kate's face."

Richard started to laugh as well. Ingrid came to the door to see what was happening. She sniggered and went back into the house. Honestly, Kate was so common. Why would anyone paint a fence when you can hire someone to do the job for you?

Richard stared at the fence and his face was still. "Have you two done that?"

"Yes, daddy, and I asked Kate to do a bit at the bottom which I couldn't do and I accidentally painted her face."

He shook his head. Kate was looking concerned. Was he annoyed that *they'd* done it and not got a professional in?

"I can't believe you've done that," he continued.

Now Jacob was looking worried. "Do you like it, daddy?"

"Like it? I love it. It's the best painted fence panel in the whole garden and do you know why?" Jacob shook his head in wonderment. "Because you two did it. Thanks Kate, thanks Jacob," he said crouching beside his son and giving him a big hug.

Richard was nearly reduced to tears, only these weren't tears of laughter, he was genuinely touched by what they had done. Kate and Richard smiled at each other. She hadn't expected him to be so appreciative. She was glad now that they'd taken the trouble.

"I think we better go and clean up, do you, Jacob?" said Kate. "I hope this comes off."

She wiped a finger across her face and looked to see if it had dried. Jacob started giggling again as he watched her. They tidied up, washed the brushes, put everything back in the shed and then the two of them went back into the house. It had started to get cold now the sun had disappeared. Jacob shivered then his face dropped as his eyes met Ingrid's seated in the dining room reading the paper. In all the mirth, he'd forgotten that she was coming to the house.

"Hello, Jacob, how are you? You seem a little happier than the last time I saw you; perhaps I just caught you on a bad day."

She'd decided against the sweets. She wasn't going to reward him for his bad behaviour. Jacob put his head down, ran past her and up the stairs.

"Hello, Ingrid," said Kate.

Ingrid looked up at her rival's face and smirked.

"Oh my, Kate, I didn't realise you were into tribalism. When does the ritual begin?"

Kate was in no mood for the woman's sarcasm and merely smiled to appease her as she walked past.

***

Doubts started to drift into Richard's mind as he stood beneath the pulsating, warm shower. What was he doing with Ingrid? Where exactly was it going? Yes, she had breeding and a bit of class, she was good at conversing but what about the things that actually mattered when the surface had been scratched away? She didn't make any attempt to get on with Kate, his friends weren't very enamoured with her, she was sarcastic, tactless and manipulative but most important of all, Jacob didn't like her. The most important person in his life didn't connect in any way with her. He wondered sometimes if he was seeing her just to please his mother. Then it dawned on him. He was seeing Ingrid because Kate had pushed him in her direction, encouraged him and in so doing, had rejected him.

When he'd kissed her the other night, she'd stopped him because he had a girlfriend—not because she didn't want him to kiss her. She'd watched and smiled at him as he'd walked away. That wasn't the action of someone who wasn't interested.

He had always harboured a nagging thought that his mother had intervened at New Year. Now it made sense. Kate had been forced to persuade him to go and meet Ingrid. Knowing Kate she wouldn't want to have hurt his mother's feelings by refusing.

He stepped out of the shower and dried himself. His dinner suit was hung on the outside of the wardrobe door. He stared at it reluctantly. He'd much rather be putting on a t-shirt and a pair of jogging pants than that. If he was being honest, he would much rather stay in tonight with Kate and Jacob than go out to some pretentious charity do with Ingrid. Maybe he would say something at the end of the evening. He couldn't back out now—it wouldn't be fair, especially as she was helping to organise everything.

He could hear Jacob in his bedroom with his television on. He was waiting for Kate to get ready before they went downstairs, scared to venture there alone in case he found himself on his own with Ingrid. What was he doing to his son, inflicting this woman on him?

Richard finally made his way downstairs.

"My, don't we look handsome?" Ingrid said floating over to him and adjusting his bow tie.

It was all Richard could do to stop himself from pulling away. He didn't want to be fussed over. Suddenly it didn't seem appropriate her touching him in that manner.

"We're going now, Kate, bye Jacob," he shouted from the foot of the stairs.

Kate appeared at the top of the stairs with her bathrobe on, rubbing her hair with a bath towel.

"Okay, enjoy yourselves."

Richard paused for a moment. She looked so lovely with no makeup and her hair dripping wet. She was so natural unlike Ingrid whom he had never seen yet without full war paint. He'd never seen her dress casually come to think of it.

"I'll probably be late," Richard emphasised. It was aimed more at Ingrid to stress that he would not be staying with her tonight.

"Don't wait up," Ingrid mouthed just above a whisper.

She strutted out behind Richard as if she'd just won him in some kind of competition. It didn't go unnoticed. Everything she did now started to chip away at his composure. Why did she feel that hurting the people he loved would raise her higher in his estimation? On the contrary, she was sinking fast.

Ingrid had offered to drive so that she had the control. She could decide when and if she was going to have a drink and consequently whether they would have to get a taxi back to Richard's so he could take her back for her car the following day. She had it all deviously planned.

***

Kate couldn't get Richard's expression out of her head. She had been trying to analyse it but was having difficulty. He seemed to look solemn, almost sad as if he was being made to do something he didn't want to. And as for those eyes, they were practically pleading her to help him to stay. Could he be getting tired of Ingrid at last? Oh, she hoped so.

Jacob appeared around his bedroom door. "Have they gone?" he asked with fear in his eyes.

"Yes, sweetheart," she smiled and rubbed the top of his head. "I'll be down as soon as I've dried my hair. Are you hungry?"

***

Richard's monosyllabic answers were beginning to unnerve Ingrid. She had exhausted the topic of work, her day appeared to be of no interest to him, she couldn't even entertain the idea of suggesting another date on Friday with him in this frame of mind. Her next question was going to be 'what's wrong', but she didn't have the confidence to go ahead with that for fear of his curt reply. She needed to make some headway or the evening was going to be a disaster. His first appearance at the Marclough Charities Society gathering would seal their impression of him for the foreseeable future.

Unfortunately for Richard, his brusqueness had an adverse effect. When they finally reached their destination and got out of the car, Ingrid clung to him as if to let him go would mean to lose him forever. She looped her arm though his as they walked through the door; a picture of togetherness to the untrained eye. To Richard, it felt like an albatross hanging from his arm and he longed to break free from her clutches. When would she get the message that he wasn't in the mood for her this evening. He eventually shook himself free when they arrived at the door and he courteously opened it for her. All eyes inside the hall turned towards them as they entered.

"Ingrid, darling, how are you and this must be Richard? How wonderful to meet you at last. We've all heard so much about you." Victoria Conley, President of the Marclough Charities society stepped forward and reached out her hand. "Plastic surgery, eh, we could all do with a bit of that couldn't we girls?"

Several of the ladies behind her tittered and carried on with their organising, each periodically taking a little peek at the handsome surgeon who had just graced them with his presence.

Victoria was in her mid fifties and looked like she'd just walked out of a scene from Miss Marple. Her plaid skirt swung as she walked and her tightly curled hair stayed firmly in its place after a good lashing of hairspray. She was a good sort though and the heart and soul of events like this. They all knew that the whole society would collapse if she ever lost interest.

"Now, Richard," Victoria continued. "Would you mind placing the chairs around the tables and Ingrid, I'd like you to put all these flowers into vases and place one in the middle of each table? Janet, could you put the cutlery out and Gwen the glasses? There, things are coming along nicely," Victoria smiled, surveying her hard work whilst mentally calculating the time versus jobs-to-do.

The hall stood ready and waiting for the throng of guests to arrive. As they filtered in and took their seats, Richard found himself seated next to Bernard Helliwell, Gwen's husband, for the charity dinner. He stared at the cutlery in front of him and had never felt less like eating in his life. There were voices all around him, chattering and conversing with each other but his world was closed to it all as his mind drifted back to Kate wrapped up in her white, fluffy bathrobe with her damp hair falling around her shoulders.

Bernard was finding it difficult to strike up a conversation with the young doctor much to Ingrid's annoyance. He seemed to be in a thoughtful mood and Bernard couldn't quite bring himself to interrupt him. The only problem was that he knew Gwen would chastise him later if he didn't attempt some kind of repartee with him so he decided to broach another topic from the one they were discussing around the table. The Banberry Horticultural Show was obviously not something that grasped his interest or he would have joined in.

"So Richard, do you have any children?" Bernard asked cheerily.

"Yes, I have a son."

"Really," he replied, pleased with himself that he had got a reply at last. "How old is he?"

"He's four."

"Oh, quite a handful then. Will he be starting school next time?"

"Yes, in September. He's at nursery at the moment."

"Ours are grown up now but I can remember when they were that small, they were into everything. It's a bit easier once they start school, but then, they learn how to be cheeky. Gwen didn't work then of course." He wished he hadn't said his last comment as he realised that Richard must be separated from his wife since he was here with Ingrid. He tried to repair the damage. "Is he with his mother?"

"No, he has a nanny."

"Oh, you'd better be careful, Ingrid. You hear stories of men running off with the nanny," he said laughing.

Gwen nudged him hard with her elbow.

"I used to be worried, Bernard, but not after this afternoon." Ingrid said turning her attention to their conversation. Richard looked at her, intrigued as to her next comment. "You should have seen her after she'd painted a fence panel with Jacob, Richard's son. Honestly, why don't people learn and get someone in to do these jobs? Her face was covered in it. She looked an absolute sight."

Gwen shook her head in disbelief. "She was actually painting the fence herself?" Gwen queried.

"Yes, her and Jacob."

"What's wrong with that?" asked Richard defensively. "Are you saying that I would find her any less attractive because she had paint all over her face?" He laughed. "Quite the opposite actually; that to me makes her more attractive because she was prepared to do it in the first place. I'd said I was going do it at the weekend and she was saving me the trouble."

It was the most he'd said all evening only it wasn't what Ingrid wanted to hear, and most definitely not what she wanted the rest of the table to hear.

"Richard, do you mind?" she whispered sharply to him.

"Well, if you're going to bad mouth her in front of everyone, I'm going to defend her in her absence," he replied equally tersely.

"Richard, will you please be quiet?"

Ingrid could feel the eyes of the table on her. Richard couldn't care less. He didn't want to be here in the first place, but she had built their relationship up to be something that was going places and this was not how it appeared at present. She was furious with him.

Gwen was telling Bernard off now.

"I was only making a joke," he sighed.

"Well it wasn't funny," Gwen scolded him. "Look what you've done now."

Richard could feel the anger welling up inside him. How dare this privileged woman have a go at Kate like that? What did she know anyway? She'd probably never done a days DIY in her life. Mummy and Daddy more than likely paid for it all. He fell silent again and stared vacantly at the flowers in the middle of the table. A plate of roast beef, Yorkshire pudding and all the trimmings was placed in front of him. He looked at it for a moment then pushed it to one side.

"Do you not want those roast potatoes, Richard?" Bernard began. Gwen gave him a second nudge. "What?"

"No, it's fine Bernard. Help yourself. It's a pity to waste them."

Richard passed the plate on. He could feel Ingrid's anger heighten but he was helpless to do anything about it. He simply didn't want to be there and he wasn't in the mood for acting the devoted boyfriend. Ingrid took a mouthful of her dinner then pushed that away too. She was sickened to the stomach. What was he playing at? She was beginning to see where Jacob got his antics from. She scraped her chair back.

"Excuse me," she announced to the rest of the table. "I can feel a headache coming on. I'm going outside to get some fresh air."

"Are you alright, Ingrid?" Gwen asked concerned. "Do you want me to come with you?"

"No, thank you, Gwen. I'd rather be on my own if you don't mind."

She marched out of the room rubbing her forehead. Richard followed; finally he had the opportunity to escape. They met in the foyer. Ingrid's eyes were blazing. Richard stood tall and prepared himself for the onslaught.

"Why are you doing this, Richard?" she asked in a slow, threatening voice. "Why are you trying to humiliate me in front of my friends?"

"To show you how it feels."

"What?"

"You sit there showing off to your friends, making derogatory remarks about Kate, expecting me to listen and do nothing."

"That woman," Ingrid said shaking her hands in the air. "If I hear that woman's name again I'm going to . . ."

"What are you going to do, Ingrid, come on tell me?"

"I don't want her in our lives anymore. You'd better get rid of her or we are through. I mean it Richard."

"Like I did the last time when you begged me to go and get her back."

"That was different, I know now that you need a nanny, but it doesn't have to be *her.*"

"Yes it does have to be her. It will always be her as far as I'm concerned because my son loves her and . . ." He stopped. It was true; he did love Kate only he'd never actually said it out loud before.

"And what?" she hissed.

". . . so do I."

Ingrid went white. The bottom of her world had just dropped out and she had no way of retrieving it. She was fooling herself to think that getting rid of Kate would solve all her problems. He had just admitted he was in love with her and it was more than she could take.

"You bastard," she shouted. "You bastard, I hate you."

She thumped him hard on the chest as the tears poured down her face. Victoria appeared around the door anxious to see what the shouting was about. "Ingrid, dear, whatever is the matter?"

Ingrid stared at Richard. "You tell her. Come on, Richard, be a man and tell Victoria why you choose this moment to tell me you're leaving me for some slut."

He should have walked away at that point but there she was again, insulting the woman who he now wanted, more than anyone, in his life.

"She's not a slut, Ingrid. Please don't call her that, she's . . ."

"I think it's time you left, don't you, Richard?" Victoria interrupted.

Her menacing glare told him not to argue. He took one last look at Ingrid. "I'm sorry, Ingrid, I should have done this better," then turned and walked out of the door.

Ingrid collapsed on Victoria's shoulder and cried.

"There, there," said the older woman stroking her hair.

"I must be . . . the laughing stock of . . . the whole place," she said between sobs. "I built us up to be . . . the perfect couple and then he dumps me . . . in front of them all."

"No one else heard, Ingrid," she lied. "They're all chatting and eating in there. Most of them haven't even noticed you're missing. Now, I'm going to get Maurice to give you a lift home whilst I conduct the auction. You get yourself to bed and in the morning, things will look a lot different. Maybe you should pop up to Scotland. Go and see your parents for a little TLC. Mother's always know what to do for the best. Or failing that, you could give me a ring and I'll come round. We'll have a nice cup of coffee and a chat."

Ingrid was gaining her composure. She'd never experienced Victoria's caring side before, only the domineering, organised one. She suddenly regretted all those looks she had exchanged with the others when she had been dishing out her orders. None of them really knew her.

"Thank you, Victoria. I'll wait here if you don't mind. I told them at my table that I had a headache, would you mind telling them that it was a migraine and I've gone home."

"Of course I will, now have you left anything behind before I get Maurice?"

"No, I have my bag and my coat's in the cloakroom."

Victoria looked into her eyes. "Now, chin up, girl. He's not worth the heartache. Life will be much simpler without his baggage to contend with."

Ingrid fought back another wave of tears as Victoria disappeared back into the hall to find Maurice.

***

A heavy drizzle filled the air. Richard pulled his jacket around him, put his head down and headed back along the driveway to the main road. He paused at the end as he tried to remember the direction to take back to the village of Marclough. He hadn't been paying that much attention on the way here. His mind had been elsewhere. He had a long time to think now as he contemplated the walk back. What would he say to Kate? How would she react? Would she want him after all that had happened recently? His mind started to recall her face earlier that day, covered in paint and how she and Jacob had laughed together. It was the loveliest sight he'd ever seen. His thoughts drove him on through the darkness.

Half a mile more, the finger post sign read. He was soaked to the skin but it fed him with a new energy. Finally he could see the street lights ahead and the sign of the Old Fox pub. Surely he'd find a phone there to ring for a taxi.

The pub was quiet for a Wednesday night. An old gentleman was seated at the bar and a couple chatted in the far corner. The barman was conversing with the old man whilst drying a pint pot with his starched, white, tea towel. They all stared at Richard as he entered. Richard smiled as if nothing was amiss.

"Do you have a phone I could use, please? My car's broken down up the road and I need to get a taxi."

"Certainly, sir, there's one over there on the wall. You'll need some change."

"Thank you. I think I have some coins on me. You don't happen to have the number of a taxi do you?"

"There's one on the wall next to the phone."

"That's great."

Richard was so relieved. He'd known he would eventually get home tonight, but up until now, he hadn't quite worked out the finer details without catching pneumonia.

It wasn't long before the only taxi in the village was beeping its horn outside the pub. Richard tipped the whisky and warm water he'd ordered, down his throat and thanked the barman again. At last he was on the final lap home.

***

Kate flicked the kettle on. Jacob was tucked up nicely in bed, Richard was out for the evening and now was a good opportunity to curl up on the sofa with a good book and a cup of tea.

Suddenly she heard the front door bang and before she had time to respond Richard was standing in the kitchen doorway drenched from head to toe.

"Richard, you made me jump. You're soaked. I thought you were going to be late, have you two had a row?" Kate started to laugh at her attempted humour.

"Yes, we have."

Kate's smile dropped into a look of concern.

"Oh, I'm sorry. I didn't mean to . . ."

"No you're not, you can't stand her, can you?"

"Well I . . ."

"It doesn't matter. Do you want to know what we were arguing about?"

He was looking intensely at her. Kate had retreated to the back of the kitchen, scared to hear what he had to say.

"It's not really my business, is it?"

"Yes, it is actually. We were arguing about you."

"Me?"

"Yes, she was telling a group of people that she didn't think I could possibly find you attractive covered in fence paint, and I said on the contrary, I thought you were more attractive because of what you'd done for me."

Kate swallowed hard. "And what did she say to that?"

"She didn't like it." Kate was staring as intensely as he was now. Her heart was beating wildly in her chest. Was he saying that Ingrid was history, that they'd split up. "But it was the part where I told her that I loved you that really pissed her off." Kate's eyes widened. She could hardly breathe now in anticipation of his next words. "Kate . . ."

"Yes?"

"Can I take you out one night on a date?"

Kate's eyes lit up then a smile spread across her face. "Of course you can," she laughed. "I can't believe it."

"Oh, Kate," said Richard throwing his arms around her.

They held each other so tightly they could hardly breathe, then his lips were upon hers, only this time she didn't pull away, this time *she* was his girlfriend and she was going to saviour them. She kissed him back with a desire that she had been holding back since the day they met. A desire that was so strong she feared she would burst. At last she could show her true pent up emotions. He had said that he loved her. She was the happiest person alive.

Richard couldn't believe it either. He had worried all the way back from Marclough that she would reject him. The further he had walked the more certain he had been of the outcome; he certainly couldn't have hoped for this. But here she was, his precious Kate, holding and kissing him like it was meant to be. He held her face between his hands and kissed her gently again.

"When shall we have our first date?" he asked.

"Why not on Friday when Jacob goes to Melissa's?"

"Perfect. It couldn't have worked out better."

"Now why don't you go and get dried before you catch your death of cold, and I'll make you a nice warm drink?"

He took one last look at her and kissed her lightly on the lips. "Thank you, Kate. We're going to be so happy together."

Kate already knew that. She'd played it through in her head so many times, but now it was for real. Now she could replace her dreams with reality.

# Chapter . . .

# 18

Mike Fenwick stared at the photographs lined up in neat, little rows on his bedroom wall. He fought back the tears that threatened to spill over as he focussed on each one individually. Why hadn't she called him? She'd said she would and now there was someone else in her life. He hadn't been given a chance to prove himself worthy of being hers. His eyes rested on the picture of her gazing down at the little boy laughing. She looked so beautiful. He could have made her so happy.

Mike relived the scene in his head; Kate standing in the doorway of the house this morning in her white bathrobe, the doctor stepping outside, turning, threading his arms around her waist and kissing her. He had kissed *his* Kate and to make matters worse, she had kissed him back then smiled and looked adoringly at him. They had both laughed as if they were mocking him.

He had been there every morning for her, hiding, yet waiting for her to acknowledge his presence, and now she had thwarted him, abandoned him for someone else. The tears started to drip down his cheek. He had waited too long to make his move. Now someone else had stepped in and taken what should rightfully be his.

Mike sniffed loudly and wiped his nose with the sleeve of his sweatshirt. He couldn't face work today; they would have to manage without him. He was far too distraught to do anything useful. He opened the can of lager beside him and sipped his first mouthful then, one by one, ripped the pictures off the wall. Finally the last picture was in his hand—Kate leaving the house, flicking her hair behind her ear—he loved that one, she looked so natural, just the way he liked her. Not like some of the girls he'd seen on a Friday night with layers of makeup and stiff, sprayed hair, he couldn't stand them. What would they look like in the morning? He would give the world to see what Kate looked like first thing, just before she woke properly and her eyes were all sleepy. He threw the picture onto the top of the pile and took them into the kitchen to put them in a drawer, any drawer, just somewhere to keep them so that he didn't have to be reminded constantly of her betrayal. The one under the kitchen sink would do where he kept all those things that he didn't want to throw away but would probably never use again, like menus from the local Chinese and kebab shops and Allen keys that didn't fit anything. He closed it quickly. *Oh Kate, why? He'll never love you like I did. How could I have been such a fool? I thought you were different but you're just like all the rest.*

Kate would carry on now, sharing her life with her new man, totally oblivious to the heartache she had caused.

***

Kate tiptoed up the stairs to Jacob's room.

"Jacob, it's time to get up now," she sang.

Jacob's eyes stirred. Kate looked at his angelic face. She loved this time in a morning when he was just wakening. He looked so adorable, but this morning she saw him in a new light. Maybe one day she would be waking him as his stepmother. She so desperately hoped so.

"Is it morning?" asked Jacob rubbing his eyes.

"Yes it is, sweetheart, and it's time to get up for nursery."

"Do I have to go today?"

Kate smiled. "Yes of course you do, what's different about today?"

She was dying to tell him that it was indeed a very special day; that all her prayers had been answered and her dreams had come true, but she refrained and pulled his duvet back, tickling him as she did so.

"Come on, sleepy head, I bet you can't get out of bed by the time I count to three."

Normally Jacob loved this game but not when he had just woken up. He reluctantly swung his legs out of bed by the time she got to two. She took him by the hand and led him downstairs struggling to keep the smile from her face.

"Do you want cereal this morning?"

"Can I have toast instead?"

"Of course you can."

"Kate."

"Yes?"

"Why do you keep smiling?"

"Because I'm very, very happy."

"Why?"

"Because I'm a very lucky person and live here with you and your daddy."

Jacob shrugged his shoulders and ventured his next question, although he knew the probable outcome. "Kate."

"Yes?"

"Can I eat my toast in the lounge and watch telly?"

"Just this once, but don't tell daddy," she answered winking in his direction

Jacob liked the new Kate; she was far less strict and quite funny. There were a few more things he might try throughout the day. He didn't want to waste an opportunity.

***

Richard saw Todd as he pulled up into the Consultant's car park. He couldn't wait to get out of the car and tell him his news.

"Morning, Todd," he shouted running up behind him.

"Richard, how are you?"

"Fine, absolutely fine, and yourself?"

"Oh, you know, up most of the night with Molly. We think she's teething."

"Ah, the joys of parenthood."

"How did the charity do go last night?" Todd wasn't really that interested but he thought he'd better ask. The less he heard about that woman the better.

"It was awful."

"What? You seem pretty pleased with yourself to say it was awful."

"I *am* pleased, no, to tell you the truth, I'm ecstatic." Todd was all ears now. "I ended up walking out of the charity dinner. Ingrid and I had a major row and basically split up."

"Really? What did you argue about?"

"Kate."

"Kate? Are you serious?"

"Yes, anyway, to cut a long story short, when I got home I asked Kate out."

"And . . ."

"She said yes. Jacob's sleeping over at Melissa's on Friday so I'm taking her out for a meal."

Richard's eyes were glowing with happiness. Todd was delighted for his friend.

"Well, you old fox. You can certainly pull the women, can't you?"

"You've either got it or you haven't."

"That's great, Richard. I'm so pleased. Listen why don't you both come over for something to eat one night so that we can meet her? It would be great if the girls got along together."

"Yes, we'd love to. I'll let you know when Jacob is staying with Melissa again, you see, I've gained the perfect girlfriend but I've lost my babysitter now."

The two of them laughed and went off to their respective ward rounds. Richard couldn't believe it. He'd been with Kate less than twenty four hours and they'd already got an invitation for dinner.

***

Jacob had his suitcase packed and was waiting with Kate for the taxi to arrive.

"Are you and daddy coming back for me tomorrow?" he asked anxiously.

"Yes, of course we are. I think it will be just after lunch time once you've said goodbye to grandma and granddad, but we'll be there." He sighed a heavy sigh. "What's wrong, Jacob? You're going to stay with mummy and your grandparents."

"I know, but Alex will be there and I don't know him very well."

"Oh, Alex will be fine. I've heard he really likes children. Maybe you should ask him to play something with you, then you can get to know him better."

"Like what?"

"How about that card game where you put all the cards on the floor and you have to turn two over and find a pair that are the same?"

Kate remembered him playing that game with his niece when she was little. The two of them would play it for hours when they went round to visit.

"Okay, I'll take my cards with me."

The taxi arrived and they were on their way. Kate had thought about little else this morning apart from her date with Richard. She couldn't wait to be alone with him and be the centre of all his attention. She would drop Jacob off, have a cup of tea with Melissa, then make her excuses and leave so that she could go back home and get ready. Thankfully this time she wouldn't be asked to have a meal with Alex.

Melissa was waiting at the door for her son. She waved excitedly as the taxi pulled up.

"Mummy," he shouted and ran up the garden path to greet her.

Kate paid the driver then followed Jacob into the house.

"Hi, Kate, come on in," Melissa called from the kitchen She was already flicking the kettle on. "Mum and dad have nipped into town to do a last bit of shopping. They won't be long. Tea or coffee?"

"I'll have a cup of tea, please. I won't stay long Melissa, I've got things to do back home."

"Okay, that's fine. I only wish Alex was here, then he could give you a lift back."

"No, that's not necessary."

The two women went into the lounge where Jacob was emptying his small suitcase of toys.

"So, Jacob," Melissa began. "How have you been?"

"Okay, Kate went out on Monday and Ingrid looked after me and I didn't like it, and a policeman came to the house but he didn't put me in prison."

Kate closed her eyes and waited for the repercussion from Melissa.

"What does he mean, Kate?" she asked frantically.

"It was all a misunderstanding but things have been sorted out now so it won't be happening again. Ingrid won't be looking after you any more, Jacob."

"Good, I didn't like her."

"Is this Richard's girlfriend, she doesn't sound suitable to be near children? Mind you, we all have our ups and downs, don't we?" she added before going in too deep and drawing attention to her own shortcomings.

At that point Alex entered the house. His tie was loose around his neck and the top button of his shirt was open as if he'd had a hard day.

"Alex, is that you? You're early," Melissa shouted to him in the hallway.

"Had a bloody awful day so I finished early. I'll do a bit of work over the weekend . . . Oh, hi, Kate, I didn't realise you were here."

"Hi, Alex, sounds like you need a drink."

"That sounds like a very good idea. Hi, Jacob, how are you?"

"Okay, do you want to play cards with me?"

"Sure, what game do you want to play?"

"Well, we turn all the cards over and then we have to try and choose two of the same card."

"Oh, yes, I used to love this game."

He briefly glanced over at Kate. Had she said something to Jacob? Kate smiled and stared at the floor. Melissa noticed their eye contact and immediately wondered what was going on. Were they just flirting with each other? Had she inadvertently pushed them together when she'd asked Alex to take Kate for lunch? Suddenly she felt uneasy about the two of them being under the one roof. She certainly wasn't going to leave them alone in the room together. She wasn't going to openly accuse Kate of anything untoward, she didn't want to make an enemy of her, but she definitely wasn't going to offer her the use of her boyfriend for a lift home.

"Kate, you must let me get your taxi fare home. It's the least I can do after all your help in getting Jacob to stop."

"It's not necessary, Melissa, it's not very far."

"No, I insist."

"Okay, thanks, I'll give them a ring now."

"Use the phone in the hall."

Kate was glad. She was becoming aware of the time and didn't want to rush getting ready for tonight.

***

Richard glanced at the clock. Only one more case and he would be able to escape. He too wanted some time to get ready for tonight. He'd felt in such a good mood today. Kate had this wonderful knack of making him feel good about everything. He'd noticed that before. She was like a fairy godmother who went along waving her magic wand at things that weren't quite right and making them better.

"Mr Anderson, next patient is on the table . . . Mr Anderson."

"Sorry, Carl, on another planet there for a minute. I'll be right there."

The sooner he got started the sooner he would be finished so he could get back home to Kate.

***

Kate took one last look at herself in the mirror. She had to look and feel just right tonight. Nothing was going to be left to chance. All her clothes were new, the charcoal grey, linen trousers, the soft, pink, woollen top, even her grey court shoe, in fact, everything down to the white, lacy underwear—just in case.

There, she was ready. She picked up her handbag from the end of the bed and prepared to walk downstairs to meet her man. The butterflies in her stomach were going wild. Why was she so nervous? She lived in the same house as Richard and saw him every day, yet somehow this was different. She wanted tonight to be so perfect.

Richard heard footsteps above him. He stood at the foot of the stairs, and with his heart racing, glanced up. Kate stopped and looked at him. He was so handsome. Her stomach churned and she wondered if she would ever feel like eating again. Then Richard smiled at her.

"You look gorgeous," he said, his eyes bright with happiness.

"Thank you," she replied, relieved. She made her way to the bottom of the stairs and they stared at each other, neither quite believing that they had finally made it to this day. "I'm the luckiest person alive," she said breaking the silence.

"Why?"

"Look at you. You're handsome, clever and extremely talented, and I'm just a nanny."

"Don't ever say that, Kate. You're not just a nanny; you're a wonderful person who changes people's lives. Look at Jacob and me before you arrived. We were a mess, then you made everything better, then I screwed them up again by inviting Ingrid into our lives and now here you are, making me the happiest I've ever been. I'm the lucky one Kate and don't you ever forget that." He kissed her gently on the cheek. "I'll not spoil your lipstick."

She laughed and they left the house hand in hand.

The Italian restaurant was just out of town. Richard wasn't going to risk Marcelle's or the Japanese Garden in case someone else had the same idea. No, he didn't want any unwanted disturbances. Tonight was special.

The journey took them along Cedar Vale High Street. She briefly glanced at the flat above the dry cleaners.

"That seems a while ago since you were living up there," Richard said following her eyes.

"Yes, thank God. That was one part of my life I'd rather forget."

"If you hadn't been there and worked in the dry cleaners we'd never have met. There's a reason for everything you know."

"That's very philosophical."

They were soon out in the countryside and heading towards the quaint village of Turnbridge. A few yards past the sign requesting careful drivers, Richard turned right and into the car park of the Bella Vista Italian Restaurant. Kate jumped out of the car and quickly grabbed Richard's outstretched hand.

The restaurant was busy but they were soon approached and shown to their table by an Italian waiter in a pristine white shirt and tight black trousers. Kate took a menu then looked around.

"What a lovely restaurant. I didn't even know this place existed."

"Oh, there are lots of places like this off the beaten track, you just have to look for them. What do you fancy? I'm going to have pâté followed by sirloin steak."

"That doesn't sound very Italian."

"No, but it sounds good."

"Mm, I think I'll have . . . pâté as well, then the sole."

"Ah, equally un-Italian. And you were calling me."

"I know, but I'll see your pâté and then I'll wish I'd had it."

Richard laughed and shook his head. The waiter took their order and brought their drinks.

"Can I ask you something, Kate?"

"Yes."

"Why didn't we do this months ago? What happened over New Year?"

Richard had always wondered about those few days with his parents. They seemed to change their relationship over night.

"Maybe it just wasn't the right time," replied Kate feeling somewhat uncomfortable as to what was coming next.

"Or maybe my mother had something to do with it. Am I right, Kate?" She looked down at the table and thought carefully about how she was going to answer that question. "I am right, aren't I?"

"Kind of."

"I knew it."

"She asked me to baby sit for Jacob because she wanted to take you out to dinner to meet the Harpers, and of course I said I would, why wouldn't I? Then she asked me to try and persuade you to go because she didn't think you'd want to without Jacob, so again, that was no problem. Then she seemed so pleased with the plan, that when she dropped the bombshell about Ingrid being there, I didn't feel I could go back on my word. I was devastated but your mother had big ideas for you. She didn't want you settling down with a nanny, she wanted you related to the Harpers."

"And in the meantime, she ruins everything for us. I thought we'd been getting on really well before that and then you suddenly changed. Now I see why. I'm sorry, Kate. I should have known better, putting you through all that. I'm going to spoil you rotten from now on."

"You don't have to spoil me rotten and take me to posh restaurants all the time you know. I'm not Ingrid. I'm quite happy with just you and a cup of coffee."

"What do you mean?"

"Well we could go out for a walk and then find a café and have coffee, or go shopping and have coffee. I've had lots of dreams about you, but one of them is that we go for a long walk across the moors, there's just the two of us. Every now and then we stop to kiss . . . and admire the view of course." Richard laughed and slid his fingers through hers.

"Carry on."

"Then in the distance, we see a pub so we walk over there and you have a pint of beer and I have a coffee and then we walk back . . . hand in hand, . . . just talking and laughing, together."

His smile was filled with affection. It was such a simple dream but meant so much. She didn't want money spending on her or gifts lavished on her, she simply wanted him.

"Tell me some more of these dreams?"

"Not tonight. You'll have to wait."

The waiter placed their starters in front of them. Reluctantly they unlocked fingers and started to eat.

"Oh, that is beautiful?" he said sliding another mouthful in.

"Mm, I was so nervous about tonight, I didn't think I'd be able to eat anything, but I'm glad I can, this is delicious."

"You know, I think we should tell Melissa tomorrow," said Richard.

"What, about us?"

"Yes, she has to know sometime."

"How do you think she'll take it?"

"I think she'll be fine. It's always easier if you're both in a stable relationship. It makes life simpler. Besides, she may get to see Jacob more. We might need a baby sitter."

"Sounds like you're pretty sure about us then."

"Sure? I'm more certain than I was when I married Melissa."

Kate swelled with joy. They'd finished their starters and the main meal was in front of them.

"Oh, I forgot to tell you, I mentioned us to Todd yesterday and he's invited us for dinner. He wants you to meet Jayne, his wife."

"That's nice, I'd love to meet your friends."

"You can bring your friends over you know, for a meal or for a drink."

"There's only really Tina now. It's funny, when you split up with someone, all the friends you shared seem to go one way or the other. They don't usually stay friends with both of you. Most of them sided with . . . him." She was about to say Alex's name then stopped herself. This situation was getting confusing now. The two couples had basically swapped partners and half of them were oblivious of it. She seemed to be getting on well with Melissa. If they were going to see each other more often through Jacob, she was going to find it difficult keeping the pretence up.

They'd nearly finished their meal. Kate didn't know why she had been so nervous. Richard was so easy to talk to. The two of them had chatted endlessly.

"Shall we take Jacob somewhere tomorrow, on his bike? I think we should make a fuss of him, so that he doesn't feel left out," Kate suggested.

"Yes, if it stays fine. That's a good idea."

He was staring at her again, looking deep into her eyes. She was so caring, always thinking about everyone else. She hadn't even wanted to hurt his mother's feeling when she ruined their potential relationship. Kate caught his stare. How she longed to be alone with him.

"Do you want a dessert?" he asked almost in a whisper. She shook her head. "Coffee?"

"No, thanks."

"Shall we go home?"

She nodded this time.

Richard called the waiter over and asked for the bill. He wanted to go too. He put his arm around her shoulder as they walked out of the restaurant. An elderly woman, seated behind them smiled as they walked past, remembering days gone by.

Richard couldn't wait until they got home. Once in the car, he reached across and pulled her towards him, kissing her passionately. Kate kissed him back, their tongues entwining. She knew that tonight, despite it being their first date, she would be making love to Richard Anderson.

***

The morning sunlight filtered in through a gap in the curtain. Kate stirred. She slowly opened her eyes and for a brief moment, wondered where she was. The unfamiliar surroundings completely confused her. Then she looked to her side and the peaceful face of her boyfriend lay sleepily beside her. She smiled to herself. Did last night really happen? Did she actually sleep with the only man on this planet that she wanted to spend the rest of her life with? She studied his face. She wanted to keep every detail in her head then she could visualise him at any time of the day or night. Richard slowly opened his eyes. The first sight that met him was Kate gazing adoringly at him.

"Good morning," she smiled, caressing his face with her hand.

He took hold of it and kissed it gently.

"Morning," he grinned back. He held his arm out and she slid under it, snuggling into his warm body. "That was the best night last night. How are you this morning?"

"The happiest person alive," she replied dreamily.

"Me too. I'm so pleased you agreed to go out with me. You could have quite easily told me where to go after the way I'd treated you."

"There wasn't much chance of that. I'd been wanting you to ask me for months. Anyway, we're together now and that's all that matters."

"Mm," he held her tightly and kissed her hair. "Are you sure you won't move into this bedroom? I don't want to let you go now."

"Only when Jacob's not here. I don't want him walking in on us. That would be a bit too much for him to understand at the moment."

"I know you're right, you always are, but it seems such a pity me here and you in the next room."

"It is early days. How bad am I, sleeping with you on our first date?"

Richard laughed. "I know, you tramp."

She tapped him gently on the chest. "Just goes to show what a bad influence you are."

"I won't be able to keep my hands off you now, you do know that don't you?"

"I don't think that will be a problem." Her face was serious. Their emotions were rising again. They started to kiss and soon Richard was on top of her.

"I love you, Kate."

"I love you too, Richard," she replied. *More than you'll ever know.*

They made love then lazed in bed nearly all morning, making the most of their free time together. Breakfast took the form of brunch eaten in bed, as the minutes turned into hours.

Richard glanced at the bedside clock. "Oh, my God, have you seen the time? I told Melissa we'd pick Jacob up at one. It's five to twelve."

To save time they decided to shower together, although once in there Kate deliberated at the rationale of the idea as their lips met again.

"This is supposed to be saving time," Kate laughed, and pushed him out of the door as soon as he'd finished washing his hair.

***

At ten past one precisely, Richard and Kate walked up the pathway, hand in hand and knocked on Melissa and Alex's front door.

"Oh, hi, you two," she said smiling.

Jacob came bounding round the corner into the hall.

"Daddy, I went to the airport and I saw some big planes and granddad said I could go on one this summer to Anteegwa."

Melissa froze to the spot, mortified. They had discussed the possibilities but not in quite that context. A little more diplomacy had been used. Melissa tried to explain. "Jacob, granddad didn't say that, he said we would ask daddy first if you were allowed to spend some time with them over the school holidays. Oh, I'm so sorry," she apologised, trying not to dig herself in even further. "That sounded awful and so presumptuous."

Richard looked at his excited son and his heart melted. How could he deny him such an adventure just to point out to Melissa who was in charge? Kate had taught him better than that.

"Well, we'll have to see how good you can be up until then."

Both Melissa and Kate looked at him in astonishment. Kate was so proud of him. That must have been really difficult to say. Melissa's worried look turned into sheer delight.

"Jacob, do you hear that, daddy says you have to be a good boy and he'll consider it. Thank you, Richard." Suddenly, she saw their hands clasped together. Her eyes widened and a smile spread across her face. "Are you two . . . ?"

Richard laughed and looked down at their hands. "Yes, we are whatever it is you were about to say."

"I don't believe it. That's wonderful. I'm so pleased for you both." She went to hug Kate, then Richard. She couldn't have been happier about the fact that her closest ally had taken her place in Richard's affections, and that her suspicions of Kate and Alex were completely unfounded. "I really do wish you both the best."

"Thanks, Melissa, now do we get invited in for coffee or do we have to stand on the doorstep all afternoon?"

Melissa put her hands to her face. "Oh, I'm so sorry, yes, come on in. I've been so excited about everything that's just happened I'm forgetting myself. So when did this all happen? Jacob only mentioned Ingrid yesterday," shouted Melissa from the kitchen.

"It was Wednesday, wasn't it Kate, when I finally woke up and saw that the best woman for me was right under my nose. Not some aristocrat who has no idea what it is to be a nice human being. We had our first date last night."

"I'm gobsmacked. Have you told Jacob yet?"

"Not yet, we'll tell him when we get home."

At that point Alex walked into the house after a lunch time meeting at The Dog and Duck.

"Hi, everyone. Sorry, I've just been conducting a little business over a pint," Alex announced as he entered the room.

"Alex, you'll never believe it, Richard and Kate are an item," Melissa said, bursting to get the news in first.

Alex struggled to look pleased. He attempted a forced smile but Kate noticed it. It was the same look she had encountered when Chris had told him that he was marrying Tina.

"Congratulations," he said half heartedly. He went to shake Richard's hand and kissed Kate lightly on the cheek. "That's great; I'll just go and get changed."

Alex wasn't sure how he felt about the news. Melissa was obviously over the moon. Kate was the answer to all her problems where Jacob was concerned and being with Richard would give her far more say than if she was simply a nanny. He just felt that he and Kate were now well and truly over, it was final, and if he ever felt the urge to go back to her, she was no longer available. He knew it was selfish, but while Kate was alone, she would possibly be missing him. Now she wouldn't give him a passing thought.

***

It was a pleasant, sunny afternoon; one could be confused into thinking that spring had arrived early. Richard dug Jacob's bike out of the garage and pushed it across the road into the park. Jacob was eager to get on. The last time he'd ridden had been a disaster and he was keen to put that encounter behind him and have pleasant thoughts of cycling instead of his current nightmares. Richard sat down on a park bench and kept hold of the bike.

"Let go, daddy, I want to set off," Jacob insisted.

"Just a minute, Jacob. Kate and I have something we want to tell you first."

"What?" asked Jacob with a worried look on his face. What could be so important that it interrupted a bike trip? Richard had been wandering how he was going to put this.

"You know how mummy has got a new partner, Alex?"

"Yes, I quite like him now, he's good at playing pairs," replied the little boy.

Kate smiled nervously hoping her secret wouldn't come out, that she was the one who had instigated the game.

"Well, daddy has got a new partner now."

"Who?" he said with utter panic written across his face.

"It's Kate."

Kate smiled happily this time. She loved Richard telling people about them, even Jacob.

"Kate? Are you going to marry her?"

Kate could feel her cheeks glow at the thought. Richard was a little taken aback. He hadn't quite got that far yet in his dreams, but he wasn't far off.

"Well, we've not made any plans yet but who knows. Are you pleased?"

Richard couldn't decipher his thoughts at the moment. He looked to Kate for moral support.

"Does that mean Ingrid won't be coming back?" Jacob continued.

"Yes, it does."

A wide grin spread across his face. "And Kate will always be with us?"

"Yes."

"Hurray," he yelped and jumped off his bike.

He ran to Kate and threw his arms around her. Tears appeared in the corners of her eyes. That was what he wanted, to be rid of Ingrid and have Kate in his life for good. She couldn't have been happier. Richard glowed with pride as he watched the two people he cared most for embracing each other. He hadn't forced his son into those actions, they were purely spontaneous.

"Daddy, can Kate come on holiday with us this year?"

"Of course she can."

Jacob seemed happy with the reply. He jumped back on his bike and started cycling.

"Now don't go racing off so we can't see you," Richard shouted after him.

"Okay," came the reply.

Richard slid his arm around Kate's shoulder and they walked together under the bowing branches of the trees, just like she had imagined they would.

***

Jacob soon fell asleep that night, in fact, virtually as soon as his head hit the pillow. He'd been so busy it was inevitable. Richard had taken him up, much to Jacob's annoyance.

"No," Richard had insisted. "Let's give Kate a night off. I'll read you a story tonight."

Jacob had reluctantly agreed on the understanding that Kate would do it tomorrow night.

"I either bored him to death or he was really tired," said Richard as he returned to the lounge.

Kate had a glass of red wine waiting for him on the coffee table. He sank onto the sofa next to her.

"Well, that was a day and a half," he smiled.

"I know. Everyone seemed pleased though."

"Why wouldn't they be, they all think the world of you, even Melissa? I didn't think she possessed feelings, but it would seem you've even brought those out of her. She's actually quite civil these days. I don't mind being in her company at the moment."

"I know, I couldn't believe it when you asked for a coffee. I thought you'd be raring to leave."

"It actually makes life a hell of a lot easier when you get on doesn't it?"

Kate smiled and nodded.

Suddenly the phone rang and Richard left his warm chair to go and answer it. Kate could just about hear him talking.

"Oh, hi, mum."

Kate went pale. What did his mother want, as if she didn't know? Obviously the news had filtered down to her that Ingrid was no longer Richard's intended, as she would so desperately want her to be.

*"I met Bea Harper today in the village and she had some very disturbing news to tell me. Is it true you and Ingrid have split up?"* she said angrily, getting straight to the point.

"That's right, mother."

"*Why*?" Her voice was shrill, almost threatening.

"Because we weren't compatible and she didn't get on with Jacob. Any problem with that?"

*"Well you hardly gave it a chance for goodness sake. She would have been a perfect stepmother for Jacob."*

"Says who, mother? You've never even seen her with Jacob so how on earth can you make that assumption?"

*"Her mother says she's wonderful with children."*

"Again, has she ever seen her with children?"

Kate closed her eyes. She could imagine the other half of the conversation and the tone of voice from his disgruntled mother.

*"I'm really very disappointed, Richard. How can I look Bea in the face now after this? She says that Ingrid is heartbroken. She said something else Richard and I hope it isn't true."*

"What's that?" Richard knew exactly what was coming next.

*"That you left her for that nanny of yours."*

"If you mean Kate, that is true?" he replied lowering his voice.

*"Richard, how could you? I mean a nanny for goodness sake. Ingrid will inherit practically all the land around here and you have to go and settle on a nanny."*

"I can't help who I fall in love with, mum."

*"It's got nothing to do with love. It's to do with Jacob's future and making sure he wants for nothing."*

Richard was exasperated. He'd never heard such utter rubbish. This was all about his mother no longer receiving dinner invitations to the Harpers and how she will no longer be able to name drop while she's buying her groceries in the village. He hadn't realised until this moment what a complete snob she was. He was the one disappointed now, in the fact that she put her social climbing before his and Jacob's happiness and he was going to tell her so.

"I'm sure the Harper's would be interested to know what you had planned for their vast fortune once they've passed away. Honestly, mum, did nobody tell you that arranged marriages aren't part of our culture any more?"

"*Now, Richard, there's no need to be like that.*"

"Yet you quite happily ring me up and try to organise my life for me. I'm quite capable of doing that myself . . ."

". . . *Well apparently not.*"

"Yes I can, and I would be grateful if you didn't interfere in future. You single handedly nearly ruined my chances with Kate, now please, it's time you stepped back and let me get on with my own life."

*"Well!"*

The phone went dead and Richard knew that his mother would not be ringing back that evening, in fact not for quite some time. His heart pounded in his chest. How dare she take it upon herself to 'sort' his life for him? She lived miles away, she hadn't a clue what was going on in his day to day events. He suddenly remembered Kate in the lounge and hoped she hadn't heard any of that conversation. He quickly went back to her and found her with her eyes filled with tears.

"Oh, Kate, I'm so sorry."

"She's not pleased I take it."

"It's not because of you, it's because she can't socialise with the Harpers any more. That's what's killing her."

"I'm sorry, the last thing I wanted is for you to fall out with your mum," she struggled to say through the lump in her throat.

"Hey, it doesn't matter. What matters is that we are happy, all three of us and anyone else is a bonus. I hardly ever see her; she'll come round by the time she wants to see her grandson again. I'll give dad a ring tomorrow and try and smooth things out."

Kate knew he was upset. She could see it in his eyes despite his best efforts to appear unaffected. He opened his arm to her and she snuggled into him, letting the tears role down freely, splashing onto his white t-shirt.

He'd felt so elated after the response of Melissa and Jacob. It hadn't occurred to him that someone may not approve. Maybe it was the way she found out, or maybe he was right; she was a snob—of the highest order and he would give her a wide birth for the foreseeable future. She wasn't going to spoil his happiness now that he had finally found it.

# Chapter . . .

# 19

It was tortuous, tormenting, but he continued to do it, day in, day out, waiting outside the house for her to leave with the little boy. He had to know if Kate was alright. It was his duty now. Gone were the days of trying to woo her or waiting patiently for her to call; Mike's role had changed to that of protector, making sure that she didn't come to any harm. She would thank him in the long run. Not everyone had the luxury of a Mike Fenwick guarding your interests.

It wasn't that he was needy or anything ridiculous like that. He had his pick of any one of the 'Friday night girls' as he called them. But that's all they were useful for, Friday nights; a solicitous bunch of desperate women who would disparage themselves for one quick, drunken fumble in the dark, hoping that by some minor miracle it would lead to a meaningful relationship. They were nothing like Kate, she was different. She was for keeps and he would be there for her, ready to whisk her away into the sunset on his motorbike, when the doctor finally gave her the push.

His eye twitched; a nervous tick developed during his hours of vigil. At that point the front door opened and Kate appeared waving a letter in her hand. She walked down the garden path and opened the front gate. There she was in front of him, heading in his direction.

Mike started to panic. What if she saw him, what could his explanation be? There was no reason on this earth why he should be seated on his motorbike, outside her house with the engine turned off, other than appearing to be stalking her. He opened the pannier at the back of his bike and pretended to look inside. Meanwhile, Kate continued to walk down the road towards him, her eyes searching. He was sure they'd rested on him. His heart started to pound as he fumbled with the key.

Suddenly, the postman appeared from one of the gardens and Kate ran towards him. She handed the letter over, obviously posted to the wrong address then ran back to the house.

Despite the cold, Mike could feel a trickle of sweat make its way down his temple. That was too close. He hadn't been given time to react to the situation. He turned the key and kick started the bike. Perhaps he needed to reconsider his position.

***

The next day, Mike permitted himself a lie-in. It was Sunday and from previous experience, he knew Kate wouldn't appear until late morning, early afternoon, if at all.

He parked his bike in the car park at the back of the park, and walked the short distance to position himself opposite the house. He found a park bench and sat down. The air was filled with a fine drizzle and the wind stirred the trees.

The old lady walked past with Mitzie, the West Highland terrier and eyed him warily. She had been on a mission to rid the park of odd looking characters ever since she'd lead the police to that malicious woman with the little boy, and this one, loitering in a sinister fashion clad in black leathers was equally worrying if not more. What was he doing sitting in the rain on his own staring at the house opposite? Was he casing the joint for a later visit? Mike nodded briefly to her as she hurried past him. Neither of them smiled. The dog pulled on the lead towards him, his nose twitching. She quickly whipped him back in the right direction. It was probably the drugs he could smell on him, she thought.

About twenty minutes later, Mike's view was blocked by a police car, as it pulled up by the kerb alongside the park. A tall policeman got out and walked towards the unsuspecting young man.

"Afternoon, sir," he said.

Mike didn't realise he'd been there that long. "Afternoon, officer. Is there a problem?"

"We've had a report of someone acting suspiciously in the park dressed in black, leather, biker's gear. That wouldn't be you would it?"

"I'm not acting suspiciously. I'm only sitting here."

"Why?"

"It's not a crime is it to sit in the park for a bit of fresh air?"

Mike noticed the curtains opposite moving and Kate's face appeared at the window. Typical, he'd waited there for ages to see her and then when he does a policeman is interrogating him. He shielded his face from her; she mustn't know it's him.

"But it's raining."

"So?"

"Okay, sir, why don't you just move on then you don't frighten any more members of the public?"

"Interfering busy bodies half of them. You should be out catching proper criminals, not innocent bystanders."

Mike picked up his helmet and made his way back to his bike. He quickly glanced back at the window but she was gone.

***

"She's lovely! I've never met anyone so easy to get on with." Jayne Hamer and her husband Todd were waving Richard and Kate goodbye as their car passed the front door. Todd closed the door once they were out of view and smiled to himself. At last his best friend, Richard, had finally found a woman who his wife could get along with.

"They both look so happy as well, don't they?" Todd replied.

He threw another log onto the open fire and lowered his head as he passed under the oak beam in the middle of the room. It could be a handicap at times being six foot two in these stone cottages. His wife noticed his movements and laughed.

"Kate couldn't believe we wanted to move out of here until Richard cracked his head on the beam. Wasn't it funny, she couldn't stop laughing? Someone's going to get concussion one of these days if we don't find somewhere soon."

"I know, it'll probably be one of the children at the rate we're going."

"Do you know," Jayne continued. "She's one of those people who you find yourself telling your whole life story to. She just sits and listens and says all the right things at the right time. I can't believe how different she is to that awful woman, Ingrid."

"I know, I'm so glad he got rid of her. You'll be pleased to know then that old Royston has invited us all over for dinner to discuss the hand meeting that's coming up, so you'll be able to see her again pretty soon."

"Oh, when's that?"

"In a couple of weeks. The meeting's only three weeks away. We're going over the final details. I don't know what Mrs Royston has to say about it. She was still pretty bad the last I heard."

"Oh, she isn't still suffering from depression is she?"

"I think so."

"Hasn't she been to see a doctor yet?"

"I don't think she'll go by all accounts. Royston has been using his secretary as some kind of counsellor, I think he just wants someone to talk to, and she was telling us about it all the other day. Apparently Marjorie has suffered from depression in the past."

"It must be difficult for both of them. I mean, she's in all day on her own and he works such long hours. That must be a very lonely house to be in at the end of a long day. Do you think she'll be able to cope, all of us descending on her?"

"I think the idea of us all going round is that we can discuss the meeting away from work and you ladies can talk."

"I hope he's not expecting a miracle."

"It'll be a chance to talk to Kate again, even if Mrs Royston doesn't feel like chatting. I think it will be just the three of you. Apparently Raj's wife won't be going and Elizabeth doesn't have a partner."

"Well, we'll do our best. I'm looking forward to it."

***

Kate looked agonisingly in the mirror as she tried on her third outfit.

"Are you nearly ready up there, Kate, we should be setting off soon?"

*That was no help*, she thought, for now she was panicking and looking for something suitable to wear. Everyone knows that is the worst combination; trying to rush a woman into choosing her attire for a dinner party would only end in tears. It had to be trousers, she couldn't start looking for a pair of tights without holes in at this point in the proceedings, and her legs were far too pale to consider going without. There was no other option; she would have to wear the same clothes that she had worn on her first date with Richard. They were classy yet demure. She was going to be in the company of several surgeons and that was the look she was attempting to achieve. So be it, Richard would just be glad she was ready, he wasn't going to fret at having seen her in the same outfit twice.

"Oh, I'm sorry, Richard, I didn't know what to wear."

"Well you look gorgeous," he replied. "Let's get going."

She was right, he hadn't noticed. She settled into the front seat of the car and tried to regain her calm exterior. What was she going to talk about? She was glad Jayne would be there, but the rest of the ensemble were a little daunting, especially this Professor Royston. She'd heard his name mentioned on several occasions and it was always done with a considerable amount of deference.

They stopped outside Todd and Jayne's cottage and Richard ran out to knock on the door. Kate slid into the back seat and waited for her newly acquired friend to join her.

"Hi, Kate," Jayne giggled. "I'm so glad you're here. At least we've got each other to talk to if no one else wants to speak to us."

Kate laughed back. "I know, please sit near me at dinner. I won't have a clue what they're all talking about. At least we can discuss shopping and the price of children's shoes."

Richard looked in his mirror at the two heads bobbing in conversation. He nodded towards them as Todd took his place in the front seat. "I don't think we need to worry whether these two are going to get along," he commented.

Neither of the women heard his remark and carried on their discussion until they pulled up outside the Roystons' house. Kate clasped Richard's hand as the four of them waited patiently for the door to be answered. It was the Professor who opened it.

"Ah, Todd, Jayne, Richard and this must be Kate. Very nice to meet you."

He held out his hand and kissed her lightly on the cheek. Then it was Jayne's turn.

"Now, ladies, my wife is in the kitchen stirring up a culinary delight, she'll be out shortly. Why don't you come in and meet the rest of the guests."

Richard glanced at Todd. Was that an excuse for her not coming out to meet them or was she truly up to her elbows in vegetables? He hoped it wasn't all too much for her. It would be sad to see her as unhappy as she was at their wedding anniversary.

They made their way into the lounge where Raj and Elizabeth were waiting each with a cocktail in their hands.

"Can I interest you in one of those ladies? They're a bit of a speciality of mine."

"Oh, they look lovely," said Kate. "I'll try one."

"Splendid, what about you, Jayne?"

"Why not?"

"I'll have one without the alcohol," said Richard.

"Ah, you're the one driving are you?"

"Yes, how did you guess?"

"A glass of fruit juice it is then."

"I'll have a beer, please," said Todd.

"Oh, where's your sense of adventure?" Jayne said nudging him.

"Richard, you introduce Kate to everyone whilst I go and get the drinks. So that's two cocktails, one fruit juice and a *beer,*" Prof reiterated looking over his spectacles in Todd's direction.

Gerald went into the kitchen to see how his wife was fairing.

"They're actually very nice," said Raj lifting his glass up towards Todd.

"I'll stick with beer thanks. I know what's in it."

***

"How's it going at the helm, dear?" Gerald gingerly asked his wife.

He didn't want to disturb the aura of the kitchen. She had reluctantly agreed to stage the dinner party despite her inability to concoct an evening meal at present. But he had rallied round throughout the day; seasoning soup, peeling and washing vegetables, marinating chicken, and washing up, in a bid to jolly her along. She seemed fairly calm and collected at the moment. Should he leave her to it or offer assistance?

"I'm getting there," she replied half heartedly.

He wished he hadn't asked. He could feel himself compensating for his wife's lack of enthusiasm. He was sure everyone would notice by the end of the evening. He knew they wouldn't say anything though; they were all far too polite. Maybe he'd overdone it this time. I mean six guests all at once. Anyway, they were here now, so he would face them alone if necessary.

"All the guests are here. I'm just getting them a drink."

"Right."

He returned to the lounge where Kate and Jayne were happily chatting to Elizabeth and Raj had joined the men in a conversation that would inevitably end up being about work.

"There we go ladies," Gerald said handing the glasses out from a silver tray.

Kate held hers nervously as she tried to think of a topic to discuss which Elizabeth would find interesting as well. She could think of a million things to say to Jayne but she had no idea what the other woman's pastimes were. Ah, maybe she could ask her that.

"What do you like doing in your spare time, Elizabeth, or do you not get much of that?"

"Oh, I'm really glad you asked me that, Kate. I've been dying to tell someone. I've just taken up a new hobby. I've decided after all these years I'm going to learn how to cook properly. I've enrolled in a cookery class."

"Oh, that's fantastic," Kate enthused.

"Oh, yes, what kind of cooking?" asked Jayne.

Kate felt really pleased with herself. Not only had she asked a good question, but she'd also sparked off a conversation which Jayne was joining in with as well.

"I'm on the Italian course at the moment, but if I like it, I'm going to go round the world. Not literally of course, but cooking around the world; Asian, French, maybe even English. Just think, when I invite you all round for dinner, you'll be able to name the country where you want to eat."

"Yes, we could dress up as well, say we're eating French, we could wear a beret and some onions round our necks," said Kate.

The other two laughed heartily. Kate was beginning to enjoy herself. Gerald was pleased how things were going. Everyone seemed to be getting on. He joined the male half of the gathering just as Dorothy entered the room.

"Evening, everyone." She attempted a smile.

"Dorothy, how lovely to see you again," said Elizabeth and she went to kiss her on the cheek.

"You haven't met Kate have you Dorothy?" Richard started.

Kate went over and took her by the hand. "Thank you so much for inviting us all. It's lovely to meet everyone. It nice to put a face to all the names."

"Yes, it is, isn't it, Kate? Why don't you all take your seats at the table?"

Dorothy brought the dishes in course by course then mechanically cleared the bowls and plates away. She pushed her food around the plate but barely ate a child's portion. Kate's heart went out to her. Her mind was turning now. She'd broken the ice with Elizabeth, what could she say to Dorothy to try to cheer her up?

The dessert was placed on the table and with a cake slice in her hand, Dorothy asked, "Anyone for lemon and vanilla cheesecake?"

A resounding "Mm" went around the table and she began to deftly slice and hand out the pieces. A jug of cream followed and all started to eat. Kate's eyes met Jayne's across the table in a look of heavenly delight as they both savoured the delicious sweet. Dorothy noticed the exchange of glances and smiled.

"Do you like it, Kate?" she asked.

"Like it? I love it. It's so . . . creamy and vanillary and . . . gorgeous."

"It's a recipe I found in America when we were there on holiday one year. We went into a wonderful café and had some. I had to buy the recipe book which wasn't cheap but well worth it."

"I'll say, I've never tasted cheesecake like it, have you, Jayne?"

Jayne loved how Kate always included her in the conversations. They were really going to become good friends. She finished the mouthful she was eating and then replied. "I know, it's beautiful. There you are Elizabeth, you can enrol on the American cheesecake course as well now."

The three ladies laughed. Dorothy smiled proudly to herself. The men all looked on sombrely, as if they'd missed out on something. The table unanimously congratulated Dorothy and Professor Royston on a splendid meal. They had all thoroughly enjoyed it but now was the time to get down to business and leave the women to their idle chatter. They had the I's to dot and the T's to cross in their final preparations for the hand meeting and sitting around the table was not getting that done. The surgeons all left the table and departed into the lounge whilst Dorothy went and switched the kettle on to fill the cafetiére.

"Can we help, Dorothy?" asked Kate, poking her head around the kitchen door.

"Yes, Kate, would you two kindly take the coffees through to the lounge whilst I do some for us?"

"Of course."

Kate carried the coffees whilst Jayne followed with the cream and sugar. The surgeons were very appreciative and Richard winked at Kate as she turned to leave.

"Okay?" he mouthed.

Kate nodded and smiled. He knew he didn't have to fuss. She'd already formed a friendship with Jayne and broken the ice with Elizabeth. He was slightly concerned as to how she was going to get on with Dorothy though in her current state of mind.

"Well, this is nice," Dorothy said placing their coffees on the table. "I very rarely get to sit and talk to the partners of Gerald's colleagues. They're usually far more interesting than their other halves. All *they* do is talk shop."

"Well you certainly won't catch us doing that," Kate added.

There was a silence as they prepared their coffees to their liking. Kate stirred in the sugar. What would they talk about now?

"Are those your grandchildren on the wall, Dorothy?" Jayne asked staring at three, framed pictures behind Kate.

Dorothy's eyes glassed over. "Yes, I haven't seen them for a while. They'll have grown since those pictures."

"Do they live a long way away?" asked Kate.

"Yes, they do but not that far that their parents can't make the effort to bring them over once in a while. We've sort of fallen out. We haven't spoken for months now. Gerald rang them to tell them what he thought of them after they totally ruined our last holiday. You see, they wanted us over for

Christmas but we decided to go on a cruise instead. Anyway, that was the last time I spoke to them. They haven't answered my calls since. It breaks my heart to think of all the things our grandchildren are doing and we're missing it all."

Suddenly the penny dropped. Kate could see why she was so upset. It was her children's thoughtlessness and ultimately her lack of contact with her grandchildren that was causing her to be so depressed.

Jayne put a hand over Dorothy's. "You know, I lost my mother three years ago. Your children don't know what they have. Time is too precious to form grudges."

Dorothy looked thoughtful.

"You're right, Jayne, my mother lives in Spain and I don't see her for months on end, sometimes it can be as much as a year. I didn't know about your mother, Jayne. I'm sorry to hear that." The three women paused for thought. It was Kate who spoke first. "I know, Dorothy, why don't you adopt us two and then we could come round and visit every week and have cheesecake."

Dorothy began to laugh. "Oh, what a delightful thought you two. Wait until I tell Gerald he has two new daughters."

"He won't mind will he? Can you imagine us turning up on the doorstep every Saturday night with our overnight bags?" said Kate.

"Yes," said Dorothy, "we could have the bedrooms redecorated. I've been wanting to get them done for years. You could have one each."

"We don't mind sharing, do we Kate? We could have a natter," Jayne added.

"Oh, no, Jayne, Gerald wouldn't stand for that. Once the lights are out it's straight to sleep."

The three of them started to laugh. It started off as a response to Kate's comment, but then it was as if something had been released in Dorothy, and Kate and Jayne wanted to hold it and treasure it.

In the other room Raj was discussing the finer points of his talk. Gerald put up a finger. "Just a second Raj, sorry to interrupt, but did you hear that?"

"What?" asked Raj.

Gerald looked in Richard's direction. "Did I just hear the sound of my wife's laughter?"

His face was motionless. He stood up and went to listen. Slowly, he opened the door to the dining room and the wonderful sight of his wife chatting and laughing greeted him.

"Oh, I'm sorry, Gerald, did we disturb you?"

"Not at all, I'm so glad to see you're enjoying yourselves."

"Yes, we are. Kate has come up with a wonderful idea. We're going to adopt the girls and they're going to come round for cheesecake every week."

Gerald's eyes glistened with emotion. He looked first at Kate then at Jayne and smiled. He wanted to individually hug them and thank them for that beautiful sound of happiness in his home. He'd missed it for so long now and had at times doubted if it would ever return.

Richard and Todd were behind him and both looked adoringly at their partners. They had done something no others had managed in the last few weeks and that was to break the despairing fortress surrounding Dorothy Royston. They'd only been in there a few minutes and here she was, a different person. The three men returned to their task and Gerald patted them both on the back as they walked.

"I hope, I just hope," he said, to no one in particular.

The ladies continued their chat over coffee and Dorothy could feel a sense of warmth emulating from them both. Had she really stumbled across two friends who liked her for who she was, not because she was the professor's wife?

Kate could feel the evening drawing to a close. She could sense the surgeons in the other room starting to move around, but she couldn't leave Dorothy to return to her solitary place, not now they had broken the ice.

"Are either of you busy next week when the meeting is on, only, I'm taking Jacob to the Shadmoor Spring Fair. Why don't you both come?"

"That's sounds a great idea, Kate, the kids would love it, well Charlie would, I doubt Molly would know much about it."

"What about you, Dorothy, will you come with us?" asked Kate.

Dorothy was overwhelmed. "Oh, I'm not sure . . ."

"Please, Dorothy, we'd love to see you again."

"Yes, we would," agreed Jayne. "I could borrow Todd's people carrier, we'd all easily fit in."

"Oh, what the heck, yes, I'll come, and what's more, it'll give me something to look forward to. I've not had much of that recently."

"That's settled then, shall we take a picnic? I think they have marquees to eat in if the weather's not too good," said Kate.

"Okay, you make the adult's picnic, Kate, and I'll do the children's, how does that sound?"

"Perfect," agreed Kate.'

"What does Jacob eat?"

"Ham sandwiches will be fine and a bit of fruit. Is there anything anyone doesn't like?"

"No, not me, I'll eat anything," Jayne smiled.

"Me too," added Dorothy. "Shall I take some dessert then?" Both women looked hopefully in her direction. "Shall I make another cheesecake?"

"OH, YES!" they both replied simultaneously, and all three were laughing again.

Gerald poked his head around the door again, right on cue to see their happy faces.

"I'm sorry team, especially you, Elizabeth," he said poignantly. "It appears we didn't have as good a time as the ladies this evening. Maybe we'll join them next time."

Dorothy smiled at her husband. It had been a long road for him and at times he hadn't been the most sympathetic, maybe understandably, but she was going to make a real effort to make it up to him now.

Richard was so proud of Kate. He would never forget what she had done tonight, but he wanted her to himself now and despite everything, it was time to go.

"Thank you, Dorothy for the lovely meal and the company. I really enjoyed it," said Kate.

"No thank you, both of you. It's been a pleasure, it really has."

Dorothy hugged Kate and Jayne tightly as if she was going to miss them over the next week.

"Thank you, Professor, it's been lovely."

Professor Royston kissed Kate on the cheek and nodded knowingly. She saw the glistening eyes again and knew what he was thinking. He didn't need to say anything.

Richard and Todd said their farewells and they turned to leave.

"See you next week, girls," shouted Dorothy from the door.

"What's this?" asked Gerald.

"We're all going to Shadmoor Spring Fair whilst you attend the meeting."

Dorothy closed the door and went to retrieve the coffee cups from the lounge. Gerald finally allowed the tears to spill onto his cheek. His bottom lip shook with sheer relief as he tried to regain his composure. Why hadn't they been introduced to Kate Forrester weeks ago?

***

"Well you two worked your magic tonight, didn't you?" said Richard looking in his rear view mirror on the journey home.

"What do you mean?" asked Kate surprised.

"That was the first time Prof has heard his wife laugh in ages."

"Oh, that was Kate," interrupted Jayne. "She was offering our services as adoptive daughters."

"Really, is that what made her laugh?"

"No, it was the part when she said we could come round every week for cheesecake that set her off. Mind you, it was lovely to see. Remember that anniversary dinner, she looked dreadful didn't she?" Jayne continued.

"I think Prof was a bit touched by it all. I could see a tear in his eye by the time we were leaving," added Todd.

"It was nice of you to invite her to Shadmoor Fair, Kate?" said Richard. He wanted to hug her.

"Jayne's coming as well with the children," said Kate.

"Oh, that's great," said Todd. "We'll be slogging away with lectures and demonstrations and you'll all be out enjoying yourselves. Seriously though, Richard, I bet old Royston is in a better mood than he has been thanks to our girls."

"Definitely, I'm quite looking forward to seeing him on Monday morning."

Kate got out of the car with Jayne when they'd arrived at their house and they hugged each other.

"See you next week, Kate. Thanks for being there tonight."

"No, thank you. I'd have struggled on my own."

"I doubt it, Kate, you have an amazing knack of always saying the right thing."

Todd gave her a squeeze and shook Richard's hand. "Thanks for the lift, see you Monday."

They waved and drove off. Kate settled back in her seat; not far now and she would be able to snuggle up with Richard in his lovely king-sized bed. Richard glanced across at her and smiled. He took hold of her hand and kissed it.

"You don't know what you've done tonight, do you?" he asked.

"Well . . . "

"You hardly knew anyone and you managed to have a laugh with Elizabeth, probably *the* most serious person on this planet, and pull Dorothy out of her depression. All in one evening. You are quite remarkable, Miss Forrester, do you know that?"

Kate smiled at him. She had enjoyed this evening despite Richard spending most of it in another room. She had also made another friend. Dorothy would be her surrogate mother whilst her own was in Spain. Prof had been quite friendly as well which was indeed a bonus. But right now, she just wanted to kiss the man beside her.

They soon arrived home and went into the house.

"I miss Jacob when he's not here, but I do love our nights together when we can sleep in the same bed and wake up together," said Richard gazing down at her.

"Me too, I've missed you this evening."

"Come on then let's go up."

They climbed into bed and Kate wrapped herself around him. Richard's arms closed around her and he kissed her on the lips.

"You did enjoy yourself tonight, didn't you?"

"Of course I did. I love meeting your friends and colleagues. It makes me feel part of your life."

"You are my life, Kate. You and Jacob are all I need to make me happy. I want you to know that; as far as I'm concerned, this is it forever."

Kate could have cried. She had dreamt about him so many times but had never dared to hope that he would say those words. Tiredness swept over them both, but once they started to kiss, that was soon forgotten.

# CHAPTER . . .

# 20

Richard rose at seven thirty in readiness for the hand surgery meeting. He could hear Kate busy in the kitchen downstairs. He smiled to himself. He knew what she was doing. She was making sandwiches for their trip to Shadmoor Spring Fair. She would be making extra special ones because Dorothy would be there. He'd seen the ingredients in the fridge the night before; smoked salmon, creamed cheese, crumbly cheese, caramelised onion chutney, bacon, lettuce, and tomato, but hadn't said anything. He didn't want to embarrass her; she was going to such an effort.

Kate could hear the shower and knew that Richard was up and about. She would get everything packed into bags then prepare his breakfast for him. It was Saturday morning; she would treat him to poached eggs on toast.

He eventually arrived in the kitchen dressed in grey, suit trousers and a crisp white shirt with a couple of buttons opened at the neck. Threading his arms around Kate's waist, he kissed her neck.

"Is that for me?" he asked.

"Yes, you're missing out on our picnic so I thought I'd make you a nice breakfast."

"That's why I love you so much." She turned around and planted a kiss on his lips. The sensuous aroma of his aftershave was making her quite heady. "I'm going to miss you both today. Why don't we do something nice tomorrow? We could go for a long walk on the moors to a pub, and maybe you could get a coffee and I could have a beer and . . . "

"And maybe you could stop making fun of my dreams and eat your breakfast."

Richard laughed as she hit him with the tea towel.

"You haven't told me any more of them yet. You said you would."

"Do you wonder why?"

"If I promise not to make fun of them will you tell me the rest one day? I want them all to come true."

"Well, when you put it like that . . ."

Breakfast finished and jacket and tie on, Kate kissed him goodbye at the door and went back inside to tidy up. She failed to notice the flash of light reflecting from the visor of the biker in black across the road in the park.

Mike could feel his eye twitch again. He hated it when she did that. Why did she have to flaunt the fact that she was with this guy, right in front of him? There he was, leaving her on a Saturday morning, alone with the kid, and she still kissed him.

He could feel the anger rise within him, and wanted to punch something. It worried him slightly. He'd never met anyone who had brought about this feeling in him before. He needed to know where she was, at all times now. The habitual surveillance had become some sort of ritual of which he couldn't break free.

The old lady with the West Highland terrier kept a safe distance. It was him again and she didn't want him to see her for fear of the reprisal she may receive after reporting him to the police the week before. She was sure he would know that it was her. She lifted out her mobile phone, a present from her son for such emergencies, and pressed the number for the police station. A police car was there before she'd left the park and the same officer stepped out.

"You still here? I thought I told you last week to move on."

"It's not a crime to sit in the park. They wouldn't put benches in if it was."

"Don't be funny with me, lad," the officer replied, removing his notepad from his pocket. "Now what's your name?"

"Michael Fenwick."

"Address?"

"Flat seven, Pottersfield House."

"Right, Michael Fenwick, I'm going to be watching for you in this park and if I find out that that house over there has been done over, I'm going to be knocking on your door, understand?"

"Yeh."

"Pardon?"

"Yeh," he said louder and skulked off in the direction of his bike.

He briefly looked over his shoulder to see whether the officer had left. He wanted to find the bitch who had snitched on him for the second time. He had a damned good idea who it was. The officer waved him on and Mike thought better of it. If he was arrested then he wouldn't be able to keep tabs on Kate. Maybe he would have to move his look out back to its original place. He hadn't been disturbed there, and although Kate had almost unmasked him, his identity was still intact, as was his covetous little secret.

***

The car was loaded and the merry band were seated inside. Dorothy sat in the passenger seat beside Jayne, whilst Kate joined Molly in the middle. The two boys sat bravely in their booster seats at the back of the car casually chatting about which cars they possessed.

"Are you alright, boys, in the back?" asked Kate as they set off.

"Yes," they sang out in chorus.

Dorothy looked cheerful. The etched line of worry on her forehead seemed to have disappeared and some contented laughter lines had taken their place around her eyes.

"Oh, I have been looking forward to today," she said looking round at Kate. "It's amazing how it changes your whole disposition when there is something in the non-too-distant future to look forward to. Gerald thinks he's living with a different woman."

The two younger women smiled, delighted that Dorothy hadn't slipped back into her unhappy place after they'd left.

"I think Richard was a little disappointed he wasn't coming this morning. I'm sure he thinks he's missing out on something."

"Gerald was the same. He kept looking over at the cheesecake and saying, "Where is it you're going again?" I think he felt a little bit of excitement in the air."

Kate met Jayne's glance in the rear view mirror and nodded. Kate was glad she'd invited them both. The three of them would be good for each other and it was nice for Jacob to have a friend along instead of just Kate's company all the time.

As they approached the fair, a small queue of traffic was slowly edging its way into the car park in a field. Jayne joined the end and they waited patiently whilst the cars in front reversed into position before they took the next available space.

"Are we here?" shouted Charlie from the back seat.

"Yes," replied Jayne. "Just let me straighten up and then we can go."

Light fluffy clouds floated across a blue sky. Dorothy stepped out of the car onto the firm grass and looked up. "We're lucky with the weather. If it had rained this car park would be like a quagmire."

The children and picnic were unloaded and they set off on the short walk to the fair. The sound of a brass band could be heard in the distance so they followed the noise. There were plenty of people already milling around when they arrived. A few stalls lined the route in, selling various plants and hand carved wooden items such as trinket boxes and ornate photo frames. Jacob stared at a little train, the carriages of which were made up of capital letters and tried to decide which ones he would require to spell his name. He picked up a 'J'.

"That's right, Jacob, well done. Now, what's the next letter?"

"A, then a curly C, is that right?"

"Yes."

"Then an O and then a B."

"Well done. I'll tell you what, as you've been so clever, shall we get one before we leave today?"

"Oh, yes please, Kate."

"You be a good boy then and we'll see what we can do."

Jacob's eyes lit up at the thought of the train with his name in the middle of it. He would quite happily have stayed at the same stall all day if he hadn't seen the carousel. As Kate dragged him from the stall, it was there in front of him, bursting with colour and vibrancy

"What do you think, Jayne?" she asked. "Do you think we should go on with them?"

"I think so, although I'm not sure Charlie would be able to hold on by himself. Dorothy, you don't fancy going on with him, do you, then I could take Molly?"

"What?" Dorothy asked. "Oh, what the heck. Come on Charlie, you can hold me on."

"Yeh, come on Jacob, you sit next to us," shouted Charlie.

The three women cocked their legs over their respective horses and pulled the children on in front of them. An old fashion band organ played music in the middle. Jacob was fascinated at the keys as they disappeared then reappeared without any one playing them. Two wooden figures, a man and a woman rang bells at either end. Suddenly the carousel started to go, the horses moved up and down and the children screamed in anticipation.

"Hold on tight, Charlie," laughed Dorothy as the wind whistled through her hair. She whooped and laughed as all the pent up, bleak emotions she had been harbouring floated from her troubled mind. It took her straight back to her childhood. She hadn't had this much fun in ages.

Afterwards it was time for lunch. Kate led them over to the marquee where they could eat. Several tables and chairs were positioned around the interior. An empty table came up and Jayne grabbed it. They removed the contents of the polythene bags and spread them around the table to the relevant person. Kate had thrown a few paper serviettes in to act as plates. Once the children were sorted out, the adults tucked into their sandwiches and drank coffee from the silver flask. The children sipped their fruit juices.

"Mm, smoked salmon and creamed cheese, how delicious," said Dorothy.

"Yes, Kate, you put my sandwiches to shame," Jayne agreed.

"The children wouldn't like these," said Kate modestly. "Besides, I had to compete with Dorothy's cheesecake."

Dorothy laughed. "Honestly you two, I've never *had* so much praise for a cheesecake before."

"Well, the others mustn't have any taste buds then," Kate added.

"Oh, Kate, you are funny."

"Has Richard heard anything from his mother?" Jayne enquired.

Dorothy looked up. "What's this, Kate?"

"Richard's mother found out that he was going out with his nanny—that's me."

"And what's wrong with that?"

"She'd virtually married him off to one of the wealthy landowner's daughter up in Scotland. I think we've messed up her social life now. There'll be no more invites from the manor house any more now that Richard has upset their precious daughter."

"Do I know this woman?" asked Dorothy.

"She was at your anniversary party, Dorothy," Jayne added.

"Really, I don't remember her at all. Well, it looks like I've got another adopted child now, Richard."

Kate smiled. "Will you have room for us all when we move in?"

"I'm sure we could find some but I'm not sure you'd stay very long with Gerald around. He can be a bit grumpy at times. Maybe we should stick to once a week like we arranged, then you won't get fed up of him . . . like I do."

They giggled. "You must have loved him at one time," said Jayne.

"Oh, I still do, especially when he goes into his study to do some work and I can have the television all to myself." They were laughing out loud now as they finished their sandwiches off and Dorothy proudly unveiled the cheesecake.

"What's that, Kate?" Jacob whispered.

"This is Dorothy's delicious cheesecake. Are you going to have a piece?"

"Are you?"

"Of course I am. I wouldn't miss out on this."

"Okay, I'll try a piece. Are you having some, Charlie?"

"I'll try some."

The children tentatively put a piece in their mouths then smiled and nodded.

"There you go, Dorothy, you should go into business. I've never known Jacob eat a piece of cheesecake before."

"Well I'm very pleased you like it, Jacob. I know what to make now when you all come round."

They'd all enjoyed lunch and the flasks were packed away whilst the children handled the job of throwing the multitude of plastic bags in the nearest bin. They made their way outside where the sun continued to shine on them.

"Shall we go and look at the animals whilst lunch goes down," suggested Kate.

"Good idea," agreed Jayne. "I'll go and get some food so they can feed the goats and the sheep."

"Okay."

"Charlie, will you stay with Dorothy for a minute?"

"Okay, mummy."

Dorothy took Charlie's hand and led him to the pony that was poking its head through a metal gate. Charlie patted his nose cautiously.

"Oh, hello, Kate, what are you doing here?"

Kate spun round swiftly and came face to face with Ingrid. Jacob disappeared behind her legs.

"Hello, Ingrid."

"No Richard I see. Still left holding the baby?"

"He's working."

"On call no doubt? That's what he says, in fact that's what he told me too; turns out he was shagging the nanny all along."

"That's not true." Kate could feel her face flush with contempt.

"Oh yes, it bloody is. You don't just say you're in love with someone else without sampling the goods first."

"Everything alright, Kate?" Jayne asked as she approached the two of them. She could see Jacob shying away behind Kate. She must have really left a bad impression on that young boy.

"Oh, how cosy," said Ingrid sarcastically. "And how are you, Jayne? I see you've fallen for Kate's charms as well."

"Mummy, have you got some food for the animals?"

Ingrid's mouth dropped as she saw Dorothy approaching with a smile on her face. The woman had practically been moribund the last time she'd seen her. There was no recognition in her eyes as to who Ingrid was.

"Sorry, Ingrid, but we have to go. The children want to feed the animals," Jayne intervened. "Come on, Kate."

Kate was rooted to the spot. She hadn't thought about Ingrid when she'd suggested Shadmoor Fair, but of course, she lived nearby, why wouldn't she be there? What else happened in Shadmoor that was worth a visit?

"Kate, come on," Jayne ordered, and pulled her by the arm.

"Don't forget to say hello to Richard for me."

Ingrid threw a departing smirk and disappeared in the opposite direction.

"Sorry, Jayne, that took me by surprise."

"Who *was* that?" asked Dorothy.

"The woman we were talking about earlier who came to your party, - Ingrid," replied Jayne.

"Oh, I didn't like the look of her at all. I don't remember her from the party. She mustn't have left a lasting impression."

For the rest of the day Kate went over Ingrid's sniping remarks in her head. How sordid she had made their relationship seem. She suddenly wanted Richard by her side to reassure her that everything would be alright. She wished he'd been here today so that Ingrid could have witnessed first hand how close they were instead of insinuating that he was with someone else.

Jayne could sense the mood change in her friend and could see how she warily glanced around her every time they moved on to the next stall. What had that woman said to change her whole demeanour in an instant? Ingrid's contorted face and scornful eyes indicated that it was more than just a mere passing of the time of day.

The old fashioned sweet stall had the children's eyes bulging with desire and diverted Jacob's thoughts away from Ingrid, for the time being anyway. Candy lollies, striped humbugs, sugared mice, treacle toffee, pear drops, aniseed balls, Coltsfoot rock and Kola Kubes not to mention the huge array of chocolates and penny chews.

"I'm going to have one of those red liquorice shoelaces," Dorothy announced. "Anyone else want one? I haven't seen them in years."

"Can I have one?" shouted Charlie.

"Can I have one?" echoed Jacob.

"You've started something now, Dorothy," laughed Kate.

"Are you going to have one, Kate?"

"Go on then."

"Jayne?"

"Well if everyone else is."

Molly was sound asleep by this point and no one was about to disturb her so Dorothy bought her some white chocolate mice then she didn't feel left out.

"Kate, could we get mummy some of those striped sweets?" asked Jacob.

"Of course we can, they're called humbugs. Does mummy like those?"

"I've seen her with some before. She used to keep a bag of them in the car."

Kate picked up a small bag of humbugs and gave Jacob the money to pay for them.

"You can give her them next week when you visit," she said.

"What can we get daddy?" he asked excited at the thought of giving his own gifts.

Kate looked around. "Why don't we get him some home-made chutney off the next stall? He'd like that on a sandwich with some cheese."

"Can we get one of those with a little hat on?"

"Yes, they look nice don't they," answered Kate eyeing up a jar of green tomato chutney with a gingham covered lid.

Kate quickly glanced over her shoulder again as she stood behind Jacob with his purchases. The last thing she wanted was some acid comment from Ingrid whilst Jacob was in earshot. He was already totally traumatised by her after her day of child caring.

It was finally time to leave and after unanimously deciding to have one more ride on the carousel, minus Jayne and Molly, they made their way to the exit via the little wooden toy shop, for the train composed of the letters J, A, C, O and B. Charlie had to have one as well with his name spelled out in letter carriages, and of course Molly couldn't be left out so she had a hand painted wooden doll to hang on the wall of her nursery with the name Molly imprinted on her dress. They were all exhausted by the time they'd finished.

"What a lovely day that was," Dorothy enthused. "Thank you for inviting me."

"Thank you for coming, Dorothy. We didn't realise you were such a good sport. We couldn't have taken the children on the carousel with just two of us," said Jayne.

"We all like a bit of fun," smiled Dorothy. "Even us old ones."

"You're as young as you feel," said Kate. "And from what we saw today, that makes you about twenty five."

Dorothy threw her head back and laughed as they proceeded to the car park eating their red shoelaces.

***

It was late afternoon when they arrived home. Kate and Jacob waved furiously at Jayne, Dorothy and the children as they disappeared in the car, then went back into the house. Richard was already there.

"Hi, how was the meeting?" shouted Kate as she took off her jacket and hung it up.

"It went very well, thanks," Richard replied.

"And what about your presentation?"

"Fine, it got a good response. Anyway, enough of me, how did your day go?" he asked picking Jacob up and giving him a huge bear hug.

"It was great," Jacob started. "We went on a carousel and Dorofee was really funny because she kept screaming."

"Dorothy went on with you?"

"Oh, yes," replied Kate. "She's amazing, she's up for anything. I went on with Jacob, Jayne took Molly, so Dorothy agreed to take Charlie on and she loved it. She bought us all red liquorice shoelaces to eat on the way home."

"Unbelievable."

"We saw Ingrid, daddy, and she swore at Kate."

"She did what? Kate what's this all about?"

Kate cringed as now she had to explain the conversation which she was hoping she could quietly forget.

"It was nothing," she said making her way to the kitchen.

"Kate, Kate, what did she say?"

He was in front of her now and wasn't about to leave the subject alone until he was satisfied that he'd been given the whole story. Jacob stood by, wondering if he had said the right thing. Kate took a deep sigh and began.

"She just insinuated that you and I were sleeping together when you were with her. Of course I denied it so then she said, "Of course it was *bloody* true" and that was it," Kate said in a quiet voice.

"Did Jayne hear any of this conversation?" Richard knew she wasn't telling him the whole story. He could tell in her eyes that she was holding something back. They looked worried and sad.

"Not really. Ingrid made some sarcastic remark to her then we left."

Kate went into the kitchen and flicked the kettle on. Richard watched her closely.

"Daddy, we bought you a present."

"Oh, thank you. What is it?" Jacob handed over the jar of chutney and Richard inspected it. "Green tomato chutney, my favourite. I'm going to have a cheese sandwich for lunch tomorrow just so that I can put some of that on."

"And look what I got." Jacob rummaged around in the plastic bag and removed the train piece by piece. "See what it spells."

"JABOC?" said Richard.

"Oh, I've done something wrong. Daddy, what have I done wrong?"

"Shall we start again?"

They rearranged the train and finally got the spelling right.

"See daddy, it spells JACOB."

"Wow, what a fantastic train. I wish I'd had one of them when I was four."

"And we got mummy some humbugs."

"My, you have been busy. That's really kind of you, Jacob, to think of mummy and daddy whilst you're out. Thanks, Kate."

He followed her into the kitchen and kissed her on the side of the face.

"It's alright. Jacob chose them."

He was still worried about her. She wasn't her usual cheerful self and he was sure it had something to do with Ingrid and what she had said to her. Kate turned towards him. She wrapped her arms around his shoulders and pulled him to her.

"I couldn't cope if you left me, you know," she said.

"What? Where has this come from? I'm not going to leave you. You've got me for life, I told you that the other day."

"I know, just keep telling me. Ingrid looked so bitter, but in a way I can understand how she must feel, because that's what I would be like in the same situation."

He held her close for a while until Jacob demanded his attention again.

***

That night Kate lay in bed going over every detail of the conversation with Ingrid. She was beginning to regret the pact she had made with Richard that she would only go into his room when Jacob was away at his mother's. She wanted him beside her, holding her, comforting her and reassuring her that everything was going to be alright.

Richard was brooding over the same dilemma. He'd unwillingly parted that night with the issue still not resolved. As much as she said she was fine, he knew the opposite was true. *To hell with it,* he thought. The pact was that she wouldn't go into his bed; it mentioned nothing of him going into hers. He tapped on the door to see if she was still awake.

"Yes?" came the reply.

"It's me, can I come in?"

"Course you can."

He sat on the edge of the bed in his boxer shorts, and ran his fingers through her hair.

"I love you, you know."

"I love you too."

"Move up."

Kate slid to the other side of the bed and Richard got in beside her. He fed his arm around her and pulled her towards him. Kate gulped hard. She was struggling to keep the tears at bay.

"Tell me what happened," he said staring into the darkness.

"She asked where you were. I told her you were working and she as good as said that when you say you're on call, you're actually seeing other women. I know it's rubbish but she was just so hateful."

"She's jealous of you and trying to put doubts in your mind. I have never been as happy as I am now. You know when you've met the right person because you start to make plans for the future, not just the next date. That's what I'm doing, Kate. I'm thinking about where I can take you and Jacob on holiday and whether we should have a short break with Todd and Jayne and the kids. I didn't do that with Ingrid, she wasn't that important to me."

He could feel her tears drop onto his chest.

"I hope they're tears of relief and not because you're still worried," he teased her.

"Yes, they are," she said half laughing.

"By the way, I'm staying here tonight. It's warm in here and I've got no intention of getting back into a cold bed."

"Good, I need you here tonight."

They held each other tight until Kate finally fell asleep. He could feel her drift off as she slowly released her grip on him. Kissing her on the forehead, he wondered how many more times Ingrid Harper was going to interfere in their lives. He thought that chapter had been well and truly closed.

# Chapter . . .

# 21

Impromptu events are often more enjoyable than those that have been planned for weeks; and so it was that Richard's idea was born. By about eleven thirty, one Saturday morning, the last of the cloud had dispersed revealing a bright mid-May, blue sky.

"Why don't we have a barbeque this afternoon?" he had suggested and from that one statement, things mushroomed.

"Can Charlie come?" Jacob had asked.

"Oh, yes, we could invite Jayne and Todd and the kids, and what about Dorothy and Prof? It would be nice for us all to get together again, we had such a nice day at the fair," added Kate.

"Okay, if you insist. I'll go and give them all a ring, see what they're doing."

Dorothy was overjoyed to be asked. Prof even succumbed to wearing a short sleeved, open necked, casual shirt. He felt virtually naked without his bow tie on but Dorothy had insisted.

Jayne was just waiting for Todd to return from work. His free latissimus dorsi flap to a lower leg from the previous day had gone a worrying shade of blue. He wouldn't be long though. He'd already rung to say he'd finished and was just writing the operation note up and then they would love to come too.

Richard had dashed off to the butcher's before it had closed and Kate started preparing salad and accompaniments.

By four o'clock the party was in full swing and everyone was enjoying a drink, the sunshine and the company. Jayne was helping Molly build a tower with some building bricks on the decking, whilst Prof, Richard and Todd were teaching the two boys to play rounders with a big sponge bat and ball.

"Look at him," said Dorothy as she joined Kate in the kitchen. "He never does that with his own grandchildren. He's having a whale of a time."

Kate smiled. "Yes, I don't know who's enjoying themselves more, the children or the adults."

"I think the men probably have the edge. Can I do anything to help?"

"No, we're ready to cook now. I don't like to interrupt Richard; he seems to be having so much fun. I think I'll start barbequing."

"I think you're right. They don't get much chance to let their hair down in their profession."

The afternoon had progressed into the evening. The delicious smell of barbequed food still hung around in the air. Music played in the background and the wine flowed. Kate decided to take a few pictures to remember the occasion.

"Here, let me take one of you and Richard," Jayne offered.

"Oh, thanks, Jayne, we've never had one taken together."

By about eight o'clock, Molly started to protest that it was past her bedtime and she wasn't going to be pacified with just a dummy and a chewed blanket. It was Todd and Jayne's cue to leave.

"Thank you so much for a lovely afternoon. We really enjoyed it," said Jayne kissing Kate on the cheek.

"It was a pleasure. We're glad you could all come. It's not often we get a nice day like this," Kate replied.

"Yes, come on Gerald, we'll get off as well then they can get Jacob to bed. Thank you so much for a lovely time."

"Yes, Richard, Kate, I thoroughly enjoyed myself," said Gerald looking quite surprised at the fact that he could actually experience fun. He rubbed Jacob on the head. "And you, young man, don't try so hard in future to get me out."

Richard felt a tinge of affection for his boss. He wasn't the old misery they all thought he was. He glanced in Todd's direction who was looking somewhat surprised; fancy old

Royston having a sense of humour after all. Dorothy was pleased. Finally he had emerged from his sullen exterior. He was really just a nice old man underneath all that pomp and bow ties. She linked his arm and steered him towards the car.

"I think that was rather successful," said Richard with one arm draped around Kate's shoulder and the other waving.

***

"Where are we going?" asked Mike as he let Alex and Chris into the flat.

"Just down The Dog and Duck. They've got a quiz night on. Wade's meeting us there," Alex replied.

"Okay, just let me have a quick shower and I'll come down with you."

"Sure."

"Beers are in the fridge. I won't be long."

Alex and Chris wondered into the kitchen and opened the fridge door. The bottles of Budweiser were evenly stacked on the top shelf. Alex took two out.

"Where's the bottle opener?" shouted Chris but there was no reply.

"He won't be able to hear you if he's in the shower. There must be one in one of these drawers. Why doesn't he just buy cans, save all this trouble?" said Alex.

They both began to open drawers in search of the bottle opener. Suddenly Alex stopped.

"What's up, mate?" asked Chris walking over to where he stood.

Alex picked up the top photograph of Kate. He stared at it then showed Chris. "What the hell's this, there are loads of them, and they've got blue tac on the back? He must have had them on his wall."

"Are they all of Kate?" asked Chris peering over his shoulder.

"No, some have got Jacob on."

"He's obviously got some kind of crush on her."

"This is more than a fucking crush; this is stalking. What's he doing taking pictures of Jacob as well?"

"Maybe he just happened to be there when he was clicking away."

"That better be the case. I'm gonna find out what's going on."

"Just a minute, mate, he's took them down now, the phase has probably passed. Maybe he lost interest when she started going out with Richard." Chris could see Alex's veins start to stand out on his neck.

Alex threw the picture back into the drawer and slammed it shut. "If he as much as goes near Kate again, I'm gonna have him for this. He's fucking weird. Tell him I'll see him down there. I can't stomach his bleeding beer."

Chris stood in the kitchen alone as Alex stormed out of the flat. Moments later Mike appeared with a threadbare, faded, blue towel wrapped around his waist. He rubbed his hair with another towel which had once been white.

"Where's Alex gone?" he asked looking perplexed.

"He forgot something and had to go back. He said he'd see us down there."

"I thought I heard the door bang, nearly took it off its bleeding hinges."

Chris looked perturbed. He could feel an atmosphere coming on and a full evening trying to keep his two friends apart. Mike wasn't aware of their discovery and would wonder why Alex had suddenly turned on him. How was he going to explain that? His immediate response was to take off home but then what would he say to Mike if both of them had turned up unannounced inviting him to the pub, then suddenly disappeared.

***

Alex was true to form. He stared menacingly across the table, practically urging Mike to say something. Chris kept Mike talking to divert his eyes from Alex's grimace. Wade looked bemused in the middle. He'd only spoken to Alex about half an hour ago and he was fine. What on earth had dampened his spirits so quickly and why was he looking at Mike in that manner?

The quiz master introduced himself and announced the rules. Chris breathed a sigh of relief. They could all concentrate on the quiz now and he could let down his guard until it was over. He would then make his excuses and go. Alex could do what the hell he wanted to Mike after that.

***

Richard rubbed the back of his neck and finished off writing the notes in front of him. He'd have a spot of lunch in the canteen then try and start his list a bit earlier. Maybe then he could get home and see Kate and Jacob before he got called out. Wednesday was always a hard day and had been known to last until the early hours of the following morning. It only took one amputated finger and he could be up half the night.

He handed over the notes to the nurse in front of him and, sliding his jacket back on, left clinic. The canteen was just a short walk along the corridor, up the stairs and off to the left past the administrators' offices. He joined the queue and immediately started to scan the metal trays warming behind the glass window. On Wednesday lunch times, he generally had a fairly decent meal, just in case he didn't make it home. He pressed the button for a white tea with no sugar then proceeded to the cashier to pay. Todd was in the far corner waving his arm. Richard went over to join him.

"Roast beef and Yorkshire pudding, eh, has Kate stopped feeding you?" asked Todd humorously.

"You never know when your next meal is when you're on call."

"Oh yes, it's Wednesday isn't it? Good barbeque the other day, by the way. Even old Royston enjoyed himself."

"Yes, he can let his hair down when he wants to do, can't he? Never seen him like that before. I don't know what Kate does to people. Melissa's the same. Complete change of character since she met Kate."

"She's lovely. Jayne thinks the world of her. Don't let this one slip away, Richard. She's special."

"I've no intention of doing. In fact, strictly between you and me, I'm going to ask her to marry me."

"Really?" said Todd. Richard nodded. He'd thought about it all weekend and now was in no doubt whatsoever. "I don't blame you. What about Melissa; will she give you a quick divorce?"

"I think so. I've not asked her in so many words but why would she want to delay it. She's got Alex. I'm going to get Arthur Bainmouth, my solicitor on it as soon as I've asked Kate."

"I don't think there's any chance of her refusing. She's besotted with you."

"Do you think so?"

"I'm sure so. The pair of you are like a couple of love struck teenagers."

Richard laughed.

***

Kate reached for her coat and slid her feet into her shoes. It was time to go and fetch Jacob from nursery, then they would have some lunch and maybe a quick trip to the park. She wanted to try him on his bike without stabilisers again. What a surprise it would be if he could master it by weekend. Richard would be amazed.

Suddenly the doorbell rang. Kate quickly looked at her watch. Time was slipping by and she didn't want to be late. Who was this delaying her? She opened the door.

"Oh, what do you want?"

***

Richard dabbed his mouth with his paper serviette. "Well, not as good as Kate's but not bad for hospital food."

"My sandwich was delicious."

"Yes, it looked it. I was just wondering how long it'd been sat there under those lights."

"Probably about a fortnight knowing this place. Anyway, enough of this, I've got a list to do."

"Yes, me as well. I want to see if I can start a bit earlier so that I can get home for a while."

"Why, there's nothing coming in is there?"

"Not yet, but you never know." At that point Richard's phone rang. "Hello, Richard Anderson speaking."

*"Mr Anderson, it's Mrs Bentley here from the nursery. We're a little concerned; Kate hasn't turned up yet to pick Jacob up and he's starting to get upset. She's never normally late you see and we've tried the house and her mobile and there's no answer."*

"Are you sure?"

*"Yes. If she was going to be late, I'm sure she'd have rung us and let us know."*

"Yes, of course she would, erm, I'll come and get Jacob and I'll try her again on the way, er, thanks."

"What's wrong?" asked Todd looking concerned.

"It's Kate, she's not turned up for Jacob yet and it's twenty past twelve. She's twenty minutes late. It's not like her, she's never late."

"You go, Richard, I'll get Carl to start your list."

"Do you not mind?"

"Not at all."

Richard walked as fast as he could out of the canteen and through the corridors to the outside world. From the door of the hospital he ran as fast as he could to the Consultant car park. A cold, stark panic started to rise in him. Where was she? He couldn't think of a logical explanation as to why she wouldn't have collected Jacob.

He knew he was driving too fast but he had to find out where she was. His phone was in its dock. At the next red light, he searched for her number and pressed the green button.

"*Your call cannot be taken at the moment, please . . ."*

He quickly cancelled the call and dialled home. *"Your call can . . ."* still no answer. Where are you Kate? The lights changed. His foot hit the floor and the automatic engine responded. His heart was racing. What if something had happened to her? He was soon at the nursery. He drew to a halt and ran in. Jacob's tear stained face greeted him.

"Hey, little fella, are you alright?"

"Daddy, where's Kate?" he sobbed.

"I'm not sure, but there must be a good reason why she hasn't arrived yet."

"Has she gone . . . again?" he asked between sobs.

"No, sweetheart, Kate loves you and she promised she would never go away again without telling you first, didn't she?" Jacob nodded. "Come on, let's go and find her. Thanks, Mrs Bentley. Sorry to keep you."

"No, not at all. I just hope Kate's alright."

Her comment made Richard all the more worried. She was obviously not used to Kate diverting from any timescales. He needed to go home first, he would start from there and try to trace her steps.

He strapped Jacob into the back of the car then rather more sedately drove back to the house. The wheels of the car scraped the kerb as he stared in horror at the open front door. A wave of sickness came from nowhere and overwhelmed him. He put his hand to his mouth as he considered how to handle the situation without frightening his son. Taking his hand, Richard led him to the door. He pushed it open and shouted.

"Kate, Kate are you there?"

There was no reply. He looked around for any signs of life on the street outside. A curtain twitched in Mrs Hamilton's house across the road. He knelt on one knee next to his son.

"Jacob, would you stay with Mrs Hamilton for a few minutes whilst I check the house?"

"Why, daddy, what's wrong?"

"There's nothing wrong I just want to have a look round and see if Kate's left anything that could tell me where she is. It probably won't be very exciting for you. Mrs Hamilton has nice biscuits doesn't she?"

"Okay."

Richard walked Jacob across the road and knocked on the door.

"Richard, is everything alright?"

"Hello, Mrs Hamilton, I wonder, could you look after Jacob for a few minutes? We're not sure where Kate is and . . ." he turned around to look at his house. ". . . the front door's open," he mouthed.

Mrs Hamilton's eyes widened. "Of course, come in, Jacob. Do you want a drink and a biscuit?"

Richard ran back across the road. He was free to panic now that his son wasn't watching his every reaction. "Kate, Kate are you there?"

He looked in every room downstairs, nothing. He stood at the foot of the stairs and looked up. What was he going to find? His breathing became rapid and shallow as he mounted the stairs one by one, his eyes still staring ahead.

Her bedroom door was open. He quickly glanced in. The room was empty and just as she'd left it, then he noticed his bedroom door was shut. He never left it like that, neither did Kate after she'd been in there. His hand was shaking as he lowered the handle and opened the door. The room felt cold inside; the window was open and the curtains stirred with the breeze. His eyes scanned the room then, he looked behind the door.

"Kate, oh my God, Kate, what's happened?"

Kate lay on the floor, her head bent to one side, her eyes closed and a pool of dark red blood on the cream carpet beneath her. Richard fell to the floor and his fingers automatically went to the artery in her neck. Could he feel a pulse or was his mind playing tricks with him? It was faint if it was there at all. He shook her slightly.

"Kate, can you hear me, it's Richard?"

Years of knowledge and training flew out of the window as his mind went blank. What would he do now? He took his phone out and dialled 999. An ambulance and the police. He would start with that.

"I need an ambulance quickly, please, thirty two Richmond Avenue. It looks like my girlfriend's been . . . stabbed." He could barely bring himself to say the word. Who would do something like this?

*"Is she still . . ."*

"Look, I'm a doctor. I'll do what I can until they get here but please be quick."

Richard tried to feel the carotid artery again. He could feel it, he was sure. It was faint but it was definitely there, weak and thready, but there.

"Kate," he said bending down beside her. "I'm going to turn you slightly."

He moved her body and soon could see the full extent of her wound. She looked so pale, as a trickle of blood ran down her chest and dripped onto the carpet, merging with the rest of the congealed mass. He reached for the towel hung over the radiator behind her limp body and pressed it over the hole left by the knife. He couldn't tell whether her lung had been perforated or not.

"Come on ambulance," he willed. He couldn't do anything on his own. There was nothing that could save her life to hand. He picked her up into his arms and pressed on hard with the towel. Her head fell back onto him She felt cold and clammy. If she wasn't going to make it, he at least wanted her to know that he was there for her.

It seemed like an eternity, but at last the welcoming sound of a siren could be heard in the distance. It was getting nearer and Richard almost cried with relief.

"They're here, Kate, hold on, sweetheart. They're here."

"Hello," came the comforting voice of the paramedic.

"Up here," shouted Richard. "In the bedroom on the left."

Two sets of feet could be heard ascending the stairs, then they appeared from behind the door carrying a full set of resuscitation equipment. Richard had never been so pleased to see anyone in his life.

"Oh, thank God you're here. I think I can still feel a pulse, it's very weak but it's there and her breathing is shallow, resps about twenty eight. She's been stabbed in the chest."

"Okay, sir, what's her name?"

"It's Kate."

"And yours?"

"Richard."

"Okay, Richard, I'm Sam, you keep pressing on the wound whilst I get a cannula in and John intubates. We're going to do everything we can now to get her to hospital as quickly as possible."

"Thank you."

Richard was unaware of the tears streaming down his face. Sam wrapped a tourniquet around her arm and expertly found a vein. He quickly connected a bag of fluid and then helped John with the intubation. Kate was then lifted onto a stretcher, the wound covered and carried downstairs to the waiting ambulance.

Two uniformed policemen were waiting at the foot of the stairs as Richard appeared covered in Kate's blood.

"I'll follow you," Richard shouted to the paramedics. "I have to take care of my son first."

"Hello, sir, I'm Sergeant Hargreaves and this is PC Vale. Can I ask you your name?"

"It's Richard Anderson."

"And where is your son, sir?" asked the sergeant.

"He's across the road with my neighbour."

"Is there someone we can call to take care of him?"

"Erm . . . yes, my ex-wife. She can collect him."

"Do you have a number, Richard?" asked the second officer.

"Yes, it's, er, . . . it's in the book, under M for Melissa."

"Do you have any idea what's happened here?"

Richard looked at the floor and tried to stem another flow of tears by pinching the bridge of his nose. "I got a call at lunch time in the hospital canteen, I'm a doctor, to say that my girlfriend, Kate, hadn't arrived to pick my son up from nursery. When I got back, I dropped him off at the neighbour's because I noticed the front door was open. When I went into the bedroom, I found her lying in a pool of blood. She was barely breathing. I don't know how long she's been there."

"We're going to bring forensics in. I'll come with you to get changed to make sure you don't disturb anything. This is obviously a crime scene and you need to be really careful as to what you touch."

"Your ex-wife is on the way," said PC Vale.

The two of them walked upstairs and Richard found some clothes to get changed into. He washed his hands in the bathroom and gave the officer the items he had been wearing as requested. He suddenly started to feel like a suspect.

"Where were you this morning, Mr Anderson?" asked the sergeant taking off his hat.

"I was at work doing my clinic, then I had lunch with a colleague of mine, Todd Hamer. He was there when I got the call from the nursery."

"Thank you, we need to ask, I hope you understand, just to help with our enquiries."

"Yes, of course."

"Do you have any idea who would want to do this to your girlfriend?"

"No, I've tried to think, but she's very popular, everyone loves her."

Footsteps were heard coming up the stairs and PC Vale appeared to announce the arrival of Melissa.

"Right, Richard, if you want to come down and hand your son over, I'll take you to the hospital. I don't think you're in any fit state to drive."

"No, I think you're right."

It was the first time the sergeant had called him by his first name. Did that mean he was off the hook—as if he could hurt his precious Kate? He followed Sergeant Hargreaves downstairs.

"We will need to take your fingerprints. Obviously yours and Kate's will be all over the house but we can do that later. We'll get you to the hospital now."

"Thank you."

Outside the house, Melissa stood in a state of shock.

"Richard, what's happened?"

"It's Kate, she's been stabbed."

"Oh, my God." Melissa put her hands to her mouth. "Is she alright?"

"I don't know. She's probably on her way to theatre now. I'll go and get Jacob. He's over at Mrs Hamilton's."

The officers waited with Melissa. Jacob walked back across the road holding his father's hand. His little face looked upset and wan as the tears slid down his cheek and landed on his coat.

"Mummy," he said sadly. "Kate's poorly, she's gone to hospital."

"I know, sweetheart. You come and stay with mummy and Alex for a few days whilst daddy takes care of her."

Jacob nodded and took her outstretched hand.

"Will daddy make her better?"

"I'm sure he will."

"I'll bring some clothes round later. I can't get back in the house at the moment," said Richard.

His heart ached as he listened to the simplicity of his young son's questions. What if daddy couldn't make her better? How would he cope with his own grief, never mind that of Jacob?

"Don't worry, we'll find something for him to wear."

"Bye, Jacob. You've been a good boy."

"Bye, daddy."

On the way to the hospital, the officer explained that a detective would be assigned to the case and that they would contact him later. But right at this moment, Richard would be left to concentrate on Kate. Once parked up outside the main entrance, he stepped out of the police car and made his way into the hospital like he had done on so many occasions before. Only this time he was a grieving relative, on the other side. Now he knew how it felt to arrive at the hospital and not know what condition to find your loved one.

After pausing briefly to explain to Todd what had happened, he continued on to the operating theatre, and pressed the intercom button.

"Mr Anderson?" came a voice from the metal plate on the wall. "We're not expecting you."

"No, I'm not here to do a case."

The door buzzed, and Richard stepped in. He wandered through reception in a fog. Several of the nurses greeted him on his way through, but he didn't seem to hear them. In recovery, Sister McBride approached him.

"Mr Anderson, are you alright?"

"Ah, Sally, is there a Kate Forrester in theatre at the moment?"

"Yes, stab wound to chest."

"She's my girlfriend."

"Oh, my goodness. Come this way."

Sister McBride took Richard by the arm and led him to the Relatives' Room. She seated him in one of the comfy chairs and switched the kettle on.

"How is she, Sally?" It was a question he was scared to ask for fear of the answer.

"She's still with us. She's fighting. Mr Firth is operating; he's the best there is at thoracic surgery. She's had quite a few units of blood already. Does anyone know she's your girlfriend?"

"Not unless Todd Hamer has said something. Mind you he's probably busy in the other theatres sorting out our lists."

He sat forward in the chair and rubbed the back of his neck.

"Here," she said handing him a strong cup of tea. "Drink this; you could be in for a long night. Can I get you anything to eat?"

"I couldn't stomach anything at the moment, but thanks for asking."

Sally wanted to sit next to him and put her arm around him like she had done with so many of the visitors. In fact she couldn't think of a member of the female staff who wouldn't want to do the same thing. But instead, she put her hand over his, and held it there for a while.

There was a tapping at the door and Richard quickly looked up hoping to find Clive Firth, the surgeon. It was Todd.

"Any news yet?" he asked concerned.

"No, nothing yet," replied Richard. "I suppose they say no news is good news, but it doesn't feel that way."

"If anything had gone wrong, they'd be straight in to tell you."

"Can I make you a drink, Mr Hamer?" Sally asked feeling somewhat uncomfortable now with her hand on Richard's whilst someone else was in the room.

"Coffee, one sugar, thanks, Sally."

Sally passed the drink and then left the room. Her services were no longer required whilst Todd Hamer was around.

"What if she doesn't make it, Todd? What am I going to do?"

"Hey, come on, don't think like that, mate. What if she does make it? The poor girl has got to marry you."

Richard nearly laughed. The last conversation he'd had with Todd came tumbling to the forefront of his mind.

After what seemed like an age, there was another knock at the door and both men looked up. The surgeon, Clive Firth walked into the room and removed his paper theatre cap. He scrunched it into a ball and threw it into the waste paper bin.

"Richard, I believe this young lady is a friend of yours, well more than a friend. We've managed to patch her up, her lung was nicked by the knife and she had quite a bit of internal bleeding. She's on her fifth unit of blood as we speak, but she's alive." Richard breathed a sigh of relief. He could feel his composure slipping as Clive Firth continued. "Because of the amount of blood loss, we don't know what she'll be like if she wakes up. We can only wait and see."

"*If* she wakes, Clive, what do you mean *if*?"

"You and I know it's a waiting game now, Richard. We've done all we can on the surgical side, it's up to Kate now to pull through."

Clive tapped him on the shoulder and went to leave.

"Thank you, Clive, thanks for all you've done."

"No problem, she'll be in recovery soon. I'm sure they'll let you in to see her."

Richard looked at Todd. Neither of them said a word but both knew what the other was thinking. *If* was a huge word. How many times had they said that to relatives in their years as junior doctors? And how many times had their patient not pulled through.

A few minutes later Sister McBride came back into the room.

"Do you want to come and see Kate now, Richard, before she goes round to ICU?"

"Of course, thank you."

"I'll speak to Prof, Richard," said Todd. "Explain you won't be in for a while."

Todd put a comforting hand on his shoulder as he walked past then followed Richard to the recovery area. A curtain was pulled partially around the bed for privacy from the other recovering patients.

Richard's face looked haunted as he first set eyes on Kate. She lay there, as pale as the sheets beneath her, still connected to a ventilator via a long piece of tubing and an endotracheal tube protruding from her mouth. The ventilator blew and sucked air, in and out of her body, her chest rose and fell in synchronisation with the machine. A monitor above was the only other indication that she was alive. An ECG trace flashed across the screen, and blipped with every beat of her heart.

A container partially filled with blood stained fluid swung by the side of the bed; the chest drain to help re-inflate her punctured lung. So the knife had been deeper than he thought. Poor Kate.

Richard stared at the monitor screen taking in all the numbers; heart rate 86, that was better than earlier today, respirations 16, oxygen saturation 96%, arterial pressure 125 over 88. Everything looked satisfactory. He took her hand and kissed it, whilst his eyes fixed on her ashen face.

"Mr Anderson, here's a chair for you," one of the nurses offered.

"Thank you," he said absently.

Another nurse recorded the observations on a chart and with an empathetic smile, went about her business. The anaesthetist appeared in his theatre blues to ensure his patient was comfortable.

"Richard, I'm so sorry. Do they have any idea who did this?"

Richard shook his head. "No, not yet, Ian," he replied, his eyes never leaving her face.

Dr Ian Curtis lifted the tubing of the central venous line in her neck, undid the bung and emptied the contents of the syringe he was holding, into it. He flushed it through with sodium chloride.

"Just a bolus of Fentanyl to keep her pain free before we move her to ICU. We'll be taking her round there in about ten minutes when they've prepared the bed area."

"Thanks, Ian."

***

Alex opened the door to the lounge expecting to see Melissa. Jacob looked up from his colouring book dressed in his pyjamas.

"Hello, Jacob, I didn't expect to see you. Where's your mummy?"

"I think she's upstairs cleaning the bath. I have to stay tonight because Kate's poorly and daddy's got to look after her."

"Oh, I see. Well that's fine." He left the room to meet Melissa coming down the stairs. "I hear Kate's not well, what's wrong with her?"

Melissa looked stricken. She put her finger over her lip and nodded towards the kitchen. Alex was intrigued. What on earth was going on for Richard to allow Jacob to stay during the week?

"Kate's in hospital, she's been stabbed."

"Stabbed?"

"Yes, just before lunch time. They had to call Richard from the nursery to pick Jacob up. When he got home he found her lying in the bedroom in a pool of blood."

"Do they know who did it?"

"No idea. Maybe it was burglars who were disturbed."

Alex shivered as an icy chill rushed down his spine. His immediate thoughts went to Mike and the contents of his kitchen drawer. Was he capable of such a deed? He certainly had a motive as it would seem he had developed an unhealthy fixation on Kate and Richard had ruined what might have been his ultimate plan. Had Kate betrayed him in his eyes and now he was carrying out his revenge?

"How is she, have you heard?"

"No, not yet. Richard must still be at the hospital. He said he'd try to bring some clothes for Jacob but I told him not to bother tonight. I'll just go and see if Jacob wants any supper."

She left him alone in the kitchen to toy with his thoughts. He had to do something. This was Kate he was talking about. The police had to know about the pictures. He went upstairs into the bedroom and took out his mobile phone.

The police accepted the anonymity of the call and Alex knew that despite the trouble his friend was in, he'd done right by Kate. He sat on the edge of the bed and contemplated his next move. Opening the small bedside cabinet, he took out an old metal biscuit tin with a picture of a Scottish glen on the front. It contained some photographs that Alex had decided he wasn't going to get rid of. There were several holiday photographs of him and Kate, a few from Christmas and the rest were of their friends at birthday parties and weddings. He stared without blinking at the one on the top. She looked so happy back then. It must have been about six years ago on a beach somewhere in the South of France. She was dressed in khaki shorts and a white, sleeveless t-shirt. Her blonde hair was long and loosely tied back. He was wearing just his swimming shorts and had his arm around her. They were both laughing at the camera.

His mouth formed a smile, but his eyes remained sad. He hadn't heard Melissa walk into the room.

"What's that?" she asked peering over his shoulder. "Is that Kate? Why have you got a picture of Kate and . . . you?"

There was no point in hiding it. He'd been caught and it was now time to confess.

"I'm so sorry Melissa; I should have said something ages ago." Alex wasn't worried about the consequences right at this moment. He just wanted to know she was alright. Melissa stood rooted to the spot. What was she about to hear? She got the distinct impression she wasn't going to like it.

"Well," she said with panic in her voice.

"I went out with Kate for nine and a half years. We lived in this house together. I finished with her to go out with you."

Melissa could barely speak.

"Why?"

"Why what?"

"Why didn't you say something?"

"I couldn't bring myself to tell you. I thought you'd leave me if you knew I'd lived with Richard's nanny."

"The tray    that's why she dropped the tray at Christmas, because she saw you."

"Yes, and I asked her not to say anything because I didn't want you to find out. I didn't know she'd end up with Richard and then we both had this secret which we couldn't tell to either of you because we'd kept it for so long."

Melissa sat down beside Alex on the bed, her annoyance slowly turning to shame.

"Was I really that dreadful that you couldn't tell me something so important?"

"I wasn't sure how you'd take it. It was stupid really to think that we could keep it quiet forever, but at the time it seemed like the right thing to do."

"It explains a lot of things like the little knowing glances."

"Sorry, I didn't realise we were doing that."

"I suppose I should be flattered that you left Kate for me. She's such a lovely person."

"I'm sorry I didn't say anything. Am I forgiven?"

"It should be me asking you for forgiveness. I don't want you to keep any more secrets from me, do you promise?"

He nodded. "Just one more thing then. One of my friends, Mike Fenwick, had a lot of pictures of Kate in his kitchen drawer. I think he's been stalking her so I've rung the police to report him." He paused for thought. "I've got to go to the police station first thing tomorrow to make a statement."

"Oh, my God, do you think he might be responsible?"

"I don't know but I can't ignore it. It'll eat away at me if I don't say something."

"Yes, of course."

Alex had no intention of going to the police station in the morning. He'd done his part already. No, he had somewhere far more important to go.

***

Prof put the phone down.

"That was Todd," he said to his wife. "Kate's in ICU. She's been stabbed."

"Oh, my goodness, is she alright?" Dorothy held on to the newel post at the bottom of the stairs. Her body was swaying as she took in the news about her friend.

"They don't know yet." Prof stared at the floor and shook his head. "Who could do something like that? Who would hurt that sweet woman?"

The two of them looked at each other in abject horror without speaking. Then suddenly from nowhere, a sharp pain pierced Gerald's heart. He grimaced and held his chest. The pain became stronger; like it was crushing him. He was struggling to breathe.

"Gerald, what's the matter?"

"Ambulance, get an ambulance."

He looked grey and sweaty as he sank to his knees in the hallway.

"GERALD!"

The pain was too much. He collapsed at his wife's feet. Dorothy grabbed the phone from his hand and quickly dialled 999.

***

The evening merged into night and Richard's exhausted body was slumped over the edge of Kate's bed. He still held her hand firmly; he didn't want to let her go for fear of losing her. DS Harman had visited earlier and promised to keep him updated on any developments.

"Richard, why don't you go home and get some rest. We'll call if there's any change. We may be able to start reducing the sedation if she remains stable." said Dr Curtis.

The last unit of blood was going through. Richard sat up and took another longing look at Kate. He was impatient for some sign to indicate that she would be alright. She had gained a bit more colour in her face now and she was stable.

"I don't like leaving her."

"Nothing's going to happen tonight, Richard. We'll keep her comfortable."

Richard leaned over and kissed her on the forehead. "Bye, sweetheart. See you in the morning. You keep fighting."

He nodded at Ian as he left the department and made his way to the exit. Outside he took out his mobile phone and called a taxi to take the solitary trip to his empty home. He couldn't remember the last time he'd been there by himself at night time. It would be an eerie place tonight.

The house was cold and unwelcoming. There was no greeting as he walked into the kitchen, there was no acknowledgement as he took his cup of coffee into the lounge, and there was no soft lighting on the landing so that Jacob could find his way to the toilet, when he finally went upstairs.

He switched the light on in his bedroom. Dirty black fingerprints were dotted around the room from the forensic brush and Kate's blood still remained as a reminder of the dreadful day he had just experienced, when he had found her lying there barely breathing. The image wouldn't go; even when he tried to think of her safe in her hospital bed.

He walked into Kate's bedroom. It definitely had a more feminine touch to the décor and smelled faintly of her perfume. He sat on the side of the bed and picked up the framed photograph on the bedside table. It was the one Jayne had taken at the barbeque of him and Kate smiling happily. Richard was on the bench and Kate just behind him with her arms draped around his neck. Her face was close to his, he could almost feel her breath on his cheek. Tears appeared in his eyes and dropped onto the glass. What if he never saw her like that again? How would he cope? She'd changed his life and he doubted if he'd ever find anyone like her again.

Richard kicked his shoes off and swung his legs onto the bed. He held the photograph close to his chest and stared into space.

"Please take care of her." He found himself talking out loud, calling upon his faith and his maker for the first time in his life.

***

Alex woke early and dressed. Melissa stirred and opened her eyes.

"What time is it?" she asked sleepily.

"Shh, it's early, go back to sleep."

"Where are you going?"

"I can't sleep so I'm going down to the police station to make my statement. I won't be long."

He went downstairs and without any food or drink inside him, left the house. It was a relatively short drive to the hospital. He rehearsed his lines on the way and prepared himself for any disappointment.

The door to the ICU unit was manned by an intercom system. Alex pressed the buzzer and a voice asked, "Yes, can I help you?"

"I've come to see Kate Forrester."

"Are you a relative?"

He paused.

"Yes, I'm her brother."

The intercom bleeped and Alex opened the door. A nurse came to greet him.

"She's just this way."

She indicated towards the cubicle to the right. Alex followed her direction towards the glass panelled room. He faltered at the doorway. He wasn't prepared for what he saw. Tubes and wires sprung from her in all directions. The only sounds were the blipping of the monitor and the hissing of the ventilator.

A nurse looked up from her observation chart and acknowledged him as he entered but Alex barely noticed her as he made his way to the side of the bed, his eyes never leaving her pale face.

"Hi, Kate," he whispered. "It's Alex; I've come to see how you are. You frightened the hell out of me when I got home last night and Melissa told me what had happened. You see, Richard didn't let us know whether you were alright or not so I've come to see for myself.

"I wanted to let you know that I've told Melissa about us. She knows that we were together for all that time and it was a relief to get it off my chest. I'm glad she knows, because I was proud of that time we had, and now I don't have anything to hide. We were good together despite everything that happened at the end. And by the way, I did still love you, I just couldn't tell you that because it was so hard to finish it; that would have made it worse. I'm so sorry Kate, I really am for all the pain I caused you.

"Mind you, you're probably happier now than you ever were with me, and I don't blame you. Richard will never treat you like I did. I was a shit, and I'll never forgive myself if anything . . . well you know what I mean. I think I know who did this, Kate, and I've told the police, so you can rest assured that justice will be done whatever happens."

He sat beside the bed. His speech was finished and he'd made his peace.

***

The door to the ICU department opened and Richard entered.

"Morning, Mr Anderson," said the nurse who had previously allowed Alex in. "You're just in time to see Kate's brother. He's in there now with her."

"Kate's brother?" asked Richard.

Panic alarms rang in his head. Who was calling themselves Kate's brother? Was the perpetrator back to finish the job? He quickly marched over to the cubicle and looked through the glass. *Alex, what was Alex doing here? Surely it wasn't him,* he thought.

"Alex," Richard said in surprise.

"Richard!" Alex sprung out of the chair. "I'm sorry, I was hoping to be gone by the time you arrived."

"I don't understand, what are you doing here?"

"I'm sorry, Richard," he said hanging his head. "I just needed to see for myself how she was doing. You see . . . there's something Kate and I haven't told you . . ." Richard looked crestfallen. Was his whole world about to fall apart? Was Alex going to tell him that he and Kate were having an affair? "We used to go out together. For nine and half years to be precise, then I virtually threw her out so that I could be with Melissa."

Alex waited for Richard's reaction. Surely he wouldn't punch him in this environment. Richard looked across at

Kate and felt an unbelievable wave of relief wash over him. He wasn't about to be angry—there was no need to be. That was all in the past and life was far too short, as he was now painfully aware, to get upset about things that had already happened and couldn't be changed.

"That's why Kate dropped the tray on Boxing Day, because she saw you," Richard surmised, his eyes still fixed on Kate's pale form.

"*I* asked her not to say anything. You two weren't an item then and I didn't think Melissa would take too kindly to finding out that I used to live with your nanny."

"No, you were probably right, Alex, she wouldn't have back then. But then, we all change don't we? You see, right now it doesn't matter what happened in the past as long as she pulls through."

"I think that's what Melissa thinks as well."

Richard glanced at Alex. "Have you told Melissa?"

"Yes, last night. She was fine. She just wants her to get better. We all do, Richard. I know I'm not with her anymore, but I couldn't bare it if she . . ."

"She's not going to die. I won't let her. It's took me forty years to find someone like her. I'm not going to let her slip through my fingers now."

A tapping on the glass of the door caused them both to turn around. It was DS Harman. As he entered the room, he flicked through the pages of his notebook.

"Sorry to disturb you, Mr Anderson, only I have a bit of news. We have a suspect in custody at the moment, a Michael Fenwick. Do you know anyone of that name?"

Richard shook his head. "No, I've never heard of him."

"We had an anonymous tip off last night and when we searched his flat we found several photographs of Kate; some with your son, outside your home. We're about to question him. I was going to ask you if you could shine any light on how he knows Kate?"

"I tipped you off," Alex announced. It was time for him to come clean on everything he knew.

The two other men looked at Alex in anticipation of his confession. Richard took hold of Kate's hand.

"Carry on, sir," insisted DS Harman.

"Mike was a good friend of mine. I've known him for years. He hardly spoke to Kate all the time we were together," he explained to Richard. "Then at Chris and Tina's wedding he became fixated on her, asking her out and then I found him trying to kiss her."

"Oh, I think I remember Kate telling me about him when she came back from the wedding," Richard interrupted.

"Well, I let it slip that I'd seen her at your house on Boxing Day and he must have done his homework to find out where you lived. I was looking for a bottle opener in his kitchen just a few days ago and found the pictures. When I heard Kate had been stabbed, that's when I went to the police."

"Thank you, sir," said the detective. "That's very helpful."

DS Harman left the room and Alex turned anxiously towards Richard.

"It's my fault isn't it? I brought them together. I should have seen what he was like."

"You can't blame yourself for someone else's actions. You weren't to know what he was thinking," Richard said trying to console him.

"But the pictures; I should have said something as soon as I found them."

"What could you have said; it's not a crime to take pictures of someone? Alex, you told the police as soon as you found out about Kate. What else could you have done?"

Suddenly the ventilator started to alarm.

"What's happening?" asked Alex in a state of panic.

"I think she's waking up," replied Richard.

The nurse went to fetch the doctor. Ian Curtis swiftly walked into the room and turned off the alarm. "Okay, that's a good sign. She's nearly ready to breathe on her own. Alright, Kate, I'm going to take that tube out of your mouth in a moment. You breathe nice and easy." Dr Curtis loosened the tape holding the tube in place. He watched as the re-breathing bag moved in and out. “Good girl, Kate, that’s just what we need.”

Richard was watching closely. She still had her eyes closed but her body was starting to function on its own. He could feel his heart swell with hope. *Come on, Kate, you can do it.*

Dr Curtis studied the monitor then the bag again. Kate’s hand started to flicker.

“It’s alright, Kate, we’re going to take that tube out now.”

The nurse removed the air from the cuff of the endotracheal tube and the doctor gently pulled it from Kate’s throat. As the tip came out, Kate coughed and her eyes slowly opened. Richard’s eyes filled with tears. He held his breath. She was awake, now would she recognise him?

It took a while before she became focussed. Richard was the first person she saw. A smile slowly formed on her lips. “Richard,” she whispered. Her throat was sore and her voice hoarse after hours of intubation.

She feebly squeezed his hand and he knew that she was safe. His precious Kate was back with him and nothing now would stop them from being together. Her eyes closed again. It had been such an effort waking up. Richard kissed her hand and put it to his face. “It’s alright, Kate. You sleep; you’ve been through so much. Don’t worry about us. We’ve got all the time in the world.”

Richard, Dr Curtis, Alex and DS Harman stood still waiting to see what she would do next. Her eyes flickered and opened again and she looked around the room. A look of surprise flashed across her as she recognised Alex’s familiar face.

“Alex, what are . . . you doing . . . here?” she asked breathlessly.

“It’s alright, Kate, I know all about you and Alex and it doesn’t matter in the slightest,” said Richard stroking her hair from her face.

Kate smiled at him and then looked in Alex’s direction. He smiled back.

“I just came to say I was sorry for everything.”

Kate shook her head.

"Doesn't matter . . . I have . . . Richard now," she answered.

"Yes, I know," he said accepting the inevitable.

DS Harman waited for his turn to speak.

"Dr Curtis, could I just have two minutes of Kate's time?"

"Two minutes and that's all. She needs to rest."

"Thank you. Hello, Kate. My name is DS Harman; I'm the investigating officer for your case. You'll be pleased to know we have a suspect in custody, a Mr Michael Fenwick. We're just about to . . ."

Kate frowned and shook her head. "Why Mike?"

"He had some pictures of you in his kitchen drawer. He's been watching you," Alex explained.

She shook her head again. "It . . . wasn't Mike." Kate turned towards Richard. "It was . . . Ingrid."

# Chapter . . .

# 22

Professor Royston lay on his coronary care bed feeling the aftermath of his heart attack. His chest felt like it had been run over by a double decker bus and he'd just experienced the worst night that he could ever remember. The plastic covered mattress and starched linen sheets had made him sweat and were not conducive to sleep causing his agitation to heighten. It had also troubled him that the person responsible for Kate's attack was, as far as he was aware, still at large

Gerald glanced behind him at the monitor to ensure that his heart was now behaving as it should and that his heart rate was within satisfactory limits. He didn't want to go through that pain again. It had scared him to think that he could be so close to death and if he didn't calm himself down, he would be facing the same fate again. His heart rate was elevated, but his ECG was relatively stable under the circumstances.

"Nurse," he shouted across the room from behind his oxygen mask.

"Yes, Professor Royston, what can I do for you?" she asked politely.

"I wonder if you could find out how a patient is in the ICU? It's a woman called Kate Forrester. She's a friend of mine and my wife's. I'm getting a little concerned at the fact that I haven't heard anything. I just hope people aren't keeping the news from me for obvious reasons."

"I'll see what I can do, Professor."

"Thank you."

***

Richard sat down and shook his head.

"Ingrid," he muttered. "I didn't think she was capable of something like this."

"Who's Ingrid, Mr Anderson?" DS Harman asked opening his notebook again.

"She's my ex-girlfriend. She lives in Shadmoor. Her parent's own vast quantities of land in Scotland. Why would she do something like this?"

"I'll need her full address. We'll send someone round to pick her up."

"Yes, certainly it's, erm . . . my head's completely emptied, Ludmere Cottage, Shadmoor Old Road, about half a mile past Marcelle's Restaurant on the right. She works at Shadmoor Antiques."

"Thanks, Mr Anderson, I'll let Kate get some rest now."

"Kate, I can't believe she did this to you. She should be locked up and the key thrown away. It must have been awful for you; I'm so sorry."

Alex had followed DS Harman out of the room.

"Excuse me," he called after him.

The detective stopped and turned around. "Yes?"

"What will happen to Mike now?"

"We'll have to let him go."

"He's going to hate me for this."

"You were only doing your duty, sir. Perhaps he'll stop taking photographs now he's been caught. Something good may have come out of it."

"Yeh, there is that."

"Thanks for your help anyway."

Alex wandered back to the cubicle. He would leave Kate and Richard alone now to try and come to terms with what had happened. Their secret was no longer burdening him and although he had a few bridges to build with Mike, Kate was still alive, which was the main thing.

"I'll be getting off now. I'm so pleased you're alright, Kate."

"Thanks," she croaked.

"Yes, thanks, Alex. Don't beat yourself up about Mike. You only did what you thought was right." Alex nodded with half a smile. "Would you tell Jacob that Kate is awake?"

"Yes, of course I will."

Kate closed her eyes. The exertion had taken its toll. Richard smiled and took a seat on the chair next to her. What a strange turn of events had unfolded in the past hour.

Ian Curtis came to the door. "Sorry to disturb you, Richard; one of the nurses from Coronary Care is here asking about Kate. Apparently Professor Royston is in there. He's had a heart attack and he wants to know if Kate is alright."

"What, a heart attack? Oh, my God, is he okay?" said Richard standing up. "Whatever next? I'll pop round while Kate has a sleep and see him."

Richard followed the nurse into the next department, and there was the Professor, sitting up in bed, awaiting the news.

"Richard, how is she?" he asked.

"She's going to be alright, Prof. She's woken up and breathing for herself. How are you? I can't believe what's happening today."

"I'm fine. Just got a bit of a dodgy ticker. Didn't take the news about Kate too well."

Richard looked at his boss. Had Kate's attack really brought this on? He must be really fond of her. He didn't think he possessed such feelings.

"Have they found out who did it?" asked Professor Royston.

"Yes, Kate managed to tell us. It was Ingrid."

"Who's Ingrid?"

"Remember the woman I brought to your anniversary meal, her."

Prof shook his head. "Never liked the woman. Not in the same class as Kate."

"No, you're right, she isn't."

***

Ingrid Harper was arrested later that morning, her whereabouts given to the police by her rather reluctant colleague at Shadmoor Antiques. She was charged with the attempted murder of Kate Forrester.

Ingrid looked like a startled rabbit caught in the headlights of an oncoming car as two uniformed policemen and DS Harman walked into the Marclough Charities Society's monthly lunch and read her rights to her. She knew why they had come as soon as they had entered the building and made no attempt to deny her involvement.

Victoria Conley nearly passed out at the embarrassment of it all. The other ladies just stared in shock and disbelief. They'd never met an attempted murderer before and had certainly never lunched with one.

Of course, Ingrid's parents would no doubt employ the use of the best lawyer and barrister money could buy, and probably plead diminished responsibility, but that was for a jury to decide. Suffice to say, Ingrid Harper would not be attending the Marclough Charities Society's monthly lunch for some considerable time.

***

Kate and Professor Royston were transferred to Fife Ward and Graseby Ward respectively. Their conditions no longer life threatening, they were now in the position to start the long process of rehabilitation. For Kate that meant short spurts of walking around the ward, not just to gain strength and mobility, but to ease the boredom of her single room which Richard had insisted she take.

Professor Royston was told to take things very easy in his side room. He was even banned from using his laptop much to his dismay. He promised he wouldn't touch it as long as they left it in his room—which of course was a complete fabrication. The nurses were at the point of drawing straws to decide who would be the one to confiscate it. Many had heard of Professor Royston's reputation and didn't relish the task. A chance visit from a certain Kate Forrester gave them an idea.

"Penny," Kate said, acquiring the attention of one of the nurses on her ward. "Could I ask a favour of you? A friend of ours is on Graseby Ward and I wondered if you could take me to see him? I'm sure he'll be as bored as I am and it might do me good, a change of scenery."

"Certainly, Kate. Give me a second and I'll find a chair to take you on."

When she arrived at the ward, she was soon the centre of attention.

"Do you mind if Kate here visits Professor Royston? She's a friend."

"A friend of Professor Royston?" They were all intrigued. "That's fine on one condition," said a well-made-up, bleached-blonde haired nurse in the doorway of the office.

"What's that?" asked Kate, anxiously awaiting the reply.

"That you sneak his lap top out of his room. He keeps trying to do his work only we've been told in no uncertain terms that he hasn't to do any. He has to rest."

The other nurses behind her laughed. "I'll see what I can do," said Kate joining in the fun.

Penny wheeled her to the door of the side room, helped her out of the chair, and left. Kate gingerly walked to the doorway. She peeped into the room and there was the professor tapping away on his lap top.

"Hi, Prof," she said gently not wanting to alarm him.

He quickly slid the computer under his bedding and looked up. "Kate, how lovely to see you; come on in."

"Hope I'm not disturbing you but the boredom is getting too much. There's no one to talk to up there."

"Tell me about it, Kate. I've been trying to do a bit of work but they keep catching me. I'm sure they're going to confiscate it when I'm not looking," he said showing Kate the offending article underneath the covers.

Kate smiled and shook her head.

"How are you feeling, besides bored?" he asked.

"Not too bad. Still a bit breathless and it's quite painful when the pain killers start to wear off, but apart from that, okay. What about you?"

"Still feel like I've got a sumo wrestler sat on my chest but not as bad as I felt yesterday. Help yourself to a grape. I think Dorothy's trying to build me up. She brought me some playing cards in but there's only so many times you can play solitaire without going into melt down, especially on these tables. There's not quite enough room for all the cards."

"Do you fancy a game? I can play rummy."

"Ah, I'm a bit of an expert at rummy. You ask Dorothy. I don't think I've been beaten in a while at that game. Rummy it is."

The cards were shuffled and dealt, and Kate settled back to enjoy an hour with the card shark professor, amused at his desperation to win, not daring to beat him in case his heart took umbrage.

***

Richard had arrived on Fife ward to see her and was surprised to find her room empty.

"Nurse," he said. "Do you know where Kate is?"

"Yes," said Penny. "She's gone over to Graseby Ward to see Professor Royston."

"Really? Thanks."

Richard smiled to himself and set off in the direction of Graseby Ward. As he was about to enter he espied Dorothy through the door. She had the fondest smile on her face. He let himself in and called her name.

"Richard, come and see this," she mouthed.

He and Dorothy stood at the door of the side room and watched as Kate threw her hand onto the table.

"Splendid," said Prof. "I do believe that's seven nil. I told you I was unbeatable at this game."

"Are you cheating again?" asked Dorothy entering the room.

"Dorothy!" said Kate turning around.

"Kate! How wonderful to see you up and about."

The two women hugged each other. "I've brought someone with me," she said nodding towards the door.

Richard appeared from nowhere. "So this is where you hide out during the day is it?"

"I'll have you know she's damned good company," insisted Prof. "Getting a good beating from the master I'm afraid, but then I don't play to lose."

"Oh, will you listen to him," said Dorothy. "I've been telling him for years that I let him win."

They all laughed.

"I'd better get her back to the ward now; we don't want too much excitement in a day now do we?" said Richard.

Kate eased herself off the chair and walked to the door. "I'll try and get back tomorrow for round two," she said.

"Look forward to it," replied Prof.

Richard waved and helped Kate back to her chair. She lowered herself down and Richard pushed her back. As they passed the nurses' office, the staff nurse with the blonde hair popped her head out of the door.

"Did you manage to get the lap top, Kate?" she asked.

"No I didn't. I kept him off it for an hour though which was a feat in itself."

The young woman laughed. "Are you coming back tomorrow?"

"All being well."

"See you then."

"Bye."

"You're unbelievable," Richard said incredulously. "What was that all about?"

"Prof has got his lap top with him and keeps doing a bit of work behind the nurses' backs. They're threatening to take it off him but nobody wants the job."

"I'd like to see them try, heart attack or not. Thanks for going to see him. You didn't have to do that. You're convalescing as well."

"I'm also extremely bored and looking for something to do to while away the time in this place."

They arrived back in Kate's side room and she carefully manoeuvred herself back onto the bed.

"Wow, I'm exhausted now. Doing nothing really takes it out of you."

"That's why you should be taking it easy. Listen to your body."

"Yes, doctor, of course, doctor."

He smiled and kissed her on the lips. "I'm really missing you, and Jacob. The house is so quiet."

"How is he? Have you been to see him?"

"Yes, I went round this morning. He's okay. He's missing you as well; I can tell. He's quieter than usual. Everything's alien to him and his routine's all changed." Richard looked into Kate's eyes. "I also went to see Melissa."

"Why?" asked Kate anxiously.

"I went to ask her for a divorce."

"And?"

"No problem. She'll be quite happy to get rid of me."

"She must be mad."

"Kate," said Richard taking hold of her hand. "When I'm eventually free, will you marry me?"

Kate mouth dropped open, and her eyes filled with tears.

"Are you sure?"

"Of course I'm sure, I love you."

Kate put her arms out and as he leaned towards her, she squeezed him as tightly as she dared. "Of course I'll marry you. I can't think of anything I'd rather do." The tears spilled over onto her cheek. "You've made me so happy."

"I nearly ruined your life with my bad judgement."

"Don't talk like that. It was nothing to do with your judgement. It was her jealousy that did it."

They held each other, like they never want to let go.

Suddenly there was a tapping noise at the door. Richard looked around and there were his parents standing in the doorway.

"Mum, dad, what are you doing here?"

"We came to see how Kate was. I hope you don't mind, Kate. Ingrid's mother told us the story, she was mortified. May we come in?"

"Of course," said Kate smiling.

The thought of Richard and his parents being reconciled just added to the euphoria she was feeling.

"How are you, dear?" asked Iris Anderson.

"I'm okay," said Kate. "Still a little sore but a lot better than I was."

"I'm so sorry, Kate. I practically threw Ingrid at Richard, never once thinking that she might be some kind of psychopathic maniac. Her mother says she must have a mental illness, but I hate to think what she could have done. Imagine if Jacob had upset her one day, what an earth would have been her reaction to that?"

Kate and Richard glanced at each other recalling the day she took over from Kate as nanny.

"Don't tell me she has done something to Jacob as well," asked Iris, her face frozen in horror.

"Nothing to worry about, mum. But needless to say, Jacob was a little traumatised every time he set eyes on her," Richard offered.

"If I ever try to interfere again, please tell me to go away."

"You won't have the chance to find me any more prospective girlfriends, mum. Kate and I are getting married as soon as my divorce comes through."

Kate was so proud. The first person they had told was his mother. She knew it was official now and that she was free to spread the word.

"Really, oh that is good news. I'm so pleased for you both."

She leaned across and kissed Kate on the cheek. Donald nodded complacently in the background. He knew his son would find happiness if he was only left to his own devices. He'd liked Kate the moment he'd set eyes on her. They would make a very good team.

"Richard," said Iris. "Come and give your mother a hug."

He embraced his mother and shook hands with his father. All was well again in the Anderson family. Richard was quietly appreciative of his mother for taking the trouble to come all this way in order to eat humble pie in front of him and Kate. That must have taken some doing. As for the Harpers, at least they weren't trying to blame someone else for their daughter's misgivings.

"Who's got Jacob at the moment?" Donald asked when he was finally allowed to get a word in edgeways.

"He's staying with Melissa for the time being. Just while Kate gets properly back on her feet."

"Do you think she'd mind if we went to visit him whilst we're down here?" asked Iris.

"I'm positive she won't." Richard was glad he'd let Kate persuade him to allow Jacob his overnight stay to see Melissa's parents. "How long are you here for?"

"We've not made any plans as such," said his mother sheepishly. "We wanted to see how the land lay, if you know what I mean?"

"Listen, you're quite welcome to stay for a few nights if you want. The house is pretty empty at the moment . . . and I could do with a few shirts ironed."

Iris smiled affectionately at her son and they all laughed whilst he went on a mission to find three cups of tea.

At the end of visiting time Iris and Donald had been supplied with tangible directions to Melissa's and confirmation that they would receive a warm welcome. They bid farewell to Kate and promised to see her soon—after all, she was their future daughter-in-law now.

Richard stayed a while until the distinct aroma of boiled cabbage filled his nostrils.

"Smells like your evening meal is on its way," he smiled.

"Mm, delicious," Kate mocked.

"Oh, by the way, in all the excitement I forgot to tell you; I spoke to your mum today and she's going to get a flight over at the end of the week. She said she'd come over and look after you for a while whilst I'm back at work."

"Oh, that's wonderful. It must be over six months now since I last saw her."

"She sounded really concerned but I told her you were out of danger. She'll have to stay in your room when she comes over which means, you'll have to move in with me."

"Ah well, I suppose I'll get over it," Kate teased him as he walked out.

"The only thing is," he said popping his head back round the door. "There's no way you're moving back when she leaves."

# CHAPTER . . .

# 23

Professor Royston waited nervously for his chair. He'd very rarely been on this side of the fence and the next few hours were going to be both uncomfortable and nerve racking. He was about to have a stent inserted into his coronary artery to try and unblock it. The angiogram had highlighted the diseased blood vessel and this procedure would stave off the coronary artery by pass graft for some time.

*The anticipation is going to give me another heart attack at this rate,* he thought to himself as the minutes ticked by. Finally the nurse arrived with the chair.

"They're ready for you now, Professor Royston," said the young nurse. "I'll take you over to the cardiology department."

"Thank you, nurse," he said trying to remain in control. "Let's get this over with then the quicker I can get home."

***

Alex was racked with guilt. He had played out every scenario he could think of between him and Mike and he couldn't think of a single, logical reason to explain why he had grassed on his friend, and had him locked away in a cell for the night. Every excuse he envisaged culminated in Mike slamming the door in his face and never speaking to him again. It was obvious that it was either he or Chris who had blown the whistle on him; they were the only two who had had access to his kitchen drawer, and he couldn't let Chris take the wrap for something he hadn't done.

He tapped on the door of Mike's flat and waited. His stomach lurched in anticipation of his reaction. Would his fist fly first or would he verbally attack him with a barrage of expletives. He was about to find out. He could hear his footsteps on the linoleum flooring as he approached the door.

"Alex, mate, come in." Alex was dumbfounded. He stepped into the hallway then followed Mike into the kitchen. "Can I get you a beer?"

"Er, yeh, that would be great."

"Have you heard about Kate? She's been stabbed."

"Yeh, I found out the other day."

"You're not gonna believe this; they arrested me for it."

"What?" Alex replied feigning surprise. He felt such a fraud.

"Yeh." Mike handed him a bottle of beer and leaned against the sink unit. He shook his head and looked at the floor. "I feel such a fuckin' idiot. I was watching her." He looked up to gauge Alex's reaction.

"Why?" asked Alex. At last he could find out the reason behind the photographs.

"I like her, well, it's a bit more than that. She's the only girl who's ever spoken to me properly, at Chris's wedding, you remember." Alex remembered her making polite conversation but that was all. "She said she might ring me, but she didn't so I found out where she was living and I started to watch the house, and take the odd picture. I had to move position because she nearly saw me one day so I sat in the park at the side of the house. This old woman fuckin' grassed on me, didn't she, and the police came . . . twice. When Kate was stabbed, the bleedin' copper who spoke to me, must have put two and two together and thought of me. They searched the flat and found all my pictures of her."

Alex shook his head in disbelief. Was Mike taking the blame for everything and he about to get away with what he'd done?

"Go on," said Alex.

"They kept me in a cell overnight and treated me like some kind of nutter. It was horrible. It wasn't until Kate woke up the next day that they let me go. Apparently it was some woman who did it." Mike looked at Alex trying to determine his thoughts. "You're not mad with me are you? I'd hate myself if this ruined our friendship."

"Why would I be mad at you?"

"Because I'd been following Kate and taking pictures. I won't do it again, not bloody likely. I've really learnt my lesson. That was the worst experience of my life."

"Then what can I say? Let's just forget it. You've been through enough, mate."

"Aw, thanks, Alex. I thought I'd really screwed everything up. I had to tell you, even though I knew you wouldn't be pleased. It would have just eaten away at me if I hadn't."

"Yeh, I know what you mean, I'm the same."

"Come on then, mate; let me buy you a pint down at The Dog and Duck."

***

Kate waited patiently with her bags packed. Her take-home drugs weren't quite ready so Richard said he'd nip over to the clinic to speak to Carl whilst she waited. She was itching to get home after just over a week in her hospital side room.

She flicked through a magazine that was three months old and smiled at the out-dated news. Several of the happy, celebrity couples were now estranged; some were even in new relationships. How quickly they fell in and out of love. Her marriage wouldn't be like that. Her's would be for keeps.

Richard was at the door sooner than she expected.

"Are you ready? I haven't actually been to the clinic. I've brought someone to see you," he smiled excitedly.

Kate looked puzzled then her mother, Pat, walked into the room. Her tanned face looked concerned but healthy and her hair was lighter than Kate remembered in a neat, short style.

"Mum," she cried holding her arms out.

"Sweetheart, how are you? Richard has told me all about it. I'd have come sooner but he said you were doing alright and you would need my help when you got home. Come here; let me give you a hug." Kate carefully threw her arms around her mother and tears of happiness rolled down her face. "Hey, what's the matter?"

"I'm just glad to see you," Kate replied.

Her mother held her face between her hands. "We've got a lot to catch up on haven't we? Now what's this news that you two have to tell me?"

Kate caught Richard's eye. Bless him; he'd waited for her to divulge their plans.

"We're going to get married."

"Oh, that's wonderful." It was her mother's turn to cry. She picked a handkerchief out of her handbag and dabbed at the corner of each eye. "Come here, Richard, you can have a hug too. I can't believe it, the first time I meet you and I get this news. Whatever will be next?"

"Come on then, shall we go? The nurse said your tablets have arrived," said Richard herding them out of the room.

Kate thanked the nursing staff. Richard deposited a large box of biscuits and chocolates in the office and they slowly left the ward.

***

The plastics ward was on the left as they made their way to the car park.

"I just want to pop in here and see if Carl's around. I need to leave some instructions for him. Why don't you come in and meet everyone?"

"You go, Kate, I'll wait here," said her mother. "They won't want us all in there."

"Okay, won't be long."

Sister Jackson was the first one to see them entering the ward. "Richard, I haven't seen you for a while," she said flashing a quick smile at him. Then she saw Kate just behind him.

"Ah, Cynthia, this is Kate, my girlfriend, well, fiancée now," he said fondly looking down at her. "Kate this is Cynthia Jackson, the sister in charge of the ward."

Sister Jackson flushed. That was the first time he had ever called her by her first name and he chooses now to announce that he's betrothed to another woman. She attempted a look of joy for the happy couple and went to shake Kate's hand, fighting back the disappointment threatening to expose itself on the surface. Life was so cruel. She'd waited years for him to notice her and now she would have to step back into the role of wall flower; patiently waiting for the next eligible consultant to come along.

"Congratulations and I'm pleased to see you're up and about. We were all very concerned about you," she said through tenuous lips.

"Thank you, that's really kind of you."

Richard took hold of her hand and led her to the office where Todd and Carl were deep in discussion over an x-ray on the computer.

"Kate," said Todd rushing over to kiss her on the cheek. "Great to see you up and about. We were so worried; you frightened the life out of us all. Jayne can't wait to see you."

Sister Jackson rushed off into the depths of the ward. She couldn't bear to hear anymore of the familiarities. Obviously this woman had made a great impression on her colleagues. Rumour had it that Professor Royston had suffered a heart attack when he heard she'd been hospitalised.

"Carl, this is Kate, my fiancée."

"Oh, congratulations," said Carl.

"You sly dog," interrupted Todd. "You never mentioned that."

"I only asked her the other day. We've not got the ring yet."

Todd went over to shake Richard's hand. "I'm made up for you both."

"Everything alright, Carl? I'll be back on Monday. I noticed we had two cases in the afternoon. Would you change the order so that Mr Forshaw goes first; I don't want that case being cancelled, he's at the point of breaching. Anything to discuss before I leave?"

"No, I don't think so, Mr Anderson," Carl replied.

"Just have a look at this, Richard, before you go. I might pass this over to you?" remarked Todd pointing at the x-ray of a wrist.

Richard stared at the picture on the screen. "Yes, you can see some arthritic changes around the ulnate and radial articulation."

"What do you think?" asked Todd.

"I'd have to see the patient first but they might benefit from a fusion of the two bones."

"What would that do, Mr Anderson?" enquired Carl moving his wrist around whilst manipulating it with the other hand.

"Well, it limits the movement but reduces the pain."

Kate looked on proudly. It was like a different language he spoke at work. One she could never fathom out.

"Thanks, Richard," said Todd. "We'd better let you go now and get Kate back home."

"Yes, your mum will be wondering where we've gone," said Richard making his way to the door.

"Bye, Mr Anderson, bye, Kate," said Carl.

"Make sure he takes good care of you, Kate," shouted Todd after them.

"Bye," Kate replied laughing at Todd's last comment. "Nice meeting you, Carl."

***

The car pulled up outside the house and Kate looked warily at the front door. That was the place she'd first encountered Ingrid on that fateful day. She'd come to see if she'd left her watch in Richard's bedside cabinet. A ploy, Kate had thought, to make her jealous at the idea of her and Richard sharing his bed. Kate had offered to quickly check before she went to collect Jacob, but unbeknown to her, Ingrid had followed her up the stairs. When Kate had turned around to come back and inform her that there was no signs of the watch, Ingrid had stabbed a knife into her chest.

She'd remembered the first drop of blood on the carpet and how she'd worried about Richard's reaction if he'd found the stain before she'd had chance to remove it. Then she'd realised what had actually happened and panicked as her breathing rapidly became laboured. Soon her eyes had become unfocussed and before she could grab the phone, the lights had gone out; the rest was history.

When she recalled the whole episode, the fact that she hadn't collected Jacob from nursery had saved her life. If she hadn't been late, the staff at the nursery wouldn't have alerted Richard and he wouldn't have found her on the floor of the bedroom. She could have been there all afternoon and bled to death. The thought made her shiver.

"Are you alright?" asked Richard putting a comforting arm around her as they walked up the pathway to the door.

Her mother took her hand. "Is this where it happened?" she asked. Kate nodded. "Then it's bound to feel a bit strange, love."

"Yes," agreed Richard. "It's going to take a while for things to get back to normal if they ever do. I'm glad your mum's here when I go back to work."

They all walked inside and Richard took the bags upstairs.

"Do you mind if I have a little lie down before lunch? I feel a bit sickly after the journey."

"Not at all, come on, I'll help you up then I'll show your mum to her room," said Richard.

Kate slowly ascended the stairs then walked into the bedroom she would now share with Richard. Her eyes went to the floor where she'd collapsed then she took in the rest of the area.

"Have you had a new carpet put down?" she asked.

'I had to, Kate. That one would never clean up and I didn't think you'd want a constant reminder of what happened."

She smiled and kissed him on the cheek, then throwing her shoes off, lay on the bed. Her eyes immediately closed and she fell into a deep sleep for the first time in over a week. The soft pillow nestled her head as she drifted off. Richard took

Jacob's duvet off his bed and placed it over her. He stared down at her and suddenly felt overcome with the enormity of what could have happened if he hadn't found her that day. He thanked God for the chance they'd been given now that she was safe again in her own surroundings.

***

It was Prof's turn to go home. Dorothy arrived with a change of clothes and handed them over.

"How do you feel, dear?" she asked.

"Remarkably well at the moment, all things considered. I can recommend these stents although the procedure to put them in isn't particularly pleasant."

"I suppose we'll have to tell the children when we get home."

"What for? Why do they need to know? If they were in the slightest bit concerned about our welfare they'd have phoned us weeks ago. The last thing I want is their pity. Now let's go home and forget about them. I don't want another episode, getting worked up about whether they're going to ring or not. I hated to see how upset you were, and I am in no doubt that it all contributed to bringing on the heart attack; so if you don't mind I'd rather we were left alone with our little collection of friends, to get on with things."

"Very well," agreed Dorothy. "If that's what you want, then I'll back you all the way. We've been having rather a nice time recently without them. I miss the grandchildren but I can't say I miss Nina's arrogance and the way she talks down to us as if we're a confounded nuisance to her."

"Then we're both agreed. We don't say a word."

# Chapter . . .

# 24

Kate was seated between Richard and Melissa on the tiniest chair she'd ever sat upon. She doubted whether she would actually be able to get up out of it once the show was finished. Nonetheless, she was looking forward to the performance and more so, to seeing Jacob in his starring role. He had one line to say at his end of term show which Melissa had practiced incessantly with him. Kate couldn't decide who she was more nervous for, Melissa or Jacob?

Mrs Bentley appeared in front of the assembled parents and grandparents, and announced the start of the play after the usual fire precautions. From a door at the back of the hall, a line of little boys and girls marched in and seated themselves randomly on the floor. They all stared in bewilderment at the audience of adults, their mouths slightly agape, as they searched in desperation for a familiar face. Once found one or two wandered off to sit with them, others waved excitedly and one little girl started to cry. One of the staff came to her rescue and the show began.

A cacophony of tambourines and triangles all started at the same time on Mrs Bentley's instructions; the noise was deafening. The singing could barely be heard above the sound, then it went quiet and it was time to tell the story. It was about a cat that made friends with a dog and a mouse, much to the dismay of its parents. The characters made their way into the middle of the room, all clothed in a pair of leggings, appropriately coloured t-shirt, home made mask and corresponding tail.

It was Jacob's turn to introduce the story. He stood to his feet. Melissa sat on the edge of her seat and mouthed the words in unison with him.

"This is the story of a cat called Trog, who made friends with a mouse and a dog," he said in his best staccato, monotone voice.

Melissa beamed with pride. Richard and Kate grinned inanely at the little boy whose face was glowing red as all eyes in the room focussed on him. They congratulated Melissa then sat back to enjoy the production now that he'd done his part and they no longer had to worry about him fluffing his lines.

The show was over after about half an hour, whereupon the moral of the story came to fruition. The cat's parents apparently turned out to be proud of their offspring for not discriminating against the dog and the mouse. Only the older children were still focussed by this time. There was a thunderous round of applause at the end. The children bowed when prompted and were then dismissed to their parents. Jacob ran across to Kate.

"Kate," he said throwing his arms around her. "Are you better?"

"Much better after watching your show. How did you remember all those words?"

"I practiced with mummy."

"Well you know what they say, practice makes perfect."

Mrs Bentley joined them, a beaming smile on her face. "Kate, it's lovely to see you. How are you?"

"Much better, thanks. In fact, it's thanks to you I'm still here. If you hadn't rung Richard . . ."

"We were getting concerned. You're never late. We're going to miss you and Jacob next term. He's been such a good boy. Any plans over the holidays?"

"We're actually going to take a bit of a holiday soon. We're going to Spain with my mum; we'll spend a few days with her then maybe do a bit of sightseeing; see how I feel."

"Well have a wonderful time, you deserve it."

"Thank you."

She went off to circulate and left Melissa pondering over the question she had wanted to ask for the past few weeks but hadn't quite found a suitable moment. Had Richard remembered the trip to Antigua with Jacob to see her parents or had things changed slightly due to Kate's indisposition?

"When are you going to Spain?" she casually asked Richard hoping not to appear too obvious.

"When you go to Antigua, hopefully." Melissa's eyes widened. "You haven't mentioned it since Jacob saw your parents off at the airport. You are still going aren't you?"

"Yes of course, if that's alright with you? We can go anytime so when it's convenient just let us know."

"I think Kate's mother will have to go back soon. She's left her partner running the restaurant. Would a week tomorrow be a bit short notice?"

"No, that's perfect, I'll start making arrangements."

***

They all went back to Richard's for coffee after Jacob's show. Kate's mother had prepared some cakes as a kind of celebration. He was a big boy now, ready to start big school, and that deserved a bit of a party.

Melissa greeted Pat like a long lost relative. Jacob hid from her for a while then slowly emerged from behind his mother when he saw the pile of butterfly cakes on the coffee table.

"Pat, am I allowed another one?" he asked politely.

"Of course you are, sweetheart. I made them for you."

"It's not my birthday."

"No, but it was your last day at nursery, and that's a big occasion."

"I like them more than Dorofee's cheesecake."

"Really, that's very nice of you but don't tell Dorothy will you? That will be our little secret."

Jacob nodded and smiled then quickly peeled the paper off.

The doorbell rang and Richard went to answer it. He came back into the lounge followed by Alex.

"How did it go, Jacob?" Alex asked. "Did you get your lines right?"

"Yes," replied Jacob.

"He was perfect," Melissa said singing his praises and taking just a little of the plaudits for herself.

"Alex, what are you doing here?" asked Pat entering the room with some fresh coffee.

"Pat, hi," he said spinning round to face her. "It's a long story but to cut it short, I'm Melissa's other half."

"Hang on, Melissa was married to Richard and you were with Kate, and now . . . you've all swapped?"

They smiled bashfully, like they'd just been caught with their fingers in the cookie jar.

"I know it looks rather strange, and it wasn't exactly intentional," said Richard before his future mother-in-law had a funny turn, "but it actually works rather well, now we've all got to grips with it."

"Well, I can't say anything. I ran off to Spain with my brother-in-law. I wasn't married to his brother at the time, so I suppose I wasn't officially related in the eyes of the law, but then, it takes all sorts."

They all laughed, relieved that Pat wasn't about to morally reprimand them.

"Yes, mum," Kate continued the story. "And his brother wasn't even my dad, he was the one before."

Now Pat was laughing with them whilst a bemused Jacob wondered what was so funny.

# CHAPTER . . .

# 25

Richard stretched out on the sofa. His bronzed face suited him; made him look healthy and refreshed. Kate was sat beside him, his head resting on her shoulder.

"That was a great holiday. It's funny, I've probably spent more time in your mum's company in the past two months than I have with Melissa's parents in ten years of married life. She's great. I felt so comfortable and Frank's a nice guy as well although we didn't see as much of him."

"I know, you probably know Frank as well as I do now. He's very quiet isn't he? Mind you he probably struggles to get a word in edgeways with my mum."

"He's a great cook. I really enjoyed our evenings at the restaurant. That was a first, eating out every night in a great restaurant for nothing. You can't argue with that."

"Mum never mentioned how nice it was. I just presumed it was some Brits-abroad fish and chips kind of café but it was far nicer than that."

"Let's have a look at the photos again. I'd love to go back there some time and maybe see Granada. We could get there from your mum's place quite easily and maybe spend a couple of nights there."

"Seville was lovely though, wasn't it?" said Kate studying the photographs. "I loved the Plaza de Espana. It was a beautiful building."

"You're right, every time I went to take a picture it was a better view than the last one. I could have spent all day snapping away there. Apparently they used that building in Star Wars and Lawrence of Arabia."

"Really?"

"Yes, I've just read it in the guide book."

"That's a good one of us in the restaurant that mum took. Wow, the Cathedral looks pretty impressive on that one. You've got a really good camera."

"Let me have a look at that one of us on the horse and cart. That would make a nice enlargement. We could get it framed. Was that a car that just pulled up outside? That'll be Jacob."

Richard jumped to his feet and went to look out of the study window. Jacob was just getting out of the car. Richard tapped on the window, waved and went to answer the door. His little boy jumped into his arms.

"Jacob, how are you? Have you had a great time?"

"Yes, daddy, I went swimming every day and granddad took me on a boat fishing."

"Wow, it sound like you've been spoilt rotten. Come on in. Kate's in the lounge, don't go jumping on her will you?" Melissa and Alex followed with Jacob's suitcase. "Hi, you two, come on in. Suffering from jet lag?"

"You could say that," said Melissa.

"Now you see, you don't get that when you go to Spain."

"Did you both have a good time?"

"Great thanks, we're just looking at the pictures now. How were you're mum and dad?"

"Relaxed and looking incredibly healthy. They were so pleased to see Jacob. I think dad'll miss his little shadow next week when he's lazing by the pool recovering."

"Ah, the joys of retirement. Can I get you two a drink?"

"If you don't mind, we'll get back, Richard," Alex insisted. "We're kind of exhausted."

"No, I don't mind at all."

"We'll just pop in and say hello to Kate. How is she?" asked Melissa.

"She got tired quickly, especially the sightseeing part, but I think it's done her the world of good; a bit of sunshine and good food."

"Well, if you need help with Jacob at any time just shout," Melissa insisted.

"Thanks for that. I don't know how she'll manage with him on her own. We'll see how it goes."

Kate and Jacob were cuddled up on the sofa by the time they all joined her. He was describing in detail his holiday and the size of the fish he'd caught. Melissa laughed.

"It's getting bigger by the day this fish. How are you, Kate?"

"Much better thanks. I'm just hearing all about this wonderful holiday."

"You look a lot better. It's amazing what a tan can do for you."

"I know, we spent most of the first week lazing around in the sun with my mum waiting on us hand and foot. She wouldn't let us do a thing. We had to do some sightseeing just to give her a break."

Melissa thought guiltily about her previous trips to Antigua where she would lie around the pool whilst her mother brought her iced gin and tonics. Valerie had seen quite a difference in her this visit, running around after Jacob, swimming with him and preparing the odd meal; she'd even accompanied her mother to the market to shop for food which was totally unheard of in the past.

"Well that's what you needed, a good rest, especially with this one back for a few days. I told Richard to let us know if you need any help. You promise to tell us if it's too much too soon."

"I promise, and thanks."

"See you at the weekend, sweetheart."

Jacob ran to his mother and kissed her goodbye. "Bye Alex," he said, hugging him round the waist.

Kate looked at Alex and smiled. Even he looked relaxed about the whole thing now. Maybe he was finally growing up and taking some responsibility on those broad shoulders of his. He smiled back. He was glad they were friends again and that he didn't have to hide their previous relationship any more.

Outside, Alex watched for Melissa's reaction.

"You alright?" he asked concerned.

"Yes, why?"

"Because you've just spent the last few weeks with Jacob and now you've handed him back to Richard."

"I know what you mean. That's why I said if Kate needs any help they only have to ask. I suppose I'm secretly hoping that she will. I've loved having him around recently."

"I'll back you all the way if you want to go for custody."

"No, but thanks for the thought. I want to take things easy and carry on as we are. It's much better for Jacob that we are all friends, than bickering behind each other's backs. Kate's really good for him and Richard wouldn't go down without a fight. It could mess up all the goodwill we've mounted up. Imagine if I didn't win because of what happened when I left. Richard would probably never speak to me again for trying."

They got back into Melissa's car, Alex in the driver's seat. They pulled away and waved one last time at Richard and Jacob who had his nose pressed against the study window.

"I went to see Kate in hospital," said Alex staring at the road in front of him.

He waited for Melissa's reaction. He wasn't sure how she would take the disclosure of yet another secret.

"When?"

"The day I said I was going to the police station to make a statement. I needed to see her to say I was sorry in case . . . she didn't make it."

Melissa watched him for a while. He could feel her eyes upon him. He glanced across.

"And?"

"I was glad I went. I got closure as they say."

"Oh, didn't you have that before?"

"No, because I thought she still hated me. But the fact of the matter is that she doesn't feel anything for me any more. She's so mad about Richard; I'm just a thing of the past."

"Are you saying you wanted her to still like you?"

"No, but I didn't want her to hate me. I wanted to try and explain things to her."

"And did you?"

"Yes, but she was unconscious at the time so I don't know whether she heard or not. She came round whilst I was in the room so maybe she did; they do say your hearing is the first thing to return."

"And how do you feel now?"

"When she did come round she was surprised to see me, but she was so happy to see Richard. I felt like a spare part; someone who was on the outside looking in. I'd spent the last nine and a half years with her yet I was like a stranger who was poking his nose into their private lives. All I wanted was to go home to you."

Melissa didn't speak. She merely looked out of her window at the people passing by; the old men and women with their shopping trolleys, the children being dragged along under duress to the shops, the young girls in their micro mini skirts, but more so at the couples holding hands, walking along happily together. Finally she spoke.

"Do you love me, Alex? You've never actually said whether you do or not."

Alex didn't reply. She eventually looked round towards him. *He was thinking about it, actually thinking about it*, she thought in disbelief.

"Yes I do," he replied. He sounded surprised by his answer.

It was strange; but by thinking about it, Melissa actually believed him. It wasn't an off-the-cuff remark to try to appease her; it was a genuine, thoughtful response.

"Well in that case, how can I be annoyed by what you've done? If that was the way you had to find out whether you loved me or not, then I'm glad you went. Maybe now you can get Kate out of your mind and think of us. I'd like to meet some of your friends for instance."

"Why?"

"Because they're part of your life and I want to be part of that life too. Kate knew them all so why have you never introduced me to them?"

"Because they're not your kind of people."

"What are my kind of people, Alex? You've never met any of them apart from Richard and my parents and . . . "

"Exactly, Richard is a doctor and your parents live in a mansion in Antigua."

"And I was going to say Kate. I consider her a friend now and she was your girlfriend."

"Yes but . . ."

"But what? What about Chris for instance? He's your best friend and I don't even know what he looks like."

"Well, if you really want to meet him you can, but it might involve him bringing Tina round as well."

"Good, someone for me to talk to."

"She's Kate's best friend," he said cautiously.

"There you go, we've already got something in common to talk about—Kate."

"Okay, I'll invite them round, but I warn you, it could be a totally different evening to what you're used to."

"Good, I like different now that I've got down off my high horse and learned to like real people."

Alex grinned. Maybe it *was* time to get Melissa involved more in his life. It looked like they were going to be around each other for a long time. He even quite liked the idea of spending more time with Jacob now that they had initiated a bond.

The journey home was complete. They'd never talked so much in all the time they'd known each other. He vowed never to keep any more secrets from her. She was actually quite understanding under the circumstances and certainly not the woman who he'd met at the gym with her designer training gear, full face of make up and not a drop of sweat to be seen.

***

The long summer holidays were finally over and it was Wednesday morning. Richard had managed to take a couple of hours off work. Kate sat beside him in the passenger seat. She sniffed loudly.

"Here," said Richard offering her a tissue.

"I'll be alright, I promise."

He laughed and shook his head. "God knows what you'll be like if you ever have one of your own." Kate looked across at him with her eyes opened wide. "Well you never know," he said.

She glanced in the back of the car. Jacob was nervously seated with his eyes firmly fixed outside. His new school uniform looked big and starched. His white collar stuck in the side of his neck as he took in the passing traffic. The words St. Bede's Primary were etched under the emblem on his green sweatshirt and his grey shorts almost met his grey socks. He appeared so small and innocent; how could they possibly let him out into the big wide world at his tender age?

"Nearly there, Jacob," Kate whispered not wanting to disturb his train of thought.

Richard pulled over at the side of the road outside a row of houses round the corner from school. Kate dabbed the corner of her eyes again and rued the moment she had decided to apply mascara this morning. Richard grabbed Jacob's hand and threw his arm around Kate.

"Come on, softy."

She blew her nose and walked in the direction of school. Melissa was stood by the school gates. She smiled when she saw them coming towards her and removed a tissue from her pocket as her eyes rested on Jacob. Her bottom lip quivered.

"Oh, doesn't he look gorgeous."

"Not you as well," said Richard.

"Are his shoes alright. Their not pinching your toes are they, Jacob?" she fussed.

"Melissa, you got him measured didn't you?" asked Richard.

"I know but I don't want him to be uncomfortable on his first day."

A few minutes later the bell sounded.

"You two take him in," Kate said. "I'll wait here."

"Are you sure, Kate?" asked Melissa.

"Of course I am. There'll be far too many parents in there." She bent down and held Jacob by the arms. "You have a great day. I always used to love my first day at school after the summer holidays because we got lots of new books and pencils. Everything was new, even the crayons and paints." Jacob looked hesitantly at the door. "And I want you to do something for me. I want you to do me and daddy, and mummy and Alex a beautiful picture so that we can say this picture was done on Jacob's first day at school. Do you promise you'll do that?" He nodded a bit more brightly then kissed Kate goodbye. "Mummy and I will be waiting here for you at home time," she said waving.

He took his parents hands and Kate allowed the tears to flow now that Richard was no longer there to mock her. She watched him disappear inside the school walls and thought back to the first day she had met him at the house. Who would have thought that she would be seeing him off on his first day at school as his father's fiancée?

Her eyes had dried by the time the proud parents joined her outside the gates. Melissa's were red and glistening though as they made their way back to their cars.

"Was he alright?" asked Kate as soon as she saw them.

"He was fine, unlike his mother. He spotted Luke from nursery and walked in with him. They'll look after each other today I'm sure."

"Are you alright, Melissa?" Kate asked putting her arm around her shoulder.

Melissa nodded. "I'll be fine. Didn't he look a sweetheart? They all looked too young to be starting school. I'll see you at the gates at three thirty, Kate, and thanks for that today."

"For what?" asked Kate surprised.

"For letting me go in with him."

Kate looked shocked. "Don't be silly; of course you should have gone in with him. He's your son."

"I know, but after the way I behaved when I walked out on him, I wouldn't have blamed you if you'd wanted to go. You've done wonders with him over the last few months and I want to thank you for that."

Kate could feel the tears pricking again and went for her tissue.

"We've all come through some really hard times, probably better people for it at the end," said Kate. "I'll see you later, Melissa; you must come round for coffee and spend some time with him after. I'm sure he'll want to tell you every little detail."

The two women hugged each other and Richard stood by wondering how everything had turned out so well. It was less than a year ago that Melissa had left him and Kate had entered his life and now look at them. They were practically best friends, all of them, Alex included.

"Come on then, Kate, I'll drop you off on the way past," Richard interrupted.

"Okay, see you later Melissa."

"See you later, bye, Richard."

"Bye."

Kate and Richard got back into the car and drove off.

"Well, my little boy has started school. What a day for him. What are you going to do with yourself later? You've got quite a bit of free time now."

"Do you know, I haven't a clue. I haven't even thought that far. Maybe I should go and see Dorothy and Prof. See how he's getting on before he goes back to work."

"I'm sure they'd love that. Get yourself a taxi, I'll give you the money."

"No you won't, you pay for everything. I've got enough for a taxi."

They pulled up at one of the rare parking spaces along Cedar Vale High Street.

"Are you sure you want to go here?" asked Richard.

"Positive."

"Do you want me to come in with you?"

"No, I most certainly do not," she said laughing.

"Okay, see you later, love you."

She kissed him tenderly and watched him disappear out of view. The high street was fairly busy. Kate noticed someone entering the dry cleaners with a handful of garments and wondered who would be on the counter today. It was Wednesday morning; that meant it was probably Edna. She wouldn't have time to pop in, not now she'd decided to go over to the Royston's. She'd have plenty more days to do that now that Jacob was in school.

She walked off to her right in the opposite direction of Patterson's Dry cleaners until she reached the shop she required; The Bridal Shop. There were two dresses in the window today; a strapless, white coloured gown made of chiffon which looked so elegant, and the rear view of a white, off the shoulder, satin gown with a row of pearl buttons all the way down the back to the waist line. The dress had a flowing train which had a tiara sat in the middle of it and some confetti thrown around. Kate wanted it there and then. She gazed in awe for a while longer, not quite believing her luck, then, instead of walking away as she had done time and time again, she opened the door and went in.

# *Epilogue*

Dorothy gripped hold of Gerald's lapel. She channelled the stem of the red rose into the button hole, then removed the pin from her mouth and fixed it in place.

"There, don't you look smart?" she smiled.

Gerald took a quick glimpse of himself in the mirror, pulled his jacket down and adjusted his red bow tie.

"Yes, not bad for someone who was at death's door only a few months ago."

"Now, don't talk like that, Gerald. You're as fit as a fiddle now. You can virtually beat Richard on the rowing machine at the gym."

"Yes, that's only because he has it on a much higher setting than I do."

"Well, nonetheless, you're doing really well."

Suddenly the doorbell rang.

"That might be the window cleaner; I missed him yesterday when I had lunch with Kate and Jayne," Dorothy said making her way into the kitchen to retrieve her hat from the worktop.

Gerald opened the door and his heart nearly stopped on him for a second time.

"Hello, dad," said Nina and Peter in unison.

"Oh, my goodness, what brings you two here?"

"We've come to apologise, is mum in?" said Nina, the nominated spokesperson.

"Yes, she is, but you've caught us at rather a bad time. We're off to a . . ."

"Wedding?" His daughter said before he could finish the sentence. "Your buttonhole."

"Ah, yes, of course," he said looking down at the flower. "Why don't you come in and I'll get your mother."

Gerald showed them into the lounge whilst he went to break the news to Dorothy in the kitchen.

"You'll never guess who's here," he said in his best stage whisper.

"Who? Was it not the window cleaner?"

"No, it's Nina and Peter."

"What?" Dorothy's handbag slid to the floor and her mouth hung open. "Well we'd better go and explain that we're going out hadn't we?" she said coming back to her senses.

"Dorothy," said Gerald catching hold of her arm. "I can ring Richard and cancel."

"Why on earth would you do that, Gerald? They're two of our best friends who dragged me out of a numbing depression. Those two in there are supposed to be our children who haven't bothered with us for the best part of this year."

Gerald followed her into the lounge.

"Well, this is a surprise," she said as if she'd just walked onto centre stage at the West End.

"Mum," said Nina. "How lovely to see you."

"Is it, Nina?" Dorothy stared for a moment at her daughter. Nina shifted uneasily. "I'm afraid we're just on our way out. You're welcome to wait for us although we might be late home. If you're not in a rush to get back, you could stay," she added sarcastically, "and we could maybe have a chat in the morning."

"Okay, mum; that would be great as long as you don't mind us staying."

"Oh, don't be ridiculous, Nina. Of course we don't mind you staying. It is nice to see you both . . . finally," she said, her mood softening, "but we really have to go to this wedding, you see, some very special friends of ours are tying the knot and we wouldn't miss it for the world. So make yourselves at home and we'll see you later. Come along Gerald."

Gerald chased after her nodding at both his children. They both looked shell shocked. Their mother had taken on a new identity. She was forceful and not to be tangled with. Had they gone too far in their militant action, punishing their parents for daring to take a holiday when it was Christmas.

"You've overdone it this time," said Peter to his sister as he heard the door close behind them. "She's not going to be a push over like she normally is. She didn't actually look that pleased to see us. In fact, if I wasn't mistaken, we were kind of in the way, a bit of an irritant."

"Don't blame this on me. You could have rung them at any time. It's always the same, you always get me to do your dirty work for you. Let's have a think about this and decide what we should do."

"We need to grovel. I thought that was blatantly obvious by our mother's disapproving look as she set eyes on us. I know we weren't expecting a tickertape welcome but that was decidedly frosty. And who are these new 'best friends' getting married? We've missed the boat, 'scuse the pun; they've moved on and they're not missing us anymore. We've got a lot of making up to do."

Nina listened to her brother. She hated it when he was right, but on this occasion, she was ashamed to say, he was.

***

Kate was glowing with happiness in her off the shoulder, satin gown with pearl buttons down the back to the waistline and flowing train. She'd just become Mrs Kate Anderson, Richard's wife, and nobody could take away the joyous feeling running through every vein and sinew in her body. She looked around the room. Twelve months ago she wouldn't have recognised the majority of people present today, yet here they all were, celebrating their nuptials.

Tina and Chris were seated alongside Melissa and Alex. She would never have put them together normally, but since Melissa had insisted that she meet them both, they had got on quite well, certainly well enough to sit together at a wedding. Kate momentarily thought back to Chris's speech and hoped Richard had something slightly better planned. She wouldn't put it past Alex to pop the question to Melissa now. He seemed to have grown up considerably over the past few months and everyone else he knew had settled down, apart from Mike of course, who still hadn't found that perfect woman yet. He had however, finished stalking Kate so at least that was a step in the right direction.

Raj and Elizabeth shared the next table with Raj's pretty, petite wife Jarvinda, and their two children Laila and Sav. They had been so good throughout the service and now they were expected to sit nicely whilst they all ate. She'd make sure the children got together later and had a little play on the dance floor. Elizabeth hadn't brought anyone but then they all knew she wouldn't. She did look lovely though in her floral dress and powder blue jacket. Kate made a mental note to talk to her later about the cooking course and to ask which country she was up to.

Dorothy and Professor Royston had been placed with Carl Walker, his girlfriend, Laura, and Jayne plus the two children. Carl had thanked Richard profusely, in a desperate manner for seating him on the Professor's table but to his surprise he had actually enjoyed his company and that of his wife. They were both quite amusing and it wouldn't do his career any harm to do a bit of social climbing. Dorothy was in fine mood; her prodigal children had returned with their tails lodged firmly between their legs, she'd whispered to Jayne. Jayne nearly choked on her Chardonnay as the image blossomed in her mind.

"What did they say when you marched out of the house?" Jayne asked aghast.

"What could they say? I've got the upper hand now, Jayne, and I'm not letting it go."

"Good for you."

Charlie was biting at the bit. He could see his father on the top table near to his new, best friend, Jacob, and was trying to find an excuse to go and speak to him so that he could perhaps get to play. Unfortunately, he wasn't quick enough, and Jacob went over to sit with his mother whilst the speeches were done. Now what was he going to do?

Richard's parents were on the top table. They had been delighted to attend today and even more thrilled to be seated alongside Kate. It meant they were welcome but even more so, they were forgiven for bringing Ingrid Harper into their lives. They had hastened to tell Richard that Ingrid was still awaiting sentence and hadn't received bail due to her unstable nature. Her parent's hadn't been seen much in the village lately. Apparently the housekeeper did most of the shopping these days.

Kate's mother sat beside Richard and flirted endlessly with him throughout the meal. Neither Richard nor Frank, who had kindly taken a few days off to attend, seemed to bother. Richard humoured her; it was harmless fun and he did like her. He was glad to see Frank. They'd obviously made some kind of impression on him despite not spending that much time with him during the holiday. Kate's mother had given her away, a job she had undertaken on the understanding that she wouldn't be expected to make a speech. That would have ruined her whole day, after all, the bride's mother was meant to be seen (in her finery), not heard.

Jacob had been the ring bearer and couldn't wait to take his tie off the moment the ceremony was over. It had been quite a battle to get him to agree but they'd finally won him over with the promise of a sleepover for Charlie.

Todd concluded the familiar line up for Kate. He had gladly agreed to be best man and would have been deeply hurt if Richard had asked anyone else. He and Richard looked so smart in their matching morning suits.

The rest of the guests were made up of colleagues, family and friends, most of whom Kate had never set eyes on before but she didn't mind. She was moving in a different world now. The previous one hadn't brought her much luck or happiness, so she was all too willing to embrace the new one.

It was time for Richard's speech. Todd clinked his glass and the throng quietened to listen. Richard stood up and took one small piece of paper out of his pocket. He placed it on the table in front of him. Kate stared in horror. Was that all he was going to say? This was going to be as bad as Chris's speech. She took a deep breath and braced herself.

"On behalf of my wife and myself I'd like to thank you all for coming . . ." There was a resounding cheer around the room, ". . . and for the wonderful gifts you've brought. We'll have a great time, or should I say Jacob will, opening them later. It really is lovely to see so many familiar faces all together in one room to celebrate our wedding. I can't believe we've actually made it to this day. There's just a few people to thank before I go any further. I'd first like to thank our parents for coming today. Mine have come down from Scotland and Pat, Kate's mum and Frank have flown in from Spain. We're both so glad you're all here. I'd like to thank my best man, Todd. We've known each other for many years now; in fact it dates back to medical school. Todd's obviously a couple of years older than me as you can tell . . ." Richard tapped him on the shoulder as several titters were heard, ". . . but despite that we've been good friends all that time. Thank you also to my son, Jacob, who so expertly carried the rings today. We were very proud of you, Jacob." Jacob sank into his mother's lap as all the eyes of the room turned to look at him. Richard looked down at Kate. She smiled nervously back at him. "This is one of the happiest days of my life. I didn't know Kate a year ago, yet in that relatively short space of time she has completely transformed my life, at home, at work, in every way I could possibly think of. She's also made me think about others in a totally different light. She doesn't know she's doing it, but she has this amazing knack of finding the positive in people and where bad feelings could linger, she puts a stop to it and pushes you back in the right direction.

"As many of you know, quite recently we were painfully made aware that life is far too short to harbour grudges. Todd, my best man here will tell you that on that very day over lunch, I was planning to ask Kate to marry me before I found her.

"I can only thank God that we're actually here today celebrating our marriage. This is for life for me. People like Kate only come along once in a life time . . ."

"Here, here," shouted Dorothy from across the room. Kate smiled affectionately at her.

". . . . and I've been lucky enough to find her. My son loves her, my family and friends love her, and I absolutely adore her."

Kate couldn't speak. She knew she would cry if she as much as opened her mouth. How could she respond to that? It was said with such love and affection and he hadn't looked at his piece of paper once. She glanced towards Tina, who was dabbing her eyes with a tissue.

"Could you please be upstanding and raise your glasses to the two most important people in my life, Kate and Jacob."

"Kate and Jacob," came the response.

Kate stood up slowly, put her hands on his shoulders and kissed him gently on the lips to the delight of the onlookers. Then, she wrapped her arms around him and buried her face in his neck. She loved him more than words could say and blessed the day she became Jacob's nanny.

The End

CPSIA information can be obtained at www.ICGtesting.com
Printed in the USA
BVOW071950051211

277651BV00003B/28/P